That's Not It

NANCY ELLEN ROW

NEW DEAL MEDIA

PORTLAND, OREGON

This novel is a work of fiction. Any resemblance to persons living or dead is purely a coincidence.

A portion of this book originally appeared as the short story "Tea" in the April 1989 issue of The Portland Review.

ISBN-13: 978-1466488632

ISBN-10: 1466488638

For Steve, Emiliana, and Ezekiel.

In memory of Mia Zapata and Yolanda Panek – peace to you both.

If love is the answer, could you rephrase the question?

–Lily Tomlin

1 *Art*

A rt major my *ass*. It was taking me forever to graduate. I kept taking time off to work, make more money, pay off bills, then go back to school. My dad's folks died the summer before I started college – they left me enough to cover tuition, if I stretched it carefully. It was sweet of them, they really didn't have to do that. As long as tuition didn't go up by too much, I'd be OK. I got a little Social Security, from Dad, but Reagan cut and cut it until there was nothing left. I didn't want to take out loans and have to repay a bunch of crap when I graduated, which would be this summer, Lord willing.

I felt self-conscious, being in school for so long. Michael didn't mind at all; he just kept taking out more loans and slacking. I didn't like owing anybody anything. Anyway.

Last week I ran into this German guy I dated for awhile last year. He was back from St. Tropez; he was there for a few months, I guess, maybe longer. All I could say when I saw him was... nothing. Not a thing. He

1

thought that was just hilarious.

He said, "How unlike you, Elizabeth." Fuck. I ran into him at this bar we always partied at; I was there with a couple of friends, after night class. We used to sleep in for hours when he stayed over. Sheer decadence. I wanted Michael out of my life was what I wanted. Michael just kept saying, "I love you, I love you." I needed that. I needed to be reassured. And, for the first time in a long time, I had someone who could stand up to me. JoJo said, "About time you had a decent father figure."

It felt like I'd been waiting for him my whole life. So that? That was nice. The sex? Good. Taking care of his baby all the time? Not good. And the rest? Fuck it. We had moved in together too fast, this was insanity.

I had been thinking about Dad a lot. I always thought about him. I missed him every day, but I'd been thinking about him more than usual. Maybe it was that time of year – his birthday coming up, and Father's Day after that. And seeing all the water, every day, going to the university, which was downtown. My wish was that I wouldn't think of him every day for the rest of my life. Just once in a while would be better. Maybe... once every few weeks. That sounded reasonable. I would like to make sense of it all. Please.

I felt betrayed by Michael. I knew he was seeing someone else. Maybe. I was pretty sure. I couldn't prove it. Or maybe I was paranoid. Possessive. Crazy. Was a gut feeling enough to go on? It should be. Why wasn't it? All I could hear was Mom saying, "Maybe you *need* to feel betrayed. Maybe you set this all up *yourself.*" Fucking '60s hippie parents.

I don't and I *didn't*. It was one thing to take some of the responsibility; it was another to take *all the damn responsibility.* Karma this and karma that. Fuck that. Fuck that *twice*. If this ended, this cozy little relationship with Michael, my life wouldn't be over. I hated him for making me feel crazy. Cozy and crazy at the same time. I wasn't some crazy, demanding bitch like he made me out to be, laughing at me, making fun of me when his friends were around, then saying, "Oh, baby, I was just kidding." Bullshit. Maybe I should draw for a while, instead of fixating. Waiting for that spark to fall from heaven.

Michael showed up around nine, after Amber was down for the night. I was in charge of her dinner. Again. Chicken nuggets, corn, macaroni and cheese, and milk. I bathed her and all of her bath toys, too ("Fishie! Bath!") She had these wind-up animal bath toys – a fish, an octopus, a shark. I read her *Goodnight Moon* once and *Go Dog! Go* three times, kissed her, cuddled her and tucked her in. Forgot to plug in the night light; apologized when she pointed at it, to remind me. All the things a one-year-old's parents should do. All the things Amber's parents didn't do. She was so sweet, she gave me a little smile when she pointed at the light.

"I was studying for my history test, sorry," Michael said when he finally rolled in. "Did Amber go to sleep all right?"

"I'm sure she'd like it if her daddy tucked her in sometimes," I said.

"Yeah, you know," he said, not making eye contact. "Studying took longer than I thought it would."

I knew his way of studying – drinking cup after cup of coffee at some hip coffeehouse, and flirting with anyone who walked by.

Study my ass, buddy.

I didn't believe Michael's excuse for a second, but I was preoccupied about the week. I didn't know how we were supposed to juggle it – classes, work, study – now that we had a baby living with us again. In the few months I had been with Michael, his daughter had gone back and forth between her mother, Kim, and us. There was no set visitation, no weekend schedule, just this crazy see-saw, back and forth. Now Amber was staying with us again, indefinitely.

"Can't deal," was all Kim said when I tried to talk with her earlier in the day. I had tracked her down at home. She actually picked up the phone. She was sick. I mean, mentally ill sick. Depressive disorder, aggravated by drinking and drugging, and who knew what the hell else. I would say, in my extremely unprofessional, biased opinion, that she was bipolar. She sure swung back and forth with the moods. *(Takes one to know one.)* She had been committed again and was released too soon. She had been in a few times, from what I'd been able to gather. It was hard to figure it out, exactly, from what little I heard from her and others.

But she was out of the hospital now and seemed to be spending most of her time at friends' houses, sprawled on their floors, watching videos and eating junk food. She was thirty-five – ten years older than Michael and thirteen years older than me. And still acting like a twelve-year-old.

"You like Woody Allen?" she asked me when we talked. I was trying to talk her into taking Amber home. Kim wanted a break. *I* wanted a damn break. She trumped. She was distracted and jittery on the phone, impossible to communicate with.

"Uh, *Manhattan*," I said, "and *Annie Hall*, I guess. Hey, when do you think you'll be... "

"Akira Kurosawa? Chuck Norris?" She laughed. "We watched Kurosawa night before last, then had a Chuck Norris fest last night. What a trip." She told me she would get back to me later and hung up on me. Sweet.

"Your baby's fine," I said into the quiet phone.

Michael threw his backpack on a dining room chair and started rummaging through it, got distracted and started rummaging through the refrigerator instead. I was half-assed trying to get my art supplies together and finish my collage. I was pleased with it – it had a mermaid theme, with real seaweed and seashells. For the ocean background I pieced together this fabric – brilliant blue, with sparkles woven through it – with some crinkly blue paper. I found the fabric in with my mom's old sewing supplies. Score.

At least Amber still liked to nap. She liked her sleep – she wasn't one of those get-up-at-five-a.m. babies. Thank God. When she was awake, she was happy for short times in the high chair, parked with some Teddy Graham cookies and *Sesame Street*. That bought me a couple of hours, between Sesame Street and the naps, once or twice a day. She was walking now, and spent a lot of time careening around, knocking shit over.

The shells weren't sticking with Elmer's. Maybe epoxy would work.

"Can you at least drop Amber at daycare in the morning?" I asked Michael, trying without success to glue a shell on again.

"Yeah, sure," Michael agreed.

"God, Kim drives me crazy! She doesn't even think about what it would be like for Amber if she was gone." I took a handful of pebbles and placed them near the shells. The seaweed was impossible to work with, it was too crispy. Maybe some crinkled-up dark green tissue paper? It would go nicely with the blue. Now the collage didn't look at all like what I was imagining. I stepped back and eyeballed it.

Michael said, "It'd be easier for Amber, if she were dead." He was too casual about it.

"Michael, God! How can you even say that? It so would *not* be easier! I know, OK? You don't know. How does this look to you? Dammit, this is stupid." Michael examined it. He was an honest and supportive critic, usually. "It looks good. Wind the mermaid's tail around here. No, here, see?"

"Yeah, maybe." It was hard to make anything – even lunch for tomorrow – when I was this tired.

"You know she used to stick herself with pins, when we were together?" Michael said. He picked up my scissors, opened them, closed

5

them.

"Yeah, you mentioned that," I said. I kept fussing with the tail.

"And she made tiny cuts up and down her legs and arms. Is it going to be better for my daughter to grow up with a crazy mother? What if she starts hurting the baby instead of herself? They should have kept her in when they had her. I don't know why they let her out."

"No insurance money, honey," I said. Kim and Amber were on welfare; the medical card covered her hospitalization whenever she needed to spend any length of time in the mental ward. Kim had been committed this time for two weeks. Last year, it had been three weeks, Michael told me. Wait, when she was pregnant with Amber and freaked out, that time it was for three weeks, I think. When she was newborn, Kim's friends took care of the baby for awhile – for a few weeks, I think. Kim had postpartum freak-out and was committed then, too. Clearly she had needed to be in for longer, this time. But she told the staff she wasn't suicidal and back home she went.

I poked a piece of the collage's fabric behind the mermaid's tail and glued it in place.

"A week isn't even long enough to get her stabilized on her medication. Doesn't it take a month or something? It would be nice if they could come up with a cure, y'know? I always hoped with my dad that they could fix it."

He was schizophrenic, though; that was a whole different deal. I was kind of relieved, in a weird way, that they didn't find a "cure" in the first few years after he died. If they had found some kind of magic pill, say? It would have been too much. Now I wished they would figure it out, already.

"Nothing she has been on has helped, anyway," Michael said. He had found some granola and yogurt and was eating that. "That one kind of medicine just made her more suicidal. She wasn't on anything when she was pregnant; she was worried it would hurt the baby."

"That makes sense. Now, what else?"

"That's fine," he said. "It looks good. You just need to get more shells glued on. No, I mean her meds, they're a joke, OK? She just starts drinking when she gets out, and what good are the antidepressants then? She's wiggy all the time. Does she tell the doctors how much she drinks? No. Does she go to AA meetings and say she's not drinking when she is? Yes."

"Like the medications work, anyway. My dad had bad reactions to all of them. So then you start self-medicating, see?" (*"Keep coming back/it works!" – Alcoholics Anonymous.*) I had gone to a few Al-Anon meetings, at Kim's suggestion. They were good. But I wasn't her family and I wasn't married to a drunk. I think her family had written her off.

In some ways, things *were* working for her. In addition to the medical coverage, the state also paid for twenty hours of childcare a week for Amber, supposedly so the unemployed Kim could find work. She usually spent the time in a diner by her house, drinking coffee and smoking cigarettes with a friend of hers, who was nineteen and had a two-year-old. Kim and her buddy always found a way, somehow, to afford booze and cigarettes. Drank coffee all day and booze all night. And watched Chuck Norris movies, what the hell?

"Living right up to those welfare stereotypes. Chuck Norris and cigarettes," I said under my breath. I had to laugh. Here I was, feeding her kid and taking care of her.

"What?"

"Nothing." I picked up my supplies and shoved them back in the tackle box where I kept them. I had spots for beads, sequins, everything. The little compartments were perfect. There was room underneath for the glue, scissors, and some scraps of fabric.

7

"I'm going to bed," Michael said. "You turning in soon? I haven't seen you all week."

"Whose fault is that?" He leaned down and gave me a kiss, scooping me up in his arms. He still made me shivery. Shoot.

"Sorry, sweets. I've just been too... too, too."

"Yes, too, too. Of course."

I stayed up after Michael went to bed. We went to the Laundromat the day before and threw everything into the baskets when it was done drying. I folded some laundry, started a paper for art history, paid the phone bill. Thought about my senior project, which was due next term.

Thought about the technicalities of suicide. End the pain, no more mornings, no more depression. Very handy, loose ends tied up in a tight little bundle. No possessions, no hopes, no art. No notes. Tonight was the most Michael had ever talked about it. He always said he didn't want to hear it. Same old song and dance – anti-manic pills, dark mornings, Kim cutting herself, blah, blah, blah. For me, it was like Dad all over again. Nothing worked for him, either. Spinning... something spinning. The color brown. Leaves falling. A flash, going by. My stomach flipping. Then the images were gone.

2 *Monsters in the Kitchen*

"Such a selfish thing to do," I overheard from the kitchen. I peeked through the swinging half-doors that led into the hallway as Aunt Tisha, my mom's stupid sister, hustled through. I stepped aside. She didn't see me. She refilled a platter of sliced sausage and cheese and pushed back out again. The house was full of people. I didn't know any of them, except for our neighbors, and the minister. And Dad's family. And Mom's. I guess I knew mostly everyone, but they all looked so different today. There was nowhere to sit. My new bodysuit was itchy and my skirt was too tight. The bodysuit was white and sheer, with puffy, short sleeves. It had snaps at the crotch. I didn't care for the outfit. I liked jeans and peasant blouses.

Aunt Tisha pushed back through the doors, the platter empty again. *What did she do, go dump it all on the rug or something? Man.*

"Honey, have you had anything to eat?" she asked me this time as she waltzed past. So she did see me. I thought I was invisible. I shook my head no, but Tisha wasn't looking at me, anyway. She was already busy talking to the kitchen ladies.

"Everyone grieves in their own way," she said, as they piled more cold cuts and cheese on the tray. This time they added some pickles and olives. "Some grieve with food, I guess." The kitchen ladies laughed. Ha. Ha. Ha. Ha.

Tisha went back through the swinging doors. I could hear some laughing from out there, too, and some talking. I had been eavesdropping from behind a chair in the living room, earlier. I was sitting up against the wall, kind of crouched down. No one noticed me. Not even one person was talking about Dad – how he liked fishing, or how good he was at basketball, or how nice his singing voice was. Was he not supposed to count? This was supposed to be his wake party-thing.

"What's *Thuringer*?" I had asked my mom that morning, while she was doing some last-minute stuff in the kitchen. I was digging in the back of the refrigerator, getting the carton of milk out for the Apple Jacks. Me and Skyler had to get up early, to get ready for the funeral. It wasn't until one o'clock, but we needed to be there early, Mom said.

"Why? Why do we have to get up so early?" I was grouchy when she woke me up. I fought her about getting out of bed. I was used to sleeping in on Saturdays. I liked sleeping. When I was asleep I dreamt that Dad was still alive – I completely forgot he was dead. It was peaceful. It was extra peaceful. He was happy in my dreams, smiling. My mom looked like she didn't know what to say to my question. She looked like she hadn't slept all night. I could hear her crying at night sometimes. It made me sad. Her forehead was wrinkly and she had purplish bags under her eyes. I felt bad then, sat up and put my feet over the side of the bed. Then I flopped backwards.

Every morning when I woke up I thought, *Dad is dead, Dad is dead, Dad is dead.* I thought it, but I did not say it out loud. I didn't say it very loud, when I did say it – I mostly just mouthed the words. I didn't yell it or anything. But I wanted to. Mostly, though, I just thought it in my head. *Dad is dead, Dad is dead, Dad is dead.*

"It's not like a party," my mom finally said. "You can't just stroll in fashionably late, Elizabeth Anne." I sat back up again and got out of bed after my mom left the room.

"I wish it took longer, to remember he was dead," I said into the mirror over my vanity table. It would be great if I didn't remember it until midmorning, that he was gone. If I could have a few hours. Have that peaceful feeling for a few hours.

"That would be great," I mouthed at the mirror, "Wouldn't it?" I got dressed fast in the stupid clothes mom had set on the chair the night before. I had these new, clunky, dark blue shoes to go with the outfit. Blech.

"Kids don't need to wear black to funerals," Mom said, giving a little snort at the black dress I held up at the store. It was pretty. It was like a hippie-girl dress, only black. Kind of loose, with white ribbons at the neck and hem. Mom picked out my whole outfit herself, and made me try on brassieres, too. I hadn't started wearing brassieres yet. I didn't really need to.

"This is too sheer," Mom said, holding up the bodysuit and looking at it. "You have to wear something under it." She got me a training bra. It pointed out how flat I was. The straps rubbed against my shoulders and were uncomfortable, but I didn't say anything. Maybe they were supposed to be uncomfortable. A tank top would have been better, but the mood she was in I didn't want to suggest that.

We had gone to the boy's department next and picked out navy blue slacks and a white dress shirt for Skyler.

"No tie for Sky," Mom said, then gave a little smile at her rhyme.

Skyler and I did not smile. Skyler looked relieved. He wouldn't have known how to tie a tie, anyway. Then she bought us both new shoes, and black socks for Skyler.

I tugged on my nylons; they were already slipping down.

"This, Mom." I put the milk for the Apple Jacks on the counter and held up a tube of meat product. "This Thuringer. What's in this, anyway?"

"It's summer sausage." She was scrubbing the sink and pulling the good platters down from over the refrigerator. "For afterward. Everyone's coming over here."

I put cereal into two medium-size Tupperware bowls, green for Sky, pink for me. I poured too much cereal into Skyler's. When I poured in the milk I splashed it all over, spilling it on the counter. I grabbed paper towels and wiped it up. I got two soup spoons out of the silverware drawer and broke two bananas off the bunch in the big yellow fruit bowl, then set them next to our bowls.

"I think it's stupid we have to feed them. I'm not even hungry." I took a bite of cereal. "I'm not hungry when people are around, anyway."

"I don't want the assholes coming over, either," my mother said, giving the sink a final rinse and starting in on the platters. "I don't even know the last time I used these things. Maybe when we had that anniversary party for Grandpa and Grandma Ryan?" she said. "Too dusty."

She filled the sink half-full with suds and began rinsing them. There was one from North Dakota, where my dad was born.

"This was a wedding present from Grandpa and Grandma," Mom said. She looked really sad again. I wanted to cheer her up, so I tugged on my nylons.

"Look... fancy!" I said. She gave me a smile.

"You look nice, honey."

"Where's the regular tray?" I asked. "The plastic one?"

"Oh, here. It's clean." It was already in the drying rack. Mom gave it a once-over with the kitchen towel and handed it to me. It was heavy green plastic and looked fancy, with black and gold trim. It had a squiggly pattern in the middle that looked like amoebas. My favorite thing about it was that it wasn't breakable. And it was big. I stacked everything on the tray and went downstairs to the family room. I could hear the television blaring the theme to *Land of the Lost*. That was Skyler's favorite. He was nuts for the Sleestacks. He loved *H.R. Pufnstuf*, too. I liked *H.R. Pufnstuf* better than *Land of the Lost*. Better theme song.

I was singing the song to myself and humming a little as I balanced the cereal bowls and sidestepped down the stairs. Sky used to be scared of our basement – he wouldn't go down there alone. He would tug on my hand, point down the steep staircase and tell me, "They's mustards down there." That's how he said the word "monsters." "They's mustards down there, Lizzie." I would have to hold his hand and walk down the stairs with him. He got over that last year, I think.

My favorite shows: *The Partridge Family, Sonny and Cher, Mary Tyler Moore* and *Bugs Bunny*. I liked TV. Our whole family did. My dad loved *Mary Tyler Moore* – he always sang along with the theme song. He had a great singing voice, the best in our whole family. He sang like that singer, Jim Croce. I didn't like TV when they showed the war in Vietnam, though, the guys in green with the guns, and the tanks, and the naked people running down the road. Things blowing up. People blowing up. Old people and little kids, even. It was upsetting, and loud. It was like the noise on the TV went up louder when they had the war on. My parents watched the war reports all the time, every night at dinner. We ate on TV trays in the basement, in front of the evening news. My parents were opposed to the war and I was, too. Sky did not seem to have an opinion on it, yet.

I slid Skyler his bowl of cereal and handed him a banana. He immediately started shoving cereal into his face.

"Say thank you," I said.

"Thank you," he said, through a big mouthful of Apple Jacks.

"Do you have a crush on Witchiepoo?" I asked. As usual, he was flat on his belly, six inches away from the screen, chin propped in his hands.

"No, she's scary! That's not on till tomorrow, Lizzie, it's the Sleestaks, then Sigmund and the Sea Monsters." He began slurping his milk. He could barely fit the spoon into his mouth.

"Their eyes are too creepy," I said. "Don't they creep you out, Skyler?" Skyler didn't say anything. It was hard to get his mind on anything else when he was watching television.

I heard a crash from upstairs, then, "Dammit. Hey, Lizzie, can you come help me with this?" Mom was yelling. So I finished my cereal and went to help her.

Now, at my dad's wake, I was quietly humming the *H.R. Pufnstuf* song again. I was still eavesdropping in the hallway. I liked that book, *Harriet the Spy,* she was always eavesdropping on people. And getting in trouble. I didn't know the women in the kitchen, but I didn't like them, I knew that much. They were worse than Witchiepoo. Ruder and uglier. One was Mrs. Groves, Grandma Ryan's neighbor. My dad's mom. Grandma Ryan was here, she was in the other room, visiting. Grandpa Ryan was talking with Dad's brothers. His sons. The other lady was a friend of Mrs. Groves's, it looked like. Maybe from church. She came to help with the food. And be a vulture.

"With those two little children, how could he?" Mrs. Groves said, all indignant. The other lady made a tsk-tsk noise and spooned potato salad from a big metal bowl into a smaller metal bowl. Mrs. Groves was cutting up more sausage, excuse me, *Thuringer,* and ladling meatballs in sweet-

and-sour sauce from a Crock-Pot into a serving bowl. She'd burned some instant white rice to go with them. I could smell how burnt it was. I hated that smell. Mrs. Groves fretted over it a little.

"I left that on just a few minutes too many."

"Just don't scrape too close to the bottom," her friend said, "No one will notice." Usually meatballs and rice was my favorite, but I didn't want it now. I didn't like burned things at all. From the living room I heard Gary's voice, my dad's brother. Dad had three older brothers, Gary, Bob, and David, and they all flew in for the funeral. They always called Dad the baby boy, which was funny, because he was taller than the rest of them. My uncles' families stayed home.

It was too expensive for the kids to come too, my mom said, but I think they didn't want them to know about suicide. And then their moms, my aunties, had to stay home with them, so *they* couldn't come, either. So there were basically no kids here but Skyler, my cousin Gwen, and me. It wasn't like Dad died from cancer. Then they all would have been at the hospital, the wives and kids and my uncles, or calling all the time, all that. One of the girls at school lost her mom to breast cancer and everybody was always going to the hospital to see her, talking about it, having prayer circles and stuff. Our neighbor told my mom about it. Mom took them a casserole, I think. Chicken and rice, probably, her specialty. *Not* burnt, and not with instant rice. She cooked with real rice and real mashed potatoes. People were lighting candles for the lady and all that. I had never heard of a prayer circle before. Maybe they didn't pray hard enough, because she died anyway. All the kids at school were talking about heaven and hell, after they heard she died. They said she was in heaven, for sure.

I didn't believe in hell, I didn't think. *("They's mustards down there.")* Maybe heaven. I was disappointed not to see my cousins. My cousins on my mom's side were kooky, except for Gwen; the ones on my dad's side were not as weird. We didn't get to see them that much. My cousin Melissa, Uncle Gary's daughter, was just a little older than me. She was nice. She liked to collect stickers, she always showed them to me and shared some.

Gary walked through and patted me on the head, like I was a dog. *Why do grown-ups always do that to kids?* I liked him though, so I didn't mind, with him.

"Hey, cutie," he said. "You spying?" Mrs. Groves and her friend jumped. "What's going on? Did you eat?" He didn't wait for me to answer. Which was fine, because my voice was kinda stuck.

"Is there more beer?" he asked the ladies.

"Outside, in the coolers," they said in unison. They looked at me kind of nervous. I yanked up my nylons and wiggled my foot around in my shoe. The shoes weren't stretched out enough, they were a tiny bit uncomfortable. The ladies were probably wondering how long I'd been standing there. Hadn't they figured it out? Tisha had already said hi to me.

I gave them both a look and walked through the kitchen and out the back door. I practiced looks in the mirror all the time; I was getting good at them. Giving someone the right look came in handy sometimes.

"You want a soda?" Uncle Gary asked, pulling a beer and a soda from the cooler. He held up an Orange Crush. "You like this kind? Melissa is nuts for this."

I shook my head no and walked down the driveway, fast, across the front lawn, and over to the hidden space, between the neighbor's house and ours, where no one could find me, where I could take these shoes off, where I could pretend like Dad was inside with everyone else, talking with his brothers, having a beer. I went as fast as I could.

3 *Nutty as Fruitcake*

MARCH 1987

I shook my head. I could hear Amber in her room, tossing in her sleep. One of her toys thumped to the floor, and she sighed. Dan, our roommate, and his girlfriend were good about watching Amber when I needed them to. My best friend JoJo would come by, if I was waitressing or had a night class and couldn't find anyone. She was good about having Amber over at her house, too. I looked at my notes, index cards and textbooks spread across the dining room table. Tea. I could fix a cup of tea before digging into the paper. Maybe it would be easier to think once the caffeine kicked in. I looked at the mermaid collage, then at the notes, then back at the collage and started working on that again. Shells. It was almost eleven now. Maybe epoxy was the ticket. If the store was still open I could just run over there now and get some. Too late though. More shells would be a perfect excuse for taking a trip to the coast. I could take Amber. She hadn't been to the ocean yet, except once when she was a few months old.

Michael kept telling me that we would get a call in the middle of the night sometime. He wouldn't even talk to Kim, at first, the week she melted down. She called us at school. We both worked two jobs apiece at the university – Michael in student government and with the outdoor sports group, while I worked in the art department, answering phones and opening mail, just a few hours a week. I used to work as a waitress at the campus deli. I quit that one when I landed a different waitressing job – more hours and better tips. Students were lousy tippers. I had just started working at an art gallery, too, just Saturdays for now. I hoped it worked out; I was sick of piecing together a few hours here and there.

The day Kim called, Michael had stopped by the art department to see me and Kim tracked us down there. She called the second he walked through the door. He and I had a half-hour discussion while the red light on the phone blinked. I was telling him to talk with her; he was telling me she wasn't his problem.

"I broke up with her to get away from this shit. She's nutty as a damn fruitcake."

"Yeah, well you have a little something that still ties you together, don't you?" I said, snapping at him. I didn't like it when people threw those labels around – nutty, crazy, cuckoo.

Finally I said, "Christ, Michael! You need to talk to her, not me." He picked up the phone.

"Look," he said to her, "Just call if you need us to take Amber. I don't want to know why, just call." Then he put her on hold again, without saying goodbye, and left the office. He ignored me when I called after him. I picked up the phone.

"Please call if you need us, Kim. I do want to know why. Just call, OK? We'll be there." She was crying. Late that night Kim called in an even bigger panic. She wasn't crying anymore, she was just freaking out. We were already asleep. The second I picked up the phone, Kim said, "I'm gonna hit this kid if someone doesn't take her. You need to come get her now. Right now. I can't get a thing done around here!"

So Michael and I drove at midnight to pick up a sleepy, confused Amber, a few of her clothes and toys and her medical card from welfare, all stuffed in a torn, brown paper grocery bag. Kim was manic when we got there, wearing a red-and-white gingham shirt, underpants and nothing else, scrubbing the walls of her apartment. A few days later she was ready for another vacation to the ward.

4 *The War at Home*

This kid up the street, Paul, kept picking on Sky. He was such a jerk. He was two years older than Sky and a year older than me. Sky was almost ten and Paul was already eleven. I would turn eleven in August, Paul would turn twelve whenever his birthday was. It was coming up. We actually used to go to his birthday parties, when we were all little! This was so unfair. The point is – I was in fifth grade, Paul was in sixth. Sky was only in fourth!!! And Paul was way bigger than Sky. Plus Paul had all these older brothers. He was the baby, so he had this big ol' spoiled attitude. I hated those guys. One of the brothers was nice, the next to the oldest one, but the rest were jerks. And their dad was a jerk, too; he hated all the kids on the block. Their mom? Super nice. Too bad she didn't have girls. You know what else I hated? Not having any friends my own age on our block. No girls lived on the block behind us, or the next block over on the other side. It was all boys, boys, boys, no girls. *("Boy germs! No returns!")* A couple of the babies were girls and that was it.

20

It was messed up, Paul picking on Sky so much – at school, on the way home, when Sky and his friends (he had a bunch) were out playing after school. We told Mom. She talked with Paul's mom. She said she would "have a talk with him," but that didn't do anything. It got worse after that, in fact. Paul didn't hit Sky or anything that would get him in trouble, he just *made* like he was going to hit him, then said, "Faked you out, ha ha!" like a younger kid would do. He and his friends rode their bikes right in front of Sky and his friends, making them crash when they were riding – "Whoops!" – stuff like that. *("They's mustards down there.")*

Also he talked in a Donald Duck voice all the time; it was quite obnoxious. He had no cool friends at school; it was just him and all his reject friends.

They liked to play army every day at lunch – they would be out behind the school Dumpsters, all pow-pow jumping out like they had guns, pretending to fall down dead. Sixth-graders! God.

Me, I did not play that much so I didn't have problems like Sky did. I read and did my art and my homework. I was not that into playing. Sky was not that into homework. Girls fought different, anyway. Even when I did play with other girls, it wasn't like it was with the boys. Saying mean stuff and pretending we were trying to be funny, handing around slam books at slumber parties, those were the kinds of things girls did. Slam books are when you get a notebook and write a question at the top, what do you think of so-and-so? (Had to be someone at the party or it was no fun.) Then everyone wrote things down and they could be quite evil. "Oh, I was just kidding!" if you said anything back or started to cry. They could say what they wanted about me, I didn't care, anyway. Maybe a little is all. If it was a best friend saying something mean, I wouldn't be best friends with that person anymore, that's all.

Mainly I got stuck with chores while Sky played. Mom was working all the time, so I was starting to help with cooking, too. I was sick of TV dinners, they were all we ate, ever since when Dad was sick. Turkey dinners, Salisbury steaks, those awful fried chicken TV dinners, with the instant mashed potatoes. *("Thank goodness for Banquet!")* Blech. I liked my Granny's fried chicken, my mom's mom's; it was good. Sometimes we still ate dinner at our grandparents' houses; that was the same at least.

Half the time we didn't even eat at the dining room table anymore; we ate at the little table in the kitchen. There was room if it was just the three of us. Last night for dinner I made roasted chicken. Easy! You just put rosemary, poultry seasoning, salt and pepper on it, and paprika. It wasn't as good as Granny's chicken, but it was still pretty good.

Mom wrote it down on an index card for me. I started a file, the cards were in a little green metal box that I kept next to Mom's recipe cards on the shelf. I had some good kids' cookbooks, too, the Betty Crocker one, and a Charlie Brown cookbook. So I could get some ideas from those.

I used chicken breasts in my recipe and roasted them for about an hour in the oven. Three hundred seventy-five degrees and done. Frozen corn, Stove Top stuffing and some instant chocolate pudding, the end. We ate it all up. Dad would have liked it. But he was also happy with pork chops, or a peanut butter and banana sandwich. I made those for me and Sky all the time, in Dad's memory. I set the dinner table last night, even, and made it fancy with a tablecloth, candles and cloth napkins instead of paper. I poured our milk into these elegant brown glasses Mom kept with the china. She called it "the hutch," the cabinet where she stored it all. I had to dust them off, we hadn't used them in so long. I just used our regular plates though, not the china. Our regular plates were thick, really heavy duty and had yellow and brown flowers on them. They matched the glasses. We did not watch TV while we ate, we just visited and enjoyed our dinner.

We didn't watch the war on TV anymore, it was over. It ended last month, actually. We didn't know, at my school. It was a regular school day. They just called us in for an assembly in the gym and told us, then we all clapped and some of the teachers went, Woo-hoo! and they let us go home early. I went and got Sky and we walked home. Mom was at home – they let everyone at her work go home to celebrate, too, I guess. Sky grabbed some cheese from the refrigerator and ran out the back door to go play. Mom was at the dining room table and was smiling and crying at the same time.

She seemed pretty happy, though.

"What does it mean?" I asked her, "It's totally over? Done?" The newspaper was still spread out on the table, from that morning. They ran pictures all the time on the front page of The Oregonian, of the soldiers. Dead, or Missing in Action (MIA they called it) or POW – Prisoners of War. There were always those pictures, on the front page at the bottom. It seemed like the war had been going on my whole life.

"No more pictures?" I asked, pointing to the paper.

"No more pictures," she said. She grabbed me hard then and hugged me for so long I finally had to break away from her. I was glad, too. Dad would have been happy, to know it ended finally. I wished he could know that it was over. Maybe there was a heaven, and he was keeping track up there. You never knew. That was a good day. Paul didn't pick on Sky that day.

But today was a different story. I was watching *Gilligan's Island* and doing my homework downstairs when Sky came flying through the back door and down the basement steps, crying. Mom was still at work.

"He said Dad was crazy, Paul did."

"What? Tell me exactly what he said." I pushed my homework away and turned off the television.

"We were trying to finish that maze we were making, in Mike's backyard, and Paul came over. We were..." He was all snorting and everything, he was crying so hard. I got him a tissue and told him to start over.

"Then he pushed me, then he said, 'See what a wuss you are? You're crazy like your Dad.' "

That was it. We went up the street to find Paul.

They were still playing in Mike's backyard, Sky's friends. Paul and one of his idiot friends, another sixth-grader, were there. They were playing army, of course.

"What did you say to my brother?"

"C'mon," Paul said to his friend. They started to walk down the driveway, all casual, trying to make a getaway. I followed them, with Sky and his friends behind me. They were excited I was standing up for them – Sky wasn't the only one who got picked on by Paul.

"What the hell did you say to my brother?"

"You know what," he said. He gave me this sneaky little smile. "You know your dad was crazy."

Everything just went red after that, in my head and my eyes. I grabbed Paul. His friend ran off. We were still in the driveway, and I knocked him down and smacked his head backward, as hard as I could against the concrete.

"You never say one word about my dad again, got it?" I was sweating, I was furious. I knew I should turn him loose but I couldn't. He started crying. He didn't try to fight back. He wouldn't have had much of a chance, anyway, I don't think. I slapped him as hard as I could across the face and spit at him. He finally scrambled up and ran off.

The little kids and Sky all looked at me. I was breathing hard. They had these serious looks on their faces, like they were little grown-ups now. Sky came over and took my hand.

"C'mon." He pulled me down the driveway. "Liz, c'mon, let's go home."

It was just a half-block walk to get home. We sat down on the front porch for a few minutes. I stopped breathing so hard and started breathing more normal.

"Thanks," Sky said.

"You're welcome."

That was it, we were done with it. The lights were all on inside our house and Mom was at the table paying bills. The back door was open and we went in through the kitchen. We weren't supposed to bother her when she was doing bills. She got in a bad mood over them and usually drank a glass of wine. Or two. But I had to tell her. I didn't need to, though, Sky did it for me.

"Mom? You know how Paul has been bugging me? Lizzie kind of beat him up."

Mom didn't look up from her work. She had a cup of coffee next to her, not wine, her pack of cigarettes, two books of matches and her big green ashtray. She hated the bills as much as she hated cooking. And laundry. She taught me how to use the washer and dryer, it was easy. Putting the bleach in was the only hard part. And folding the sheets, I couldn't get that right. Mom said not to worry about it.

"Mom?" I said. Now she was making me worried. Was she mad?

"I know, his mom just called me to apologize."

"Are we in trouble?" Sky asked.

"Let me pay the bills, guys. Did you have any dinner?"

"We can just get some cereal," I said. "We're not that hungry, right, Sky? Or we could have leftovers from last night."

"I had some," Mom said, "They were good. Eat up."

25

"Naw, we're not really hungry," Sky said. He wandered off to his room.

As I walked by Mom, she still didn't look at me, but she held up her hand to me, palm out. So I smacked her hand with my palm, like how my dad used to do when he was saying, "good job," and tried not to smile. It didn't work. I was smiling as I headed to my room.

Paul never bothered Sky or me after that. He should have apologized, not his mom, but he didn't. We heard later, from the other neighbor kids, that when Paul's dad heard what he'd said to Sky about our dad, he beat his ass, too.

I was glad.

5 *Rock 'n' Roll*

WINTER 1976-77

12/25/76

It is Christmas Day, obviously. What all do you want to know about me? I will be twelve and a half soon. Well, in a couple of months. My mom gave me a diary as one of my Xmas presents. It says, To Lizzie, with love, Mom, on the inside cover. Her boyfriend/not boyfriend, Everett, says you should always write out the word "Christmas" and not put an X because Christ was our Savior and deserves more than to be X'ed out. Whatever.

I like to write, but I like doing art more. I got a bunch of neat stuff for presents. Tons of art supplies, paints, crayons, oil pastels, small and large pads of paper. Some charcoals – I've never used those before. You can turn them sideways and shade stuff. My art teacher, whose name actually is Art, showed me. This bumper sticker my friend JoJo got me says, "Get really stoned... Drink wet cement!" Ha ha! I think I'm going to get a KISS Alive! album from Aunt Tisha and some other stuff too. We're leaving for Granny and Grandpa's in a little bit.

Sometimes I get so mixed up, like with people hating each other. I am sick of being me. Me and JoJo got some really good pot, this Hawaiian-Mexican. It tasted like eggs. We were in my room yesterday and we got so stoned. We drank some Mad Dog, too; I had a couple of bottles hid in my drawer. We stole it from Fred Meyer. Here is the thing about Fred Meyer – it's like they want you to thieve. They have a turnstile at the far end of the store. You stash everything over there, walk casually around, out the other way. Walk by the cashiers, then go pick up your stuff and boom right out the door. One-stop shopping! There is a shoe repair guy there; he just ignores everyone. They keep all the dog food and firewood and all that out in the drive-through area. You can pick up your groceries and be out of the rain. They have benches out there and stuff, where the old ladies can sit while their husbands go get the cars. So everyone from the neighborhood just drives up, loads up what they need, and drives off. Nobody around here has any money, so it's helpful.

We got stoned, JoJo and I, drank some wine and were listening to Led Zeppelin II really loud. We heard all this knocking, like from far, far, far away. It was Gwen, and when Jo finally answered the door she said, "It took ya long enough!"

JoJo said, "I didn't have enough energy" and we both started laughing and couldn't stop, even when Gwen said, "Have you two been smoking that funny green stuff? Did you get a lid?" I just nodded. Then my mom came in, and Gwen looked at us and said "You two have such small pupils!" so Mom knew we were stoned. Gwen thought it was funny getting us busted. Ha. Thank you, Gwen. JoJo had to go home after that. And Mom said she wants to talk to me, "When you're not high." She likes JoJo but she thinks we don't bring out the best in each other. I think we do.

⊗⚮⊗

It seems like I've never been scared of anyone or anything in my whole damn life practically and here I am scared of my mom's boyfriend/not boyfriend Everett. Whenever he gets near me or grabs me by the arm when he gets mad, or when he gets that angry look in his eyes, he just freaks me out. He pushed me down once. I fell between the couch and the coffee table. I smacked my shoulder really hard – it left a bruise. It didn't hurt, not that bad, but my friends were here, they were just leaving, and it embarrassed me. The next day one of them asked, "Did that hurt, when your dad pushed you?" And I was all, "That was not my dad."

My dad never did crap like that.

I told Mom that and she said that I didn't need to be scared of him. But I still am. Also, do you think they apologized, either of them, for him pushing me? No. Mom saw it happen. She stood right there with this little sneaky smile on her face like, "You deserved that."

It was my fault, I know that. I was in my nightgown. My friends were leaving, like I said. They had stayed too late, it was a school night, Mom had already told them to leave a few times, blah blah blah blah blah blah. Then I joked like I was leaving with them and walked out on the front porch. I was wearing my nightgown; I wasn't going anywhere, right? It was a stupid joke. And Everett was all, "Oh, no, you are not, missy," and then he grabbed me.

So. So that's about it on that subject.

What do you do when you want to hide? I mostly go to my room and make art. I glue collages together. I did one for my little brother with all animal pictures. Last night it was the carnival at school. I went and it was boring. Not that many other seventh-graders went, mostly younger kids. No eighth-graders. I have four dollars and Gwen is going to get some money and we are going to get a lid and smoke it with Chip and Mark. They're brothers. I like Mark. He's in my class. Chip is in eighth.

❦

2/11/77

Right now it's 11:25 at night. I held three joints for Kevin all day at school. I had a birthday party here for him – Mom and Everett were out at a party. I took speed for the first time, and I got pleasantly hyped out. It just made me feel like I had lots of energy, which I did. I had pot, beer, speed, cigarettes, pizza, pop, donuts, cake (I got Kevin a cool cake, it had rockets on it), cookies, chips, and a few other things. I got him a KISS bicentennial poster. He saw it and said "Alright, oh I LOVE you, Lizzie!" – and a card. When he came upstairs to get his stuff before he went home, I came up too and he put his arms around me and kissed me and said, "It was a great party, Liz, thanks for giving me it. I love you." It was really neat. I love him so much.

❦

3/2/77

We skipped class yesterday, me and Kevin, and went to his house and made love. I am no longer a virgin! Then we went to the drugstore for lunch. I had a hamburger and hot cocoa. I wonder if I'm pregnant? I won't know for seven more days or so because that's when I should get my period but then I'll have to wait another month before I can have the test. God, what if I am pregnant? I'm not ready for this. I'm only twelve and one half, ya know!

❦

4/21/77

I'm not pregnant, thank God! Kevin broke up with me. He just wanted sex. I told him that, and he said, "I didn't break up with you right away!" Yeah, that makes me feel better. Jerk. I'm going to Planned Parenthood. They tell you stuff about contraceptives. Neat, huh? I got a referral in Mr. Martin's class for saying something smartass but he gave me all four copies so I tore them up and went home instead of to the principal's office. I just painted my toenails pink. They look nice.

I'm leaving in a few minutes to go play foosball at the place up the street. I'm getting pretty good at it! I can't play pool that good, though! Ha. I came home at 11:30 p.m. last week so I'm supposed to be grounded but Mom doesn't really care if I leave. Everett wants me to leave. I hate him, the fucker. Later. Much.

⚜

5/1/77

Kevin got caught taking a pair of sunglasses and a candy bar from Fred Meyer. I was with him. We are boyfriend and girlfriend again. I yelled at the security lady. I didn't have anything. She let me go. I did have a pack of cigarettes I stole, but she didn't see me, ha. I told her Kevin didn't have a home phone. Quick thinking, huh? Kevin went along with it. So the cop drove him to our house. I jumped out of the car first and ran in the backyard because I knew Mom was mowing the lawn. Everett was not there, thank God. He was at his wife's. They are trying to work things out, supposedly.

I told Mom what happened, and to please, please say she was Kevin's mom. She just rolled her eyes, but she went along with it. His dad is an asshole. He'd kick Kevin's ass if he found out. Mom thinks he's an asshole too; she's said it before. Anyway, the three of them talked, Kevin, Mom, and the cop. I left and went over to JoJo's. It was too weird for me. And my pot was over there. And get this, my mom told me that the cop told her that he's a single parent himself and maybe she needs some help with her kids and to call him. He wanted a date! Ha! Gross.

He said he has four kids and they're really a handful, so he should know. But Mom said she couldn't call him because then he'd figure out Kevin isn't her kid. She said she didn't like the way he put his feet up on the coffee table and wanted to tell her his problems. Plus she misses Dad still. She didn't say that, I just figured it out. Two of her boyfriends have proposed to her already, but she said no. Everett hasn't asked her. My guess is because he still has a wife.

⌒꒜

5/3/77

Today in social studies we handed in our booklets on China and started one on India. I brought some work home, and I've finished three things already. It was raining again, I hate the rain, it's so gray and it makes me feel awful inside. It makes me think of Dad, when he left. I don't think it was raining that night, though. But it was in April, and April is always nasty in Portland.

Kevin was over at Gage's this afternoon, JoJo's boyfriend? And Kevin was really drunk. I mean, needing to pass out and not passing out drunk. Gage called me and told me. He was worried. Gage put Kevin's head under cold water, under the bathroom faucet, and Kevin went wild. He shoved everything off the bathroom counter. Gage told me – all of his mom's hairspray and makeup, toothpaste and toothbrushes. He broke the drinking glasses and the holder the toothbrushes go in and everything.

JoJo told me that part. Gage called her, too. All of the other guys were there, too, their friends. They're always all together. They all get along pretty good. They stopped by later, after Kevin had sobered up, to see if I wanted to go run around with them. I asked them, "Jesus, do you guys live in a commune or something, there's so many of you!" They said that they did. I had to do my homework though, so I just stayed home. Later, later, later, later, later, later, later, much.

6 *A Day at the Park*

MARCH 1989

A mber was three now, Kim was still a mess and back in "the nervous hospital." That was what my granny called it. The day after Kim entered the mental ward, I dropped off some things for her – a coat, some pajamas, a couple of magazines – and left them at the front desk. Same old routine for us, Amber back and forth, Kim committed and then out again. They weren't letting her have visitors yet.

That weekend, Michael and I took a break from fighting to take Amber to the park by our apartment. I had taken a couple of terms off from school to work, and was back in now, still trying to graduate. It would happen, eventually. I was aiming for summer. Again. We were still in the same neighborhood, living with Dan. His girlfriend had her own place and they were back and forth a lot, so it was all right. We didn't get too sick of each other. The apartment was rundown, but cheap, and close to the university. Amber loved the playground. She immediately made a friend, a cute little red-headed boy who had as much energy as she did, and they raced off to play on the swings. She always wanted me to push her on the merry-go-round, but it made me too dizzy. They were dangerous, anyway, with the kids jumping on and off again, getting stuck underneath or thrown off or something.

I sat on a bench, soaking up the thin sun, smiling at Michael. He was wearing a pair of my old gym shorts, and one of Kim's old T-shirts, from the food co-op where she used to work. His hair was long – it needed to be trimmed. The resemblance between him and Amber was strong. The same huge, cocoa-colored eyes, with long, fringy eyelashes, the same half-smile. She was a cute kid.

"Michael, go grab Amber," I said, "She just bonked that kid on the head." The red-haired boy looked like he was going to cry. Dang it. So much for the new friendship.

"Whoops!" Michael said, and headed over in Amber's direction. The other boy's mom was already there and stood towering over the children, tall and skinny, looking tense. Her son seemed to have recovered. Amber, spotting Michael, gave him a big, angelic smile. "Daddy! Will you push me?"

"Listen, sweetie," I heard him say, "When we're playing with other kids..." He knelt down, and I couldn't hear what else he was telling her. He might be an asshole, but he was good with his kid at least. When he was around, anyway. Amber nodded and pulled Michael toward the swings. Michael shrugged his shoulders in the mom's direction, gave her a big smile, and headed off with Amber. Little girls could get by with murder.

I leaned back, enjoying the peace and the warm sun, and closed my eyes. A few minutes later, I heard a weird noise behind me, in the bushes. There was a girl hiding there. Young — maybe fourteen, fifteen, tops – and wearing all of these hippie/gypsy clothes, a long purple skirt, a loose tie-dye T-shirt, filthy men's gym shoes that flopped around on her feet. She didn't have any socks on. Her dark hair was matted and greasy. I couldn't look away. She looked like a girl I went to school with, years back. Weird. She held some kind of cloth in her hands – it was a pair of dirty nylon biking shorts. She put them up to her face, sniffing them.

Why do the freaks always gravitate to me? Is it pheromones or something? I knew I should move, but I had strange shivers now. I sat frozen on the bench.

The girl's face was smudged. She smiled at me. Bad teeth. Michael and Amber were done swinging – they were playing on the big wooden climbing structure. Michael climbed to the top; Amber played at the bottom of it. It occurred to me that the girl maybe had a knife or a gun hidden beneath all of those crazy clothes, that if I moved too suddenly she'd hurt Amber, she'd hurt me. I was suddenly positive, without having any proof at all, that the girl had a weapon on her.

I finally got unstuck from the bench and walked slowly toward Amber. The girl jumped in and out of the bushes; Michael was oblivious, as always. I began to pray for the girl to go away. I would, I would keep praying to God and promise him anything if it meant keeping Amber safe. I got to Amber and picked her up.

"Michael, please come down here," I said. I kept my voice quiet. He was perched at the top of the slide.

Of course the girl headed for Amber. She came up too close to us. I held Amber closer. She grabbed me around the neck and stared at the girl. Michael looked down and smiled at the girl.

"Michael!" I called out. He laughed, throwing his head back like someone had just told him a good joke. He kept smiling at the girl, as if he was flirting with her. *No, he couldn't be flirting with her.* My imagination had run completely, thoroughly wild. God, he *was* flirting with her – he was giving her that little almost wink he did when he thought someone was cute. He'd forgotten that Amber and I existed.

"Bastard," I hissed under my breath.

"Are you innocent?" the girl asked me. She was still clutching the gym shorts. She was stretching them out and releasing them, repetitively.

"Michael!"

He finally climbed down, not wanting the show to end. Amber with her big soft brown eyes was still watching the girl, not saying a word.

"What is it with this baby?" the girl asked. I walked away, once Michael climbed down. He stood next to me, but it was as if he wasn't there at all. Worthless as a cocker spaniel in a man's body. I wanted to run away from him. When we were a block away from the park, he said, "'Are you innocent?' What a *great* thing to say! It's so cool — 'Are you innocent?'"

"Get the fuck away from me!" I screamed at him. Then something inside me broke loose and I couldn't stop screaming.

"I hate you. I hate you. You wouldn't answer me. Get away from me." Then I ran, finally I broke loose, heart pounding, Amber grabbing on tightly, thinking it was a game.

"Just get away now, Michael! You think the whole fucking world is a television show. I hate you." I was trying not to cry, I would not let him make me cry. I ran home and when I got there, locked the deadbolt behind us so Michael couldn't get in. So he broke in. He climbed up on the balcony and jimmied the door lock. I couldn't keep him out. But I wouldn't talk to him for the rest of the night. He slept on the couch.

"When you're all uptight like that it just makes it worse," he sang at me through the door. "People can see how scared you are. It shows." My stomach went flip, spinning. Thinking of merry-go-rounds, spinning.

Inside my room, I curled up in my quilt, ignoring Michael and folding origami frogs for Amber. She was nestled in beside me. I had fixed some bowls of cereal for us, and brought in two oranges, too. I peeled one and handed her a wedge. I finally calmed down a little. We were waiting to hear when Kim would be released. Michael's parents, Rick and Penny, had called earlier to say they'd stop by to take Amber out for a burger. They were trying to spend more time with their granddaughter, get to know her better. Michael hadn't encouraged it before but was now. I needed the break. I still had homework I hadn't gotten to.

Michael told the story about four hundred times during the following weeks – at parties, at the university. He started by telling Rick and Penny when they came by to get Amber.

"I don't get it," his mother said, puzzled. "Was she mentally ill?" He talked about it with Kim, who came to pick up Amber a week later when the doctors released her. She was in good spirits, the new meds seemed to be working. She thought it was hilarious.

"My baby girl!" she said, snuggling up with Amber, who beamed at her. Kim shot me a smug look that said, *Paranoid idiot!* as I gathered up Amber's things and put them in a new pink backpack I had bought for her.

"Are you innocent?" became Michael's new catchphrase. He cracked himself up every time he said it, delivering the punch line again and again.

7 *You're Not Smiling*

APRIL 1989

The whole thing, the pregnancy, was just one huge separation between body and mind. I knew I couldn't keep the two apart, not for nine months. I was splitting in half. Michael was playing invisible man. My body was thoroughly into growing a baby. I was all... glowy. My mind was racing in the opposite direction. *Why hadn't we used anything?* I was so stupid, thinking it would be safe.

I couldn't sleep, couldn't eat, except for every afternoon around two when I had this insane craving for an egg salad sandwich. I hated egg salad. I ran a high fever, broke out in a rash, wondered if it was all the egg salad, broke down and made my second trip of the week to the campus clinic. They gave me my pregnancy test results (positive, no surprise there) and waited for the doctor to make an appearance. I was about six weeks gone.

The nurse was in her early sixties and bore a physical resemblance to my Grandma Ryan, my dad's mother. She had short gray hair cut into a tight helmet, brown eyes, and loose skin on her upper arms. She wore a short-sleeved nurse's top with a floral pattern, and blue scrubs for pants. She acted like Grandma Ryan, too. Stern on the outside, but looked like she would be a soft touch. She took my temperature and blood pressure, then laid a hand on my arm.

"You're not smiling," I said.

"I don't know if I'm supposed to be, dear," the nurse said. "You're pregnant – the test was positive. And you're running a fever, it's 102." I looked down and began picking at my cuticles.

"Are you ready for a baby?" the nurse asked.

"Do I look like I'm ready for a baby?" I asked. No answer. "I'm not. I hate being sick, I can't even think. My boyfriend doesn't want a baby, and he's an ass... jerk, sorry, and I want to finish school. I'm supposed to graduate after spring term."

The doctor knocked and the nurse let him in.

"Check with me before you leave," she said, and slipped out. The doctor was in his early thirties. Just out of med school, probably. Blond. About five foot ten, solid build. Pretty buff, with a great tan. He must have just gotten back from somewhere warm.

Or maybe he just liked the tanning beds, who the hell knew? My mind was wandering. But damn, he was quite good looking. No wedding ring. *Shit. And here I am, knocked up by some jerk. Excuse me. Asshole.*

"My mom could have diagnosed this twenty minutes ago," he said, after examining my ears, nose, throat and rash. He closed my file and set it on the end of the examination table.

"You have the measles," he said, "in addition to being pregnant."

"The measles? But I had my vaccinations when I was a kid."

"Sometimes they wear off. What about the pregnancy?"

"I don't want to talk about that," I said. I turned around and yanked my shirt back down.

"Are you going to go through with the pregnancy? If you are, the measles are a problem."

I slipped on my shoes and headed for the door.

"Elizabeth, please wait. Do you want this baby?"

I stopped.

"There is a chance the baby could have deformities, from the measles. I'm just saying, it's something to consider. It's probably not the best time."

I kept my hand on the door. "I need to go now, I'm late for class." *I'm late for everything.* My hands were shaking. The fever made me feel sideways.

The nurse stopped me in the hall. She gave me some Tylenol to bring down the fever.

"Every four hours, and lots of liquids, OK? Might be good to get home and get some sleep." She also handed me a bottle of sweet, sticky syrup she said would help with the morning sickness, and information on the abortion clinic. She had insurance papers from the college – my school medical coverage would pay for the abortion.

"But you don't need to mention that to anyone. It's a little secret." She tried, and failed, to comfort me. I bolted. I had to find Michael. He already knew, but he didn't know officially. And he didn't know I had the measles.

I remembered a conversation Michael and I had, when we first started going out. We went to high school together; we sort of knew each other already. We talked about everything – our old friends, ex-lovers, past jobs, our family histories and what we both wanted out of life. Everything. We talked about everything. It was easy and natural with us.

We never wanted to go back to the old neighborhood, we agreed on that. We would go to visit our families or our friends who still lived there, but we never wanted to live there again. Michael talked the most about Amber, and Kim, and the abortion she had had, the first time he got her pregnant. How freaked out he was. "But I was so relieved when she walked through that door at the clinic," he said.

Not ready, not ready. Not time, not yet. Not the best time. Besides, we had Amber to worry about. I stopped by a drinking fountain, took two of the Tylenol and several big gulps of water. They splashed around together in my stomach. Soup sounded good, I could probably keep that down, with some crackers. I hadn't eaten much all day.

I was twenty-four, Michael was twenty-six. We were adults, but we couldn't even handle the kid we already had.

His mother came by to see me at home the next afternoon. Horrible, horrible, horrible. She dropped by unexpectedly; she heard from Michael that I had the measles. He didn't tell her the rest, of course. He under-reacted when I told him, then disappeared. She brought me soup, a little bouquet of flowers and a get-well card. She wanted to know whether there was anything else she could do (no), was Amber with Kim? (yes) and then she asked where her son was. It was after his classes had ended for the day, he should have been home already. I started crying.

"Oh, don't, honey, please, don't," Penny said. "Shh-shh."

"It's Michael, isn't it?" I nodded. I wanted so badly to confess to her, tell her I was pregnant, tell her I had messed up. That I was scared.

"Michael has always been a disappointment to us," she said. "I am sorry that he is disappointing you. You deserve better." She said it in a very flat sort of way. *That* I did not expect, what she said or how she said it. I stopped crying.

She went to get some tissues for me. She spied one of my collages on the windowsill and picked it up to admire it. It was all skeletons and dark colors, with splashes of red and two tiny vases of paper flowers. Very Day of the Dead.

"Nice," she said, sounding like she meant it. She picked up a smaller collage next to it. Plastic dinosaurs, with little trees all around them that we had cut out of construction paper.

"Amber's?" It was in a kid-size shoebox that her tennis shoes had come in.

"Yeah, how did you guess? She does art with me, while I work."

"Lucky you. Most kids wouldn't be that good. She really is an angel, isn't she? So well-behaved?" I agreed. "Most kids don't entertain themselves the way that little girl does. You're good with her, Elizabeth. Thank you."

She rose and stood up. I started to stand, too.

"No, please, sit. I'll let myself out."

"Again, I'm sorry," she said. She leaned over and patted me on the shoulder. Then she walked out the door.

She was sorry but I was even more sorry. Damn.

8 *The Misery Index*

APRIL 1989

Ever since I told him I was pregnant, Michael had been lazing around in bed as if he were the one with morning sickness. The look on his face when I told him. Jesus. He looked like he wanted to throw up and then run away. So this was some kind of lame sympathetic pregnancy, I suppose. He did fix me an egg salad sandwich – with pickles, the way I wanted it. We were staying at his parents' house while they were away for a weekend church retreat.

"C'mon, Michael, let's do *something*. Get a movie, go for a drive, *something*."

"My girlfriend's pregnant, I'm depressed."

I threw one of his mom's needlepoint pillows at him. It said, "Happy Heart's Make a Happy Home." Why were there always so many misspellings on these kitschy pieces of crap? Michael finally got up. The abortion was scheduled for the following week. I refused to talk about it anymore. I had talked with JoJo, Gwen, my mom, Skyler. None of them offered me any words of wisdom, let's just say that. And there was the measles – that kind of negated everything. I felt like I didn't have much of a choice.

"Let's go for ice cream," he said, "and to get some movies. Something light, huh? A girl movie, how about?"

"I don't care, anything. Anything is fine." I wanted to keep my mind occupied. I jumped into our VW bus first, anxious to leave. As Michael walked around to the driver's side, he kicked out the block he had propped in front of the back tire to keep the bus from rolling. The emergency brake hadn't worked since Michael had brought the bus home. He bought it for a hundred bucks from someone who was broke and desperate. The guy should have paid us. In spite of no brakes, Michael had parked it at the top of his parents' steep driveway. The bus wasn't in gear, which I hadn't realized. And I had forgotten about the goddamn emergency brake. Also, I hadn't realized that Michael was going to kick out the block – he usually, what? Drove over the top of it, I guess. I hadn't really thought about it. I hadn't really thought about any of it.

Which is why I didn't expect the bus to start rolling. Fast. With me in it. With Michael trying to jump back in, attempting to jump in and slam on the brakes. I tried to jump over the console but couldn't reach the brakes, and Michael was in the way, anyway. He managed to steer the van enough so it missed sideswiping the cars (a BMW coupe, Volvo wagon and Mercedes sedan) parked in the neighbor's three-car garage across the street. The Volvo was parked out in the driveway; the other two cars were in the garage. We careened through the neighbor's terraced front yard and bumped down their stone front steps, riding up and over their wrought-iron handrail.

He's trying to kill me, I thought. Then I hurled that thought right out of my head.

It all happened so fast, the wreck. It took about one minute. It felt like forever while it was happening, though. It took ages for it to stop. Michael disappeared as the bus crashed into the house. Someone pulled him out from under the bus, then, "Oh, no." A woman's voice.

"There's someone in the car."

I was scared but OK. Relieved out of my head that the car had stopped. No broken bones, no going through the windshield. I started to call out to them, to tell them not to worry, but gave it a second thought. Once they knew I was OK, they would start bitching about all the damage we had done to their yard. I kept quiet for another minute. But I couldn't worry someone, even someone I didn't know. I rolled down the window of the van.

"I'm fine. I'm not hurt."

The entire front end of the bus was smashed in. Second to that, the yard was the biggest victim. The car had broken all of the bricks used to line the walkway. The plantings – shrubs, flowers, trees – were annihilated, the handrail bent in half. Michael's left arm was gashed, but not deeply – he scraped the skin off when he slid through the yard. He was limping from where he fell on his ass and had a goose egg on his forehead.

"You should probably see a doctor," someone said.

"No, I do not need to see a doctor," he said, snapping a little.

"I think you should," the neighbor said, "Maybe have that head looked at? You have medical insurance, don't you? How about car insurance?" Michael did not answer. The neighbor didn't push it.

He shut down and I had to deal with everyone, then. The neighbors, the tow truck driver, the police officer who came out to take a report. Michael stood aside from it all, as if he didn't know how all this mess had happened. Dazed.

"Are you really OK?" he asked me, finally, about half an hour after he should have.

"I'm fine, honey."

"You sure?"

"Really. But Michael, we have to get you to the hospital." The neighbors were being more than understanding, considering the condition of their yard. *Probably relieved the Mercedes wasn't smashed.* The neighbors even loaned Michael the money the tow truck driver demanded on the spot to have the bus towed out of their yard – Michael didn't have towing insurance. Or car insurance. The Misery Index was up, especially when Michael's parents got home the next day and found out what happened.

"Oh, Michael!" Penny said, and ran to him, as if he'd fallen off his bike and skinned his knee. His dad just shook his head. No one asked how I was.

"The neighbors are going to remember that one, for sure," Michael's dad, Rick, said. He frowned. Michael hung his head and looked embarrassed.

9 Accidents

APRIL 1989

"Could you forgive someone for an accident?" Michael asked me out of nowhere. We were cutting class again. We had already missed Monday classes, and the previous Friday's, too. It was 10 a.m. on Tuesday morning. We were in the living room of our apartment. The sun was shining through the windows, and the dust motes were dancing. I was eating a bowl of vanilla ice cream with chocolate syrup poured on thick and watching some crap on TV. Michael was working on his fourth cup of coffee. We had stayed up late the night before, watching a stupid video about Sting on tour with his jazz band.

"What accident?" I was joking – I thought he meant the car wreck. "You should have known not to park in the driveway," I polished off the last bit of ice cream and licked the syrup off the spoon. The morning sickness wasn't as bad as it had been the day before.

"No, I meant if someone was messing around, and they hadn't intended to."

I put the bowl down. "Like what? Unpremeditated fucking? It's still fucking around. Are you sleeping with someone else?"

"Never mind."

"No, what did you mean?"

"My parents, I meant. My mom had an affair, after they adopted me. And my dad forgave her." They had adopted Michael and his sister as babies. I had heard Penny refer to it as "borrowing" them. Yeah, babies on permanent loan, so to speak, from teen mothers at their home church.

"How did you happen to find all this out?"

"She mentioned it, when I told her maybe we'd get married someday. She said that you had to be willing to forgive someone their transgressions."

"Are you a sinner, Michael?" I asked him, laughing. "Are you on fire? *Transgressions?* Jesus. I don't think I'd be able to forgive or forget that one." We both dropped it. I didn't want to think about Rick and Penny or their sex life. They were nice enough, but I hadn't really bonded with them. They were pretty conservative. They let us house-sit when they were gone; this was the third or fourth time we had done that for them. But we had to pretend we slept in separate bedrooms. Ha. Michael even washed the already-clean sheets on the spare bed and re-made it.

They were good with Amber, though. Supposedly his mother hadn't been able to conceive, a barren woman, right? In the olden days, it was never the guy's fault. Anyway, I sure wouldn't have pegged her as an unfaithful wife. She seemed so devoted to the family and her crafts projects. For Christmas she gave us half a dozen crocheted stars to hang from the tree, along with four half-walnut shells she had turned into mouse baby beds, complete with tiny plastic mice and miniature bedding.

"See? I make art, too," Penny told me when she presented them. Pretty sweet. I gave them a guidebook to Portland and some homemade cookies.

I had no idea whether they liked the gifts or not. Michael hadn't had any ideas on what to give them. Amber made them a card that she covered with hand-crayoned stars, floating above a big Christmas tree dotted with purple, yellow, and red dots, representing ornaments. She told me to write "I love you Grandpa and Grandma" on it. I did. She scribbled her name below the words. She was so proud that she had learned to write her own name.

Amber had gone nuts for the little mice. They were pretty cute, if you liked that sort of thing. Michael's parents probably wouldn't ask us to house-sit now because of the car wreck. I didn't like their house that much, anyway, what with all the pretending-not-to-be-sleeping-together thing.

God knows what they would think about me being knocked up. Talk about "transgressing." Seriously? Fuck them.

Staying at their place also made it a hassle to get to and from school. They lived way out in the boonies, in our old neighborhood. I didn't care what his parents *or* the neighbors thought about Michael's wreck. It wasn't my wreck. I still had a car, thank God. Also I had other things to worry about.

The appointment was scheduled for that Saturday. "You promise me," I said when we drove up to the abortion clinic. "You promise me that you won't feel relieved when I walk through that door. You are not allowed to feel relief over this."

Michael nodded and took me in his arms.

I cried for three days afterward, feeling guilty and relieved and guilty about feeling relieved. I hurt. I didn't want to leave Michael, especially now. Someday, maybe, but not now. I didn't especially like him anymore, but I needed him to hold on to me. So tired, empty, and cold inside. I didn't know if it was all because of the baby being gone, or because my feelings toward Michael had changed.

I regretted my decision.

But there was nothing I could do about it now – it was over. There had been extra tension between us, anyway, since we had that huge fight over the girl at the park. I mostly hid in my room. I didn't have an appetite, I felt sick to my stomach. I kept thinking about the measles and birth defects to the point of obsession.

On Wednesday, I asked Michael to bring home groceries. He stopped and got Taco Bell instead. I made it to school Monday and Tuesday, but bailed after that. I had to go back, I was going to get lousy grades this term if I kept this up. Amber was back with Kim, it was all right that I was a mess. But still, I wanted to have some real food in the house. Just in case I ever felt like eating again.

"How hard is it to grocery shop, Michael?" I screamed at him. "We're out of milk. We're out of everything. What's Amber supposed to eat when she gets here? Thought about that?"

"Jesus, Liz, calm down. So I'll do the shopping later, big deal. Why can't you go? I mean, aren't you feeling better?"

I threw the textbook I was reading right at his head. He ducked. "Don't you dare tell me how I'm feeling! This happened to *me*, not you, got it? This is *my* body!" I stopped yelling and went into the bedroom. Michael left without saying goodbye. I didn't know if he'd be back or not and didn't really care. Unlike Michael, I was post-partum.

I heard the mail slide through the door and found an envelope from Michael's mom along with the circulars and some stuff from the university. Dan had some mail. He had been staying with his girlfriend and hadn't been around.

Penny had included a bill from the neighbors in her letter. They were asking Michael to cover the $200 deductible from their homeowners' insurance.

"We paid back the money you borrowed from them for the tow truck," Penny wrote in precise cursive, "but you need to pay this part of it." I knew Michael would never send a check. I called Kim. My excuse? Making arrangements to pick up Amber. But I was really looking for sympathy. I felt awful, I didn't know I'd feel this awful, no one had clued me in. So hormonal and up and down. Michael didn't understand at all.

"Did you get depressed? After you had your abortion?" I had climbed in my bed. I felt like hiding under the covers until summer started.

She waited for a minute, "Well, sure. You get over it. It's just hormones, out of whack."

"It's driving me crazy. I just threw a book at Michael."

Kim laughed. "I hope you hit him."

"Naw."

"Too bad. You know, it'll happen again," she said, all matter-of-fact, with a little edge to her voice. "I bet you anything he gets you pregnant again within six months, and he won't want a baby then, either."

"I won't," I said. What was I thinking, seriously, calling my lover's ex-girlfriend for sympathy? I knew Kim had had two abortions – one with Michael, before Amber was born, and one when she was sixteen.

"Is he fixing you food, at least?" The question caught me off guard.

"What? Yeah, he's been getting burgers for us. Take-out mostly." I regretted the words as soon as they left my mouth. Taco Bell. Jesus.

"That's all?" Kim said. She snorted. "After I had the abortion he made pasta for me. And vodka tonics. Have him mix you a drink when he gets home. *If* he gets home, that is." Another dig. She shifted gears again – her favorite trick. "After I had the first abortion, I promised myself I'd never ever have another one. And I did."

"That's you. Kim, I need to go. Drop Amber off when you can this week." Nothing was going to make me feel better. Certainly not Kim. Or

Michael. I hung up before she could squeeze in another zinger, and started crying again. Kim was just jealous. She wanted Amber to be Michael's only child. She wanted the two of them to be the only females in his life. God, girls were such... cats.

"Kim's not the only cat, is she?" I asked my own cat, who had jumped onto the bed for some attention. Billiam was always in favor of taking a nap. He was only a year old; he was my baby. Orange kitty with big green eyes. Michael had not been a comfort to me, at all. The cat babied me more than my lover did. He knew I was sad – Bill was always butting his head against my hand, trying to comfort me.

Every time I tried to talk with Michael about the sadness, how it kept hitting out of nowhere, he just said, "Honey, we'll have babies someday. We'll have four," then changed the subject.

I didn't want four, I wanted just that one. I had changed my mind. And it was too late. I moved to the living room and sat there in the dark. I went to bed finally. The cat was still in there, sprawled out. I slept for a bit. I woke up.

Michael came home at some point. He was sound asleep beside me, his arm thrown up over his head. He looked sweet. Maybe he did the shopping? I checked the kitchen – nope. No groceries. No Dan, either, his door was open and his bed was empty.

It was 2 a.m., then 3, then 4. I was rocking back and forth on the couch, crying. It was like this every night. I could hear Michael snoring in the other room. I was pro-choice. A feminist. I hadn't changed my mind about that, but I wished I hadn't done it. Had it done, whatever. But the measles...

A couple of years back, I had even worked a few times as an escort at the abortion clinic, the same one where Michael took me. There were six or seven of us, all women. We guarded patients from the protesters who shouted when they entered the building. "Two lives go in, one comes out!" I remembered one yelling at the teenager I was escorting. She had a slight build, this girl. Tired face, with large, serious hazel eyes hiding behind granny glasses. She wore a jean jacket, Levi's and a beat-up pair of black Converse.

"He didn't want it, my boyfriend," she told me. She said it plain like that. No tears, no drama. He wasn't with her that day; she went alone. Said her parents didn't want her to go through with a pregnancy; they were embarrassed and didn't want any of the rest of the family to know. She said she couldn't deal with carrying a baby for nine months, then giving it to someone else to raise.

"What choice do I have?" she asked me. I didn't have any answers for her, it was her decision. I held her hand and got her past the protesters. *Pro-choice my foot, they should call it no-choice.* I looked around the apartment – Michael's mountain bike leaning against the wall, my half-finished art projects spread all over the dining room table, as always. The kitchen table, where we sat at night until eleven or twelve, eating a late dinner, or playing cards. Michael had already proved himself to be a lousy, half-there father, at best. And maybe I didn't want another baby. Maybe I wanted the art supplies spread all over, only needing to be picked up when Amber came for a visit.

Selfish bitch. You are one selfish bitch. I wanted the voice in my head to shut the hell up. I was glad abortion was legal. I was glad the doctor had figured out I had the measles; I never would have known. I was not glad about the abortion.

Maybe a baby, someday. (*"We'll have four."*) I knew "someday" wouldn't be with Michael.

My mom didn't think having the baby was a good idea, she had said so when I asked her opinion. Michael's parents, of course, didn't know.

And my brother didn't think it was time, either. "Think of yourself first, Lizzie. Think of yourself first, always."

The cat pressed against my side. He loved our new hours, my new habit of sitting still, staring off into space and not doing anything. It was cat behavior. Billiam played hard, then crashed hard, always, big green eyes pressed tightly closed. His striped fur was the softest thing I'd ever felt. He stayed asleep while I stroked him, purring and stretching. He made me feel not so lonely. I scooped him up and laid him across my chest. He stretched his legs and purred harder. It was getting late. I'd try to make it to my end-of-the-week classes. Michael, on days he left for school without me, would say, "I love you. And I'm leaving. But just know I love you." Like he was trying to convince himself, and me.

I stepped out onto the balcony. The night was almost gone – it was dawn now. I saw the neighbor across the street, Dorothy, fixing breakfast in her kitchen. Every night when I hadn't been able to sleep, I had seen Dorothy's light on. Maybe she was an insomniac too. Just for different reasons. I kind of wished we knew each other better. I missed having older people in my life. Maybe we could play cards and talk. We could play the games I loved, kings corners and gin rummy and all those. Both sets of my grandparents were big card players. Skyler and I played with them at their houses just about weekly, growing up.

All I knew about Dorothy was that she had lost her husband several years earlier, and she loved to garden. Her immaculate yard could have been photographed for one of the home and garden magazines. There was something blooming, year-round. Her daffodils were spectacular, and so were some orange and yellow flowers I always forgot the name of, that bloomed during the off times of the year. Grandma Ryan had grown a big patch of them; they were gorgeous. Calendula, they were called. She had a lot of the old lady flowers, too – foxglove, hyacinth, iris, and those cabbage-y looking ones with the purple flowers, that were nice for borders. They had dark green leaves. I didn't know what they were called. Grandma Ryan had a lot of those, too. She was gone now, Grandpa, too, but at least we still had Mom's folks. And the memories. You know.

I stepped back inside, pulled on my coat and shoes and got a grocery list ready. I could go shopping; it wasn't like I was going to get back to sleep. The Safeway up the street was open twenty-four hours now. And it was within walking distance. I left a note for Michael, quietly locked the front door behind me, and left.

10 *Wonder What It's Like To Be Crazy*

Spring-Summer 1977

5/4/77, 11:29 P.M.

I've been happy, sad, mad, worried, scared, screwed, foxy, fickle, lovable, bitchy, bitched-at, dumb, foolish, wise, me! Kevin thinks I'm a hood and wonders if he got me that way? He says it's his fault. I wonder. I'm a sosh that smokes pot, hangs around with park rats, plays foosball, etc. I like this new guy, he doesn't go to my school. He has long, long straight blond hair and we played foosball and talked, he likes me. I was wearing that red and brown flowered shirt, it's like a tube top, with my white shirt over it. I looked good. I'm too tall! But this new guy (I don't know his name) is tall, too. Kevin isn't that tall and he's not so cute since he got his hair cut. He wrote the words to "Beth" on my desk at school, only he changed "Beth" to "Liz." Aww, that was sweet.

Tonite me, Mom and Skyler are going to the Ice Follies. I really want to see it! Later folks!

~

5/13/77

His name is David, the blond guy. His friend has the most fantastic car you've ever seen. It's a Mustang, it's tricked out. The only time those guys go play pool is when they have lots of money. They always lay some on me, that's cool. And they pay for all the pool and foosball games, and pay for the pot and beer. They're sweethearts. David bought me a bracelet, lip gloss, a really nice spoon ring, and a Motocross shirt, and two Everlasting Gobstoppers. They each turned five colors. Blue, green, purple, red, yellow, and orange. I'd like to do a painting with all those colors, swirled together. I like that show *One Day At a Time,* it's pretty funny. I like that it's two sisters, like JoJo and me, or Gwen, too, if there were three sisters. I pretend they're my sisters all the time.

~

WEDNESDAY MAY 25, 1977

Today is my dad's birthday, he would have been (math) 35 years old. Make that, it would have been Dad's birthday. Much, much, much, much later.

~

5/27/77

We're here, finally, in Eastern Oregon. It's gorgeous. I saw three deer on the way up and a bunch of cute lil chipmunks. Aunt Tisha isn't here yet but everyone else is, all my uncles, aunts, cousins, Granny and Grandpa. As soon as Tisha gets here they will all start fighting. It happens every time. Today it snowed, rained, hailed, sleeted, and sunshined. In May! What weird weather. Now I'm sitting in front of the fire. We just had dinner. I slept most of the way up. The creek is really icy-cold and it's gorgeous all around. Grandpa and Mom went for wood.

5/28/77

Everything iced over last night, the bananas, pails of water, and even the ink in this pen. I was freezing last night, but tonight I have a sweatshirt on so I'm warmer. We had spaghetti for dinner. Hardly any animals are around, just deer, cattle, frogs, ducks, and geese. The fish won't come out, the uncles couldn't catch anything. The sky is all around, everywhere you look. Tisha and them haven't been fighting too bad. The sunset was bright red. Grandma said, "Red sky at night, sailor's delight." It should be nice tomorrow.

9/12/77

I wonder what it's like to be crazy? I mean, I don't want to find out from experience or anything, but I wish I knew. I'd like to be able to find out what it's all about, if you can get over it or what. I bet that I'd just get more confused than I am now. Mom said that you feel like your world is caving in on your head, that everyone is out to get you. Dad used to think he was Jesus. That scared Mom. She said they gave him shock treatments. He was in his own private world, she said. They gave him this medicine and that one and none of them worked for shit. Mom said, how did she put it? That the prescriptions made him feel, sometimes, normal enough so he knew how messed-up he was the rest of the time. And that it was too much, realizing that. Does that make sense? No. That his sickness made him not there for us, and he hated that. He used to cry and say, I am a bad father. And I would tell him, No, Daddy, you're a great Dad, I love you! But I do not think that it helped.

I remember he could draw very well. He drew my school picture from first grade and it looked excellent. It was neat because in the picture they only got part of my necklace, a Lucky Locket Kiddell one with a doll inside, but Dad drew it so it all showed. I was so mad at them for not having the picture include my necklace. It ruined the picture. But my dad fixed it. He used to draw Mickey Mouse all the time, for Sky and me. I asked him once what he dreamt about (when I had a dream I remembered and was telling him about) and he'd say that him and Mickey Mouse went somewhere. I used to love the smell of his coats and stuff. They made me feel very secure, that Old Spice/Dad smell. Him and Peaches, our dog, hit it off real good. Peaches used to wait at the door for Dad to come home from work or the hospital, she'd look so sad. She would've hated it without him. I miss Dad, and I love him. I'll never stop doing either one of those. I hate it when kids want their parents to die. No matter how mean they are, you'd miss them something fierce. Later.

11 *Like an Old Tattered Quilt*

NOVEMBER 1989

"S hit! Amber. We weren't going to use the glitter, remember?" The tiny silver, gold, metallic blue, red and green flecks that Amber dumped out of the glass canister made a pile on the edge of the table. It was a good-sized jar, and it had been completely full. Most of the mess drifted off onto the thick red and orange Berber rug Michael's mother gave us. We were trying to make Christmas cards, and were having a few artistic disagreements.

I grabbed a paper towel and pushed the glitter on the table into a pile, scooping it up. It wasn't just the glitter, it was everything. I was supposed to be working on an assemblage for studio. It was overdue, and I'd already asked the prof for two extensions. I hadn't even started it yet and had no idea what to make. It took a few months, after the abortion, but my hormones were quieted down and back to normal. Whatever "normal" was for me. I was on the Pill and making Michael use condoms, too. The Pill didn't always work.

Amber stood next to the table, her three-year-old hands clasped behind her back so she wouldn't knock anything else over. She was so tiny – not even three feet tall. She weighed thirty-four pounds. Her straight brown hair was getting long, almost past her shoulders. *I need to stop being so hard on her, she's a sweetie. I'm a shitty parent. She's having a hard time, not me.*

"It's just glitter," I finally said. "Look! I got it all." I wadded up the paper towels and threw them in the garbage.

She bounced a little from foot to foot. "I'm sorry, Liz. It was on accident."

She was wearing my favorite shirt. It had alternating light and dark purple stripes. She had a pink flannel shirt over it, patterned with little bunnies. Both shirts were gifts from her grandma Penny. They were her two favorites. With them, she wore her brand new five-pocket jeans, another Penny present. I gave her shoulder a little squeeze.

"No, it's no big deal. Sorry I was cussing. Glitter really gets all over, huh?" I hated, in order: glitter, Elmer's glue, scissors. They should all three be outlawed, as far as children were concerned. I needed a locking cabinet for all my art supplies, to keep them out of sticky little fingers.

Kim was breaking down again, and Amber was staying with us. *Why weren't her parents cleaning up her messes? We had already had the milk incident, earlier, and the toothpaste squeeze-out, last night. And there was the cat food and water, kicked all over the floor. Soggy mess after soggy mess. Where was her dad? Her mom?* Oh, right. I was all she had. Michael left that morning before Amber and I were awake, leaving a note in big block letters on the table.

"Going for bike ride and to study. We're out of coffee. Sorry. Love, me."
I should leave him a note of my own: "Had an abortion, still depressed and
hate you. No love, me." He had apparently forgotten about the abortion.
Problem solved. For him. And he had a babysitter (me) for the kid he did
have, so problem solved, again. God. But if I didn't watch Amber, who
would? Kim was estranged from her family and none of them lived in
Oregon, anyway. She didn't have many friends, except from Alcoholics
and Narcotics Anonymous.

She had Amber in daycare, but it was a crummy one. I got a sick
feeling in my stomach the two times I'd left her with those people. I
usually could find someone to watch her – Michael's mom, or mine, or a
friend – instead of leaving her there. She was on the wait list for the
university's daycare; it was supposed to be better. We took a tour when we
filled out the forms. It seemed a lot nicer than where she was now, for sure.

Amber smiled her crooked little half-smile, her mother's smile. It
didn't reach up to her eyes. She was worried I was still mad about the
various messes (glitter, milk, toothpaste, cat food, no time alone, no, I was
fine. Mostly...).

"You have glitter on your arm," Amber said. She reached out her
finger and pressed hard on my forearm. I dipped my finger into the flakes
and touched the end of Amber's nose.

"You have glitter right *there*." I smiled all the way up into my eyes,
then took her into my arms. I carried her into the kitchen. She smiled, eyes
and all finally. She put her thin arms around my neck and rested her head
on my shoulder. She smelled like little girl sweat, sharp and warm and like
the earth. I set her on the kitchen counter and washed my hands. The
water took forever to warm up. Baths were especially a drag – once the hot
water did finally warm up, it always ran out before the bathtub was even
half full. The apartment was built in the 1920s and the plumbing was about

63

that ancient, too. My hands were chapped from always washing in cold water and I could never remember to put on hand lotion. Amber's skin was sensitive – she couldn't use anything with alcohol in it. Just this one type of cream in a big tub was about all that worked. It worked well on my hands, too, when I remembered to use it.

I caressed Amber's scalp and lifted her down. She clung to me. Her hair was matted down on one side. I ran my fingers through it, fluffing it.

"Bedhead," I said.

I hadn't bathed her last night before bed. "I can vacuum later and get up the rest of the glitter. We'll give you a bath, too. But your mom is on her way over now. She wants to see you before she goes to the hospital." I took Amber down from the counter and set her on the kitchen floor. She frowned at me, squinching her left eye almost shut.

"She'll be in the hospital a little while. Remember? We talked about it, before?"

"How long?" she asked.

"No idea."

"OK. She'll be here in five minutes? Or three?"

"Probably ten. Want to help me get ready?"

"Are we having cookies?" Amber asked. "Are they the good ones?"

"Yes," I said. I pulled out the plastic tub of Mexican Wedding Cakes that we had baked and gave her one. She loved powdered sugar. I hoped to God that Kim wouldn't start the suicide talk in front of Amber. I had asked her not to, several times, for my sake and Amber's. But it was her favorite subject, and she wrapped herself up in it like an old tattered quilt: how she'd kill herself, methods: razor, bridge or pills; when it would happen: not soon enough, when Amber was not with her, anytime now, who knew?; and that she was ready to go: tired of her depressions, tired of: no money or food, not enough welfare money, not enough food stamps;

also tired of: anyone who pissed her off or refused to help. See: Lizzie and Michael. As if we had abandoned her like everyone else.

"I'm almost forty. That's old enough. I've put up with shit for too long already."

"You shouldn't go," I told her, and I meant it. But I still wondered daily when or if it would happen. I already knew what they called it in AA: "holding someone hostage." How apt. Maybe Kim *would* overdose, or slit her wrists again. She tried it before, when her lover left, the one before Michael. She did it "the right way," according to Michael. He meant up and down, not sideways. Kim's ugly scars were glaring white jagged wounds, raised red in the middle, on her thin, pale arms.

Michael laughed a tight little mean laugh when he said it. "But it still didn't work. She's cursed to be alive."

Kim tried to cut herself with Michael, too, but he slammed the bathroom door open and grabbed the blade. They both told me their stories, and Michael's mom, Penny, puttied in the chinks. According to Penny, Michael was afraid to go home because he thought he'd find Kim dead.

"The poor thing," Penny said. She meant Michael, not Kim.

According to Michael, he slept around a lot so he didn't have to go home. According to Kim, she and Michael were very, very, very happy. For three months. The rest of the time she couldn't find him.

"Every winter she's like this," Michael said. She'd had a bunch of meltdowns since I met her, three years earlier. A meltdown for each winter of Amber's life, basically. The depression started in late October, after her birthday. As soon as the daphne started blooming in February she felt a little better.

"Not much better," she told me last winter. "But enough to know I need to be here, for Amber." Her depression the rest of the year was a low-grade fever. Enough to slow her down but not shut her down.

"No one would miss me if I was dead," she said.

"I'm not saying that to feel sorry for myself," she said.

"What is true is no one would miss me. Amber would be better off," she said.

There might be some truth to this. It was a guilty thought I squished right away. I twisted and untwisted the phone cord during that call. I needed water. We had been talking for close to two hours. It was 11:30 p.m. Michael wasn't home. He was never home when I needed him. *Motherfucking son of a bitch prick bastard worthless fuckwad.* Honestly. Was he around to help me deal with this? No.

I had worse thoughts about him than Kim did. I felt almost bad for her. She just kept making excuses for him: he wasn't good with little-bitty babies, but would be good once Amber was older; he was busy with school; his family had screwed him up; it was because he was adopted, that was why he couldn't bond with people. On and on. I didn't give a shit about any of that. Potential doesn't count, it's what you do with what you've got. I sighed.

"What is it?"

"Nothing, I'm here. Continue." Was Michael having an affair? Probably. I squished that thought, too, as soon as it entered my mind. My eyes stung. I was in too deep. I hated them both and loved their kid. I loved them both and resented their kid. I loved their kid and that was as far as I could take it. I wanted to inhale her, care for her, watch her grow up.

I was not going to lie and say, *I would miss you, Kim,* because I wouldn't. I didn't want Amber to be without a mom, but truth was? Kim was a pain in the ass. *What is true,* as Kim was so fond of putting it, was that she was a major, class A pain in the ass.

66

"I don't have any reason to live," she said.

"Hang on a second, OK? I need a drink of water, and I've got to check on Amber." Kim sighed. I set the phone down and peeked in on Amber. Sound asleep and snoring a little. I ran to get a drink. I got back and grabbed up the phone.

"Look, I don't know exactly what to tell you, Kim. Trust me. It's a bad idea."

"Amber would have you guys. She doesn't need a mother who's, you know, like me. Hitting herself all the time." My stomach seized up. I stuck my hand into the waistband of my pajama bottoms and massaged my stomach. The knots calmed.

I am 25, I have a kid-who's-not-my-kid who's almost four, I am getting an ulcer, fucking prick asshole jerk-off Michael, I hate my boyfriend but not as much as I hate his ex-girlfriend. I took a big breath in and made my voice go calm. Four breaths. Silence from Kim.

"Why hit yourself? Doesn't it hurt?"

"I do it so I don't hit Amber. Sometimes I bang my head on the wall."

"You do this in front of her?"

Kim hesitated before answering. "Sometimes. Not all the time."

"Do you hit her?"

"No!" Kim said. "I've just spanked her a few times is all. I try not to hit her."

"Try? Shit, Kim, don't hit her, OK? Or yourself. No hitting." I couldn't think of what else to say. I wanted to spank Amber sometimes, too. Three-year-olds were tough – headstrong and stubborn, and always thinking they were capable of doing things that they were just too little to do. I had spanked her a couple of times, until I realized it didn't help. Kids were crazy. And mean sometimes. She had just gone through a phase where she threw tantrums, flung herself on the floor, windmilled at me when I tried to pick her up. She shrieked, caterwauled, flipped out and then flipped out some more. Sometimes people turned and gave me dirty looks when we were out in public.

I wanted to defend myself to them, call out to them, "This isn't even my kid!" I'm sure they would believe that.

She kicked me hard with her shoes, smacked me in the breasts with her little clenched fists when I finally contained her. Supposedly girls weren't as wild as boys? Ha. Ha and ha. How could somebody so small hit so freakin' hard? My response to it was usually patience and more patience, but on a bad day? Pure animal rage that flew up and horrified me. I had to give myself "time-outs" more often than I gave her time-outs. Seriously. I would shut myself in the bathroom and hope she didn't take a header from the apartment balcony. Then I'd panic, thinking she was going to turn on the stove or something nutty, and that would be the end of my time-out.

"Kids are hard, Kim."

"Yeah, tell me about it." We laughed. I was not a mental health professional, for fuck's sake. *And not even a decent parent myself, obviously. Who am I to tell her, no, that's bad, you're wrong. What the hell do I know?*

"Look, I need to get going, it's late," I told her. *And I've got problems of my own,* I wanted to say. *For starters, your three-year-old, asleep in the next room. And a boyfriend who can't keep his dick in his pants.* Kim was quiet. I changed tactics.

"The kids would tease her, you know. If you killed yourself."

"They would not!" Kim said, pissed. And sounding protective and maternal, for a change. Huh. That was something new.

"Yeah, they would. They teased me and my brother about it, all the time." I was remembering that neighbor kid, Paul, and wondering what kind of asshole he had turned out to be. Thank God his family moved when we were teenagers.

Kim said, "Huh," on the other end of the line. "Really? That's ugly. I'm sorry that happened, Liz. I am. Give Amber a kiss for me, OK?" Funny, how fast she got off the phone once the conversation wasn't about her. I'd need to remember that one. We said goodnight.

The next day Kim decided the best place for her was the mental ward. I agreed. Michael, who had stayed out until 2 a.m., then disappeared again the following morning, agreed. Her shrink checked her in by phone.

"Sooner would be better than later," he told her. But Kim wanted a day to pack and figure out feeding arrangements for her nine inbred gray cats.

"I need to water my plants and feed the cats, and see Amber. Can I stop by on my way to the hospital? Tomorrow?" She insisted on driving herself, even though I offered to take her. The doorbell rang. Kim was shivering in a pitted-out white T-shirt and a pair of men's work pants, brown, that were a little too big, with the cuffs rolled up. They were filthy. She was wearing a thick, black leather belt. They would take the belt away, once she got to the hospital.

Her face looked four million miles away. "Hi," she said.

"Where's your coat?" I asked her. I moved out of the doorway for Kim to come in, but she didn't move. She looked down, folding her arms across her chest. "I forgot it. I've been staying with these friends, you know. My stuff is mostly over there. Maybe you could swing by their place?" She stepped inside.

"I could give you the address? No. I'll have them leave it all at my place, they have a key. Then you could get it all from there?"

My head was spinning, but I nodded. "Yeah, make me a list, once you get there. I'll bring you whatever you need. You coming in for a minute or what?" Amber appeared. She wouldn't come to the door at first, but now she hung onto my legs, almost hiding behind the front door. She was eying Kim but not going to her. Kim stood there, frozen.

69

"Have some tea with us, Kim," I said. Amber took a tiny step out from behind me.

"Yeah, Kim," she said. "Have some tea with us. And cookies!"

Kim was scrawny and only five foot four. I was half a foot taller than she was. She weighed 115 when she wasn't depressed and 105 when she was. I hadn't weighed that since seventh grade. I wasn't fat, but I had curves. She could pass for thirty but actually had just turned 37. No hat in addition to no coat. She was carrying a small purse, like a teenage girl would carry. It was baby blue and sparkly, with flowers on it. I wondered where it came from. Maybe someone had given it to Amber. Her overnight bag must be in the car. I hoped Kim had a real bag packed, anyway, not just her usual brown paper grocery bags.

The only makeup Kim ever wore, besides pink lip gloss, was heavy black eyeliner and mascara, which overwhelmed her pretty, light blue eyes. She had messiah eyes, sparkling and a little hypnotic, equal parts wild and unnaturally calm. People would get busy staring at them and wouldn't hear one word of what she was saying.

"Couldn't you tell she was unhinged, once you saw those eyes? And her scars?" I asked Michael after meeting Kim for the first time. We ran into her and Amber, who was just a tiny baby, when we were out for breakfast. "Wasn't it a little bit of a clue?"

"Sure," he said, "But I thought she was sexy as fuck." I just shook my head at that. Idiot. Kim's straight blond hair, usually pulled back in a ponytail, was down loose and limp today. Her dark roots fought out for new territory, making a path down her scalp. Amber raced up the staircase through the French doors at the top. I walked up the stairs, hoping Kim would follow me. She did.

"It's cold, have some tea," I called to her. Amber ran across the hardwood floors from the entryway, through the dining room and into the kitchen. She pulled a chair from the square hardwood kitchen table over to the cupboards. She climbed on the chair and started pulling tea strainers and tea bags out of the cupboards, and waited for me to put the kettle on. She started chanting, "Raspberry, I like raspberry, peppermint and lemon. Lizzie, this is lemon, yeah?"

I pulled three cups from the cupboard. "Yes, that's lemon. You want that kind? It's tart."

"No," she said, "Raspberry. And honey." Amber settled herself at the table and began finishing the drawing she had started that morning, some animal superheroes she was fixated on. She didn't like princess anything – she liked action and things blowing up. She had wanted the glitter for the Christmas cards and for her picture. They had funny names, the superheroes, plus weapons and masks. A girl hung out with them. "But she doesn't do anything," Amber told us as she drew. "She doesn't have a power pack or a light saber or anything. That's her job, just to hang out with them."

As she drew, she ordered Kim around. "Mom, sit. Isn't this a good drawing, Mom? Kim? Mama, are you going to have tea? Cookies, too?" Kim pulled out a kitchen chair and sat with her back straight and rigid, running her hand through Amber's messy hair. She smiled at her, half a smile.

"You need a haircut, honey."

"What kind of tea would you like, Kim?" I asked.

"Uh, licorice spice? If you have it?"

"I don't," I said, pushing the boxes aside and looking for the glass jar where I kept the loose bags. I rifled through them. "Sorry."

Amber shook the drawing in Kim's face. She ignored her. Kim rummaged through her purse. "Can I smoke in here?" I shook my head. "Sure, that's cool. I don't have to." She started to take out a pack of smokes, like she was going to light up anyway, then put them back.

"All that tea and no licorice spice? I use it for Amber when she has a cold. You should get some. Peppermint is fine, then." The kettle whistled. I fixed the tea and set out the platter of cookies I had fixed earlier.

Amber was a true tea lover, with her own rituals. She liked the tea cooled with two ice cubes, to begin. And with a spoonful of honey or sugar stirred in. She was especially nuts for the sugar cubes they sometimes brought at restaurants. When the ice in the tea melted, she took a sip, dumped the tea leaves out of the tea strainer onto her plate, then dropped one or two crackers or cookies into the cup for texture. After that, she ate as many cookies as she was given. She never drank more than that one sip. It made a mess and it made her happy. I set her mug in front of her. It was her favorite – it was white, with blue letters that spelled "Grant's Grocery & Bible Bookstore, Madras, Ore." on the front.

"Liz, you already put the ice cubes in, right?" Amber asked, knowing that I had. She grabbed her spoon and two cookies. "And the honey?"

"Yes. Go ahead."

Kim looked ready to cry. She took two sips of her tea, then kissed Amber, who refused to make eye contact with her and did not kiss her back. The drawing had fallen to the floor.

"I love you, baby girl," she said and walked out, leaving the cookies untouched on the plate. It was too abrupt. I didn't try to stop her.

"Goodbye, Kim," Amber called as her mother walked down the stairs. She picked up her drawing and put it back on the table.

"See?"

"Yeah, it's good. I like it a lot. I like you a lot, too." I picked her up and put her on my lap. She wiggled down and went back to her chair. She ate the rest of her cookies, then started whining – about the glitter, about wanting more cookies – and suddenly she flipped into tears. Sometimes she hit herself on the head with her fists after seeing her mother, rocking back and forth while she did it. Or she banged her head on the wall, hard, other times. Now I knew where that came from. I hated Kim's visits. I hated seeing her with Amber; she was horrible with her. I didn't have any other friends with little kids, really, I didn't know what was "normal." This didn't feel like what normal should be.

"It's not the 'terrible two's' it's the 'terrible three's,' " her pediatrician told me at her last checkup. "Tantrums are normal for three." I had to take her; Kim's car was in the shop. He didn't know about Kim hitting herself, possibly hitting her kid, did he? Probably not. And I sure wasn't going to ring him up and tell him to add it to the chart.

That day, after seeing Kim walk out, Amber did not hit herself. *She just wants her to be a normal mommy, and that one is never going to be anywhere near normal.* Maybe it was better, that she figure this out early on. Maybe she wouldn't hope so hard for something she'd never have. Kim had no idea *whatsoever* about the implications of suicide. The abstract and the practical issues. She just thought about the technicalities: how to do it, when to do it, whether or not to do it. To be/or not. End the pain, no more mornings, no more evenings, no more depressions. Very handy, loose ends tied up in a tight little bundle. No possessions, no hopes, no art, no dreams. Anti-manic pills: gone. Dark days: gone. Banging her head and cutting herself: ended. No more responsibilities. I got that. OK, how about a fast game of "what we talk about when we talk about suicide"?

For instance? For instance, whenever someone finds out that Dad killed himself, their eyes kind of light up. Not everyone. But a fair number. More than you would think. They say, "Oh, did he...?" or "How did he...?" and then they just... pause. If I say, Hejumpedoffabridge, then it's like *I'm* the one killing him, and he's dead all over again. It's too much. Mostly I don't talk with people about it. Also, if people are feeling suicidal, they get all chummy and want to talk with you about it. Cuz you're the big expert and all. That sucks, too. And then there are the ones who tell you *you're* crazy, cuz it must run in the family.

The story I don't tell people goes like this: My dad killed himself in April of 1974. Sky was eight, I was nine. It was the depressing rainy gloomy mush springtime of the year. He took our dog, who he thought of as his dog, not ours, in the middle of the night, drove our '66 Chevy Nova to the Fremont Bridge and jumped. With the dog. That was what bugged us the longest, Skyler and me. The bridge, the time, the season and the lack of an explanatory note, that was all understandable — but not the dog. Peaches. She hated it every time he went into the hospital. And he was in the hospital more than he was out, it seemed like. The dog wouldn't eat, she just waited for him by the front door. She didn't whine or howl or anything. Just sat and waited. She was a patient dog.

Mom drove around afterward, searching for Peaches, in the neighborhood, at the pound. But we all knew he'd taken her. Finally my mom, not knowing what to say to us, her dry-eyed, grieving children, said, "Look – maybe he knew she'd be miserable without him here?"

"But maybe he just didn't want to go by himself," Sky whispered to me later. "Maybe he was scared." *("They's mustards down there.")* I didn't want Amber to have to deal with any of that. No kid should have to. No *person* should have to, it's messed up.

Amber came close to never being in my life at all. When I first started dating Michael, he told me right away he had a baby. That he didn't see her much, and that he and the mom had problems dealing with each other. I got that. And Michael was in college, after all. We both were. Class, study, work, sleep, busy. We had some friends from the old neighborhood who had kids, but we didn't run in the same circles anymore. We spent a little time with Amber, not enough. I thought, at first, that he was trying to get a degree so his kid could have a better life. *Ha.*

Then Kim asked me out for coffee, after we ran into her that first time. Amber slept beside us in her beat-to-hell stroller. The plaid lining was dirty, and Kim had patched the tears in the blue canopy with duct tape. Kim leaned close to me across the table.

"He would listen to you, if you asked him to spend more time with Amber. Michael would listen to you."

Her head bobbed as she talked. She wore a tiny red tank top and khaki shorts. She reached her hands out to me, palms up. Her scars were visible. I tried not to stare at them. I didn't take her hands and she finally drew them back. She nibbled a biscotti and took a drink of her coffee.

"Until I was eight months pregnant, we planned to give Amber up," Kim said. "We were broken up; I was dating this other guy already. But I realized finally that I'd be giving Amber up for Michael, not me." I listened, my stomach twisted and sick, didn't say much, and left. Amber slept through the whole visit. She was a cute kid; she wasn't even a year old then. I couldn't see why Michael didn't want to get to know her better. Who could resist a sweet little baby? I figured out later that Michael was never going to win father of the year.

So where was he now? The air was getting colder. A steady breeze blew in under the balcony door. I used my toe to push a throw rug against it, blocking the draft. Amber stood at the front window. It overlooked our balcony and the street below, and adjoined with the neighbor's balcony. She didn't play with her toys, scattered beneath the sill. She stood there crying and shook her head back and forth.

"Mama is not happy," Amber said.

"I want her to be happy, too. She will be, someday." *(Possible lie.)* "Want to watch Sesame Street with me?" I held two cookies behind my back.

"Guess which hand?" Amber pointed to my right hand. I turned on the television, gave her both cookies and sat on the floor, pulling her onto my lap. Her warm little body fit perfectly into the curve of mine. She stuck an elbow into my ribs, getting comfortable. I picked up the remote control from the coffee table and turned up the sound on the television. Big Bird was prancing. Amber's limbs relaxed.

"You want to bake some Christmas cookies with me?" I asked her. "We can cut them into shapes, like reindeer, and Christmas trees? What do you think?" Our neighbor used to bring reindeer-shaped sugar cookies over, every Christmas when I was growing up. They were so good.

Amber finished her second cookie. "Yes. Can we put sprinkles on them? It's kind of like glitter." She almost smiled when she said it.

12 *Heart*

9/6/78

I'm now *officially* in high school. Yeah! My classes are from 8:20 a.m. to 2:25 p.m. and are drama, general business, PE, algebra, lunch, English, social studies. Mom and Jake seem to be getting along OK; they go out a lot, to parties and stuff. All of the adults in our neighborhood are friends – they party harder than we do. I mean it. I'm all, don't even tell us not to party, look at you guys! They go to the bar, to get started, then go from there.

The other night I had a dream that Daddy was alive and well and living with my grandparents. It was strange. If he did come back, it would be very different here. Mom's lifestyle and the way I am. Skyler would be fine though. I wish he could come back, but they found his body. It took them two months to find him. It was awful, waiting. When Sky heard them say, "They found Leo," he thought they meant he was alive. He was crushed when he found out the truth; it was horrible. No, Daddy's dead and gone forever. And forever is a long time. Later on.

⌘

10/9/78

Jake has been staying with us for a week and two days. He's OK. He's kind of growing on me. He's been spending time with Sky, helping him with homework and stuff. He struggles with it. School is a drag on my creativity, but I can't complain too much. But sometimes I still do. I'm worried about JoJo. I haven't seen her since Saturday, but she hasn't been home since Sunday. No one knows where she is and her dad and mom are worried. I think she got herself into trouble she can't get out of. I hope she's OK.

13 *Sweet Sixteen*

SUMMER-FALL 1980

JULY 16, 1980

If I go in and get my license on my birthday next month, before my permit expires, I'll only have to test behind the wheel. I've got to call up that driving school about some lessons. It costs $5 to get a permit and $13 for a license. I'll get some money for my birthday and I need to babysit and earn some cash, too. I have to get insurance and all that shit before my mom will let me drive her car. We're going to see *The Blue Lagoon* tomorrow night at the Bagdad. That Brooke Shields has got some eyebrows. I like her.

⸎

AUGUST 12, 1980

My birthday was alright, I guess. It was a few days ago; I'm just now getting a chance to write. I got a nightgown, a summer top, and a makeup bag, lip gloss, an album, and a stuffed panda bear. I got $10 from Aunt Tisha, and a spirograph from Grandma. Kevin got me a bottle of Tickle Pink wine, with a pink ribbon tied around it, and a pink card. He said it was for "Sweet Sixteen." I think all the pink was his aunt's idea, he's not mushy like that. He's living over here with his aunt now, and will be going to school with us.

⚜

SEPTEMBER 1980

I've got a rotten cold. It makes me mad. I can't breathe half the time. I haven't gone anywhere this weekend I've been so tired. I keep having these coughing fits. I'm gonna stop smoking, that's all there is to it. Oh God. I saw David last week. He's the one who had to carry me into my house when I got really fucked up. I blacked out from the time we left Rocky Butte until the next morning. It was spooky. We always party up at Rocky Butte, it's private. They've still got the jail up there. When I was a little kid, our uncles would drive us by there, me, Skyler, Gwen and our other cousins and say, "You kids better be good! There's the jail! Better get down!" and we'd all hide on the floor of the car. Haha not funny.

Kevin was in JDH. He was in there for assault, the asshole. He didn't even used to fight! Not that much, anyway. One of our friends, Michael, this old friend of Kevin's and mine, ran into him after he got out. I ran into Michael at the movies. He said Kevin is really built. He weighs 170 now. He said, "I sure wouldn't want to mess with that dude" about Kevin. Kevin told Michael that he's reforming. Get it? Ha. Ha. Ha. Mom says he's a thief and won't ever change. She is so protective of him, anyway. He's been like a part of our family for so long now. Kevin's brother's the thief.

His sister, Krystal, is a little bitch. I really don't know if Kevin could reform, to tell you the truth.

He was hitting on me, Michael. He kept saying, "You're lookin' good, Liz," over and over. I told him thanks. He kept on and on so I said shut up (nicely) and he keeps on saying it! So I said, "What do you want?" Michael says, "Nothing, I got a girlfriend. In fact about three too many." I said life's rough and he started laughing.

I'm taking accounting, typing, English, Spanish, history, drama and as an alternate, stage production for classes this year. I'm gonna try to make it all work out. I need something positive in my life. Junior in high school this year.

✑

Kevin says he's never going back to school. I stayed over at his house on Friday, at his aunt's. It was alright. I said, "Why do we always end up like this?" and he says "love." I said, "Love, huh?" He says, "Really, it is." He started saying, "Liz, I really do love you." That was sweet of him. His uncle let him borrow the Torino to give me a ride home. He's going to start doing some construction work with him, I guess. I try to make him jealous, but it's dumb because he gets really insanely jealous. I've got a bunch to do so I'm signing off. Love lots of love later on...

✑

Yeah, after all that niceness, then we fought about some stupid girl. Kevin was pissed! That girl was ugly, anyhow, roach clip peacock feathers for earrings. Shit. I saw him kissing her! They were out behind the pool hall, where we play foosball. He had her up against the wall. Nice.

We made up, left, ran into Michael, hung out with him for awhile. He's been living with his grandma again, watching *Star Trek* re-runs in her

81

basement. When we left he called after us, "You look nice, Lizzie. Your eyes are like melted chocolate. But Kevin, you look like scum." Guys are so weird. Later on love.

14 *Animal Crackers*

APRIL 1990

Springtime, and Amber was always with us.

"Should we just try to get custody of her?" I asked Michael. "It would make sense." We were at the grocery store. Amber was inhaling animal cookies from their small red box and drinking apple juice from a sippy cup. I picked up a package of macaroni and cheese. It was the same orangey crap I had lived on as a kid, along with frozen fish sticks and canned peas. I looked at the ingredient list on the box – it was about a mile long. She didn't like the homemade kind; I had tried.

"Does she really need all that artificial crap? I mean, read this list of ingredients!" I put two boxes in the cart, anyway, and handed a third to Amber to use as a shaker. Amber threw the box at Michael.

Michael, who didn't know what the hell to do with a kid, especially not one who looked just like him, said, "We can't get custody. She's not even mine, legally."

He picked up the macaroni and cheese from the floor and handed it to

Amber, who threw it at him again and laughed. Michael picked it up again, this time putting it in the cart.

"You're getting too old for that," I told her. "Stop throwing."

"No," she said, smiling. I shook my head.

"Huh?" I asked Michael. I put a package of spaghetti and a jar of sauce in the cart.

"Really, I'm not even on her birth certificate. I didn't tell you that?"

"No. I would have remembered that. Why aren't you?" I headed the cart down the aisle where the cleaning products were. We were out of dishwashing soap, laundry detergent, everything. Amber threw an animal cookie at Michael, then started shaking the sippy cup upside down so the juice spattered out. She tossed the sippy cup on the floor. Michael retrieved it.

"Lizzie, what does she *want*? Isn't she hungry? She's acting like she's not hungry, throwing everything around. Are you full, honey? What?"

I cracked up. They were better than a comedy routine. I gave Amber a little tickle and took the animal cookies from her. She grabbed the box from me. I took it back again. She laughed.

"It's a game, see? Smile at her; she'll smile back." I stuck my thumbs in my ears and made a goofy monkey face at Amber, then handed her some fruit leather from the cart.

"Monkey faces," I said to Michael. "That's the ticket, pal." Amber reached her arms out to Michael and smiled.

"Out," she said. "Get me out, Daddy." God, she was so cute with him. Yummy.

"That's a good place for you, honey, you stay right there." Amber tried to scale Michael's body, but he gently wedged her back in the cart.

"Why aren't you on the birth certificate?" I asked again.

"You know, Kim was on welfare, and I told her I didn't want them coming after me for child support," Michael said, taking the cart from me and pushing it.

"What?"

"You know, I just give the money straight to her, instead of the state. I mean, when I have any. When we have any," he amended it. We had separate checking accounts, but split most of the bills. "My parents help her out, too." We had been living together for a while, and I knew he gave Kim a little money, but I had never known the details. That's what I got for not intruding.

"You like that gooey stuff?" he asked Amber, who was trying to cram the rest of the flattened circle of fruit into her mouth. It was a big hunk.

"Fruit," Amber said, mouth full.

"Yeah, that's hardly fruit," Michael told her. "Maybe we should get the monkey girl a banana?"

"You look just like your daddy, don't you?" I said, "He's kind of a monkey, too." I'd rather not talk about the money thing with him; it wasn't my business. Maybe someday it would be, but not now. Michael stopped the cart to let an elderly woman shove past us.

"She's the only person I know who looks like me," Michael said, gazing at his daughter. Amber smiled. Then she stood up and dove into the cart for another piece of fruit leather. She held up a piece and waved it at us, then ripped it open. We had no control over her; it was pretty obvious. A middle-aged couple stopped to smile and wave at her.

"Don't encourage her," I said. They laughed and walked off. I wrapped my arm around Michael.

"Is it nice to have at least one person who looks like you?" I knew exactly who I looked like – Dad. I act like him, too, or so I have been told. Clamming up when I'm angry, giving people the silent treatment. Expecting them to guess what I want. Not very fair of me. Sometimes I don't want to snap out the wrong thing, y'know? That's all. Silence is golden. Dad used to say that, too, ha. I'm allergic to filbert trees, excuse me, hazelnut trees, and pollen, just like Mom. And I look like Mom when I smile, I have heard from everyone my whole life.

Michael didn't answer my question.

"I never thought about it before," I said, after the pause had gone on for a long while. "My whole family looks like each other. Skylab could be my twin, practically. Except I have brown eyes and he has blue. So isn't it kind of cool, finally knowing someone who looks like you?"

"Yeah, I suppose. No, of course it is. It is," Michael said. "It's just weird." Amber beamed and reached her arms out to Michael again.

"Out!" she said. This time, Michael picked her up and held her, a little awkwardly.

"Your baby." Amber stuck a hunk of fruit leather to Michael's clean white shirt. Michael picked it off and dropped it on the floor.

"My baby," Michael said.

15 *Thought Parade*

MAY 1990

L ook, I didn't believe all of the rumors when they started. Michael said guess who they're nailing to the wall this week, and I said who, thinking it must be Tanya, from Spanish class, who is Such a Slut. Or Keith and Beth.

And he said, "Us."

I hadn't believed, I mean truly believed, that Michael was cheating, until I talked with (of all people) Tanya. Served me right, having all those mean thoughts about her. You know what I had to go on, before? Not much. Just a bad feeling, that was all. I never busted him. I hadn't caught him with anyone. He flirted some, but he had always been a flirt. There was that weird thing, with the girl at the park. That was ages ago. Michael didn't have a reputation for being a player, he never had. I was just being too possessive, that was all.

"I didn't want you to be the last to know," Tanya said. "I haven't heard much, because people know you and I hang out." We didn't really, but we were having coffee at the moment. Tanya had dark, sleek, glossy hair. She had freakin' perfect hair. Susan Dey from *The Partridge Family* hair. Mine was a tangly, crazy mess. I used to get called "mophead" when I was a kid.

"But supposedly what's her name, Amanda? the new student government secretary? has a thing for him. She's always sticking her legs in his face. One of my friends heard her ask him, 'Don't I have great legs?'"

Oh, vomit. Seeing what must have been a panicked look on my face, she added, "Hon, Michael is true-blue loyal to you. Don't worry. And this girl, she's a whore besides. She wishes she had a boyfriend as sweet as Michael."

"Yeah, well, he has been gone a lot lately. I'm not worried, though," I said. But I was. I stayed up late worrying – about Amber, Kim, Kim's mental health, Michael and his invisibility game. Occasionally I even worried about my grades, if I would ever manage to graduate, if I would ever be able to support myself painting. I could always go to business college if it didn't work out, right? Did they even have business college anymore? (Mom's idea for me. *It's always good to have a backup plan, honey.*) Maybe I'd do my graduate work, after I finished my undergrad degree, and get a master's in business. That sounded daunting. But so did business college. So I drank worry in my coffee most mornings.

"Thanks," I told Tanya.

"Sure, no problem!" She seemed really happy to have shared. Uh, yeah. *Thanks a whole fucking lot, I appreciate the sisterhood and all.*

Finally, after biting my tongue for a few days, I got up the nerve to talk to Michael.

"I know you're lying about something."

We were at the river, basking in the sun like snakes. It was early in the season for river-going, and still too cold to swim. In Oregon, anyway. We had been out a few times already, though. Leftover habits from our teen years – we were all river rats then. A lot of the guys in my neighborhood had boats. Everyone either fished or water-skied or both. It was supposed to be a peaceful afternoon, just Michael and I getting away from everything. There went that idea. I swear I wanted to avoid this whole topic, but I just blurted it out.

Amber was with her grandparents for two days. Rick and Penny were taking her to the zoo, and they had something planned with their church for the second day. They were doing a group tour of the science museum, I think they said. They were even more excited about it than Amber was.

"What are you lying about?"

Michael pretended he didn't hear me. We were sunbathing nude; there was no one around. Everyone took their clothes off on this stretch of beach, even though the sand was dirtier than it had been the year before – it got worse, more garbage, the water more polluted, every year.

"I don't know what exactly you're lying about but I know you're lying."

Michael turned to me, smiled, and said "I love you. I. Love. You. Nobody else. Honey, Lizzie, why do you worry? You're going to get an ulcer." He reached for a sandwich, handed me half. I pushed the sandwich away, ready for a fight.

"Liz, I mean it. Nothing is going on," Michael said, putting both hands on my shoulders and pulling me toward him. "Let's have lunch. We can go for a walk. I. Love. You. And you love me. And we have a better relationship than any of the other couples we know. You just look for problems." Unbelievable. Believable? No, unbelievable.

"And now," he said, seeing that I wasn't going to respond, "I am going to go for a walk. And when I get back, we can read for awhile."

Off he went. "Oh yeah," he added, turning toward me and blocking the sun, "don't get in a fight with yourself while I'm gone."

I started laughing and couldn't stop, watching him stroll down the beach. He looked so... goofy. So intent on the horizon. So naked. I ate my sandwich and started in on a bunch of grapes and some chocolate chip cookies, washing it down with a glass jar of iced tea. It made no sense, him having an affair. We were having great times, great sex. Michael was thoroughly, completely mine. Mine, mine, mine.

He worships me. He couldn't make love to me like that, every day, and give it to someone else, too. Could he?

You know what you call that, when your mind starts zipping along? A thought parade. I needed to shake that shit off, fast. I grabbed my air mattress and walked up the beach, then out in the river until I could barely touch bottom. I liked this beach, it was better than the one we went to when we were kids. It was sandy and didn't have as many rocks. It was more like the ocean and less like the river. It wasn't as cold as I thought it would be. I pushed the air mattress beneath me and floated away, letting the current carry me downstream. I closed my eyes. It felt good against my skin, being in the water with no clothes on. No tan lines. I couldn't wait for summer. Amber was learning how to swim. She was like a little fish whenever we went to the pool or river.

I didn't care where I landed, as I floated along. I trusted the soft, chilly water. I floated for what seemed like forever, then bumped against the shoreline. It did seem like a silly thing to do, worry about some stupid rumor involving some stupid whore. Why worry about someone who wanted what I had?

Man, if I could talk to her. I'd like to rip into her. She needs to work for it herself. Find her own guy and make it work, not just nab someone else's. Then she would see it's not easy, when you have a kid, who isn't even your kid, who's staying with you all the time because her mother keeps threatening to kill herself. And she's throwing up (some kids throw up all the time, it's the little secret parents don't share) and when she's not throwing up she has a fever, and when she doesn't have a fever, she has a runny nose or the chicken pox or some weird rash, and you have to stay home from class and work to take care of her. Or him.

I was tired. I needed a week off, not just a day here and there. The gallery had been keeping me busy, and classes and family stuff on top of that.

What if it was an accident? Michael had asked me that time when he told me about his mom's affair. Affairs? Had there been more than one? *Someone fucking around "by accident"? Like they just kind of fell into it? Oh, please.* We had talked about it twice now; it was on his mind. I told him what my mom had told me my entire life: "There are no accidents." Then I asked, "Is there something you want to tell me?"

"No, Jesus, Liz, calm down," he said. He said it as one word nojesuslizcalmdown.

Thought parade wins. When it wasn't some bullshit about "what if?," some lofty "this isn't really about me, I'm just wondering... in general... uh, forget I asked" kind of thing, we fought about money, because it wasn't like there was a goddamn lot of it floating around. It wasn't like we were leading the life of luxury or something. And whose career was more important – that was guaranteed to be a good fight, too. Michael didn't even *have* a career in mind, really. But he fancied himself an up-and-coming young politico, who would run for city council someday. Maybe president, eventually! Or something. In his dreams, maybe.

I had my art. That was a reality, not some "I wish" kind of dream. It had been there for me, my whole life – the collages, the paintings, the sketchbooks full of drawings. And now I was selling some of it.

Lately I had been having fun punking out Barbie dolls. I bought the cheap ones at Fred Meyer; you could get them on sale for a couple of bucks. I liked to cut off their hair, shred their clothes, put them in sexual positions, with some doll furniture and broken toys for a backdrop. I sold them as fast as I could make them. Ken-on-Ken, Barbie-on-Barbie, Barbie-on-Barbie-on-Barbie. They were hilarious. My bosses let me keep some on display by the front desk at the gallery. I charged twenty dollars for a small display, thirty dollars for a bigger one. The only trick was hiding them from Amber, so she didn't help herself to the dolls and the toys. She was actually the one who gave me the idea – we were picking out a birthday present for her little friend, and she chose a Michael Jackson doll. Oh. My God. It reminded me of Skylab, when I bought it – he used to chop the hair off all my dolls and strip them down.

"Nothing there," he would say, pointing between their legs. He took my mermaid doll when I wasn't paying attention – she was rubber, I don't even know where she came from. He stuck her inside our living room lamp, balanced her right on the light bulb. Which would have been fine, except then he turned the light on. The smell, yick. Oh. My God, our poor parents.

I made a couple of unsexy dioramas, assemblages, whatever they were, for Amber, and we decorated the top of her dresser with them. My latest real-life human model was Amber, in fact. She was interesting to draw, and changing all the time. She was going through a big growth spurt. I wanted to someday soon finish enough pieces to get a show mounted. A real show, not just Barbie dolls. I had shown some of my work at student shows, but I wanted more than that. It would be nice to make some money. Maybe I should teach? I was lounging on my air mattress, staring up at the big blue sky. What a nice day. Michael was right, I worried too much.

The basics gobbled up all my time, that was all. Cooking. Cleaning. Classes. The three Cs. And then there was the waiting because Michael was always late every goddamn place he went. He always got by with it, with everyone, including me. He had an auto-pass or something. Too much of a charmer.

Big smile, shrug, "Lizzie! Hon! Don't kill me, you'd miss me!" *Yeah, maybe I would and maybe I wouldn't. (I would miss his kid, though, if we were to split up.) (On the other hand... being single had its advantages.)*

"Gar." I wanted my mind to settle down, just a little. I carried my air mattress back up to our blanket and flopped down in the sand. I could see Michael, walking toward me. He made me laugh, like a six-year-old being tickled. He made me happy, at the end of the day. Comforted me. Held me when the bad memories pressed my head like a vise. And we had things in common, similar points of reference, from growing up in the same neighborhood. It wasn't like with Kevin, where we slept together and broke up and partied together for years. Kids growing up together. Michael had had his own crowd, he played soccer. We weren't super-good friends. He ran with some of the jocks, some of the kids from the nicer parts of the neighborhood. I used to see him at the river, though, at parties. He'd smile at me and wave. The last I heard, Kevin was still living on the east side, with a girl he met at the car parts place where he worked. I hoped they were happy.

We were having fun, Michael and I, with our friends from school and downtown. Out at the clubs, whenever we didn't have Amber with us. Or one of us would stay home with her so the other could go out, on nights we had her at our place and couldn't find a sitter. We saw bands all the time, there were so many good shows – national acts, local bands.

Skylab liked all the hardcore stuff. Gage was into it, too, JoJo's husband. Sometimes Kevin would show up. We all went to high school with the Oily Bloodmen's lead singer. He was a total jock then – big surprise he became hardcore. Kidding – it was not even a surprise, it made complete sense. All the jocks at our high school were badasses, too. It wasn't just the partiers and thieves who got in trouble. Those punk shows were nuts. I only went to them once in awhile. JoJo and I called them all white dopes on punk. The guys would head-butt each other. We called it disco destruction, in high school – when you'd all get out on the floor and slam into each other, while the DJ was playing some *Saturday Night Fever* crap. JoJo would call me and say, Let's go dance disco destruction, and we'd go out to the bars. We started getting into bars when we were fourteen. We always looked older. Then it was called slam dancing. After that it was called moshing and stage diving. The guys would do all kinds of stupid shit. Spit beer into each other's mouths, slam into each other until they bled. I would only go if I could stand between a couple of my brother's big friends, so they could sandwich me front and back and no one would smash into me. Sky would be off in the crowd, or stage diving. He was a maniac. Gwen used to go with him and Gage all the time, she was reckless like that.

We liked to play grown-up, too. Our friends threw these formal dinner parties, with the men dressed in thrift store suits, or they'd go retro and wear black T-shirts, flannel shirts and torn jeans; white cotton long johns underneath during colder months. Very 1970s. And only the girls would dress up. It was a good contrast, visually. The boys liked to play music, most of them were in bands. The girls liked to wear vintage dresses, when we played grown-up – Chinese silk things, taffeta party gowns, or these frumpy cotton granny dresses. We paired them up with black tights and smaller versions of our boyfriends' work boots. Or we just wore lacy slips with nothing on under or over. Big earrings and cucumber perfume oil. Everyone was into that natural hippie thing again. Michael, especially. I think his secret dream was to go on tour with the Dead. Double ha. He could do the baby tree dance *all day long* then. Seriously, the man loved to dance with his hands waving all around his head.

One night, to surprise me, Michael opened up the balcony doors, strung Christmas lights all over, and put out bouquets of hydrangeas, roses and carnations. We lived in the upper half of a four-plex, so we had both a front porch and a balcony we could use. He lit lavender and vanilla candles and put them everywhere – all over both porches, and on the steps leading to the French doors of the apartment. For dinner, he fixed homemade pasta with a perfect alfredo sauce, a loaf of homemade olive bread, a huge chopped salad, and my favorite, chocolate chip cake with whipped cream. Afterward, we made love for hours, then got up and drank wine at two in the morning, played cards and stayed up talking. It wasn't all bad, what we had.

Michael sat down next to me on the blanket. He had gone swimming, he was still wet.

"Did you leave me anything?" he said, teasing. "Did you have a good float? I could see you, from down the beach. Nice day, huh?" He was trying. I dug through the cooler. The cookies were gone, and the grapes, too. I handed him a sandwich. I was ready to go home now; I didn't want to talk with him about any of it.

Because the more I thought about it, the possibility that Michael wasn't mine and mine alone? The bigger the thought got.

16 *Things That Terrify Me*

I became obsessed with this girl, Amanda, thought about talking to her, this girl Amanda whom I'd never even met. I made lame excuses to go see Michael in the student government office, hoping I'd run into his little friend. Who maybe was a friend and maybe was more, who the hell knew? Maybe I'd ask him to have lunch with me. You know, in an innocent, not being paranoid way. Yes. Great idea. And I didn't have class for another hour and a half.

The student government office was deserted, so I wandered down the hall to the outdoor program. Michael was still working in both places. And avoiding class as much as he could, which was why he was flunking out of school. Bingo. He was renting kayaks to some shaggy-headed granola guy wearing sandals and cargo shorts. He kept nodding vigorously at everything Michael said, interjecting, "Oh, right on!" every thirty seconds.

Two girls were sprawled in the office's easy chairs. One of the girls was nondescript. Messy, strawberry blond hair, and a plain face, with a snub of a nose. She was wearing jeans and a white peasant blouse that she didn't have the right breasts for. Her backpack, with notebooks spilling out, was open at her feet. She glanced my way, then quickly dropped back into conversation with her friend.

The other girl was delicious. Pale, freckled skin; jumbled masses of dark curls pulled up on top of her head and fastened magically with chopsticks. Petite, and wearing a tiny blue Chinese silk dress, in keeping with the chopsticks theme. She carried a miniature version of a doctor's bag for a purse, and one small notebook. Pretty legs. The kind of girl who would never wear work boots, especially not with a dress. She didn't laugh too much or talk too much or stare too much. All of which I did. Those were my trademarks. Pretty much.

Amanda. I didn't need to be introduced, I knew who she was. And she knew who I was, too. Shit. It was true then. If nothing had happened yet, then it was going to. Shit. She gave me one fleeting look, then asked her friend if she was ready to go for coffee. Michael finally interrupted what he was doing to tell me to hang on a second. He was careful not to look in the girls' direction. I wanted to be a smart-ass, to say something clever to Amanda like … That was the problem. For once, I couldn't think up something clever to say. *How unlike you, Elizabeth.* So how about something not clever? How about getting right to the damn point? Maybe: *Is this true? Why are you telling people you're sleeping with him? Because I don't think you are. He's home with me every night, and he's at school and work during the day. He calls me six times a day on the phone. We make love all the time. He's relentless.*

(It didn't occur to me that he was maybe calling me from her bed.)

(It didn't occur to me that someone who wants to find time to fuck around, will.)

(It didn't occur to me that although I made his daughter a priority, he never ever would.)

Nancy Ellen Row

Things That Terrify Me

by Lizzie

- Hawaiian shirts
- Fat guys wearing Hawaiian shirts
- Fat, super-hairy guys wearing Hawaiian shirts
- Those little troll dolls with bright green or red hair
    - see "childhood nightmare about trolls"
- Troll dolls in Hawaiian shirts
- Suicide
    - see "of others"
    - see "of close family members"
    - see "my own thoughts of"
- Throwing up
    - see "carsickness and never outgrowing it"
    - see "stress and upset stomach"
- Space heaters
- Baseboard heaters
- Things that randomly explode
- Things that spontaneously combust
- Infidelity
    - see "AIDS"
    - see "big liars and how they make you crazy"
    - see "STDs"
    - see? I could be seeing someone else. This is not worth my time. Ha.

How about if I said, if I asked her: *How is this possible? He loves me. Us. His kid and me. What is going to happen to our little family? Besides, he loves me. Why would he mess with you? Why would he throw away his good thing?*

Maybe not *all* that, all at once. But something like that. But I didn't talk to her. I waited and watched and the girls walked out the door. Michael finally finished up with the kayak guy and gave me a hug, then refused my offer to take him out for lunch.

"Naw, I've got to stay here," he said, "Someone's coming by to rent a tent in a little while. Raincheck?"

"Maybe," I said, not mentioning the girls. Not offering to step 'n' fetch it, get his lunch, bring it to him. Fuck it. That girl. Michael, just that past weekend, asked me to marry him. Actually, he said he *wanted to* marry me, it wasn't a direct proposal. I didn't want to marry him, anyway, but it's the thought that counts. (Says the slighted woman.) *("Honey, we'll have babies someday. We'll have four.")*

"We could fly away together," he said. "Somewhere tropical." I talked in my sleep almost every night. I woke up in the morning with a sore jaw, from jawing all night. Michael listened.

"None of it ever makes any sense. You were talking about needing to be somewhere or something, and art class." Amber and Michael kept wrecking my artwork. They hadn't seen one of my drawings on the table, it got a cup of cold coffee spilled on it. Amber didn't mean to cause messes, she was just excited and wanted to touch all of the materials. She would unscrew tubes of paint and they would dry out, just stupid little things like that. But paint was expensive, damn. I was constantly harping on her to leave my stuff alone. She had her own stuff, why mess with mine? I loaded her up with glue sticks, tubes, vials and containers of this and that. Glitter and more freakin' glitter. Stacks of colored paper. A kid-size pair of scissors. I suppose my stuff was more intriguing. The apartment was getting smaller all the time, we didn't have an extra room for a studio.

I was making more collages, along with the assemblages. The mermaid one had turned into a series. I made seven all together, all with different themes and colors. My favorite was the last one – I gave it to my cousin Gwen for a birthday present. The mermaid kind of looked like Gwen, with her sleek, black hair and big green eyes. Their eyebrows were different though – Gwen's were thick and arching; they defined her face. The mermaid's looked like those you'd find on a 1930s movie star. I cut out all these words and phrases from magazines, in French and Spanish, and decorated with those. There was a magazine/cigar store downtown I loved for getting ideas for graphics. They sold all kinds of foreign magazines, and I picked up the *New York Times* there, too.

Now I was making three collages at once. First, I used paint, for the backgrounds, then I layered on feathers, jewelry, fabric and pieces of construction paper I swiped from Amber. I took toys from her, too – little plastic dogs and cats, tiny airplanes, baby dolls. I bought more to replenish her stock. She didn't seem to mind – she wasn't possessive of her toys the way most kids were. She sure wasn't possessive the way I was, say, of my art supplies.

I finished them off with headlines from the tabloids – "Two-headed pig discovered in man's garage!" and "Woman gives birth to alien triplets!" I used a photocopier to play with the newspaper clippings. It all had something to do with an old childhood dream of mine, being alone in the back of the car, with Mom driving.

In the dream, we had stopped at a store. I was sitting in the back, alone.

"I'll be back in a minute!" Mom called.

As soon as she went inside, the car began to roll, and I couldn't get over the front seat, couldn't stop it. *That* dream. And there's the other one of course, where you're at school or work with no clothes on. I had never had that dream, myself, but it seemed more common than the car dream. Just based on anecdotal evidence.

The car would roll downhill. (Of course, the car was always parked at the top of a hill, in those kind of dreams, that's when it all goes black and they turn into nightmares.) I would scream as the car kept rolling, rolling. It was alive by now, like a Stephen King character, taking corners wherever it wanted. Then... something spinning. Spinning around. Rolling me into the blackness until I woke myself up, sick.

So when I put a tiny doll of a girl, or a little car into a collage, and painted black clouds in the background... Hmm. Analyze that, why don't you? I couldn't deal with it anymore, having the same ugly nightmare pop up again. It was triggered by the car wreck with Michael. I hadn't had the dream for years, but after the wreck it came back to grab me by the throat again. Maybe it was a warning of more wrecks to come. I didn't know or care, I just wanted the nightmares to stop. So I started making a new piece, hoping I would exorcise the nightmares. This one had seven tiny toy cars, plus an old model car of Michael's, a red Mustang. I smashed the front half of it with a hammer, then put it all in an old suitcase, a child-sized one, that I picked up at a yard sale. It was pale green, with musty yellow fabric inside, patterned with roses. For a background, I hot-glued two small watercolors to the inside of the suitcase. Amber and I painted them together. One was a stormy sky, all gray and black, with streaks of purple, like in the nightmare; the other was a beach scene, calm and tranquil, with palm trees. I painted a whale, an octopus, and schools of fish. And a little brown-haired girl in a pink gingham bikini, digging in the sand by the water.

"That's me, huh?" Amber said. It did look like her. But it was me. Amber added more trees, and a dog.

101

"Dogs are good at the beach," she said. She wanted a dog so badly. I promised her – foolishly, perhaps – that someday we'd have a house and two dogs. I broke some old dishes and glued the pieces in a heap near the cars, and put a small baby doll, covered with a quilt in a tiny basket, over to one side. One of my neighbors saw me working on it on the front porch and loved it. She paid me cash for it.

"Looks like you've got a career, hon," she said, "I can say I bought something from you before you got famous." Then she made me sign it.

17 *To the Body of Christ*

Our roommate, Dan, told me he was worried about me. We were having coffee one morning on the balcony of the apartment; Michael had left early.

"It's weird, Liz. I think Michael is up to something."

"Like? Running around on me?"

He didn't answer me. "You want a refill?" he asked.

"You know it," I said, and handed him my cup. He stepped back inside the apartment. It was a warm morning; we had all the doors open. I spied on the neighbors. They were setting up for a yard sale.

"What are you talking about?" I asked when he returned.

"I've known Michael for a long time now," he said. "Since we worked together at the bike repair shop. But it seems like I know him *less* every year. Does that make sense? He's being weird, hiding things, even from me. What the hell does he need to hide from me?"

I took a sip of my coffee. Dan had fixed it the way I liked it, with two spoonfuls of sugar, and a generous amount of milk.

"Anyway. I don't know what he's up to, but it's something freaky, I think. I heard you talking in your sleep the other night, when you fell asleep on the couch. You were saying 'Michael, where are you going?' Any idea what that's about, Liz?"

My hands went cold. I wrapped them tighter around the coffee cup. When Dan said that, I remembered hearing the front door click shut quietly, in the middle of the night. Before that, footsteps on the front stairs. Michael, leaving our apartment. To see a lover? To go get high with a friend? Who knew? I didn't remember any of this until Dan mentioned it.

"I think, maybe, I might know," I said. "I think he's been sneaking out, at night. To see other women." Dan patted my arm, the way a parent would, then touched two fingers to my forehead.

"You're a great woman, Liz, I mean – any guy would be lucky to get you, you know? Forget about Michael, he's a prick." I laughed and started to cry a little at the same time.

"I think he's been seeing this girl, Amanda. I mean, I'm pretty sure he is."

"Aw, God, I didn't mean to... Here, I'll get you a tissue, all right?" Dan said. He hurried inside and grabbed a box of tissue for me. "It'll be fine, you're cool. It'll be all right. I don't know anything for sure, OK? He wouldn't want to drop anything to me – because I would tell you." He gave me a hug.

I buried my head in his shoulder, calming a little. He was a great guy. His girlfriend was lucky.

"Yeah, I know. I'm fine now. Thanks. Really. Thanks."

The next day I got home first. I grabbed the mail on the way in. Dan was at work; Michael was studying for a test "with some buddies." He was attending summer school, trying to make up some credits. I was done with classes; I had finally graduated. I now was the proud owner of an art degree. My final project was actually fun to work on – I took a bunch of assemblages and bolted them in place. They took up almost one whole wall by the time I was done. Thank God for the Salvation Army is all I can say. I found so much good junk. The people who work there started saving stuff for me.

The graduation ceremony itself was low-key, just an outdoor commencement at the university. I was relieved to be done.

I gave Billiam a quick stroke on the head as he wound around my legs, meowing at me. He wanted the catnip and kitty treats that Amber always doled out to him. The mail contained a bill from the electric company; a phone bill; a letter from Michael's church, Stinson Memorial, probably wanting more money; and two fat manila envelopes, addressed to Michael. I opened the church letter first. It was from the minister and his wife, addressed "To the Body of Christ," blah blah blah. All about someone resigning as director of women's ministries, two other guys resigning from the elder board and the treasurer, gone. *Cut to the chase, why don't ya?* They never give you the juicy details in these newsletters.

"Phone conversations built upon what we had heard," the letter continued, "… we had a respected Elder and his Wife over for dinner the following evening to listen to their version and gain prospective…"

Perspective, they meant.

New goal in life: to become a "Wife" with a capital "W." And according to the senior pastor, the people who left the church were unwilling to talk, as they had "been there, done that." It was getting interesting, though. It was fun reading other people's mail; I should have started the habit years before. Even though I didn't know any of these people, being a heathen. I never attended church with Michael, but I sort of remembered him saying something about an affair with two of the parish members, something

105

involving a drunk teenager who was no longer "part of the flock" – who may or may not have been a slut. ("Slut" equaling "asked for it." Abuse of children never being mentioned.)

"Did they rape her?" I asked Michael flat out when he told me about it.

"She didn't press charges, if they did," he said.

Why does he even go to this skanky church? He wanted to take Amber; Kim and I wouldn't let him. Too many freaks. I kept reading. "We could leave the Church as countless others had done. Or we could remain at the Church pretending what we knew did not matter or did not exist." *That's always your best bet.* I smiled.

The letter ended with a request for everyone to attend a special meeting, an "informational" ("not divisive," the writer hurried to explain) meeting to discuss the resignations. It was going to be held at a nearby elementary school, not the church. Neutral territory. They had included directions to the school. And an acknowledgement that "some may even call us evil," but with contrite hearts, after spending a significant amount of time in prayer, blah blah blah, God would grant wisdom "through knowledge and understanding." Signed, "In Him, Dave and Kitty Matthews."

"Okey-doke, Dave and Kitty," I told the letter as I put it on the table with the rest of the junk. "Best wishes. *Vaya con Dios.*" I ripped open one of the fat packages, not even trying to cover my tracks. I figured it wasn't anything important, so why should Michael care if I opened it? He was funny about the mail though – it was almost as if he got home first on purpose, to get the mail before I did. I rarely saw it. He and Dan took care of the bills – I just wrote them checks to cover my part.

At first it looked like the glossy magazine inside the first envelope was a camping catalog, like one the outdoor program would get at school. It had a picture of a waterfall on the cover. Then I realized that the couple on the cover at the base of the falls were fucking.

"The Best Sex" was written in small type at the bottom of the catalog. I looked at the return address – it was generic, just a P.O. box from somewhere in California. Inside, images of gadgets, videos, and magazines, all with the same goal in mind. "Constriction rings," loads of lube, a "Chinese dragonfly" that looked horrifying and potentially painful – some kind of strap-on that also included a piece described as an "anal bead stick." And a lacy little G-string, free with purchase, "to enjoy with your special someone," if an order was placed within seven days.

"Nasty!" I dropped the catalog like a hot potato. You know what feels good? White lace feels good. Maybe some silk. The breeze blowing in through the window, a blender full of margaritas. *What a priss.* I didn't know what I was in for next, but I ripped into the second package anyway. Fat people, fucking. All day, all ways, and looking pretty blissed out. OK, everyone is entitled to a good time and all, but damn, I didn't wanna see pictures. I couldn't stop. I flipped four more pages and ew... I shut the catalog and put it on the table, too. Then I took one finger and shoved them away from me. My stomach took a big lurch. So this was part of Michael's secret. I was not into it. I wasn't into Amanda, either. I just didn't like sharing, I was lousy at it.

I threw all of my clothes and most of my other junk in two duffel bags, put them in the car, then went back and gathered up the cat toys, food and basket Billiam slept in. I left Amber's stuff, except for the art corner. She was outgrowing all of her clothes, anyway. I could pick up more at Goodwill.

I had always suspected something like this with Michael, but I was still a little surprised. I knew there was a lot worse shit out there, but I was sort of innocent about all this. Plus, Michael was so... uptight. I didn't think he liked smutty stuff. But wasn't it usually guys like that, though, who were the kinkiest? He had sure never let on in bed what he was fantasizing about. Our sex life was good. It was enough for me, but not enough for him, apparently.

I didn't want to go through the kitchen and sort out whose was what. I could set up a time later, with Dan, to get the kitchen stuff and everything else. Kim was supposed to drop Amber off soon. Michael had talked with her. For once, he would have to care for his daughter all by himself. I was in no shape to play mommy right now. I could go crash with JoJo and Gage.

I kept getting drawn back to the catalogs. I wanted to rip them up and throw them in the garbage, but I also wanted him to know I'd seen them. Too weird. I'd never seen anything kinkier than *Hustler*. What. A. Prissy Priss.

"Fascinating," Michael would say. It was his favorite word. Yugh.

"Are you innocent?" I said out loud. I spread out newspaper on the table and found some glue. I layered the church letter with the fatties catalog with the sex toys catalog and made a little collage for Michael. Scissors, tape, glue. I found a roll of white ribbon in the kitchen drawer and curled some lengths of that, glued them down. That was for me – pure and virtuous and all. Ha. Then I dug through his file cabinet. I found a stack of snapshots of various women – some naked, some not; some hot, some not – along with love letters. Amanda's name was scribbled on a note that was in with the photos. A few of the pictures were of Kim, including some of her nude, mugging for the camera. Some were of women I'd never seen before. I hadn't snooped through his stuff before, but now I wish I had thought of it earlier. I took three of the letters and a bunch of the pictures and glued those to the collage, too.

It was calming, somehow, seeing the letters, with the picture of the G-string, next to Dave and Kitty's looped signatures. "...*we would encourage you to spend a significant time in prayer before the meeting ..."* meshed with *"a sensual statement at just the right moment"* with *"Michael, I hope you understand"* (in Amanda's handwriting) over to the side. Yeah, I know just what you mean, sweetie. I hope he understands, too. I really do. God, he just wanted to be caught, how stupid could I be?

The Chinese dildo next to directions to the grade school where the churchies were having their meeting. *God grants wisdom to the curvaceous female lead, who is chased through the woods by three feral creatures, finally succumbing to her primal urges in a cave, where the rowdy males enthusiastically ravage her.* I wrote that at the top, my hand trembling. My mind was rambling, thinking of a painting I could do. It was kind of funny, putting it all together like that. It gave me a little distance from it. And just because they were fat, so what? Adam, David and Goliath could have a four-way with Eve. *Orgasmic bliss and contrite hearts.* I wrote that along the other side, across from Amanda's words. All these women who believed everything Michael said. All of us. I set a photo of Michael and me on top of the collage, glued like the angel on the top of a Christmas tree. We were up in the Columbia River Gorge, in the picture. The wind was blowing through my hair. We looked happy. *Dude, I thought we were happy.*

The cat walked in, stretching and yawning, to see what I was doing. He was plenty happy. He knew what happiness was. I took all the cat paraphernalia out to the car, then went back to put kitty in his carrier. As I was walking out the door with him, Michael pulled up.

"What's going on?" he asked, confused. "Are you taking the cat to the vet or something?"

"It's like, it's like I've been *brainwashed* by you or something," I said, spitting the words out at him, "It's like you're some cult guy, and I'm saying 'Oh, you want me to drink poison Kool-Aid? OK!' And you know what else? You're *never* going to graduate from college and you know why? *Because you're an idiot."*

Michael looked like he was going to cry.

"Lizzie, I have fucked up everything in my life and now I'm going to lose you. I don't want to lose you." He started toward me, but I waved him off.

"I'm not going to see you anymore, Michael, do you understand?"

"I can't blame you," he said. And I left.

18 *Alphabet City*

"What else was I supposed to do?" I asked my girlfriend Kat, who was gracious enough to house JoJo and me while we sought temporary employment and a one- or two-month sublet. It was our first day in New York. JoJo was staying two months, at the most; I was undecided. I'd hauled along some of my paintings and two of the assemblages, in case I found someone to show my stuff. I brought slides of the rest of my work, the stronger pieces. Kat had a big crowd of friends and promised to introduce me around.

My brother was keeping my cat for the summer, or until I figured out what I was doing, and Kim promised to stay stable for Amber. She said she would call Michael if things got bad, or, emergency backup plan, Michael's parents, if she couldn't find Michael. JoJo said Gage could bite her, she was coming with me. My bosses, for a graduation present, bought me a round-trip ticket to New York and told me to take as much time as I needed. And to stay there permanently, if I wanted. Too nice of them, really. They found someone to cover for me and said, "Go, go, go."

"No, it's good you split," Kat said, "Michael is such an asshole."

We were in her tiny, one-bedroom (illegal) sublet in Alphabet City, on 12th Street, between Avenues B and C. It was scary as hell. The Hells Angels down the street did offer some degree of protection, but we didn't want it.

"Whoa," JoJo said when she first saw the place, and immediately left to go get wine. Kat and I proceeded to split the one beer left in the fridge and fried up some ham and eggs for a midday snack.

"How's it going with Kevin?" Kat asked.

I'd brought pictures to show her – the two of us at a party, the two of us at a picnic at his mom's house, with all his family making bunny ears behind our heads. Just like old times.

"Kevin is on hold for a while," I said. "Too much coke! He gets nosebleeds from it, it's ridiculous. He's working this summer; maybe he'll be too busy to party."

Kevin had heard I was single and called to ask me out for drinks, the week Michael and I split up. Like an idiot, I went. But he was as familiar to me as JoJo. And we'd always gotten along. We had a shorthand we spoke. Lizzie/Kevin code. That was nice. He and his girlfriend had split up.

"I missed you," he told me. Like fun he did.

Kat nodded. "You needed a fling."

Kat had lived in Portland for awhile but she hadn't grown up there. She was the one who got me the job at the gallery. After she heard about Michael, she nicknamed me Heartbreak Kid and told me to wise up and come to New York. So I did.

I downed the rest of the beer and sopped up my eggs with a piece of toast. "Here's to New York, girl," I said.

19 *Summer in the Hamptons*

JULY 1990

Shelter from the storm... JoJo and I got an offer from a friend of Kat's to go stay at her place in the Hamptons, and we were gone. The friend, her boyfriend, the modeling agents they were splitting the cost of the place with, assorted girlfriends, boyfriends, models – it was the crash pad for everyone. Two more bodies didn't matter. Kat said she would try to make it out for the weekend.

"Bloody Mary this morning?" Olivia, one of the models, yelled out to me. I was only barely halfway awake, and getting dressed in one of the bedrooms. I'd pulled an all-nighter talking art with a dealer – coke, not art – the night before. He did know art dealers, though, and offered to introduce me. I told him thanks to that, but no thanks to the coke. We had strawberry margaritas and swam in the pool in the dark. It was nice. Interesting guy, but not my type.

"We're going out for breakfast," I said.

"This *is* breakfast," Olivia said, winking at me when I emerged from the bedroom. "What should we drink next? Melon daiquiris?"

I pulled on my suit, a black string bikini that I'd had forever, and went for another swim. The pool was gorgeous, as was the rest of the house – four bedrooms, three bathrooms, all white. No personal touches anywhere, other than an occasional basket of seashells. And a person could breathe on Long Island, an added bonus. All that clear sea air.

"How long can you hold your breath?" was the first thing Kat asked us when we got to Manhattan.

"Until mid-September?" I said. "Maybe October?"

I was still irked about Michael, whom I really did consider a lovely man when we first started dating. Even back in high school, he had a reputation for being a total sweetheart and good friend. He used to go hear feminist speakers at the university with me. He liked my paintings – he'd seen some of them at a student show. He seemed like he actually understood them, even. My abstracts weren't for everyone, too much red and black.

"I was so completely duped. He was a bushwhacker," I said to JoJo over breakfast at a local diner.

"Yeah, no foolin'," JoJo said, inhaling her coffee.

"No, not like that, I mean... he's the kind who will tell you – princess of course I support your art, and then whack! You're pregnant and the only art you're doing involves finger paint. Not that I'm opposed to finger painting, I mean, if that's your thing."

"Woof," JoJo said. "Body paints – with chocolate. I'd be into that. Hey," she said, signaling the waitress for more coffee, "what about when he decided to do his AA shit for ten minutes? That was a good time."

"Oh, my," I said, "It changed his life, don't you know? He got sick and tired of being sick and tired, his worst day now was better than his best day then. He never stopped drinking, you know. He used to lie at the meetings. 'Clean and sober' my ass. He only stopped drinking for about two weeks, total. Then he said he had learned to drink in moderation and went right back to it. He and Kim. Freaks."

JoJo swiped a piece of my toast and dunked it in her coffee. "He always seemed like a freak show to me, babe. I never saw what the allure was. Just eat, OK? Man, this is good." She was eating some kind of seafood hash with fried eggs on top.

I slammed the rest of my Bloody Mary and ordered another. "Oh, you know – I was going to leave him, I found out I was pregnant, I found out I had the measles, he didn't want the baby, we totaled our car, I had an abortion. And then there's Amber and Kim. I've gotten attached to them, you know. Even though Kim is the biggest damn pain. You know. Next thing I know, it's been three years."

"Yup," JoJo said, finishing her hash and reaching for my hash browns. "So when are you going to really leave him?" Kat showed up with a guy friend, later, and we stayed a couple of more days at the house. Then we rode her motorcycle back into the city. JoJo rode with Kat's friend, on his bike. So much easier to get around on bikes than to drive. A wall of squirming, toxic heat hit us as we entered the city, and then our magical vacation was nothing but a memory. I tried to hold my breath, thinking of Kat's advice. I thought she was making a joke.

I tried to stop thinking of Amber and Michael on a hot summer day, wearing shorts and tank tops. Holding hands and smiling at me. Michael, taking Amber swimming. Amber and Michael, eating ice cream at the shopping center. Michael, in bed, with his leg thrown over mine, pressing against me, kissing the back of my neck. I shook my head. Would he still spend time with Amber, now that I was out of the picture? He hadn't spent enough time with her, even when I was around to work on it. God, it was stinky and hot.

"Escape to New York!" Kat had encouraged me over the phone. "What do you have going there?"

"Only it's like I can feel Michael thinking about me," I told Kat, after we got back to the city and were hauling our gear inside. "Even three thousand miles away. Is that possible?"

"Of course it's possible," Kat said. "He probably *is* thinking about you. Kim, too. Every time they can't find someone to watch their kid. Try to stop thinking about them, just for a little while." I thought about Kevin, too, sometimes. He wanted to fly out for a week, but I told him to save his money. I couldn't stop thinking about the family I'd left behind, especially the baby I never had. In New York, I dreamt about the baby nearly every night. We were in a house, in this dream, and Amber was watching Disney movies. The baby was sleeping in her crib by her. She was nine months old. And she was beautiful, stretched out and covered with a quilt. In this beautiful old house with the hardwood floors and lots of big bay windows, with the sunlight pouring in. I woke up crying every time, thinking I was at home, instead of in some crappy apartment in the East Village, with JoJo snoring quietly next to me on the air mattress. Our apartment was populated with mice, roaches, and those god-awful water bugs. They were bigger than rats. The East Village was a little rough, but supposedly up and coming. It was nasty, and there was a lot of crime. But it was what we could afford.

I was worried about Amber. I had never been away from her like this before, for this long. But it forced Kim to take care of business, without me to rely on. Maybe Michael would come through and surprise us all.

"What you do is what we call en-ab-ling," JoJo said, "Say it after me, en-AB-ling..."

Kim seemed happy; we had talked once or twice since I left. It was good to hear her voice, actually, hers and Amber's. She had found a job at a clothing store a few weeks earlier and loved it, although welfare was still helping with their medical coverage and subsidized some of her child care, too.

New York City in the summertime smelled dead. Worse than dead. Dead plus... something else. I started to retch sometimes, just walking down the street. I quickly learned to cover my nose and breathe through my mouth (Kat's words rattling around in my head: "How long can you hold your breath?"), making it past the same motionless shape in a sleeping bag that I had passed for three days in a row on my way to work. I was at a temp job, it was OK.

He could be a dead person, that guy in the sleeping bag. He could have been dead for days, weeks maybe, and would anyone notice? Did I really care? I didn't, I am sorry to say. Just move along. I cared the first few days I was in Manhattan. After that I started thinking, *There really are too many goddamn people on this tiny island.* I headed around the corner, heading to the bodega for something fast for dinner.

"No one would care if I *did* puke on the sidewalk," I told Gwennie during our weekly phone call. "They would just step around it and move along. Maybe one of the homeless guys would stop to hold back my hair for me. If I paid him."

This made Gwen laugh. She had a sick sense of humor, that one. Much like JoJo. She couldn't wait to come visit. She wanted to go by the Dakota, where John Lennon was killed, and the Chelsea, where Sid killed Nancy. A tour of death, so to speak. And she wanted to see the Alice in Wonderland sculpture in Central Park.

"New York sounds so punk rock!" Gwen said, excited.

"Yeah, especially Alice in Wonderland. We'll go to CBGB's and all, we'll have some fun," I said. "Oh! I bought a new futon; it smells yummy. Way better than it smells outside and it's more comfortable than that damn air mattress. Queen-sized – room for guests. I think it's stuffed with alfalfa.

117

I almost have to sneeze it's so good."

We talked for a bit, about Gwen's hunt for a new apartment, about my various temp jobs. I was at an accounting firm for a few weeks. JoJo and I had been spending a lot of time at Life Café; it was only a few blocks from our place.

"I'll take you there; it's great. Everyone there is super nice. And we can try to go to a Broadway show, too. And we'll eat all kinds of good stuff." The food in New York was everything everyone always said it was. The Indian food, my new favorite, was fantastic, and I was addicted to the Polish food at Veselka's. I had never tried pierogis or samosas until New York. The best part was that you could have anything delivered – Chinese food, Italian, hot soup, mashed potatoes – pretty much any time. Perfect for insomniacs. Or people like me, who needed to be babied.

And then, the elephant in the room.

"You're not still in love with him, are you?" Gwen asked me.

There was silence from my end.

"Who?" I asked.

"Michael. Are you?" Gwen asked again.

"You've been talking to JoJo, haven't you?" I asked her.

"Maybe. God. You're not. Tell me please, right now, that you're not still in love with that prick. What is *wrong* with you, anyway?"

"Gee, thanks, Gwen."

"Seriously, listen to me. He and Amanda completely deserve each other. Completely and totally for sure, forever. OK? What's that expression? 'If they weren't together, there would be four people miserable, not just two.' "

I smiled on the other end of the phone.

"God, no," I said. "Of course I'm not in love with him. I just... I wish it would have worked. I'd like to get married, someday. Not to Michael. And

I want kids. Just not with him. I wish... You know."

"Sheesh, thank God that's all it is," Gwen said, and let out a little sigh.

"And Skylab? What's he up to?" I asked. "Partying too much? He won't come visit."

"Sky is Sky, you know," Gwen said. "A guy. See you next week!"

"You bet," I said, and hung up.

20 *Things That Work To Put Out Fires*

AUGUST 1990

Friday night. The US invaded Kuwait – it was all over the news. I kept the television turned off; I didn't want to see it. Like Vietnam all over again. JoJo loved her TV and kept flipping it back on. It was going to get bad politically, I knew it. I didn't want any more wars, ever. United States politics equals *fucked up as usual*. And there was AIDS, too. The East Coast was in much worse shape than the West Coast. Maybe it just felt that way because we were in the city, I don't know. At least people were talking about it more, here. Talking about safe sex and all that. Clean needles. But I didn't want to think about any of it; it was all too much.

JoJo and I were having a guest over for dinner – an aunt of one of JoJo's friends from back home. It was nice to find some people we knew in Manhattan, however tenuous the connections were. Besides, we wanted to show off our lousy apartment. We had found the place through Kat; we

120

were neighbors now. Our housemates were rarely home, which was convenient because the place was tiny. We were also waiting for Gwen; her flight was scheduled to arrive at 11 p.m. In honor of the aunt and Gwen, we would cook food. That was our first mistake.

We bought some meat that looked like chicken legs, but it wasn't. I threw them in a 350-degree oven for an hour. That's how Betty Crocker always said to do it. When I opened the door, figuring they were close to done, I found the mystery meat had turned bright red. Quite bright red. Also the legs had started a grease fire in the bottom of the oven. Flames began to lick the sides of the stove once I opened the door.

I slammed the door shut. My first thought: I was a Campfire Girl. I can handle this. My second thought: I got kicked out of Campfire. My third thought: I screamed for JoJo, who was watching the news and drinking wine in our dollhouse-sized living room. We had mice and water bugs, a laundry line hanging across the living room, a bathtub in the kitchen and bars on the windows. It was the worst apartment I'd ever lived in in my life, but that didn't mean I wanted to burn it down.

"Throw water on it!" JoJo yelled, not budging from her chair. The New York news was engrossing, she had me there, but I needed help.

"It's a grease fire," I yelled back, "I can't throw water on it!" And that brought her to the kitchen.

"Baking soda," we said at the same time. JoJo got the huge box of soda from the refrigerator and tossed it into the flames.

Nothing.

They grew larger. So, like the kids in *The Cat in the Hat*, well. We didn't know *what* to do.

⁓

121

Things That Work To Put Out Fires

by Lizzie and JoJo

1. Baking soda, allegedly.
2. The lid of a pan often works, for a stovetop fire.
3. Fire extinguishers are also helpful. If you have one.
4. A throw rug can occasionally smother a fire.
5. Or, say a younger sister has caught her nylon robe on fire, playing recklessly with a sparkler? Roll her on the ground to put her out.
6. You could try calling the fire department.

***

It was sheer, goofy luck we even had any baking soda, because the only other things in the refrigerator were beer, a mostly-empty bottle of ketchup, wine and film (one of our housemates was an NYU film student). I slammed the oven door shut again and the flames kept coming out. JoJo and I both screamed.

It was out of control now. The flames licked the kitchen walls, not content with being confined to the stove. JoJo grabbed the phone and dialed. I fumbled with our five door locks. Half of them were unlocked, but I couldn't tell which ones and kept unlocking and relocking the same ones.

"I hate these locks."

I finally undid them all. I ran down the hall and banged on the nearest neighbor's door while JoJo talked with 911. The neighbor ran and filled up a bucket of water in her kitchen bathtub, then ran down the hall fast, with her little girl flying behind her, big brown eyes wide and excited.

"But it's a grease fire," I told her.

JoJo was on the phone with the fire department, trying to stay calm.

"East Eleventh Street! No, Eleventh. East Village. Can we use water to put it out? It's a grease fire. No — East Village."

She paused, then screamed, "Not West Village, East Village! Listen, can you please just tell me if it's OK to use water on this fire?"

"Fuck it," the neighbor said.

She opened the oven door and dumped the whole pail of water in. The fire went right out. The little girl clapped her hands and smiled at her mommy.

"Good job, mama," she said. "Good job."

"Thank you," I told her. "Thank you so much." Neighbors had come from upstairs and downstairs and were gathered around our front door. The whole thing lasted about five minutes, total. I heard the fire trucks and went to the front window to look. The window was open and smoke was rolling out. I noticed, for the first time, the neighbors clustered outside, and the Hells Angels parked on the street, alongside the neighbor kids and their trikes. The junkies had stopped making their swaps and were looking up at our window.

"Man, you can really make a lot of smoke fast, huh?" JoJo said from the kitchen.

The Cuban men who spent their days playing cards at the restaurant right across the street had paused their game long enough to squint up at the building. One pointed me out to his friend.

"Fire's out!" I yelled out the window. One of the bikers gave me a thumbs-up.

"It's OK," I heard the Cuban guy tell his friend. They went back to playing cards.

JoJo told the dispatcher, "It's OK, it's out now." She hung up and joined me at the window. "Firemen are on their way."

"They're here," I said.

123

"The Hells Angels are out there, too?" JoJo asked. "Nice of them to help, the fuckers." She waved at them and smiled. They waved back. We turned and walked over to our neighbor, our hero, and her daughter. The rest of the neighbors had backed off from the front door when they heard the firemen.

"My name's Cheryl," the neighbor said, sticking out her hand. "This is Bianca." Bianca gave a little wave, then sat down to pull off her sandals.

"Lizzie and JoJo," JoJo said. "Thanks. *Lo siento.*"

"Yeah, I'm sorry, too," I said.

"You girls just moved in, huh? Maybe you should eat dinner out tonight?" She gave me a little pat on the shoulder.

JoJo poured us all glasses of wine – Bianca had water – then the four of us watched everyone in the street, watching us back, as the fireman stomped in. They stood crammed together in the tiny kitchen, coughing.

"The fire," the lead guy said, "did not start in the oven."

"Oh yes it did," I said. "I started it myself." The pan of mystery meat was still on top of the stove where I'd left it.

"No. No, it definitely did not start in the oven. There is too much smoke for that. It started somewhere else in the apartment." They split up and started examining the entire apartment.

"Look at those nice axes," JoJo whispered to us. "I know they want an excuse to use them." Cheryl and I laughed. They looked in all four of our cramped rooms, moved some piles of panties around, checked the bars on the window, and pulled the armchair out from the wall. Then they pushed it back again. JoJo and I were sharing a room; our housemate (the film student) and her boyfriend shared the other bedroom.

"The fire," he said, "started in the oven. Maybe you girls should eat dinner out tonight."

He gave me a hard thump on the back, almost knocking me over, and

124

they tromped back out. Bianca clapped her hands together and put her sandals back on.

"Maybe we should just drink up the rest of this wine," JoJo said. "And maybe you should go get a couple more bottles, Lizzie dear, before our company gets here."

"They were cute, eh?" Cheryl said. "The firemen?" She let Jo pour her another glass of wine. At the store I had to ask the guy to open the three bottles of wine for me. The corkscrew fell behind the stove at some point, during the fire. It could stay there – I was never touching that stove again.

"So, you like this wine," he said, pulling a cup out from under the counter. He tapped the cup twice on the counter and gestured for me to pour. I filled the cup half full.

"Yeah, my roommate and I were going to fix dinner at home tonight," I told him, "but the kitchen caught on fire."

"That was you?" he said with interest in his voice. He drank the wine and gestured for more. "Over on Eleventh? I saw the fire trucks go by. So. You girls eating dinner out tonight then?" I added a couple of loaves of bread to the bottles on the counter. Cheese, a couple of apples, and some olive oil, too. Dinner.

The aunt, when she arrived, said wine, cheese and bread were fine with her. We poked at the meat and tried to determine what it was.

"Goose?" the aunt suggested. "Who knows?" I took it and the pan of grease out to the trash, along with the empty box of baking soda.

When Gwen arrived in her cab later that night, she said the flight was without mishap. She brought a coffee can full of Granny's homemade chocolate chunk cookies and a twenty-five dollar check, on which Granny had written in the memo line, "So you girls can have some fun."

"Did you guys barbecue tonight?" Gwen asked, sniffing the air.

21 *Hey, Chris!*

AUGUST 1990

They stopped my train between stations when I was riding home. I was already late – the accounting firm where I was working had kept me an hour and a half extra doing data entry. I got paid for it, but I was starving now, and I had plans for the evening. At this rate JoJo, Gwen and I would never make it to the movies.

"Injuredpassengeronthetracks," the conductor mumbled over the loudspeaker. The power went off, the air went off, and everyone became still. We held our collective breath. We were herded from the front car, where I was riding, to the second car back. We had already been crowded; now we had even less room to move. One guy panicked. He grabbed the conductor as he herded us back and slid the door shut.

"Just tell me, please just tell me," he said.

"There's a guy cut in half on the tracks," the conductor snapped at him.

"Oh God, oh my God, oh no," the guy said. Someone started telling people-killed-by-subway jokes. Everyone laughed except the Oh-My-God guy. Two subway workers walked down the tracks and threw a body bag onto the first car, then hopped in after it. The train started moving. The workers tossed the bag onto the platform at the next stop, then jumped out after it. Everyone moved back into the first car. The man who had panicked was quiet. He looked in shock. No one talked to him.

My stop arrived. I bought us hot dogs and papaya juice for dinner. We decided to stay in for the evening and watch bad TV. We also decided that our favorite new Biblical passage was: *"Shout unto the Lord — you are my rock!"*

"That's so good, isn't it?" JoJo asked. "It sums it all up."

When we went out in public, we played a game we made up to tease guys. When we were half a block or so from a group of dudes, we yelled, "Hey, Chris!" Usually one of the guys would turn around; then we'd head the other direction. It killed time.

On my lunch break one day, I discovered black squirrels in Central Park. I'm sure someone else had discovered them before, but it was a first for me. It was amazing.

"No, it's not from the pollution," I told Skyler over the phone when he asked. "They're really black. It's a fashion statement, see?"

I talked to Amber long distance a few times a week. I called her at preschool from my work line and got her out of her nap. "What toys did you buy me? Did you see those dinosaur bones again?" She had already made me promise to take her to the Museum of Natural History when and if we were ever in New York together. She wanted to see the Alice in Wonderland sculpture in Central Park, too. I had described it to her.

"Did you know there's a war now?" she asked me. "My mom and I lighted our candles, to pray for everyone."

"Honey, that's sweet. That was really thoughtful of you. Tell your mom I'll do that, too, over at my apartment. Thank you for the idea." I was getting all teary now. Also, I'd have to rethink the whole candle thing. I was still kind of twitchy around open flames.

Always, Amber's last question was, "When are you coming home, Liz?"

Jo was gone all the time, wearing high heels and little tiny black dresses. Guys named Huber and Dominick and Freddy were in love with her. They rang the bell and waited on the stoop, hoping she would come out. It was the long legs, blond hair and freckles; she looked like she was from Kansas or somewhere. Me? I didn't really feel like dating. For once.

"Them, again?" was all JoJo said about her fan club. I just called her Holly Golightly. She adjusted well to New York, but it was too noisy for me. And stinky. Sometimes the men sat together on the stoop, waiting for JoJo, smoking cigarettes. Everyone seemed to get along. They went out dancing. JoJo's favorite spot was the club that used to be a church; my favorite was the club that used to be a subway station.

None of the men realized that JoJo had a tall, tough-guy husband back in Oregon, Gage, who could bend any of them in half. Were he not three thousand miles across the country, unaware of his girl's escapades. JoJo eventually started to miss him. She flew to California and met Gage at Disneyland and didn't come back. They did love Disneyland; they'd already been three times. He was thrilled to have her back. He was even more stupid for her than the guys on the stoop. He called her "kitten." It was cute, but kind of obnoxious. She didn't even have to work much while we were in New York; he kept sending her money.

I was lonely, after Jo left. I caught a virus and ran a fever for a week but didn't start any more fires. My granny's favorite expression (she'd written it on a picture postcard of a cow she'd mailed me the week before): "Men are like streetcars, honey. There's another one along every 15 minutes. Miss one, catch the next." She knew I was discouraged about my love life. She said Grandpa wasn't feeling great, "But he's a tough old bird, he'll be all right, I expect."

I was ready to split New York. I was lonely. I was sick of jokes about the subway. I was having fun with Kat, but she knew I missed the big trees and the clean air. It was time to head home. I picked up the phone and dialed Kevin.

22 *Rain and Flowers*

SEPTEMBER 1990

*R*ainy Portland has never looked so beautiful to me. We caught a tailwind on the way back and shaved twenty minutes off the flight time. I took off my headphones and started gathering my gear as the plane landed. I had most of my stuff shipped. I sold some of the art to Kat's friends, but no galleries nibbled. I made the rounds. Maybe another time, who knew?

It was late, almost midnight. In New York it was almost 3 a.m. I would have just been getting home from the clubs, or deciding to go to another party. Or staying up late watching bad television, ha. I was tired but happy to be home.

I stepped off the plane and saw a bouquet so huge I couldn't see the person's face behind it. He was wearing black jeans and work boots. Whoever he was, he had nice arms and was holding a sign, hand-lettered in black ink, that said LIZZIE. Kevin stepped out from behind the flowers, an explosion of asters, lilies, roses, and baby's breath.

"Never leave me again," he said, "Promise?" He grabbed me,

smothered me with kisses, smoothed my hair back from my face. He looked at me as if he were seeing me for the first time. He stepped back, then took me into his arms again.

"You look too skinny," he said, finally.

"Thanks." I took the flowers; he picked up my backpack and slung it over his shoulder.

"Nice flowers," I said. "Did you steal them?"

23 *Forever Young*

FEBRUARY 1991

It was just for fun, that's what I was telling myself.

"Not a permanent thing," I told JoJo, "just a fling thing."

"When has it ever been a fling with you and Kevin?" Jo asked.

"So, hey babe, wanna get stoned?" He pulled a joint out of his shirt pocket and handed it to me after we got into the car when he picked me up at the airport. He would say things like that. Like a forever-young teenager. We had always, always partied, since we were just little kids. We grew up together, going to parties with all of the parents and families in our neighborhood. Then some of the parents would split up and date some of the other parents. Then maybe they'd get back together with the original parent, or maybe they wouldn't. It was lively. Seriously – all of us kids started drinking and smoking when we were about ten. If a kid found a joint in an ashtray and smoked it, the parents would think that was hilarious. There were no boundaries. They didn't want us growing up all repressed like they had. Hello, 1970s.

So, I said yes to the joint and glossed right over what I knew about

Kevin and heroin. No needles. But everyone else I knew had tried needles – they thought it was so daring or something. Bullshit.

The only needles I knew about were at the doctor's office. This was foreign territory to me. Yes, Kevin had tried it. Everyone had their pasts, yes? At least I knew what most of his consisted of. Unlike Michael, the sneakiest person I'd ever known.

"Does Kevin have a steady job now, or what?" JoJo asked.

I nodded my head. "Yeah, he does construction. And deals, a little. Just pot. But he's going to stop."

Kevin made me feel protected and loved and sexy. He was entertaining. He was sexier than Michael, for sure. And his jokes were funnier. Michael's jokes were stupid. Also, not funny.

We were in the scummy little bathroom of a nightclub downtown, JoJo and I. Our friends' band was playing. They weren't good, but they were loud. Someone had scrawled, "Witch one's Pink?" on the wall in crimson red lipstick. There was no toilet paper. The toilet was barely attached to the wall. One bolt held it into place. JoJo found a pack of tissue in her purse.

"Voila!" she said. "Now we can pee."

No toilet paper, and no soap or paper towels, either. But at least the toilet didn't come crashing down. We did a fast rinse under the cold water and dried our hands on our tights. All of us girls wore the same uniform – short black skirts, ribbed or fishnet black tights, black boots (motorcycle, in JoJo's case) or clunky shoes (in my case), low-cut shirts. Vintage jewelry that we had purchased at thrift stores or begged from our grannies. JoJo had a fuzzy green cardigan, in a stunning shade of lime, that she adored. She wore that thing every time we went out. She was like Mr. Rogers with that damn sweater.

"I love this place," I said. Someone had scribbled, "do a little dance" on the wall, too.

"Jo, you remember how much you used to love KC and the Sunshine Band?"

"You did, too!" she said, swatting at me.

"Not as much as you." I fixed my eyeliner; it always got all smeared.

"I would have married them and had their babies, it's true." JoJo put on more lipstick. She liked this dark purple stuff, it was almost black. It looked good against her pale skin.

"Woo woo woo woo woo woo woo woo woo woo," I sang to her.

"What about you and your ZZ Top fixation?"

"Shoot, I still love ZZ Top." We headed back to the bar, where the bartender slid a pitcher of beer across to us.

"Already been paid for," he said, and gave me a wink. Some guys across the way smiled and waved at us. The bartender gave me two (relatively) clean glasses; JoJo took the beer and gave a little wave and smile to the guys. Porno movies were playing on the televisions over the bar.

"Not as sexy as you would think," JoJo said, eying the porn. "What the hell is he doing to her, anyway?"

24 *You Took Kindly to Me*

1983-1987

MARCH 6, 1983

I look at my life now, how it's the same as when I was younger, slightly crazy. How it's different. Seeing that I am the same child. I saw Kevin this morning. We went out for breakfast at Pappy's, this place up on 82nd Avenue, and this nice old guy paid our check. He said, "You took kindly to me. I like that." All because we'd laughed at some jokes he and his buddies were making. They were sitting at a booth right next to us. That was sweet, that he covered us. We stopped by Michael's house, but he was still crashed. His grandma yelled at Kevin (jokingly), "Don't you wake him up, Kevin! You two always go, go, go! You just go and then come back!" She was funny. Then she asked who I was; I hadn't met her before. He introduced us, and she looked at him and said, "She's beautiful." Aw, it made my day.

Kevin dropped me off at Portland State after that. I didn't have class until 10. I miss him. I'd like to see him again, but I just can't start that insanity again, I can't. I need to be sane again. Sometimes I get so frustrated I just can't breathe.

⌘

MARCH 19, 1983

I'm having the best time this spring vacation. I'm doing all of my English homework ahead of time for my Shakespeare class. I just finished Hamlet, and I want to start on *Measure for Measure*. I'm getting ahead on Spanish, too, and I've been working on some drawings, for a painting I want to do. Xoxoxoxox love my art.

I get so lonesome for my mom sometimes. I never realized how nice her house was until I left it. It's OK now, my roommates I'm living with are pretty nice. But it's not my mom. She's strong, and pretty, and smart. She is cool. My roommate's mom comes over all the time to (get this) borrow money! Or pot. She likes to sit around (the mom that is) getting loaded and bitching about how screwed up her life is. Oh. My God. I can't wait until I'm not living with them anymore.

My mom plants gardens and cleans the house and cooks good food. She has always been there for me and for my friends, too. She used to date, now she says she's done with men. I told her she might change her mind. She still says that I'm her baby. How sweet is that? When my dad died, the whole world just went cold, but she was there for me, to always hold me. I don't think she's ever gotten over Daddy, that's what I think.

⌘

OCT. 6, 1986

Met up with Michael again, from high school? He's at Portland State, too, he's straightened up. We've been seeing each other pretty steady. He said he doesn't want to see anyone but me; he's given up on all other women. I will believe it when I see it. I'm not seeing anyone else. I like him a lot. We have a past, present and (hopefully) future together. He has a kid! Her name is Amber. He and the mom broke up before the baby was born. He showed me a picture; she's cute. She's almost 8 months old. Not walking yet. I love babies.

MARCH 3, 1987

Michael is pissing me off. He makes comments that he tries to pass off as jokes, but I think that they're the truth and I hate him for that. I feel sick to my stomach when I think of all the money I've blown on meals out for us, clothes. Michael said he'll leave me if I'm ever broke. Ha. Ha. Ha. I've been waitressing for awhile, and I always babysat and did odd jobs, when I was younger, so I usually have money on me. I just started at this art gallery. My friend Kat introduced me to the people who run it, they're great. I like to keep busy, but now I'm a little too busy. I think I'll have to quit waitressing, even though it pays better. The schedule isn't working with my night classes, anyway. I'm taking two this term because it was the only time they were offered. Anyway, I'd rather be around art than food. Michael barely works; he has some little job stocking the shelves at this girly shop. Clothes for girls, I mean. He just counts on his parents and his grandma. Mom doesn't have any money, but I am lucky because my grandparents – Grandpa and Grandma Ryan – set aside some money for my college. It was thoughtful of them. But I don't ever take it for granted, like Michael does.

They died the summer after my freshman year in college – my Grandma in June; my Grandpa in late August. They were fantastic grandparents. They never got over losing my dad.

Michael told me, "Once your money's gone, I'm history," and then did this baby I'm just kidding thing but you know he's not. I want to not be self-destructive anymore. Kevin is being way too self-destructive right now, I heard. I don't see him; he's running wild again. Michael is more self-destructive than I am. He's flunking all of his classes, as near as I can tell. He refuses to talk to his profs about incompletes or extensions. He won't do his papers, even though I told him I'd type them for him. He said "Oh honey, that would be great!" then still wouldn't write them. Oh, he's a strange one. If we ever get married we're keeping separate bank accounts. As soon as he got off work last night he handed me his paycheck. Just like that. "Here's something to put in your checking account," he told me. He needs a real job; he has a kid to support. He needs to get serious.

I adore JoJo all to pieces. She is better than chocolate candy. I love her more than the color green. Today I was so bummed, so I talked to her and she cheered me right up. She says, "Well, you're laughing. It can't be all that bad." And overall, I am happy, with Michael, with life. I think I'm just stressed because of school. It's hard! But I haven't felt this happy since before Dad was sick. Michael and I play all the time. I had forgotten how to. OK, what about this? I'm working on a paper for Greek mythology and want to tie in modern fairy tales. When Dorothy gets hit on the head in The Wizard of Oz, is it a symbolic death? Can she be compared to Psyche? Athena? Is this a stretch? More later.

25 *Mr. Runaround*

"**O**r for something different, you could take care of your own kid, Michael," I said, trying to be all smooth. He had called to see if I would take Amber for the weekend, but I had to work. He heard about Kevin and was not happy.

"I'm ready to take out a restraining order against you, Lizzie! You need to control yourself," he screamed. "You have a shit temper!"

"I have a shit temper? You fuckwad. You need to take out a restraining order for your dick, Michael!" I screamed back, no longer smooth. This had been going on for months now; I was sick of it. But I couldn't stop. Worse? I still wanted to sleep with him. OK, maybe I had slept with him a few times. Kevin didn't know. Yes, we used protection. (*"What the fuck?"* – all of my girlfriends, if they knew.)

Amber was with Kim and didn't hear either end of this conversation. I felt embarrassed by my behavior, once I remembered Amber. This was such bullshit for a little kid to be around. But I wasn't her mom, and that was that. I looked in the mirror. I looked like hell. Skin blotchy, circles

139

under my eyes. I hadn't been getting enough sleep. Kevin was at his mom's finishing up a remodel on her guest room. We were supposed to meet up later, for dinner. I found out (after the split, natch) that during our three-year relationship Michael pretty much slept with anyone and everyone he wanted – male, female, friend, foe.

"Oh, honey, you didn't know?" was a refrain I got used to hearing. When it's your lover, doing you wrong and all, that's one thing. You can get screwed over by anyone, anytime. It's unpredictable.

But from my friends I expected more. JoJo and Gage didn't know, my family didn't know, Dan didn't know, for sure. Kim didn't, either. Mostly everyone else did.

I didn't take it well, even though it was what I had suspected. People still kept letting little bombs drop. I went to get my hair colored and my hairdresser said something about, "I still can't believe he was running around with that nail tech."

"What nail tech?" I asked. Just numb. How dumb was I?

"Oh, Elizabeth, I'm sorry," she said, ripping up some foils to finish wrapping my hair. "Oh, honey, you didn't know?"

Here is the thing about people who run around – they don't have their "real" partners with them when they do it. So if you see a guy with some girl, and she's not his wife, and his wife isn't there, that probably means The Wife doesn't know. Because she's not in the room. Shh! Then everyone thinks it's *so* fucking funny. "She must have known, we all knew" or "He was just looking the other way, he knew!" Sometimes, we don't know. Suspicions but no proof. I knew Michael had always been Mr. Runaround, from when we were younger, but I (foolishly) thought he had cleaned up his act. So maybe if you see something, and it doesn't look right, maybe you should say something. For example: "I saw your woman kissing some guy the other day, and it didn't look like her brother." That would be helpful. Also, with AIDS and STDs and all? What kind of bullshit is that, to be pretending you're faithful and then bringin' it on home to your (other) lover. Cheating can be a death sentence, get it? Argh. I was lucky I wasn't dead. I had been tested for everything so many times. It all seemed to be OK.

Michael moved out of our old place – he knew Dan hated him – and promptly moved in with Amanda. What a surprise. So I got the apartment back, after all. Kevin wanted to move in, but it was fine for now, just with Dan, Amber and me.

I called JoJo, after the phone fight with Michael. Every time I talked with him it was like phone sex, only not as fun.

"Dogs?" I asked. "You think Michael has sex with dogs? He screws everything else he can find." Seriously, I was so dumb.

"Do you want to come over and drink beer on the porch?" JoJo asked.

Before I left, I picked up Amber's stuff, flung as usual from one end of the apartment to the other. I hated waking up to a mess in the morning. And waking up without Amber was always depressing. Worse, with all her stuff thrown around as a reminder that she wasn't at the apartment. She would be back on Tuesday; it was fine. With Michael and his crap gone, I finally had room to make a better art corner for Amber in the dining room, where we kept her easel, paints, crayons and books. "My studio," she called it.

She was awfully sweet. I was enjoying my time with her more than ever. I was like her auntie now, more than her stepmom.

"You are the one who transgressed! Get out!" Michael had yelled at me when we fought it out, after I found the weird letter from the church and his porno catalogs. I was at the apartment, packing up. It was the first time I had seen him, after I told him I was dumping him. I think the art I made of it all freaked his shit out.

"A sinner? You're calling me a sinner, Michael?" I yelled back. "I *am* moving out, you fuck. I'm already gone."

And I was. I stayed with JoJo for awhile, then found some roommates to stay with. But Dan said forget it, Michael should move out. And Amanda was glad to snatch him up.

"I'd rather live with you and Amber, Liz," Dan said. So I moved back in, and Michael moved out. Before he did, he hid or stole most of my clothes, including my favorite blue bikini panties, just for spite. I had this flannel bowling shirt I just loved, it was leopard-print and said Wildcat on the pocket. That disappeared, too, along with a lot of other stuff. He refused to leave any of the furniture we'd purchased together. I didn't want to fight him for it; it would have been a losing battle. He gave me Kim's old textbooks and hid all of mine. I returned Kim's books to her and found my own in my hall closet, buried under a mound of Michael's dirty laundry, and reclaimed them. I didn't need them anymore, but the art books cost me a ton, and I wanted to keep them for reference.

Some of my clothes were hidden in there, too. But not the panties or the wildcat shirt. It was a little weird. The laundry? I left it on the front porch for him to get the next time he picked up Amber.

Kim needed the help now more than ever. Amber was upset we split up – she asked me to take Michael's new place away from him. Michael wasn't spending much time with her; he and Amanda wanted to be alone. I got the idea she didn't like kids.

Dan was a reliable roommate. Loyal. Our apartment was a lot emptier, with all of our furniture at Amanda's. She was welcome to it, and Michael.

"Good riddance," I said to the empty spot where our couch used to be. It had been a cool couch – fifties era, orange, patterned with gold amoeba shapes, with a low, curved back. A low, uncomfortable back. Good to look at, not good to relax on. Michael's mom had found it for us at a garage sale.

Dan and I both chipped in and bought an easy chair and coffee table at Goodwill, and some rugs at Fred Meyer, but the place was still pretty bare. Amber was enjoying the freedom of no furniture – I noticed new purple crayon scribblings in one of the corners. She asked for Michael, sometimes. Mostly at night. We left him messages, if Amber wanted to say goodnight, but he didn't return the calls. Sometimes I took Amber by Michael's office on campus, to say hi. Michael always seemed glad to see her, but distant. We were chilly, but not screaming at each other, at least not when Amber was around.

I surveyed the living room again. We needed more plants. And another floor lamp. I found Amber's favorite picture book in the corner, near her studio. It was about a little girl who ran away to a Caribbean island. Not Manhattan. That was my problem – I should have gone to Puerto Rico or somewhere, instead of New York. This magical little girl had no parents, no chores. And a hammock, to boot. The book was gorgeous – it had some illustrations of what they called picasso fish. Were they real? I wondered, or just crazy-looking fish? Hot pepper sauce, barking frogs, a tranquil, inviting ocean. That's where I should be. That's who I should be – that little girl, lying on the beach and getting dark dark dark.

I turned off the light and left for Jo's. I picked up beer, chips and two kinds of salsa on the way. Four beers later, sitting on JoJo's cushioned porch swing, I was feeling a lot better. She and Gage had a nice place; they had made it really homey. I said what we needed was another trip.

"Somewhere not as stinky as New York."

JoJo gave me a look. "We're broke though, remember?" She tipped up her beer bottle and drank the last bit. "But yes, you could use a break today."

"I have been a little nuts," I said.

"Really? Who can blame you?" Jo said. She was always willing to give me a break. Ditto me with her. It kept our friendship alive and healthy.

"He's a crazy-maker, that guy. I'm sure he didn't have sex with dogs, though."

"Sure?" I asked. I opened two more beers.

"Pretty sure," JoJo said. "Not completely sure."

26 *Thrill Hill*

SEPTEMBER 1992

"Amber, you ready?" I called from the living room. I buttoned up my brown corduroy barn jacket one-handed while I dug for my mittens in my left coat pocket. Then my right. There they were. I always started wearing my grandpa's old coat when the weather got cool. Summer was gone, and the air was already smelling like burning leaves and autumn. The kids were throwing footballs around in the street; that was always the giveaway. School was back in session. The kids all had new clothes, but I loved my beat-up hand-me-downs. Grandpa's coat was a little threadbare, so my granny bought him a new one and gave me the old one. It still smelled like his soap. I wrapped a fuzzy orange scarf around my neck. We were running late.

"Amber!"

"Ready!" Amber said. She emerged from the bathroom. Her hair was pulled back into an uneven ponytail, and she had changed into a purple blouse with a squiggly pattern on it. She picked up her raincoat from where she'd left it on the floor. At least it wasn't wet.

"Hey sweetie, nice shirt!" I told her. Amber smiled and pulled her coat on, then sat down by the door of our apartment to put on her cowboy boots. It was a lot easier getting her out the door, now that she was six. We had been living here with Kevin for more than a year.

"My grandma showed me how to do a pony tail," she said. She pulled a lip gloss out of her coat pocket and rubbed some on.

"Grab your backpack," I told her. "Do you have extra clothes?"

"Yep."

The car took a few minutes to warm up, and we were off to Amber's weekly dinner with her grandparents. To be polite, they always invited me, but I liked Amber to have some time alone with her grandparents. They adored her. They usually kept her for the night, then took her to school the next morning. She was still with me about half the time. On the nights she was with her grandparents, I usually got something to go from Burrito Loco. Or I would run by and see Jo. Gage was out all the time; she was lonely. She wanted to divorce him but didn't have enough money to get a lawyer. Sometimes Kevin would be around, and we'd go out for Vietnamese food. But tonight, he and Gage were over at some friend's place, fixing cars.

"Can we go by your grandma's old house?" Amber asked.

"You mean the Thrill Hill way?" I asked. "I'm not flying down that thing, don't get excited." I stuck out my tongue at her, teasing, and shook my head no.

"C'mon, Liz," Amber said. She tugged my arm and pulled my scarf off, "Oh, sorry." She reached up and wrapped the scarf around my neck.

"Thank you, ma'am."

"You said we could drive down it fast sometime," she said. She's right – I did say that. She was a daredevil – always wanting to go on the fast rides she was too short for when I took her to Oaks Amusement Park.

146

Michael's parents lived up the street from the house my granny and grandpa owned until I was nine, the home my mom spent her teen years in after the family moved out to Oregon from Louisiana. We could see it, even from the far end of Thrill Hill. There it was – a sprawling ranch-style house with double driveways, perched at the south end of the hill. The new owners had painted it dark blue. "It used to be light green," I told Amber.

"I know," she said, "You always say that." My brother and I used to live for snow days, when we'd go to Granny's and sled Thrill Hill. Bad weather made it too slick for cars. The rest of the year, though, teenage boys liked to gun it down the three blocks that led to the hill, then fly their cars and let them drop at the bottom.

"The thrill of the hill, Amber," I said, and rode my brakes all the way down. "Wheeeee!"

"Faster, Liz!" Amber said, bouncing up and down in her seat. "C'mon, faster!"

"People get in wrecks on this hill..." I said.

"...even die!" Amber said at the same time I did.

"Yeah, what do you know, kid?"

"But sometime you'll go fast, right?" she asked me.

"Yeah, sometime, sure." The daredevils stayed away for a while, after a bad wreck, then started up again within a few weeks or months. In the summer when I was a kid, the aunts and uncles (who were only a few years older than my brother and I were) would walk us up Thrill Hill to the Shop-A-Rama for popsicles. Then we'd go to the park and swing.

"You can ask your mom about Thrill Hill," my uncle told me once. I must have been sixteen or so. Driving age. My mom gave him a wink. Her eyes sparkled.

"I never hot-rodded it in my life," she said, and gave me a kiss on the cheek. She used to kiss me on the top of the head, but I was taller than her, by then.

"Hey, what's up with that?" I asked. I pulled over, across the street from the house, and parked. A large red, white and blue For Sale sign was stuck in front of the old house, in the middle of the lawn where we spent hours playing freeze tag and red rover.

"My brother and I used to hang out here all the time," I told Amber. "With our cousins." We ate Granny's homemade spaghetti with tons of meatballs and mushrooms for dinner, then hand-cranked chocolate ice cream for dessert.

"My mom makes really good spaghetti," Amber said. "I'm hungry. I wonder what my grandma's making me for dinner." I tried to take in every detail I could about the place.

"Are we gonna buy it? Will Kevin buy it for us?" Amber asked, starting to unbuckle her seatbelt.

"We're not getting out, hon. Buckle up."

"My grandpa and grandma sold it to a minister and his wife. I wonder who owns it now?" I jumped out to get a flyer. There weren't any. I ran back to the car to get a piece of paper and a pen from the glove box.

"Hey, let me go with you," Amber said, reaching for her seatbelt again.

"One minute, I'll be right back." I ran back across the street and scribbled down the real estate agent's name and phone number. I walked a few steps closer to take a look at the house. Light was fading. It wasn't painted blue, after all – they put up blue vinyl siding and added white trim. It didn't look like anyone was home. There was an old black Ford truck parked in the driveway. A porch light was on, but no other lights.

"Liz!" Amber yelled.

"I'll be right there," I called back. I stood under the massive Douglas fir at the edge of the front yard. Granny swiped it from the Mt. Hood National Forest when I was a baby. It was one of our family legends, and kept getting more detailed as the years went on.

"It was the middle of the night," Granny's story began, "and we were driving home from deer hunting. I saw this little bitty tree way off on the side of the road and made your Grandpa stop the truck." (*How did she spot the tree in the dark? Why were they driving home in the middle of the night, anyway?* Granny's tales never left room for questions. And Grandpa never stopped for anything when he drove – not even bathroom breaks – so the entire story was suspect.) The tree was at least thirty-five feet tall now. I made a mental note to give Granny an update on her baby.

Amber popped up next to me. "Why are you taking so long?"

"Honey, I told you to wait."

"What? I looked for cars. It's pretty nice, huh? Look how big that tree is."

"Yeah, my grandma always said it was my tree. She planted it when I was a baby." We walked to the far end of the yard, to the other driveway. It wound back behind the house to the two-car garage. It looked like there were some junkers in the backyard. We walked back to the fir. My stomach clenched, hit with a memory of standing on the front porch with my parents and my brother; Granny framed by the doorway, reaching up to hug my dad. He bent his six-foot-four frame almost in half to accept her hug. Still, Granny looked bigger than he did. She seemed to hold him up.

"We'll be right here, Leo," she said, "We love you. You're going to be just fine." Old memory: We were taking Daddy to the mental hospital; he'd had a breakdown at work. He thought he was Jesus Christ and tried to bless everyone. That was the last of a number of visits – he died not long after he was released. I shook my head fast and looked away. The daphne bush Granny planted was still there, beside the front door. Mint grew by the back door, and lemon balm flourished in the backyard garden. I remembered it all at once.

"Have you ever smelled fresh mint, Amber? Or lemon balm?"

"Huh?"

"God, they smell so good. You can pinch the leaves off and just inhale them." I slipped the paper with the agent's name and number into my pocket. We got back into the car and drove up the street. I dropped Amber off, and honked and waved goodbye at her grandparents. They were framed by the doorway.

Kodak moment. That was one of Amber's favorite expressions. I drove home thinking of homemade chocolate ice cream. My dad loved two scoops of it in a Coke float.

⚘

"Kevin, I want you to buy me my grandparents' old house."

"Welcome home to you, too," he said. I loved coming home to him. We moved out of my old place and got a smaller apartment. Dan had moved in with his girlfriend, finally. It was going all right for us. A lot better than it ever went with Michael, that was for sure. Kevin and Amber had become fast friends – Kevin didn't seem to mind having another guy's kid around. A kid who didn't even belong to his girlfriend. Presto! Insta-family.

I threw down my keys and dropped my coat and scarf. Kevin must have just taken a shower – his long, dark hair was wet and slicked back.

"Did you guys get the car fixed?" I asked.

"There is no hope in hell for that car," Kevin said. He had on Levi's and a worn-out yellow T-shirt with a blue star on the front. On the back was the logo – Mr. Zog's Sex Wax. He was playing guitar with his feet up on the coffee table. He had lit a dozen candles all around the living room and was sitting with the lights turned off. I set down a bag of burritos and chips that I picked up on the way home.

"Hey, food. Thanks. Sure, baby, I'll buy you a house. You need a new

150

car, too?" He started tuning his guitar. "Thanks for not chucking this T-shirt. I love it. What is it with chicks and T-shirts? You girls recycle too much."

He strummed a chord, then sang: "Leave my T-shirts/alone/ they do not smell/that bad..." I'd given the apartment a clean sweep the week before and took four boxes to Goodwill. We had to downsize a little, with a smaller place. Two full boxes were T-shirts. Plus I wanted to be ready to move, if we ended up getting a house. We had been toying with the idea – prices were good right now. He stopped playing, in the middle of trying to rhyme "Goodwill" with something, and caught the look on my face.

"You're serious about the house?" he asked, putting the guitar down. "I was thinking we'd rent a house for now, buy one in a year or so?"

"It's my family's house," I said. "It's where I grew up."

27 A Real Fixer-Upper

SEPTEMBER 1992

e drove over the next night, after we got off work. We didn't have Amber with us – she was staying with her grandparents an extra night. They even picked her up from school for me. I had found a real estate agent that morning and given her the number for the owner's agent. She checked the price while we were on the phone. "Why is it so cheap?" we both asked at the same time.

Our agent drove up in a new-model sedan a few minutes after we got there.

"Our own little slice of paradise," Kevin said to me. "I likes. How much did they want, again? Our house payment would be cheaper than our rent."

"Oh, really?" I asked, trying not to smile.

"Well, almost. I talked to a mortgage guy, and that's what he said."

"Hello there!" the agent called, pasting on a big smile. "Are they home? They're eager to sell, I heard. He's supposed to meet us here, their agent."

The same truck was parked out front, and the junkers hadn't budged from the side driveway. One of the blinds was open, and we could see a man inside, sitting in a recliner, watching television and having a smoke.

"Maybe he's the owner?" I said.

"Let's go find out," the agent said. Her name was Mitzi. Mitzi Fitzgerald. Try saying that one fast when you're drunk.

"I've been saving money for awhile," Kevin told her. "For a down payment. The financing would be OK, I think. I talked to someone at the bank. It's too cheap – what's the deal?"

I knocked on the door.

"As-is," Mitzi said, clearing her throat.

"Meaning?" Kevin asked.

"It needs a few improvements."

"That's fine by us," he said. He had been working as a general contractor for years now – first getting trained up with his uncle, then starting his own business. He was good at it.

"I've been wanting my own house to rip into," he told me. "You know that. We could do a lot ourselves. Most of it, probably."

I knocked on the door again, harder this time. Was the guy deaf? "What kind of improvements?" I asked Mitzi. The TV guy came to the door, didn't say anything, and let us in. He flopped back in his chair.

We stepped inside. It smelled like pee and cigarette smoke. "Ew," I said, without thinking.

Mitzi cleared her throat again. "What was that you said, about wanting a project?" she asked Kevin, sounding a little too chipper. I stepped closer to him and took his arm.

"Ew," I said again, more quietly this time. It was stinky, and dark, except for the television.

"Hot damn," Kevin said. He was smiling. The walls in the living room and hallway had a few good-sized holes in them. We tentatively made our way through the dining room. Dirty, but no holes in the wall. A beat-up table and three chairs, one of them broken and listing to the side. A bar stool was pulled up to the table. No signs of life, other than the guy parked in the living room, which also contained a brown plush couch, sagging in the middle. An organ was the only thing in the den. We peeked into the bedrooms. Two were carpeted, two weren't. The carpeted rooms were filthy and smelled like beer and dirty feet. There were unlocked locks in place on all of the bedroom doors. I noticed at least three broken windows that hadn't been visible from the street. Three bathrooms, all tiny and filthy. One was a half-bath, toilet and sink only. One had a tub and shower; the other had just a tub. I spotted a gallon of bleach on one of the counters.

"For, you know," I whispered to Kevin. "Right?"

"Yeah," he said. For sterilizing needles. "At least someone's trying to be safe." The place looked vaguely like my grandparents' old house.

Some other people came in from the garage, through the laundry room, heading toward us. One of the men had large scabs all over his inner arms. We went back out to the dining room, where Mitzi was waiting for us. It was a big house, bigger than I remembered, and even had a small den, but... But, but, but. What about all those people?

The owner, at least I assumed he was the owner, waved a hello at us and strutted through. He was short, about five foot five. I got a better look at him when we went through the bedrooms again, where he and his friends had re-grouped. He was a tiny Nazi biker guy. He dressed like one, anyway. Wore a black leather vest, black tank top underneath, with Levi's and motorcycle boots. He had a big tattoo that said "Aryan Nation" on his left forearm, right below a swastika. There was an elaborate snake and flower tattoo along his right arm. He looked like half the guys we'd gone to high school with, just older.

"Did that third bedroom have a closet or not?" Kevin asked. Mitzi stuck close behind us, not commenting. We walked back into the third bedroom. The house was split into two wings, with two bedrooms on each side. A big guy had appeared from nowhere and was parked in the third bedroom. He looked ready to fix – he had his arm tied off with a belt. He gave us a dark look, and we headed back out the door.

"Yes, there's a closet. Jesus," Kevin whispered to me. "What the hell?" Mitzi stepped over a pile of wet, dirty clothes thrown in the hallway. She finally spoke.

"It needs a bit of work," she said, nudging a dirty tank top away with her black leather pump, "as you can see." Mitzi held on tighter to her black leather purse. It matched her shoes and looked expensive.

"It's a wonderful house," a woman called, walking down the hall toward us. She must have come in through the garage, too. How many people were actually here? All the doors were slammed shut now. From behind the bathroom door, across the hall, I heard a toilet flush once, then again.

She was a dead-ringer for Cruella de Ville, this one. Maybe six foot two, with her heels on. She was built like a scarecrow, with a head full of straw-like bleached blond hair. She had on leopard-print leggings, four-inch bright red stilettos, and a tattered black halter top. An itty-bitty red leather handbag hung by a strap from one scrawny shoulder.

"So... you were the ones drawn to my home?" she said by way of introduction, tripping toward us and blowing cigarette smoke in our faces. She forced us to walk backwards into the living room. The TV guy was nowhere in sight. Everyone was coming and going too fast. I was feeling like Alice in Wonderland.

"I'm Jake's wife," she said, then corrected herself. "Ex-wife, pardon me. We are the owners of this home?"

"It was my grandparents' house a long time ago..." I started to say. I heard the toilet flush again, and was interrupted when the guy in the vest walked out of the bathroom and down the hall toward us.

"So. We ready to talk? Wanted to give you a chance to look 'er over. Do you like what you see? Jake Lee Grant," he said, sticking out his hand. "Get it? Grant? Lee? Like the Civil War – both sides!" He chortled.

"Princess, you're scaring the kids," he said, motioning his hand and shooing his ex-wife away. She took a big inhale from her cigarette and her face caved in. "She dunnit own the house anymore, she just likes to pretend she does."

"Piss up a rope, Jake," Princess said.

"She thinks she runs the show around here," Jake said to Kevin. "I find it's best just to let her go on believing that, if you know what I mean, bro."

Princess stomped into one of the bedrooms, slamming the door behind her. We heard voices rise and fall. The TV in the living room was still turned on. Professional wrestling, but no one was in there now.

"Your grandparents? So they're the ones who sold it to my folks, huh?" Jake asked.

"I think that's right. He was a minister?"

"Yep, yep, that was my old man," Jake said, bouncing on his feet a little. He raked his fingers through his hair. It was dark, shot through with gray, short in front with a long, thin ponytail in back. "They're both dead now, him and my mother. God rest their souls and all that. They moved their folks in, didn't want to send them to a nursing home. They all died here. Two of them, anyhow." Kevin's left eyebrow went up. He looked sideways at me. I opened my eyes wide like, How was I supposed to know? I mean, honestly. None of my family had died here. As far as I knew. Kevin was a little superstitious; he had been since we were kids. Avoiding black cats, not walking under ladders, doing weird counting things with his food. I could relate; I was a little superstitious, too. I always had to count the squares on the sidewalk when I was out walking. I didn't like to get too close to the number thirteen – I avoided twelve and fourteen, too. Just to be safe.

Jake squinted at Kevin and leaned toward him a little. He pulled a toothpick out of the pocket of his leather vest and started picking his teeth.

"You're not superstitious, are you?"

Kevin started picking his own teeth, with his fingernail. "No," he said finally, not quitting until he had cleaned the whole upper row. Jake quit, too. He put the toothpick back in his pocket.

"My folks, they got sick finally," Jake said. "I moved back up here to take care of them and all. Anyway, they left me the house. But I gotta sell it. Too many problems with the cops in this town. I'm going back to New Mexico, man. Fuck this place, it's a mess." He pulled out another toothpick and started cleaning his teeth again. They were little brown nubs, like root beer jellybeans.

My shoulders tightened. I stood up taller and tried to relax. Breathe in, out, in … Seven good breaths. In through your mouth, out through your nose? No, it was the other way, I always got that wrong. Four good breaths. Ten good breaths. Something. I coughed, trying to catch my breath. The house didn't just smell like pee and smoke – it smelled like funk and mold, too. Blech. Kevin started to sit in the recliner, then changed his mind.

"How are those teeth feeling?" I asked him. "You're not superstitious, are ya?" He smiled at me. Jake didn't seem to hear. Mitzi had slipped away from us. She stood against the front door. She hadn't taken her coat off and was still clutching her purse. She was pawing at the floor a little, with the toe of her pump, like she thought that would get her out of the mess she was standing in.

"Hey!" Jake said, seeing how stiff we had all gone. "There's nuttin' what can't be fixed up. You bro, you look like you know your way around tools, am I right?" Kevin smiled bigger.

"Sure!" Jake said. "You know how I go on? I believe in myself. With a capital M. Yep."

"Uh, yeah," Kevin said, "Me, too." Mitzi flinched and stepped back toward us. She tripped over a hammer on the floor. Her purse slipped. I caught her by the arm and smiled at her. She smiled a weak smile at me, then at Kevin, smiles all around, and righted herself.

"Shall we write up an offer?" she whispered. She glanced at her watch. "I have another appointment I need to get to."

Yeah, like fun you do.

"And hey bro," Jake said, going serious. "I want to tell you something. Nothing was ever cooked here, it's clean."

Mitzi looked puzzled. It took me a minute to realize he was talking about cooking methamphetamine.

"Speed," I whispered to her, and smiled in what I hoped was a reassuring way. Big, big smiles. C'mon, Mitzi. She really looked like she wanted to throw up.

Good. That was good news. No, not Mitzi puking, or wanting to. Bleach on the counter, clean needles, not a meth lab, things were really shaping up. I smiled at Jake, also in what I hoped was a reassuring way. I read a novel once – the girl, the main character in the book, had a dad who was a therapist. He ran his office out of their New York apartment and always told her to "smile at the patients in a reassuring but not condescending way."

I made two notes to myself: 1) smile reassuringly, not condescendingly 2) get a New York apartment. Jake was so pleased, that I was pleased, he began to bounce up and down again, this time on his tiptoes. He also started picking his teeth again in a nervous tic.

"Oh! Good to know," Kevin said. I was thinking, hard, Please don't pick your teeth, please don't pick your teeth, at him. No luck. The men shook hands, like they were sealing a deal. Which they were.

"Good to know," Kevin repeated.

"Was your agent planning on joining us?" Mitzi asked Jake. I had forgotten all about him. You think he'd want to unload the place.

"Naw, I don't think so," Jake said. He rummaged through his vest pocket. "I got his cell number here, somewhere. Aw, fuck it." He dropped a handful of receipts and slips with phone numbers on them onto the floor. He squatted down to retrieve them and all his change fell out of his pockets.

"Aw, goddammit," he said. He scooped everything up and shoved it back into his pockets. I heard loud laughter from the other room. Another door slammed, down the hallway. On the television, one of the wrestlers was jumping up and down on his opponent. Jake turned off the TV. "Nobody ever watches this goddamn thing but it's always on. He's kind of an asshole, the real estate guy. You want to buy it, or what?" We made a full-price offer.

"He is asking way under market value," Mitzi said in an aside to me. She wrote up the offer sitting on one of the beat-up chairs in the breakfast nook, still with her coat on, purse balanced in her lap, while I sat in the other unbroken chair. Kevin perched on the barstool next to us. Jake went back to check on his guests/housemates. I heard yelling, but couldn't make out the words, then heard Princess's voice as she opened the bedroom door and walked into the bathroom across the hall.

"You do not know the art of the deal, Jake," she said.

We added a clause that the owners were required to remove all automobiles, debris and possessions. We had peeked into the garage; it was stuffed full. As was the backyard.

"And tenants," I whispered, "Can we put in a line about making sure they're gone?"

"There isn't really a clause for that," Mitzi said. She handed the paper over to us to sign. "Checkbook? They'll want something for earnest money."

"Sure," I told her, and got the checkbook out of my bag. "You sure?" I asked Kevin in a low voice. I was re-reading the offer. "Because I'm sure. I want them all out of here."

"I'm never sure of anything," Kevin said, and signed.

"Yoo-hoo," Mitzi called down the hall. "We have paperwork for you."

Jake and Princess emerged from the bedroom.

28 *Good Bones*

SEPTEMBER 1992

"Oooh, yes," Granny said when I called to tell her the news. "Fix it up.

"Robert!" she yelled to Grandpa, "the kids are buying our old place!" She was so excited she hung up on me. Grandpa was still having health problems, but they both lied about it so I wouldn't get worried. I still worried.

"Love you, goodbye," I said into dead air, then realized what had happened and hung up. "No one in my family ever says goodbye," I told my cat. "Is that strange, to you? Stranger than a girl who talks to her cat?" I grabbed a stack of old newspapers.

"Time to start packing."

The cat blinked his green speckled eyes at me, licked his lips, then yawned and sat down to wash his leg. I headed to the kitchen to start wrapping dishes.

Our financing was approved, God only knows how, and we gave notice at the place we were renting. Between the two of us we had enough saved for a reasonable down payment. I was still working at the same gallery. I didn't make a lot, but it was enough to make my half of what would be our house payment. We would save a ton of money with Kevin doing the repairs to the various holes in the walls and everything else. I could clean, tear down the old wallpaper and help him with everything.

The home inspection report contained fifteen pages of careful notes, but no major scares, other than a brief note, "Plumbing needs overhaul." My grandpa had done good work on the place when he owned it.

"Good bones," as the home inspector said.

Our friends and family promised they'd help us. Three weeks later, we were homeowners. It was almost too fast.

On the Friday night we took possession of the house, we both left work early, grabbed burritos to go and changed into old clothes. We brought along two large bottles of Lysol, soap, two buckets, paper towels, rags, scrub brushes, a toilet brush, toilet paper, a king-size pack of garbage bags and flea bombs. I had a plan for the flea bombs.

"Good," I said, "their agent got the drop box here." The big trash bin was set up in the driveway. We'd need it.

Four cars were parked out front – a yellow Duster, an old Chevy truck, a banged-up brown Toyota Corolla, and a Charger, plus one motorcycle. A Harley-Davidson.

"Nice Duster," Kevin said.

"Ewww," I said. "Give me a Mustang. Mach 1. Two-tone, black and that really pretty shade of dark red." Kevin wrinkled his nose at me.

"You and your Fords," he said.

I knocked on the door, then rang the bell, then knocked again.

"Isn't Mitzi supposed to be here?" I asked Kevin.

"Yeah, I don't think we'll be seeing much of her," he said.

Finally a young woman let us in. She had long, permed hair that was blond on the ends and black at the roots. She looked about seventeen.

"Oh, hey," she said, like we were all buddies. "Cool beans! Jake! They're here."

"Looks like they haven't had a chance to move out yet," Kevin said, setting down the cleaning supplies inside the door. "I'll go get the rest from the truck." I waited for him. He had two vehicles – a Honda Accord, blue, that used to belong to his mom, and a work truck, a Chevy, also blue, that was about fifteen years old.

Princess was nowhere in sight. I set down my cleaning supplies. Kevin returned carrying the rest of the supplies and we ventured in.

"Hey," Jake said, jumping up from the kitchen table. "There you guys are!" Baggies with a brownish-yellowish substance went into the pockets of the other two men at the table; Jake gathered up some bills and stuffed them in his vest pocket. They had some old-school Aerosmith playing, their first album.

"Hey, dudes, take it somewhere else," he said to the men, clapping his hands three times. "Chop-chop."

One was a Native American guy, dark-haired and stocky. He was wearing a pair of jeans that were ripped in both knees, a too-small green striped tank top and high-top Converse with no socks. The other guy was white. He was small, only a bit taller than Jake, blond and ratlike. He had a sharp little nose and small, closely-spaced eyes. His face looked lonely without rat whiskers. He made up for what the other one lacked in clothes. He had on two or three shirts, including an unbuttoned plaid flannel, with a red silk dress shirt underneath. He also had on a nice pair of black dress slacks, beat-up brown loafers, and a gray track jacket with a black and orange Oregon State emblem on it. Also, his hands and face were scabby.

They stood and gathered up their beer cans, matches, and cigarettes. They made sure their drugs were still tucked in their pockets. The guy with the rat face started to say something to Jake.

"Why didn't you …" it sounded like, in a little bit of a whine, then his words trailed off. They went down the hall. I could see down the hall – two of the bedroom doors were closed.

"Sorry we weren't out on Wednesday like we said," Jake said. He shrugged, then limped over to the wood stove to throw in a cigarette butt. "But hey, you know how it goes, trying to get packed and all." I took a fast look around the room. One half-full moving box sat in the corner of the darkened dining room.

"What was there to pack?" I whispered to Kevin out of the side of my mouth. Jake busied himself gathering up his things.

The guy with the rat face came out of the bedroom.

"Do you guys need roommates?" he asked Kevin. He stood with his back to me. He seemed a little nervous. He kept ducking his head.

"No, I think we're good," Kevin said, walking around the guy to stand next to me. I was still holding a mop. Kevin took it from me and leaned it against the wall.

"It's a big house and all," the guy said.

"No!" Jake said, "They said no, Pete." Pete dug around in his pocket.

"You got a lighter, Jake?" he asked.

"You already took all my matches, maggot," Jake said. Pete dug in his other pocket.

"Ha," he said, pulling out two books and waving them at Jake, who grabbed one of the books. Pete, smiling, walked back down the hall and into the bathroom.

Jake sat down at the kitchen table and took off his left motorcycle boot. He began massaging his foot.

"Whew! That thing's sore," he said, "Someone stomped on my foot today, asshole. Yeah, well, he'll get his, huh?" He slipped the boot back on.

"Hey, did you see my new bike? I got it with some of the money from the house. I'll pay the guy after I get it, anyway. So, you guys ready to stay the night or what?"

Someone knocked at the door, and we avoided the question. It was the locksmith we had called before we came over. Kevin showed him the three doors that needed locks changed.

"Nice dent," the locksmith said, spying the huge divot in the front door.

"Ah, yeah," Jake said, "That was from the cops, when we got busted. They always got to fuck a place up, you know." Pete and his buddy reappeared and began watching the locksmith.

"Picking up tips, guys?" I asked them. They thought that was hilarious.

"Ha, tips," Pete said. "We oughta give him tips!"

We left the locksmith to his work and made a quick tour of our new castle, starting with the backyard. A bedroom door opened as we walked outside, down the hall, through the laundry room, and out the back door. A doe-eyed, underfed, fawn-colored pit bull eased out from the bedroom and followed us. We stopped for a second, waiting to see if any humans would come out. None. The door shut again. We heard some Lynyrd Skynyrd playing.

"Aw," Kevin said, "memories of my childhood."

A little white cat, crossing the concrete patio outside the back door, fled when he saw the dog.

"How are you doing?" Kevin asked me.

"Freaking out a little. I'm glad I locked my purse in the car," I said. I stood on the moss-covered patio and turned to face the house. All of the blinds were pulled; the rooms were lit. I turned to face the yard. A banged-up Pinto and a red VW with the engine missing were up on blocks near what could be my garden, eventually. It was difficult to imagine tomato plants and squash in the middle of the junkyard, but it was possible, if I squinted hard enough. I walked over and examined some canes, half-hidden behind the VW. Raspberries. They needed cutting back, but looked healthy enough. There were ferns along an outside wall of the house, and three rosebushes in the corner. A lilac sprung up in the middle of the yard, and two blueberry bushes were at the far end. Other than that, it was nothing but blackberry vines, climbing all over the back half of the yard and the fallen-down fence. It was two full lots, the agent figured out when she ran her information through the computer. That made it an even better deal than we originally thought. I'd always thought the yard just seemed big because I was a little kid. My mom wanted to come over right away, but we were holding her at bay.

"No need to terrify your family," Kevin said. I agreed. We'd take out the trash – literally – then have everyone over to help clean and paint.

A battered washer and dryer were parked near the cars in the yard. The lid was up on the washer. It was half full of rain water. Three towers of old tires were piled against the fence. A trailer, nearly full with old tires, car batteries, battered boxes and miscellaneous junk, sat on the patio. Other than that, the damage didn't look too bad. Two steps led down to a sunken garden space next to the garage.

"That's where my granny had her garden," I told Kevin. I'd forgotten. It was gone, but I got socked with a memory – a warm summer day, out in the garden with my mom.

"I saw a tiny frog right there one time," I told Kevin, pointing. I squinted my eyes again and could just about see it. "It was sitting on a tomato plant."

"I don't think there are many frogs around here right now," he said. He wrapped his arms around me. It was a lot to take in, this whole mess.

166

"How are we going to get them out of here?" I asked him. I whispered it, in case someone was eavesdropping on us.

He knelt down and picked up an empty plastic pop bottle and chucked it into the trailer.

"The flea bombs, right?" he asked, "That's the plan? And the new locks."

The double garage was stuffed full of garbage, spilling out of bags and cans and covering most of the floor. The overhead door was closed, but the side door was open. Kevin poked his head in and called out.

"Hello! OK to come in?" I peeked over his shoulder. Two large, ancient trucks were wedged into the space, plus four car engines, a canoe, miscellaneous clutter, a broken propane barbecue and some lawn furniture that had seen better days. There were traffic signs and cones, seven or eight yellow plastic recycling containers full of old newspapers, and glass and plastic bottles and jars all over the place. So much junk.

Three men, a woman and the teenage girl were congregated in the back of garage, by the workbench. They stepped forward as we edged our way in, stepping over a case of motor oil and a box piled high with loose lightbulbs. I saw a couple of dozen used syringes in a pile and sidestepped them. A stray spoon was kicked to the side, next to an overflowing black garbage can. Once the people stepped aside, I spotted a pallet on the floor and two stained mattresses in the back, to the left of the workbench.

An old man turned around. "What?" he said.

He had on blue striped coveralls, stained with grease, and his hair held back under a blue bandanna. At first glance, he looked eighty. At second glance? He was around sixty-five. Possibly a few years older or younger.

"What do you want?" he said, then, without waiting for an answer, "Mmmph. That's what I thought." He began working under the hood of one of the two trucks, an old International. He climbed halfway in the truck. The others had stopped talking. They started arranging something on the workbench. I couldn't see what they were doing. I moved a little closer. They had a bag of flour and were spooning it into some small baggies. I stepped back and watched the old guy for a little while, fast at work, banging on things with a wrench.

Rip Van Winkle. He had the same long scruffy white beard and hair, and was dusty. He was wearing motorcycle boots like Jake's. We moved back by the garbage can. I didn't know how Kevin wanted to handle this one. The old guy popped back out from under the hood.

"Hello? Can you hear?" he said, "I said 'What?' "

"Just stopping by to say hey," I said, "We're the new owners."

"I know who you are. I'm Bill," he said, "You can call me William. I'm Princess's dad."

"Jake's wife?" Kevin asked, "That's her real name? I thought that was her nickname or something." He started to laugh, then stopped dead when Bill – William – glared at him. At us.

William drew the words out as if we were a couple of slow learners.

"Ex-wife, and no, it is not her nickname. Her name is Princess. That is why we call her that. Why the hell would we call her a name if it wasn't her own name?" He spat on the floor at our feet and climbed back into the truck.

"Maybe we should get back to the house?" I asked Kevin.

"Probably," he said, but didn't move. We were mesmerized. There was a bookshelf, to the right of the workbench, full of tools, half-folded clothes and some canned food. Typewriter ribbons, yanked out of their cartridges, were wound around everything. A blender caught my eye. It was half-full of murky water and some kind of mossy-looking greenery, with two anemic, but very much alive, goldfish swimming around. Was it plugged in? Yes, with a duct-taped extension cord. My stomach flipped.

"Excuse us," I said to no one, "please." I grabbed Kevin by the arm and pulled him toward the house, through the back door and into the laundry room. The pit bull trailed behind us. We heard a big burst of laughter from the garage, along with something that sounded like a growl.

"Hot damn, have you ever seen anything like that?" Kevin asked. He was smiling.

"Yeah, I've seen worse at my uncle's place. Shut up!" I whispered, and pulled him into the kitchen, shaking my head and laughing. We needed to be alone for a second. I looked out into the living room. Two new men I had never seen before had shown up. They were keeping the locksmith and Jake's other buddies company. One of the new guys was tall, with a pockmarked face. He was wearing a long, black raincoat. The other guy was chubby, with dark hair. Jake was nowhere in sight.

"Oh, that was precious," I said, "Did you see the fish?"

"Why do you think I couldn't leave? I couldn't stop staring at it. Let's hope no one hits the 'on' switch, huh? Grandpa Bill, goddamn. How the hell are we going to get rid of this crew?"

"Did you see the bag of flour on the workbench?" I whispered. "And the baggies? Are they going to bake cookies for us?"

Kevin started pulling open kitchen cupboards. "There's one here, too. And another one. Yeah, they're cutting the speed, I guess. Who knows. There's no other food around. Shouldn't take them long to clean out the kitchen." He checked the refrigerator. Empty. The freezer contained an ancient-looking bag of frozen peas and what might have been a freezer bag full of spaghetti sauce.

"Oh. My. God," I said, picking it up between my forefinger and my thumb. "That looks like frozen blood." I grabbed a pair of rubber gloves from our supplies, picked up the blood bag and ran outside with it. I threw it in the drop box. I climbed up the side and looked in. It was the only item in there, so far. I came back in to wash my hands, but the kitchen faucet wasn't working. And there was no soap.

Kevin was exploring the cupboards over the refrigerator.

"Didn't this sink work before?" I asked him.

"Yup."

I took the soap and paper towels we brought and headed for one of the bathrooms. It stunk of gardenia room spray and mold.

Kevin began cleaning up the kitchen, filling a garbage bag with trash from the counters, mainly take-out Chinese food and hot sauce packets.

"Hey, why don't you run to the store, Lizzie? Get some fresh air. Maybe get us some beer. I think we're going to be here awhile."

The light throughout the house was dim. There was one working bulb in the fixture over the dining room table, which should have held four, and one in a floor lamp in the living room, next to the locksmith.

"We need lightbulbs, I can't even see in here. How's the locksmith going to see to work?" I remembered the box of light bulbs on the garage floor. "That old man stole the light bulbs, didn't he?"

Kevin laughed. "We'll get 'em out of here soon enough, don't you worry about it."

"Maybe I should pick up a bag of dog food, too, huh? That pit bull is breaking my heart. Did you see his ribs sticking out?"

"Feed the dog, get a snack, buy some lightbulbs, buy us a six-pack, go." Kevin walked me to the front door.

"Need a police escort, ma'am?" he asked me. The locksmith looked up from his work. The four men were sitting on the living room floor now, smoking and playing cards.

"Almost done with these two locks," he said. "They were a mess. I'm putting a better deadbolt in, is that cool?"

"Sure," Kevin said, "You don't mind the wildlife, do you?" The men looked up. One of the new guys laughed.

"Naw, not you guys," Kevin said. He pointed to a large aquarium in the far corner of the room. Funny, I hadn't noticed it when we first toured the house, but there had been a lot going on that night. There were two huge snakes inside. One was coiled in an artificial tree; the other was stretched out on the floor of the tank.

"Neat. I'll see if they have some rats at the store, next to the dog food."

"Dude, I can't stand snakes!" the locksmith said, shaking his head. "Have those been there the whole time?" He turned his back to the tank and began working faster.

"That boa's Jack Daniels," the chubby guy said, "and the other one's Mustang Sally. Like the song." He started crooning the lyrics, then couldn't remember more than the chorus. "She's a python. Ooooh, man, do the neighbors flip out on hot days when we take them out to the front lawn. You guys better watch it with the neighbors. They're too uptight, man! They thought we was torturing kids over here, but we was just feeding bunnies to the snakes."

Talkative! At least they weren't as surly as the ones in the garage.

"Out of here," I said, giving Kevin a quick kiss and stepping over the locksmith. "Excuse me. And thanks."

"Yeah, no problem. Wait till I tell my fiancée about this one. She's gonna flip." Kevin and the locksmith laughed.

"Hey, you guys," I called back at the card players, "I don't mind if you stay a little bit longer, but y'all had better help us get this place cleaned up. Then you have to split, later. OK? OK!"

"No problem," the rat-faced guy said, "I know where the vacuum is!" He scooped all the cards into a pile. "Come on, dudes."

When I returned, the floor lamp was out, too. I checked it. Yep, the light bulb had disappeared. I stepped inside the house to all darkness and no Kevin. Now the only light in the living room was the headlight from the ancient Hoover one of the druggies was pushing around and around in circles on the beat-up gray carpet. He was the tall one, with the scarred face. I started putting new light bulbs in every fixture I could find, starting with the floor lamp.

"It was working before," I said to myself. "Hey!" I shouted over the roar of the vacuum, "Thanks!"

He flipped off the switch. "Huh?"

"Thanks. Looks great!" I said. A lie. It didn't look any different from when he'd started.

"Oh, it's nothing," he said. He took the vacuum outside and dumped the bag on the front porch. I didn't ask. I could see down the hall to the back bedroom, next to the laundry room. The other three guys were working hard on some kind of project, involving the baseboard heater and a box overflowing with spare parts. I'd bought three pie tins at the store. I filled one with dog food, one with cat food and one with water and gave a whistle. I heard a thumping noise. Then a bedroom door opened and a large pink pig, weighing at least two hundred pounds, trotted out of one of the bedrooms.

Kevin strolled around the corner, from the other wing of the house. He spotted the pig, cracked up and started humming the theme song from *Green Acres*.

"Dang," he said. "Wilbur. No wonder the dog is so skinny. Where have they been hiding you, guy?" The pig snarfed up most of the food and trotted back to bed. Someone closed the bedroom door again after he went back in. I poured out more food, this time for the dog, who was waiting patiently by my side.

I opened two beers and handed one to Kevin. The tall guy came in from the front porch, holding up a pill he had apparently discovered in the vacuum cleaner bag. He showed it to Kevin.

"Hey, man," he said, "Want half?"

"No, dude," Kevin said, "It's all yours."

"Cool!" he said, and swallowed it whole. He trotted in the direction the pig had gone. I shook my head.

"No beer for him, he's good," I said. "Oh, dear God. What have we gotten ourselves into? I'd like to get all this on video, you know? I mean, if I didn't think they'd shoot us for taping them." Grandpa Bill came down the hallway, out of the laundry room. He walked casually into the living room, took a greasy rag out of the pocket of his coveralls, and unscrewed the light bulb I had just put in the entryway light. He put it in his pocket and started in on the floor lamp.

"Listen, Bill," I said. He shot me a dirty look and removed the light bulb from the floor lamp, then started toward the porch. He stuffed the greasy rag into another pocket. "William, I mean. We need those light bulbs, we can't see much in here." Which is probably not such a bad thing, I thought, getting another look at the carpet.

"So leave them!" I said. I clenched my fists at my sides and gave a little jump. It surprised me, and startled him. He handed me the two lightbulbs.

"Thank you," I said.

"Yeah, thanks, William," Kevin said, and gave him a nod.

Grandpa Bill turned and headed back down the hall, grumbling under his breath.

"It's only a goddamn lightbulb," he said.

"He's burning through lightbulbs like crazy in the garage," Kevin said. "Maybe there's something wrong with the wiring, I don't know. I'll check it out after we get him out of there. Freak. I need to go get some boards at the store; you OK alone?"

"Yeah, it's fine," I said. "I'll just sic the dog on them if they try anything." The dog had finished his dinner and was again parked by my side.

"Besides, the locksmith is here. Go."

"He's working on the back door, in the kitchen. He'll get started on the door in the laundry room after that. He'll be awhile," Kevin said. "Good thing he works nights. We just need some plywood, to nail over the broken windows. I've got my hammer and nails out in the truck. I'll get out tomorrow to buy some new glass." When he got back, we dealt with the windows together, then took a look around.

"So, what's up with the rest of the house?" I asked. I had spent the time Kevin was gone working on the kitchen. All of the kitchen garbage was now bagged and in the drop box. It hadn't been too bad.

"I can't deal with the bathrooms yet," I admitted. "The maid squad is coming by tomorrow, they can deal with those. Have you checked that other bedroom? The front one?" When my grandparents owned the house, they converted the one-car garage at the front of the house to a bedroom. It was tiny but usable, with a closet and built-in drawers.

We tried the door – locked. The locksmith came down the hall. "You guys need anything else?"

"Good timing," Kevin said, "Can you get us in here?"

The locksmith popped the door open, and we entered.

"Holy Christ," Kevin said. An amazingly lifelike nude mannequin stood in one corner, with a garland of condoms around her neck. A water bed took up most of the rest of the room.

"Safe sex, that says something," Kevin said.

"Foxy lady," the locksmith said, peering around the door.

"Can you come back tomorrow and remove the bedroom locks?" I asked.

"Sure," he said. "Meet you out front? I'll get the bill together for you.

We'll have some more fun tomorrow, yeah?" He walked down the hall, whistling the theme from *Green Acres*. We flipped on the overhead light – Bill hadn't gotten to it – and assessed the damage. Broken window, no screen, a small hole punched in one of the walls. Other than that it looked salvageable. I flipped back the covers on the water bed and unearthed a foot-high stack of porno mags between the grimy sheets; several pairs of women's high heel shoes, including a sparkly pair in silver; and an economy-sized jar of Vaseline.

"Oh, ick. Dang. That is just ick," I said.

"I don't really need to think about that one much longer," Kevin said. "What do you say we wrap it up for the night? We've got everyone coming by in the morning." He looked at his watch. "Make that 'in a few hours.' It's already two."

We hammered plywood over the last window and went to pay the locksmith.

"Let's light the flea bombs off and go get some sleep," Kevin said. "We'll need one in here." We tried the doorknob on the front bedroom. It was locked again.

"What's up now?" I asked. Grandpa Bill came strutting out of the master bedroom next door.

"That's Roscoe's stuff in there," he said. "He's in jail." He jangled a bunch of keys at us. He'd seen the locksmith leave.

"William," I said, "Unlock the door. Now." He glared at me and took a step toward me. I pointed my finger at him and shooed him off. He stepped back, still jangling the keys.

"Hand over the keys," Kevin said. "Now! And don't take any lightbulbs on your way out!"

Grandpa Bill thought for a second. "Two more?" he asked.

"Fine," I said. I grabbed a package of four bulbs from the dining room table and handed them over. "Have four." Grandpa Bill smiled, showing his remaining mossy gray teeth, unlocked the door and handed us the keys.

Kevin started in one end of the house and I started in the other, setting off the bombs. Everyone, including Jake, was standing on the back patio. They had the pig (his name was Dirty, we had found out) and the dog (Rexxie) with them, and they'd moved the aquarium and the snakes out to the garage while we were covering the windows. The cat (Cat?) had already left on his (or her) own.

"We're out of here, guys!" Kevin called to them, locking the back door behind us with the new keys from the locksmith.

"The whole place will be toxic," I said, stressing the word toxic. "Toxic. You need to take your pig," I began counting off on my fingers, "your pit bull, your cat, your snakes, and all your friends, and skedaddle. Savvy? The house is locked; you can't go back in."

"Sure, sis!" Jake said. Everyone else was silent. At our request, they had come back into the house and packed up the porno magazines and everything else they could carry from the front bedroom. Jake was picking through the boxes now, looking over his loot.

"Look at all these new socks," he said, shaking them at the pock-faced guy. "Still in the package!" Pretty happy, considering he was about to be homeless. "We've already got rooms at the Rainbow Motel," he said, as if reading my mind. "We just wanted to make sure you guys were settling in. So, we're out of here. No problem. Cool if we come by tomorrow to get the rest of our stuff from the garage?" They had moved what little furniture they had out into the garage, at some point, along with a box of kitchen things I'd put together.

"Sure," I said. "We'll be here early. Come on by." Jake took off down the driveway with his box, trailed by the pit bull.

"No loyalty," I told Kevin. "After I was nice enough to feed him." I'd given the dog food to Jake, who was touched, I could tell. We headed down the driveway behind them, into the cool, starry night for our apartment and a few hours of sleep.

29 *Grandpa Bill's Potatoes*

Washing windows, when it's your own place, not just a place you're renting, is about the best. Especially when it's kind of overcast, so they don't get streaky. I gave the front window a final scrub and threw my rag into the pail. Someone was pounding at the back door. I hoped it wasn't anyone looking to buy drugs. We had a few of those come by. Once they saw me, though, they usually left pretty quickly. The past month had been a ride.

The day after we took possession of the house (so to speak, since the garage still wasn't vacated) we found the drop box in the driveway half full – of the neighbors' unwanted possessions. Bastards. A few things were on the front lawn – a couch, a stained mattress, and a suitcase and cardboard box, both spilling over with clothes.

Kevin and I climbed up the side and looked in.

"I don't think any of this is from the house," Kevin said.

"Isn't that table from the living room?" I said, spying a small pressboard end table with one leg missing.

"Nope," Kevin said, "and I bet you those old cans of paint aren't from the garage, either."

"You see any car engines in there?" I asked. "Tires?" Kevin sighed. It was all someone else's junk. We jumped down. It was quiet, and there was no sign of Jake and his crew.

"We'd better get to work, eh? Jake and those guys probably won't show until noon, if then."

"Let's go throw all those tires away, at least," I said. We got work gloves from the truck and began our attack. There were seventeen tires.

"Will they even take these at the dump?" I asked.

"Yeah, but they charge extra, though," Kevin said, and pitched another one in. "Doesn't matter. We're not the ones paying for this." The tire bounced off a broken microwave and settled in the corner.

"What is all this junk? Potty seats? Someone's file cabinet?" A torn-up love seat took up the majority of the box. Old Christmas lights, a bucket with a hole in it, a broken guitar, clothing, a pot with no handle, dead houseplants, all flung together.

"Nice neighbors, welcoming us this way," I said. I threw in another tire. "Will you remind me to call Jake's agent later? We're going to need another drop box."

As Kevin pitched in the last tire, the overhead garage door went up with a screech and a bang. Grandpa Bill stepped out, tying his hair back in a bandana. He didn't look happy.

"Do you grow potatoes or not?" he yelled at us. He knelt down to adjust his boot.

"What?" Kevin asked.

"Potatoes!"

He walked up to the dumpster, climbed in, and started throwing the tires back out.

"Hey! Knock that off!" I said. He threw another tire toward the garage. It bounced and rolled into the fence.

"I. Grow. My. Potatoes in those!" he growled at me.

"Too fucking bad," Kevin told him. "We're having an 'all-you-can-throw-away' sale today. All tires must go."

Grandpa Bill stormed back into the garage. I could see the teenage girl stirring from a pallet in the back. The door came down with another screech and bang.

"Should we call the cops? About that girl?" I asked Kevin.

"No cops. She would just lie and say she was twenty. Hey, look who's here!"

"We need to get the wood stove," Jake told us, without a hello, as he strolled down the driveway. I had a copy of the real estate agreement in my purse. I pulled it out. I knew it was going to get like this.

"Woodstove – staying. All debris, cars, appliances and all owners' possessions must be removed by the owner..." I read aloud. "That means your grandpa, too."

"Hey, sis," Jake said. "He is not my grandpa. He is my father-in-law. Excuse me, my former father-in-law. And I do not take responsibility for him."

"And I'm supposed to?" I said, getting irritated.

"He's not a bad guy," Jake said. "He's pretty good at handyman-type stuff. The plumbing needs a little work; he could do that." He headed into the garage. Kevin and I went into the house.

After a few days with the druggies, I learned to tell when they were on speed and when they were on heroin. Heroin was definitely preferable – they didn't talk much, just sort of nodded out and disappeared down the driveway. With the speed, they chattered like magpies and tried to rewire the house to "help" us. Jake almost burned down the back bedroom, attempting to fix the baseboard heater his friends had started on. Whenever Jake started arguing, he was high on meth. Grandpa Bill? Always high on meth and didn't seem to have an "off" switch.

"They'll be gone soon," Kevin said, "Good Lord willin' and the crick don't rise."

"Liar."

"At least we got them out of the house?"

"Yeah, until Jake wants to rewire it again," I said. "Ha." Kevin took Jake through the house one last time, to show him that all of his stuff was gone. Then we wouldn't let him back in.

Merry Maids came by to help clean. We had a load of family and friends stop by, too. Some of them even pitched in.

One afternoon, Amber and Kim stopped by for a visit. We had already told Amber she couldn't stay the night until we had the place ready. She raced down the hallways, checking out the house. She ran into the back bedroom, next to the laundry room, slamming the door wide open.

"Wow!" she yelled, "Can this be my room?"

Grandpa Bill and everyone else? The neighbor helped us out a few days later and we finally got rid of them. He helped Bill roar the old International to life (I would have guessed the truck was a lost cause), and even helped them pack their trailer. Three dumpsters later (fill/haul, fill/haul, fill/haul) they were gone.

"I wanted them out of here as bad as you did," the neighbor told me. "Possibly worse. I'm Todd." He stuck out his hand. I shook it.

"Lizzie," I said. "And thanks."

"Sorry about all the crap everyone threw in the dumpster."

"Not a problem. Their agent paid for it," I told him. Did he ever.

Kevin came out to check on me.

"I think it's ours now," Kevin said, "unless there are some more living behind the garage or something." He was taking a break from painting the front bedroom, the one that had belonged to Roscoe.

I laughed out loud.

"Come see what I've done!" Kevin said.

It was a different room. It really was becoming our house now.

The holes in the wall were gone – Kevin had filled everything in and painted. We had both been working so hard. I had never cleaned so much in my life. It was like we were erasing them – it was a good feeling.

I heard the doorbell ring. It sounded like the back door. Kevin went back to his painting. I headed to answer the door. No one there. Then the front doorbell rang, three short rings in a row.

A guy was there, looking anxious. "Sorry – you went to the back door, huh? You got my stuff?" he asked.

It had to be Roscoe, the jailbird housemate.

"Yes?" I asked.

He was around forty years old, maybe a little younger, about five-foot-eight, thin, with short, light brown hair. He had the most alabaster skin I had ever seen and wore a lime green V-necked polyester top, with yellow and green plaid pants. No coat, even though it was a chilly day. His fingernails were cut short and clean.

"You must be the new owner," he said, "Sorry. I'm Roscoe."

"Come on in," I said, stepping into the dining room and sticking out my hand. "Lizzie. Nice to meet you. We tried to send it all with Jake, but they left it in the garage for you, instead. Last we heard they're at the Rainbow Motel, on 82nd."

"You need a housemate or what? I'm available," Roscoe said, and glanced around. "Hey! The house is looking nice!"

A paint-splattered Kevin walked into the room.

"I love this house," Roscoe told him. "I'm Roscoe, hey."

"Hey. I'm just finishing up painting your room. I mean, old room."

"Really? What color?" We walked into the dining room and Roscoe began stroking the knotty pine paneling on the walls. "I've always loved this. I could help you work on the house … Paint a little and whatnot." We both hated painting. I didn't mind canvas, that was fine, but walls? No.

"You guys have been working hard."

"Thanks," Kevin said.

"You know what I always thought would look so nice? An indoor waterfall, right there." Roscoe gestured to the right of the entryway.

"You could enclose the porch, baby," he said, turning to me. "Make it more of a foyer-type situation going on." He smiled like a little kid. He waited for us to respond. He smiled bigger.

"Wa-ter-fall," he said, making his fingers flutter up and down, like water cascading. "Waterfall! Whaddya think? So. You need a roomie?" Oh, my God – he was funny. And he didn't remind me of the others.

"Can we think about it?" Kevin said.

"Sure," Roscoe said. "But could you think about it maybe fast? I don't really have a house anymore."

He gave us references – his mom, sister and a couple of friends.

"My mom said she would help, if you want a couple of months' rent in advance." He had been taking classes at the community college, before things got "out of hand," as he put it. "Some landscaping and design classes, you know. I could help with the yard? Or cook for you?"

I called his references while he and Kevin smoked outside. Yes, could he please still live there, oh, we just love him, he's not a bit of trouble, etc. And we had ourselves a roommate.

30 *Rosebush w sm pnk roses just across from grge*

OCTOBER 1992

"Amber? Where are you, honey?" I called. We had been outside working in the yard since early morning. Roscoe had drawn up a whole "exterior design plan" for me. I was supposed to talk with him about the "bones" of the yard before I did anything major, working around the shrubs and trees we already had.

"Don't do anything stupid," were his exact words. Good God.

You know who loved Roscoe? That's right, my granny.

She would.

She drew up a list of all the plants she could remember that had been in the yard when it was hers. She color-coded it and put down the locations of where everything used to be. She abbreviated everything, Granny-style. For instance, "Rosebush w sm pnk roses just across from grge" and "prple lilac (wht would be good tho) in back R corner of yard.

Roscoe you call me this week." Last time she came over she gave it to Roscoe, so he could get started. He undrstd all her notes of crse and studied the list like it was th Bble. They had already made three trips to the garden center.

My job was to get everything cleared, weeded and composted. I kept finding weird stuff buried in the dirt – a heart-shaped ceramic plate decorated with flowers that looked like they were made of frosting. They rose up from the plate in bas relief. The plate was broken neatly in half and thrown onto a junk pile I found out back, under the blackberries. I wondered if it had belonged to Jake Lee Grant's mom. Probably. Amber was digging in the way back of the yard one time – in an area we had already cleaned up – and unearthed first the sleeve to a man's dress shirt, then the rest of the shirt, then some rolled-up heavy plastic sheeting.

"What *is* this?" she asked, excited.

I told her to stop digging before we found the whole body. Now if only the dogs would stop, too. We had adopted two pound puppies as soon as we got settled – Sasha, a female German shepherd mutt, and Junebug, this wild little terrier with an attitude. Perfect for Amber.

The house was in good shape, at least structurally, but we found all kinds of other nasty crap inside the house and out – needles, spoons, empty condom wrappers *(Safety first!)*, and a whole bunch of bags of kitchen garbage – tin cans, soda pop bottles, chicken bones – alongside the garage. Tons of take-out containers. They hadn't wanted to pay "the man" for garbage service, it appeared. All of that we had hauled off in the dumpster, while we still had it. But broken glass, nails, dead bodies, all that would most likely keep surfacing with every fresh rain. Bones. Bad bones, not good ones.

I was in the front yard at the moment; it wasn't as bad out here. I was plotting, mentally, where I wanted to plant my sunflowers and petunias.

185

Amber poked her head around the corner. She was in the back still, playing with her new pups.

"I'm here, Liz! Guess what? I'm working on your garden! I'm pulling up weeds."

"Hang on, hang on," I said, opening the gate and walking quickly to where she was. "Remember we talked about the icky garbage I keep finding? You don't have gloves on."

"It's OK, I was just pulling the weeds, I didn't touch the dirt. But which ones are the weeds, exactly?" Amber asked. "The dogs were helping!" Their noses were covered with dirt, both of them. I swear they looked like they were grinning at me. Amber was standing next to a pile of formerly rooted plant starts I had just put in, with Roscoe's permission, and two weeds. I looked at my African daisies, pansies, and marigolds and gave a little sigh.

"Flowers/pretty, weeds/ugly. General rule," I told her, "Don't pull up anything else, all right? Promise? This one is a weed, this one isn't. See?"

She had already run off. I replanted the starts and tossed the weeds in with the yard debris. Maybe we should have stuck with the inside work, like Amber's room. It was small, but all hers. We had organized a nice studio in one corner. I was hoping to get her more furniture, soon, a desk and whatever else she needed. Amber had been more rambunctious than usual since we got the house. She was over a lot. Kim was tripping. Still trippin'. But not institutionalized, so that was a good sign.

Michael was still Michael. I didn't have to see him or Amanda, ever, and that was great. I did pick-ups and drop-offs from school, Kim's place, or Michael's parents. They were bummed that we had split up but seemed to enjoy Amanda. They liked Kevin, too. I loved having Michael's folks up the street – they kept finding excuses to drop by, with houseplants, food, little things for Amber. They even brought over a basket of goodies, all wrapped up with bows, for the dogs.

Amber had never lived anywhere but an apartment; this was uncharted territory for her. Within a two-hour period she had stepped in dog poop, poked herself in the eye with a sharp stick *("Better than a poke in the eye with a sharp stick!"),* and come about two inches from hitting me in the head with the shovel she was wielding like a bat. City kids. Now, she was using a mallet in an attempt to knock down the garage door, with the dogs at her heels, panting. What a team.

"Hmm," I said. I had discovered I could bite my tongue and say "hmm" at the same time. I also had perfected the evil snake-eye, for emergency situations. If I ever had kids of my own I would be all set.

"Stop hitting the door, huh? Maybe we should work on the gardening later?" We packed up the gardening tools and headed in for lunch.

31 *Dimes for Dudes*

FEBRUARY 16, 1993

Champs, our nearest restaurant and bar, was hurting for business. Seems the AIDS crisis was killing not just lovers, but the pick-up scene, too. So the owners struck upon a brilliant idea – every Tuesday would be Dimes for Dudes (not dollar drinks, but dime drinks) and Thursdays would be reserved for the ladies, with Dimes for Damsels.

Brilliant. Unlike the decor. In a former incarnation, Champs was called Good Fortune Chinese. When the new owners took over and wanted to give it a sports-bar theme, they kept the fish tanks and the gold foil and red wallpaper. They added sports banners and a big screen TV and called it a day. They hadn't been able to make up their minds about the music, though. During the daytime they played mostly '80s stuff, at four in the afternoon, they switched to country, and at nine, the karaoke party started and dime drinks abruptly ended.

Business was nuts on dime-drinking nights, and the other nights of the week were picking up, too. My only problem with the concept: The word "damsels" didn't match up with the word "dudes."

"Happy VD," I said, lifting my drink and toasting everyone. "Clap, everybody, clap!" We clanked glasses. I was there with Gage, JoJo and Kevin. We'd gotten there early and snagged a corner booth, as far away as we could get from the karaoke machine. We were celebrating Valentine's Day late. Because we had cheap-ass men in our life, that was why.

"They should have called it something else. Dimes for Dykes, maybe," JoJo shouted over the country-western music blaring in surround sound, "if they were looking for a different crowd."

"Dimes for Da Bitches?" I suggested.

"Naw," Gage said. "How about Dimes for Da Ladies?"

JoJo and I groaned.

"There you go," Kevin said. "You know what sucks about this place?" All four of us perused the room.

"Well?" Kevin asked. "It's so obvious."

"Everything?" I asked.

"No salad," Kevin said, pulling a celery stick from his shirt pocket and plunking it into his Bloody Mary.

"Did he just get that out of his pocket?" Gage asked. "Tell me that man is not carrying celery sticks around with him."

"He's packing," JoJo said.

"Got an olive for me in there?" I asked him, sticking my fingers in his pocket.

"No, ma'am," Kevin said, "But I do have something you might like …" He reached into his other pocket and pulled out a jalapeño pepper.

"Kevin! You got to be kidding me," I said.

"Yeah, Kevin, ewww… Isn't your pocket all lint-y?" JoJo asked. "Use plastic bags next time. Or bring a little picnic basket."

Gage grabbed the appetizer menu from its metal stand. "I could go for some jalapeño poppers. Chicken wings, zucchini pucks … What else they got? Jojos... your favorite, Jo!"

"Hardy-har," JoJo said. She tried flagging down the waitress for another round. It was Thursday, so Da Ladies were buying.

"Hell, yeah," Kevin said, "Order some wings."

"Forget it," JoJo said, spying the waitress four tables down. She was heading the other direction. "She's never coming back." Jo got up to wend her way to the bar.

"Come rescue me if I'm not back in half an hour," she said. "Wanna help me carry drinks, Gage?"

"Sure," Gage said. "Want any food, guys?"

"Naw, we're all right," I said. Gage and JoJo started off on the obstacle course to get to the bar. I didn't know anyone in here; they all looked like they needed fake IDs to get in.

I snapped my fingers. "Dimes for Dames. That's perfect. Kinda '40s." Kevin pulled out a cigarette and lit up. He gave me a quick smile, then leaned over and lightly pressed the outside of my ear, so I could hear him whisper. It was our bar trick.

"I've got it all, Liz," he said.

"Yeah, you and your vegetable medley."

"No, I mean you," he said, putting his arm around me and drawing me in for a kiss.

"Want to get married?"

"Us?" I said, thrown by his question. I pulled away. "The two of us, married? For real?"

"Yes, us. Who did you think I meant?"

"I need to think about it. Is that OK?" I just blurted it out. Oh, God.

"Sure, that's fine," Kevin said, looking worried. "I didn't mean to spring it on you like that. Sure, maybe we can talk about it later."

32 *Hope Chest*

I called my mom from work the next day. I had already left a message for JoJo; I hadn't told her yet.

"He proposed. At Champs."

"That icky place, that used to be the Chinese restaurant? Not the most romantic setting. What did you tell him?"

"I didn't know what to say!"

"Did he give you a ring?"

"No."

"Hmm," Mom said.

"What, hmm?"

"Nothing, just hmm."

"He caught me off guard. I felt like I got sucker punched. Then JoJo and Gage came back to the table, and I changed the subject."

"Sucker-punched?" Mom asked, amused. "That's an interesting way to describe it, when a man professes his undying love."

"I didn't mean it like that. I don't think so, anyway," I said. "What do you think?"

She said what she always said when the topic came up. "I'm opposed to the idea of marriage at all. Why do you think they call it an institution? You want to – "

"You want to live in an institution?" I broke in. "I know, you've told me that, like, eight billion times. But I do love him."

"Maybe you two could just keep living in sin?" Mom asked. She sounded hopeful.

"Don't you want me married off? It's not like either of us is going anywhere. And besides, he doesn't have health insurance."

"That's a lousy, although practical, reason. Want me to put together a hope chest for you?" She was laughing now.

"Oh, hardy har, Mom. Yes, why don't you start one for me. No, I do not need a hope chest. I'm freaking out. I need to call Gwen. Besides, don't most parents want their kids to get married? You hippie parents are all, 'Why bother? We didn't ...' I might get married someday. Maybe even to Kevin."

"Yes, go ahead and rebel," Mom said.

But as I said it out loud, I realized it wouldn't be Kevin. Ever. Dammit. And it was more than the fact that he proposed to me in a sleazy bar. Gah.

"What's in your heart, Elizabeth?" Mom asked. "You'll figure it out. And I *was* married to your father – legally, even."

I hung up the phone and opened my day planner. Potential buyers were scheduled to come by at 10:30, for an early viewing of the new exhibit we were putting up. I shut the day planner. I couldn't get my mind off Kevin.

A hope chest – oh, please. I was smiling. My ma was never one for sentimental tradition.

"Way too much pressure to put on a little girl," she told me, once I found out what hope chests were and asked for one. I was ten years old at the time. I had seen one at a friend's house – it was pretty. It was made of pale blond wood, and the girl's mom and grandmas had filled it with crisp, clean white sheets and pillowcases trimmed with hand-tatted lace. Her grandma had made the lace. My grandma made lace, too, it was like a sign. I was always looking for signs, as a kid. Some things you never outgrow, like me with signs and superstitions. Step on a crack and all that. Remembering not to watch someone as they drive away. Skipping around the number thirteen. There were sachets and towels and other odds and ends, tucked in. There were even a couple of hand-sewn white nightgowns, trimmed with more of the delicate, soft lace. It was amazing, really.

"How vile," Mom said when I described it to her. That kind of discouragement made me want a hope chest more than anything in the world. I asked Mom about it a few more times, then gave up. I should have gone straight to my grandmas. They would have put one together for me.

Granny. I needed to talk to my granny about this. I grabbed up the phone. Granny answered on the second ring.

"Lizzie," she said, "Whaddya know? Uh-huh. Really? Sure, why not? I like him. That poor boy needs a family."

"Grandma, he has a family," I said. "They live right in town. They're idiots, but they exist."

"Then, he wants his own family, I suppose. Maybe one that's not so stupid." She laughed. "Did I tell you we're having the senior luncheon at church this week?" Grandma started telling me about the menu – roast beef, mashed potatoes, pasta salad, and a pea and cheese salad. She would be bringing the rolls and cornbread.

"Homemade, none of that store-bought stale crap." I listened to her go on, saying, "Um," and "uh-huh" in the right spots. Why shouldn't I marry

Kevin? Why shouldn't I? I'd bought a house with him, after all. I didn't want to marry him, that was all. Great.

"What if I don't want to marry him?" I asked her.

"Well then, you don't marry him. Honey, what is wrong with you today? This is not like you. I have to get ready for the luncheon now, I don't have all day to try to fix your life. I wouldn't mind some great-grandchildren, though. Before I'm dead."

"I ordered two for you – they just haven't shown up yet. Love you."

"Love you, too, baby. Don't do anything you don't want to."

We hung up. I called Jo again. This time she answered.

"Headache," she said, by way of greeting. "What?" I told her.

"Ring?" she asked.

"No ring."

"Tell him if he's serious he needs to buy you a fucking ring. I gotta go, I need more sleep." She hung up.

I finally started on my workday. Enough torturing myself, already. Enough.

33 *The Marriage Question*

It was Amber's seventh birthday. I got her a bunch of excellent presents. A big set of Legos, to build a castle; colored pencils; a roly-poly ball with a plastic ladybug inside; a how-to book on drawing dogs; a pencil shaped like a branch; a pencil case, with an Egyptian scene on the front; a wind-up dragon that shot sparks out of its mouth (to go with the Lego castle); a map of the United States for her room; and a miniature license plate with her name on it.

Amber was in awe. She opened the case and shut it, opened it back up and put the pencils in, then went to grab paper to start drawing. I baked her favorite cake – chocolate, with chocolate frosting and raspberry filling (I cheated and used jam). I decorated it with icing in her favorite colors, purple and blue. I made icing flowers and little seashells, and wrote "Happy Birthday Amber!" across the top. I let her use seven kinds of sprinkles on it, too, remembering her comparing them to glitter. Lots of smiles, thinking back to all the good times we'd had so far, and hopefully lots more to come.

It was all a good distraction from the Marriage Question. I kept trying to talk Kevin out of it; he kept pushing it.

"You want kids, Lizzie? Fine, we can have kids."

He had never wanted kids. I was silent.

"How about in..." he paused. He was looking a little frantic now. "Seven years or so?" We would be how old then, almost forty? Yeah, right. Sure thing. We finally agreed to let it all be.

"I'm not going anywhere," I told him (blatant lie), which seemed to satisfy him for the time being. Great. Just what a girl wanted – to buy herself some time. I would keep folding laundry or watering the plants and change the subject whenever it came up.

Kevin had never been one to swap stories, but since we had moved into the house, he was telling me all kinds of stuff I'd never heard before. Mostly about his family – legendary in our neighborhood for their rowdy ways. We had been so close, when we were kids, I thought I knew him. I never knew how bad he felt about dropping out of high school. That he wanted to go back someday and pick up his GED, but he had been working construction his whole life and it didn't seem like there was a point to it. And there were other things he had hidden from me. Big things. I think he wanted to protect me. Keep it safe for me, because it wasn't safe at all for him. There was a reason he had spent so much time at our house – he didn't want to go home.

"He'd come home so loaded," Kevin said of his father, "He threw me across the room one time because I was sitting in his chair. Remember when my arm was broken? I told everyone I'd fallen out of a tree, but it was him. My mom finally starting calling the cops, and then he left me the hell alone."

"Can you believe I lived through that shit?" He laughed about it, but I was horrified. I did remember his broken arm. We were in the fourth grade

196

and had all signed his cast. In my childhood home, hostility was measured by the lengths of silences, cut, chilled, and left out for everyone to see and not discuss. But no screaming. Screaming not allowed.

"Didn't it make you mad at your mom?" I asked him. "I mean, didn't you want her to take you kids and get out of there?"

"Naw, I mean, she was in the same boat as me, y'know?" Kevin said, pushing back his sleeve and rubbing his arm. "How could I get mad at her?" I was glad Amber wasn't hearing any of this.

That night, though, it was all about Amber. Kevin made her favorite dinner – his world-famous Rice-A-Roni extravaganza, with a side of tortilla chips.

"They have to be the round ones," I heard Kevin tell her, in all seriousness. "They work the best." We had egg rolls, too, with sweet and sour sauce. Sodium overdose. I scooped up more. It was a fine night. I wanted to forget about all of our bad memories, Kevin's and mine. Forget about all the time we had spent apart and just focus on the future. Marriage? That was a big question mark.

34 *Watch Out for LaLa*

"**B**abe, don't be mad," Kevin began. "I was at Tom and Heather's and the coolest thing happened. You know their roommates?"

Cute Chris. The words ambled through my sleepy mind, like an old familiar stranger. He was Tom and Heather's newest roommate. I hadn't met him yet, but there he was, waltzing through my tired brain.

I had been asleep for four hours. When most people said, don't be mad, it was for something small. With Kevin, it was usually followed by something like, "I need money for bail? For my buddy?" or "My engine caught on fire, but I had the car towed." The digital clock's numbers glowed 2:17 a.m. Kevin buzzed around me like a happy, stoned mosquito. I swatted at his head when he leaned over to kiss me, then shoved him away, but he didn't leave. He started tickling my arm under the covers. I pulled all of the pillows over my head.

"So, are you awake?" he asked, perching on the edge of the quilt. He reached under the pillows and ran his fingers through my hair. I smacked his hand away.

"Does it fucking look like I'm fucking awake?" I asked.

"Yes?"

"Dammit, now I have to pee," I said, and got up. Kevin followed me into the bathroom and flipped on the light. I blinked in the glare, then threw a magazine at him.

"Christ, Kevin! Leave me alone!"

"All right, all right," he said, turning the light off and stepping back into the bedroom. He switched tactics. "I'm so psyched about this! They made this cool thing with their roommates, this artwork. Lizzie?" He followed me into the kitchen, where I was headed for a drink of water. Something about peeing always makes me thirsty.

"Watch out for LaLa!" Kevin sang out as I tripped over something large, bulky, and … with arms?

"Aiiiiii!" I almost caught myself, then fell backward, whacking my elbow on the table and landing on my ass. The thing was silver, and gleamed in the moonlight. It had breasts.

"Kevin, what the fuck?"

He flipped on the light and yelled, "Ta-da! That's LaLa!"

I stayed down on the floor, staring at this glowing thing sitting in our dining room. The reclining – sprawling, really – sculpture of a woman had six faces, a bald head, four breasts and four legs. It was nearly life-size, made of plaster of paris and painted silver. All over. The dogs followed behind me. They had both been sleeping on the floor next to me. Sasha started to walk over to the sculpture, then backed away slowly, growling.

Kevin was smiling and dancing from one foot to the other. "Isn't she incredible?"

I got up from the floor, rubbing my elbow. I was going to have a huge bruise on my ass. Goddammit, I was sleeping so good. "This is the most heinous thing I've ever seen in my life," I said, walking around it slowly and looking at it from all angles. "It's hideous."

"Heinous or hideous, which is it?" Kevin asked. He looked wounded. "It is art, Elizabeth!" He stroked the sculpture, comforting it.

"Hideous," I said again, "I know bad art when I see it. That thing is crap."

"You don't like anybody's shit but your own, Liz," Kevin said. This was somewhat true. "You have to appreciate this ..."

"No, I don't. It's shit."

"... for the integrity of the piece," Kevin said, "and for its rather nutty robust flavor."

I rolled my eyes. "The only thing nutty and robust around here is you. I was sleeping so good," I said. "I'm going back to bed. Leave me alone, pretty please?"

"And, besides, they gave it to me for free! Can you believe it? Cool of them," Kevin said. He was walking around LaLa, looking at her, happy. He was in love.

"Honey, they should have paid you to haul it off. I want it the fuck out of my dining room," I said. "I'm going back to bed." I smacked LaLa in the head as I left the room.

"Ouch." I hurt my hand.

"Lizzie!" Kevin said and smiled. "You're jealous!"

35 *Every Pill in the House*

APRIL 1993

A few weeks later I got the call about JoJo. She was in the hospital. She was alive, at least, but that was just luck. I called Gwen, and we went to see her. The receptionist, bored, buzzed us in to the psych ward when we got there. She dutifully inspected the bags of fast food we'd brought, dug through our purses to make sure we didn't have guns, and pointed us in the right direction.

JoJo sat up in bed, blond hair pulled back in a ponytail. Without makeup, the freckles on her face stood out. She looked about fifteen years old. She looked not much older than she was when I first met her. Except she was wearing a pink sweatshirt with a teddy bear on the front over her pale blue hospital-issue nightgown. Even preteen JoJo wouldn't have gone for that. I hugged her and set the bag of tacos and burritos on the ledge. I handed her an iced tea and four packets of sugar.

"You almost died," I said.

"Yeah," JoJo said, "I heard. Did you know they pumped my stomach?"

"Hon, they had to," Gwen said, giving JoJo a hug and kissing her on both cheeks. "They thought you were dying on them." The room wasn't awful. I had expected *I Never Promised You a Rose Garden* or something along those lines. Kevin and I watched that movie once, in the middle of the night. We drank a half rack of cheap beer and bawled our eyes out. We were sixteen then, I think. Maybe a little younger.

This room looked almost like a college dorm. All it needed were the beer signs and band posters. There was one poster in the room – a print of a country cottage, mounted on cardboard and still in its original cellophane. It looked like generic motel room art. The walls of the room were painted a soft pink.

"I wasn't that bad," JoJo said. "I was just passed out. Gage found me, it was OK, OK?" Gwen sat down on the bed. I leaned against the windowsill. I checked the windows – they didn't open.

"I was!" JoJo said. "I was alright. All right, it could have been bad. But that sure woke me up, when they stuck the hose down my throat." She laughed, but it kind of hiccuped in her throat and stopped before it really got started. Not like JoJo's usual laugh, which could make everyone in the room look around, wanting to know who the chick was with the big bray.

JoJo pushed some wisps of hair out of her eyes. "I'm sorry, you guys; I'm sorry this happened."

"Jo, it's OK," Gwen said. "It's OK, OK? Right? S'alright!" She looked to me. I nodded. "I'm glad Gage called Lizzie. Damn. I mean, it could have been bad."

"It was," JoJo said. She was almost cheerful about it. "God, I took every pill in the house. And I was drunk, OK? I wasn't thinking straight." Gwen took both of JoJo's shoulders in her hands, leaning in close to her face and grabbing her hard. She made her voice deep and serious.

"Obviously," Gwen said. "Here, have a taco."

JoJo poured all four packets of the sugar into the cup of iced tea, unwrapped a straw and used it to stir it in. "It's like I don't even remember it," JoJo said. She pulled at the sweatshirt she was wearing. "Jesus, I mean get this teddy bear. The nurse found this for me; I was freezing. Can you ask Gage to bring some clothes for me? I'm so cold all the time. They don't have robes here. Because of the ties on them, I guess."

"It seemed like you and Gage were doing great," I said.

"Not really," JoJo said, drinking her tea. "He's been seeing someone else."

"What?" Gwen said. "*What?*"

Gage had told me that JoJo was nude when the rescue crew got there. He also said he was too pissed off at Jo to even talk to her yet about what happened.

"Do you think I'm pretty?" JoJo asked us.

"You're gorgeous, Jo," I told her. "You are a beautiful girl."

"I don't think Gage loves me. I don't think he's ever, ever loved me." She finished her taco.

Gwen handed Jo some hot sauce and another taco. "Of course he loves you. He's just an idiot, that's all."

Gage and JoJo's wedding had been astounding. They had it in a little chapel across the river. I was maid of honor, Gage's airhead younger brother was best man. A bunch of our teenage friends were guests. Gage's mother spent the entire ceremony sobbing. Not happy tears, either. JoJo's divorced parents had refused to attend, but her Aunt Katharine had brought Tiffany, JoJo's little sister. The chapel's blue-green shag carpet was worn and stained. The rest of the building was just as rundown. The minister and his wife lived in the back. There were four rows of small, banged-up and scratched wooden pews. The family and guests crowded into the front two rows. The wedding march was a tinny version, played on a small cassette deck the minister perched on the pulpit. Midway through the ceremony, the minister's puppy trotted in and started gnawing on a frayed end of carpet. At the end of the ceremony Tiffany shouted "Oh, gross!" when Gage awkwardly kissed JoJo. Their teeth clanged together and JoJo winced. I winced. The minister's wife looked depressed.

At the reception, Gage shoved cake into his bride's startled face, her mouth twisted sideways, her shell-pink lipstick smeared all over. Gage's friends thought it was funny. "Give it to her!" his brother yelled, hooting. Their mother poked her head out of the kitchen, where she was opening a carton of orange sherbet and vanilla ice cream to serve to the guests.

"You asshole!" JoJo shrieked at him, then shoved cake into his face, neck, and suit.

"Payback, dude!" one of his friends said. JoJo and Gage started wrestling, ending up on the shag carpet of his mother's tiny combined living room/dining room, with JoJo astride him, beating him in the face and chest. He grabbed her in his arms and they laughed their stupid heads off. His mother shook her head and went back into the kitchen. Going to their wedding made me never want to get married. Gage was drunk as hell by six o'clock, along with his buddies.

"Hey, are you paying attention?" JoJo asked me. "I was supposed to get out tomorrow, I said, but they're saying now they want to keep me two more nights just to be sure nothing's going to happen. Nothing's going to happen!"

"It's so stupid. I'm sorry," she said again.

"Hey, why the hell did you guys get married so young, anyway?" I asked. "Y'all were just babies."

"Dunno. I think he just wanted to make sure I wouldn't get away." JoJo yawned.

"Who can blame him?" Gwen asked. She crossed the room, threw her taco wrappers in the garbage and pulled out a Marlboro Light.

"All right to smoke in here? Is this a smoking room or what?" she asked. JoJo grimaced. "No, they won't let me. My sister brought me two packs. They took them away. Who cares? Give me one." Gwen passed the pack and pulled out her lighter. I started wishing I had snuck in a flask. And that JoJo had never married Gage in the first place. Another girl. Nice. JoJo flirted, but she didn't run around.

"So has Gage been up to visit, or what?" I asked her. She got up out of bed and stretched. "Yeah, he was here yesterday, of course. He brought his mother, of course. She gave us a big lecture about how it's time for us to stop acting like little children, blah blah blah. We've made it this far, which is a goddamn miracle, really, blah blah blah."

"Gage told her at least *he* acts like an adult, *he* has a job and all that. Goddamn, I have a job, too. Waitressing doesn't count to him, just his stupid welding job."

"Of course it counts, honey," Gwen said. "Screw him. Gage couldn't wait tables if he tried." She had gotten JoJo a job as a cocktail waitress at the pub where she worked. It was in the neighborhood where we all grew up. JoJo opened the lid to her iced tea and dropped the live cigarette in. It sizzled and went out.

"He says he'll come by tonight, but I know he won't."

"What happened, exactly? How much do you remember?" Gwen asked.

"We got drunk. He dumped me at home and told me about the girl. He's not in love with her, allegedly. It's over, allegedly. He left. Then I went nuts. The end." JoJo spit it out, rapid-fire, then stopped for a big breath and sighed.

"Fuck," she said. She lit another smoke and took a puff. She grabbed her datebook out of her purse on the nightstand, and started flipping through it.

"They went through my purse." She rearranged a few things, put her lipstick back into her makeup bag.

"Shoot, Gage and I were supposed to go to the dentist this week. I'll have to reschedule that one. Damn, it takes forever to get in. You think the nurse would call them for me, to cancel it? Or else they'll charge us."

"Probably," Gwen said. "Ask her."

"Sorry," JoJo said. "I can't focus for shit." She took another long drag off her cigarette. I looked at it longingly, wishing I hadn't quit. "Jesus. People. I can't believe they went through my purse."

I stopped paying attention. Now I really, really wanted a cigarette. I scratched my head and closed my eyes. Breathe in... out... in... I did seven breaths in and eight breaths out. I hadn't smoked in years, I wasn't starting again now.

"... you know they are," JoJo said.

"Huh?" I asked.

Gwen lit another cigarette. "Fucking idiots," she agreed. "Don't you know it, girl. They're just dumb. Put Gage at the top of the list. JoJo, you cannot kill yourself over a guy, OK? It's not allowed." That made us all smile.

"Hey Lizzie, you want more chips?" JoJo asked. She was eating like a starving person. I shook my head no and finished my iced tea.

"Sheesh," JoJo said, scooping up bean dip, "I wish they'd let me out of here. I'm really sorry, you guys. This is so fucking, fucking, fucking stupid."

"Stop saying you're sorry, please?" Gwen told her. "It's OK, sweetie. Really."

"God, I'm sorry," JoJo said again.

"Stop!" I told her. "No more apologizing. It's fine. You're alive. That's all that matters. You're alive."

JoJo's big, blue marble eyes filled with tears. Gwen and I both held her, stroked her hair and tried to comfort her. JoJo broke hearts with her eyes alone. Even when she was at her most wasted, her eyes were still astonishing. We all took acid one time, when we were teenagers, and saw the same spiders climb out of the walls, build webs and surround us. Gwen asked us later, "Do you think I made you guys see them, because I saw them? Or was it because we're all friends and think alike? Or were they really there?" We thought that was hilarious for a long time.

I thought I saw a lizard crawling on my arm once, when I was tripping. JoJo said she could see the blood rushing through her veins. Even loaded out of her skull, JoJo was the most beautiful girl in the world. TFF: True Friends Forever. Going out to the river in the summer, standing on the beach wearing string bikinis, flagging down guys in boats to go for rides. Drinking their beer, smoking their dope, then giving them fake phone numbers. But it was JoJo whose number they always asked for first. JoJo, with her long, honey-colored hair, her freckled face, her legs like a colt. She didn't want them, so they wanted her. And she always had Gage.

"Is this weird for you, Liz?" Jo asked, "I mean, because of your dad?" I couldn't picture my dad in a nice place like this. I mean, it really wasn't too bad. The nurse hadn't come to check on us even once, and it smelled OK in the halls, walking in. There was a view, even, onto the park across the street. It was almost pretty. It was a chilly day, for spring, but there were still a few walkers out. Two women were race-walking; a young guy was throwing a ball for his Irish setter; an older man sat on one of the benches, reading a book.

"No, it's OK," I said finally. I had visited my dad a few times, when he was hospitalized; the place where they had him was nothing like this place. And the memories, the reality, were all mixed up with memories that weren't even mine. Sylvia Plath and *The Bell Jar*, *One Flew Over the*

207

Cuckoo's Nest. And that awful old movie, *The Snake Pit*. I think that was the title. With Olivia de Havilland. That Frances Farmer movie, with Jessica Lange. Yick. God, why had I watched all those movies? I was so morbid, as a teenager. It all blurred together. I didn't really remember much, from those visits. Just how cold the hospital was, and that there weren't any windows, to speak of. That bothered me.

It was dark there, too, I remembered that. Sky and I stayed out in the waiting room alone one time while Mom went in to check on Dad. I remembered little moments: That at first we thought we weren't going to be able to see him, but then we finally did. That we thought he was coming home with us, that day, we were so excited. We thought we were going there to pick him up. But we were wrong. Dad cried when Skyler and I asked when we could all leave. I thought we would all leave together. It didn't seem fair we got to leave and he didn't. I didn't want to make my dad cry. It made my stomach twist up. Then Mom started getting teary, too.

"He'll come home soon," she told us. "Soon." Dad let us climb on his lap and eat some of the chocolates Grandma Ryan brought for him. I shook my head at the memories. Maybe it was good I didn't remember more.

He must have been embarrassed, to have his little kids see him like that. Or maybe he wasn't. He really lived in his own world so much of the time. Especially those last few years. Then we were gone, the visit over.

Then he was gone, not much longer after that.

"There weren't any windows, I don't think," I told them. "I don't remember any, anyway. Where my dad was." They looked worried. JoJo walked over and reached out for my hands. She took them both in her hands. JoJo's hands were cold and still. Mine were warm and shaking a little.

"Uncle Leo was a good guy," Gwen said. "He was a good person." He was.

JoJo brought me joy, from the first time we met. Jo taught us all to do the Hustle. She helped start a dance team at our school – I was the first one to join.

Gwen cut into my thoughts, as if she knew right where I was. "Y'know, we've all been friends for a real long time now."

JoJo let out a sigh and dropped my hands.

"Think about it," Gwen said, smiling and trying to cheer JoJo. "I was in fifth grade, you guys were in sixth, remember? I was always staying over at your house, Lizzie. Auntie Sue just took me in. I practically lived with you. Lizzie! Remember? You were dating what's-her-name's brother?"

I groaned.

"And you found out he asked JoJo out and you hit him in the head. Do you remember? Then she hit him, too."

JoJo nodded her head and laughed. "He deserved it. Didn't get either one of us."

"I don't remember some stuff," I said. Those two, they were my collective memory sometimes. And my brother, he had a good memory, too. He could hold a grudge worse than I could.

"I'm sorry, honey," Gwen said, crossing the room to me and giving me a big bear hug. My cousin. She wasn't that big of a person, but her hugs were enough to lift you off the ground. I sighed. I would flip out without the two of them. Thank God JoJo wasn't dead. Thank God twice.

"JoJo, you remember when we first met?" I asked, smiling, resting my head against Gwen's. I remembered, like it was ten minutes ago, seeing JoJo for the first time in the sixth grade. It was midmorning, we were all sitting at our desks. It was the first week of school. The door opened and in walked JoJo, wearing green crushed velvet pants. A black-and-white striped shirt. Big, gold hoop earrings. The guys in the class, hormonal, wolf-whistled at her and JoJo blushed, trying to hide behind the door, which Mr. Hendricks was trying to close.

"Class," he said, clapping his hands in a vain attempt to quiet us. "This is Josephine Wagner, your new classmate."

"Watch out, Lizzie!" Donny Cottrell yelled. "You got competition." JoJo's blond hair was almost down to her butt. She was as tall as me; we were both so long-legged. But we never competed – we were in cahoots. We were best friends from the start. JoJo shot Donny a wicked look and took the empty chair next to me.

"What'dya know?" she asked me. She spent the night at my house that weekend, and we were inseparable from then on.

"Hey, we gotta get going, girl," Gwen said. "I've got to get to work."

"Are they pissed? Because I can't work this week?" JoJo asked.

"No, darling," Gwen said. "You're fine. You know the night manager's in love with you. He's going to send you flowers, I think. He likes to piss off Gage. He wanted to come by and see you, but I told him please don't."

"Ah, dang. That's sweet of him. He doesn't have to do that." JoJo twirled a piece of hair around her finger. "Maybe I can get a shower now." She smiled a full, lazy smile, pleased that flowers were on the way.

Then her big smile faded. "I don't know what I was doing, you guys," JoJo said, "I mean, ending up in here. Something must have set me off. I know what set me off. Her. I guess he started seeing her when I was in New York. He claims he used rubbers."

"I'm sorry, Jo, that is such a drag," I said. I mentally made a note to remind her to get an AIDS test, later. It sounded like they were coming out with some new drugs to fight it. Maybe they'd find a cure, someday. I was lucky – all three of my tests came back negative.

"I messed around in New York, but I didn't sleep around," JoJo said, pissed. She abruptly dropped it. "Have you heard from Michael?" She walked us to the door. "Is he leaving you alone?"

"We've talked a couple of times. He wants me to take care of Amber or whatever."

"Yeah, or whatever," Gwen said, teasing me. "I bet he wants you to take care of 'whatever.' We'll see you, girl," she told JoJo, giving her a hug and kissing her on both cheeks.

"Not if I see you first," JoJo said, waving as we walked down the hall.

"Just kidding!" she yelled. "TFF, yeah? Yeah!" The nurse at the station told us to keep it down. I squeezed my eyes shut together fast, to keep back the tears. I turned around and waved at her. And we left her there, alone.

36 *One of the Breasts is My Girlfriend's*

APRIL 1993

The next weekend, I went to pick up Heather, and who should be there but... Cute Chris. He lived up to his name. And no girlfriend in sight.

Jesus God. I couldn't talk.

"You here for Heather?" he finally asked.

"Yes," I said.

He just looked at me, he didn't call for Heather or say anything. So I stood there, looking back at him. He smiled and he just gave me this look... this look like, I know you. It said everything, this look. I realized that I was holding my breath, so I let it out, and tried to act normal. He had long, black, mostly straight hair that curled neatly over his ears. He really did have violet eyes like Liz Taylor's that crinkled when he smiled. Heather told me that but I didn't believe her. His arms were muscular and tanned. He was skinny and a couple of inches over six foot. He smelled good.

I had never seen eyes like that before.

He kept looking at me; I kept looking at him. It should have been awkward, after awhile, but it wasn't. It was funny, though. It was nice. My nose started itching, so I scratched it.

Then he gave me this kind of sideways smile, and asked, "How do you like LaLa?"

I didn't know if Terrie was home, their other roommate, so I said, in all honesty, "She's something else."

"Yeah, one of the breasts is my girlfriend's, my ex-girlfriend's, I mean. Do you want to come in? Sorry, I should have asked you that already. Do you want to come in?" Now he was acting a little nervous. He stepped aside to let me in.

"I plaster of paris'ed it..." Which I already knew. Honestly. Honest to God. Honest to Mike. I didn't want to hear anything else about LaLa, the creation of LaLa, the placement of LaLa, LaLa's thoughts on politics, nothing. I especially didn't want to hear about breasts.

I don't want his hands on anyone's breasts but mine. What? Where did that come from? He was still talking. I had no idea what he'd just said. What I said was, "That sounds interesting," and hoped that was the right response. He kept talking, so I guess it was. *They look like loaves of French bread, those breasts. I hate LaLa.*

"Yeah, Terrie did the sculpture for a group art show, blah blah, everyone really liked it, blah blah..." And really, I couldn't tell you much about what he said, because I was thinking, *If I'm ever single again, I want to marry this man. And then he wouldn't touch anyone's breasts but mine. Ever.*

We were standing too close together. I had to move back. I felt like I was going to pass out. The room was too warm. I took off my coat. Heather finally appeared at the top of the stairs.

"Liz? Hey, I didn't know you were here." She walked downstairs and grabbed her coat from one of the hooks by the front door.

"Liz?" Heather asked. She jostled my arm. "Planet Earth to Liz. Shall we?" she asked, and we left. "Bye, Chris."

"What was that?" Heather asked me.

"What was what?"

"I'll see you, OK?" Chris called to me. I wouldn't see him again until our first date.

37 *Beautiful Woman*

AUGUST 1993

"Where am I taking you for your birthday?" JoJo asked. She grabbed the newspaper off the table and leafed through the entertainment listings.

"Cinema 21, revival of *All About Eve*," I told her. "Drinks first. On you."

"On me. You got it, my friend."

On a hot August night, six kamikazes and one nacho platter later, JoJo and I, the happy birthday girl, staggered arm-in-arm from a Tex-Mex restaurant on the Northwest side of town. We were celebrating another year for me and another successful happy hour.

"I'm twenty-nine now; another three hundred and sixty-five days closer to the grave," I told JoJo.

"So morose, Elizabeth, always so morose." She patted my arm, and we walked down the street to get in line for the movie. "You're not old until next year."

"What's better? The dialogue in this movie? Or the clothes?" I asked her. "Or Marilyn Monroe? What if Marilyn had had the lead, though, that would not have worked."

"The dialogue," Jo answered. "And Marilyn, God rest her soul. And Bette Davis saying, 'Fasten your seat belts, folks...'" JoJo threw her arm around me.

"I love you so much, Liz. You're the wind beneath my wings. I mean it. Without you, I'm nothing. You're the top." She started humming a medley from *Anything Goes*. JoJo, tough as she was, was the biggest, maudlin sucker for musicals and old movies.

"I love you, too, you little maniac," I told her. "Think up some original lines, huh? I love this movie! I haven't seen it in ages. Will you buy me popcorn? With butter? And a big box of Milk Duds?"

"Sure, sure," JoJo said. The line started to move.

"Are they letting people in?" Jo asked. I stepped out of line and looked to the front. There he was. Michael. I hadn't seen him in a long time, but it hadn't been long enough. Oomph. He was snuggling up with a date. A tall, skinny woman, with long, sleek hair the color of a melted cherry popsicle. She most definitely wasn't his petite, curly-headed new bride, she of the chopstick hair accessories and the nice legs, no, she wasn't. Amber and Kim were invited to the wedding; I was not.

"Bumpy evening indeed," I whispered to Jo, pointing out Michael. "Look at the girl he's with."

JoJo gave her a quick once-over. "That's no girl," she said.

"Oh, my," I said. It was true – she was he, and all done up in '70s vintage purple hip-huggers, a striped Bobby Brady T-shirt and big clunky platform shoes.

"Look at that jewelry!" JoJo said, spying the date's accessories and tripping up for a better look. Literally, she started walking toward them and then tripped. She had to grab this woman's elbow to stop from falling. Kamikazes should be outlawed.

"Sorry," JoJo said to the woman, who was in line with her husband, and gave her a little pat. The woman looked confused and stepped away from JoJo. I laughed.

"Sorry," I told her as JoJo walked off. "We just saw an old friend. And a new one!"

Michael's date was carrying a oversized multicolored patchwork suede handbag. She was listening to Michael, with her head tilted to one side. She laughed at something he said, then reached out to stroke his arm.

She is in love with him. It made me feel kind of glowy inside.

"*Amor*," I said to Jo. "*Amor, amor...* What a sucker."

Michael noticed Jo, then me, then ducked his head and pretended he hadn't seen either of us. Priceless.

"Michael, woo-hoo!" JoJo called. "Who's your friend?" She tripped again and grabbed for my arm this time. We really didn't need that last round of drinks.

"Dang, I need to learn to walk in heels, eh?" she said, winking at Michael's date. She smiled back at her, a huge, warm smile. Everyone loved JoJo.

"Look at that!" JoJo said, fingering Michael's date's necklace. "Sea glass? Michael! Are you going to introduce us, or what?"

I stood back, laughing. How satisfying, to catch Michael in an infidelity. Even if he was no longer my lover. Especially since it was with this well-dressed, friendly woman. Who wasn't Amanda.

"Jo," Michael said, "Lizzie, this is..."

"Kimchi," his date interrupted, smiling and clinging to Michael's arm. I stuck out my hand.

"Lizzie Ryan, Michael's ex," I told her. "I'm sure he hasn't told you anything about me."

"Beautiful woman!" Kimchi said, clasping my hand in both of hers.

"He's mentioned you, actually, several times."

"Where's Amanda?" JoJo asked, then asked Kimchi, "He's mentioned Amanda, too? Hasn't he?" Kimchi looked at Michael and smiled.

"Maybe not," JoJo said. The line started to move.

"We really should do this again sometime," Michael said, buying their tickets and then steering Kimchi into the theater. "Really. I mean, later rather than sooner."

"Come see me perform sometime!" Kimchi called out as they vanished into the crowd.

JoJo snapped her fingers. "That's where I know her from – she works at Darcelle's. She's a really good performer. And pretty, huh? That necklace was great, wasn't it?" She paid for our tickets and we walked into the theater. The people behind us were all laughing and whispering to each other.

"Maybe they'll want to go for drinks after the movie? Probably not," I said. "We could always ask? Did you know Michael flunked out of school?"

"Finally," JoJo said.

"Uh-huh. Kim told me. Wait! Kim/Kimchi, nice. Which makes me happier? Busting him, finally, or that he flunked out? Hmm, let me think..."

"Bumpy evening my ass," JoJo said, "That was fun." She bought me a jumbo box of Milk Duds, a box of those sour-sweet candies we were both fond of, and a large popcorn, extra butter. We split a soda. Michael and Kimchi, sitting a half-dozen rows ahead of us, started making out.

"Ah, young love," JoJo said, munching on a handful of popcorn. We'd thrown all the candy in with the popcorn and were making pigs of ourselves.

"I like her so much better than I like him," I said. "She's nice. Doesn't she seem super-nice? And pretty. Too pretty for Michael."

"Maybe we could steal her away from him?" JoJo said.

"Shh! I'm watching the movie!"

As soon as I got home I called my cousin Gwen, even though it was late.

"... with a man," I finished. "Good looking, too. Wake up, Gwen! This is important. She performs at Darcelle's? JoJo said she's really good, great singing voice and all."

"Get down," Gwen said. "Did you already call Kim? You know she'll be dying to pass along the happy news to Amanda."

"She's my next call," I said. I sprawled back on the couch and gave Junebug a shove so I could stretch out my legs. He jumped down and flopped out on the floor. "Why does this make me so happy? Am I wrong to be so happy? I just hate that little bitch." Amanda-shmanda.

"You should hate Michael, that's who you should be hatin' on," Gwen said, yawning.

"Yeah. I know that. I do. I mean, I did. After tonight I don't anymore. I'm happy for them. This could be just what he needed." I carried the cordless phone into the kitchen to get some water. Roscoe was watching a movie in his room; I could hear the sound from the set. Kevin was at his buddy's, working on cars.

"In New York, I overheard these girls talking in Little Italy," I said. "They were sitting outside, having their cappuccinos. They were dressed so great. Those New York girls can dress." I looked down at the long vintage thing I was wearing. I'd picked it up in the East Village, come to think of it. And the tights, too. Eh, I looked OK.

"I'd kill for a cannoli from one of the Italian bakeries," Gwen murmured. "I would. I love New York. Or a bagful of those little cookies. And some shoe shopping."

"Anyway," I said, "they were talking about some girl they knew, and the one told the others this girl was sharing an apartment with a guy 'and they weren't even married!' The other girls just about choked on their cappuccinos. I kid you not. So what would they think about a girl like Kimchi, eh?"

"Ah, they'd love her at the Pyramid Club," Gwen said. "I love her. I've never met her, and I love her."

"I have met her, and I think she's a honey," I said.

"Now you call Kim."

I called her, even though it was even later by then. Kim didn't really sleep, so much, so it didn't matter. She sighed when I gave her the news.

"He did tell me awhile back that he'd been struggling with his sexuality," Kim said, all tender. "Poor Michael. He's never happy."

"Poor Michael? Hello! If you want to struggle with your sexuality, then struggle. But don't get married and try to push it in the closet."

"I'd better call him," Kim said. "He's probably pretty stressed right now, knowing you're telling everyone."

"You tell him from me," I said, "that I'm sending out a press release tomorrow. And congratulations – I'm happy for them. I mean that." I hung up. Half the time it seemed like Kim was still in love with Michael. Ah, well, they did have the kid together and all. Amber was getting older now, bonding with her mom and off with her little friends all the time. It seemed like she was pushing me away a little, so her mom's feelings wouldn't be hurt. I understood that. No kid wants to choose sides, but if they have to, they will.

Kim was having a much easier time with her, now that she wasn't a little baby anymore. I missed her being snuggly, crawling in with me at night and wanting me to read to her. But it was fun, seeing her get big and all. She loved books – she was reading *Charlotte's Web* now, and the Boxcar Children series. She liked these new ones called the Magic Tree House, too.

We didn't see her as much as I wanted to, but that was OK. She needed to be with her mom. How much was Michael seeing her? I really didn't know. Not enough, was my guess.

I went in the bathroom to get ready for bed and stared at myself long and hard in the mirror while I brushed my teeth.

"Are you still in love with him?" I asked aloud, smiling halfway through the question. I spit out the toothpaste and rinsed the sink.

Nope, but it sure felt good to bust him.

I got a call back from Kim, a few days later, reporting that Michael had confessed all to Amanda. "She's out for blood now," Kim said, and gave a little chuckle. "Especially because Michael told her he wants to make their marriage work – but he doesn't want to give up Kimchi. His name is David, by the way. He's super nice, oh my God. We had coffee, the three of us."

"He really is. He's probably the best thing that's happened to Michael in his entire life. So, what does Dave think of all this?"

"He thinks Amanda needs a visit with a fashion consultant, probably," Kim said. "Maybe a little freshen-up of her closet. Get rid of the kimonos and the chopsticks."

God, I had been so sad and hurt over Amanda. Why? I didn't even like Michael that much when we were dating. No wonder he wasn't happy.

"So? What's going to happen with them?"

"You happy now?" Kim asked me. "They've split. She's already saying she's going to file for divorce."

"Hmm. Yes, that does make me happy, thanks for asking. What does Amber think?" I hadn't stopped to think how she might be feeling. Pang of guilt.

"She was never crazy about Amanda, anyway," Kim said. "She said she was too 'fakey' and wore too much perfume. She made her sneeze. She would have been an all right stepmom, I guess. David will be better with her than Amanda was, though."

We hung up, and I went to get dinner ready, tripping on a chair as I went through the living room. I yelled at Kevin, who was watching TV in the living room with Roscoe and smoking pot, for having so much crap strewn all over. They called pot "binky." They were always taking little "binky breaks." Kevin left some boxes of car parts in the hallway, instead of taking them to the garage, and his dirty dishes were all over, left for me to pick up.

"You keep yelling, and I'll hit you with that chair," he yelled back at me.

"Hey!" Roscoe snapped at him. "Be cool."

Kevin said things like that a lot. But he didn't mean it. Probably. Sometimes people say things and they just come out wrong. With Kevin, practically everything out of his mouth came out wrong. His family was the worst – no tact. When they joked it was always crude. I'd known them my whole life; it wasn't anything new to me. Kevin wasn't anything new to me, either.

38 *Wine and Cheese*

B uying a house with Kevin wasn't one of my brightest ideas. It was a winter evening – cold and wet, like most Oregon winter evenings. It was dark all day. By the time I left the gallery that night at seven, downtown was deserted.

I was managing the art gallery full-time now for the same people I had always worked for. I still appreciated that they sent me off to New York for a while; it was a good experience. But I loved Portland, and working for them had been a steady gig for me. I needed steady. I had medical benefits, even.

Sammie was the woman I worked for, along with her business partner, Xavier. They started the gallery, One Fish/Two Fish, in the industrial part of downtown because of the cheap real estate. It was fairly successful, and some of that I could take credit for. I was good at selling other people's stuff. The key was to play kind of hard to get, like you didn't really know if the piece of art they wanted could actually go home with them or not. Sammie and Xavier both were artists; they studied together at the art college in town. I wanted to go there instead of the university, but it was too expensive.

At first, they tried to sell their own work, mainly, and had some wild group shows with friends. They knew all the hipsters. They put up exhibits no one else would dream of showing and got lots of attention for it. Themes: nudes, blood, copulation, death, more blood. They slept in two tiny rooms in the front of the store, when they first started out. That's where they were sleeping, like window displays, when I met them. They put in long draperies for privacy at night. Now they made enough money that they both had been able to buy decent houses, plus rentals, too. No more sleeping in the window.

I had been able to buy my house, too. Even though it was beat-up, run-down, and not in a great neighborhood, like theirs both were. It was all right, though. I could be doing a lot worse.

Sammie and Xavi liked my work and had included me in a few shows – four altogether. My little stuff I still kept for sale by the front counter. I had developed kind of a following with those Barbie doll dioramas. They were cheap to make, but they looked great. Clients knew I was into them and collected stuff for me to make more – their kids' old toys, things like that. We were all about recycling in Portland; it was our trip – one man's garbage and all that. The clerks at Salvation Army and Goodwill still saved stuff for me, too; I made weekly runs to my stores for pickups.

It was all right, the whole wine and cheese thing, when we did openings. Everyone wearing black and pretending like they knew what they were talking about. Michael loved it, of course, when we were together; Kevin refused to have any part of it. The industrial district had turned into this industrial-sized scene, with street musicians, expensive lofts and overpriced cafés. Sammie and Xavier took their monthly gallery openings and started First Thursday, this gallery walk that all the yuppies went ape for. Sammie married a lawyer and ran the business as a lark, now. A lucrative lark, at that. She had a baby, then another baby, and stayed busy with family stuff, charity work, that kind of thing. Xavier had invested wisely and still did his art, too.

A handful of Sammie and Xavier's former schoolmates went on to become popular artists whose work sold well – I mean, really well. It was a trip how good their stuff had gotten over the years. I was a tiny bit jealous. My stuff was seen as just... folk art or something, I guess. Sammie had had the luck to represent her friends from the beginning. This was at a time when everyone else in town was exhibiting landscapes of the coast and watercolors of floral arrangements.

I was working in one of the spare bedrooms at home, but the light was lousy and it was a teeny room. I wished I could just turn the whole living room into a studio, but Roscoe and Kevin were parked there eight days a week, watching crap on cable television and smoking their binky.

Kevin and I had talked about turning half of the double-car garage into a studio for me, putting in some more windows for better light. Now he and Gage were talking about starting a car detailing business and taking over the whole thing. Detailing my ass; chop shop was probably more like it. Gage made good money welding, but he had these big plans to go into business for himself.

"I don't even want to know what they're up to, half the time," was what JoJo said. I had to agree with her. The less I knew the better off I was.

"Can't you just keep using that extra room, Liz?" Of course I could, but I wanted the damn garage. Oh, right, women aren't allowed to have garages, only men. He must have read the look on my face, because within five minutes he was calling me names, singsonging them, then escalating to screaming at me and racing around the house having a temper tantrum. This time the damage was minimal – nothing broken. Last time, he'd broken a pottery bowl into shards and put a dent in a door, punching it. He kept saying, "Don't you want to fight? Don't you?" and poking me in the ribs. I'd finally yelled at him to stop, and he did. Mostly when he got like that I left and went to the movies by myself, or did the laundry or gardening, anything to stay out of his way. I stayed away from my studio, those times, and didn't use it as a place to hide. I was worried he'd come in there after me and bust it up. Or bust me up.

He wasn't the same person I'd known, and fallen in love with, when we were kids.

He finally left, after an hour of freaking out. He was calm when he got back, and apologetic, like always. The most recent time we'd made love, a month earlier, he asked me afterward to promise I'd never kill him. It was... odd.

"You got so mad at me last night," he'd said. He was quiet. And he was right – I had been furious. I was so sick of his lies.

"And promise me you won't ever have me killed," he added. I wouldn't. I wouldn't promise not to kill him, or have someone else kill him.

I wasn't promising shit.

"How about you promise me you'll start behaving?" I said.

"I will, from now on," he said. He already had blown that promise, six or seven times. He'd started dealing drugs again, even though he'd given it up, or said he'd given it up, at least. Maybe he never had, maybe he just kept it secret so I wouldn't give him a hard time about it.

"I like dealing," he told me. "I'm good at it."

He said he wanted to go legit, but he didn't show any signs of stopping. He was lukewarm about the construction work; he was sick of it. Going into business with Gage was just another pipedream. I couldn't see those two doing anything legal or aboveboard.

"I'm just dealing pot, it's nothing," he said. It wasn't coke, not anymore. He had dealt cocaine all through high school, to support himself. I had looked the other way then, too. It was still riskier than I liked to live. We had a house together – we could lose it.

What wasn't a problem in my life? Roscoe. Still doing the cooking and coming up with his share for the bills. Not a problem. And he stayed the hell out of our business and always took my side in fights, but in a low-key way. He'd tell Kevin, "Be nice to your lady." Just to defuse things.

Kevin kept the dealing separate from our life with Amber – nothing illegal was ever going on when she was around. Amber. She still saw us more than she saw her own father. She told me that her "new schedule" was to see him for the afternoon, once a week.

"But sometimes he can't make it."

She would be eight soon and was starting to pick up some clues about Kevin's lifestyle. Just the week before, she had interrogated him when he was leaving for the evening.

"What friends are you going to see?" Amber asked. "What do you do with them? Watch movies or what? When are you coming back?"

Kevin promised to take her to the park – but it would have to be another time. Amber seemed content enough, but I knew she would have more questions, later.

I picked up a stack of bills from the holder on the kitchen counter. It was stuffed to overflowing. I started to rifle through them, then shoved them back in. No money, so what was the point of writing the checks? I had already spent the money Roscoe had given me on the last round of bills. Kevin would give me a little money, but I'd have to shake him down for it. What happened to drug dealers having money?

I grabbed the basket of laundry from where I'd left it earlier on the dining room floor. I went in Amber's room to put away her clean clothes.

227

Thank God she didn't mind thrift store clothes. That was still where most of her stuff came from, along with whatever Michael's parents gave her. While I was in there I spotted a sketch pad she'd left on the bed. I grabbed some of her colored pencils and sat down in the dining room to draw.

Right in the middle of my first sketch – I was drawing an arrangement of cattails I had dried and put in an oversized vase – the phone rang. It was Krystal, Kevin's younger sister.

"We're having Sherrie's birthday party on Saturday," she started in. She wasn't one for asking how I was, was I busy, no formalities like that. She was all about the princesses, as she called them: Sherrie, Merrie and Kerrie, her three girls. Krystal made sure to invite anyone and everyone to their parties so they could rake in the gifts. The girls were sweet, but I wanted to buy gifts for my own babies, someday, not someone else's, every week. Kevin never wanted kids, anyway, he'd been saying that since we were teenagers. He was fine with Amber, but that was just because he was stuck with her.

If I wanted babies, it would have to be with someone else.

His oldest niece, Sherrie, was from Krystal's first, failed marriage, but no one bothered to tell the kid. The marriage was kept hidden like an old, crazy aunt. She thought she belonged to Kerry, father of Merrie and Kerrie (his namesake – they were hoping for a boy). I wasn't going to burst that little bubble, no way.

"Want to join us? It'll be fuuuuuun!" Krystal sang out. "Maybe you could bring the ice cream? And the paper plates? We're getting a big cake, one of those ones with whip cream frosting, from Costco."

"I'm working Saturday, and I think Kevin's got something going. With Gage." By "something" I meant "taking bong hits and watching TV."

"Are you sure you can't drop by, maybe just for a half-hour or so?" Krystal asked. She sounded disappointed. "We're going to maybe barbecue. The deck is covered and we can do it out there."

I still remembered the last time Kevin's family had barbecued. No one remembered to bring the food. Kevin's mom finally ran out and bought a tub of potato salad and a jumbo pack of chicken thighs. They were served burnt on the outside, raw at the bone.

"Really, I'm calling to hit you up for money," Krystal said. "We want to buy Sherrie a pony! Wouldn't that be great?" I waited for a second, convinced she was kidding. She wasn't kidding. They lived in the boonies and had some property, I guess they would have room for a horse. Next thing, they'd want us to build a barn for it. Or maybe their Amway sales would pay for it. *Gah gah gah gah gah.*

"Geez, Krystal. I'd do anything to get out of working, but my boss is a prick, you know? And we're broke as hell, I need the money." It was too funny to think of my boss Xavier, who usually stopped by with coffee and a croissant for me on Saturdays, as being a prick. I smiled. What did Krystal know about it?

I didn't see much of Sammie, but Xavi was a doll – he had just given me one of his old cameras, said he thought I might like giving photography a try. I liked it. I'd gone out a few times – taking pictures of bridges. And rain. Bridges in the rain. Portland was good for that. I sighed.

Your brother's a dope fiend, I could tell Krys. *You wanna buy him a pony, too?*

They wanted to buy her a pony? They couldn't even take care of the menagerie they already had. And they had this weird pet theme going, for all the birthdays. Merrie, who was four, got a pair of ferrets for her last birthday. They gave Kerrie a pair of screaming lovebirds on her last birthday. Krystal and Kerry bred Chihuahuas to sell, and in addition to the lovebirds had parakeets, finches, three parrots, an ailing Rottweiler, mangy cats, and about two dozen lizards, along with rabbits and a few gerbils.

If it walks like a duck and quacks like a duck, it's probably a ferret. Who said that? JoJo. I stifled a laugh.

"What?" Krystal asked.

"Nothing, just sneezing," I said. "Allergies."

"Maybe next time?" Krystal said. "Kerrie's birthday is next month – we'll call you. Hey! You know something funny?"

I was dying to hang up on her. Why had I even answered the phone?

"What's that?"

"Kerry was putting a new rolodex on our computer, and under Kevin's card, he put you for spouse ..."

(Because Kevin and I weren't married, Krystal, who was a born-again Christian, thought we were immoral.)

"... and under 'kids' he put 'ha-ha.' Isn't that funny?"

"I think someone's at the door, Krys," I said, going flat.

I hung up and smoked part of a joint Kevin had left in the ashtray. I had cut back but hadn't stopped completely. Stopping would be good. I stubbed it out and leaned my head against the back of the couch.

Krystal knew good and damn well that I wanted kids and marriage, and Kevin didn't. Witch. Krystal always had to make some crack about not being able to see Kevin with kids, that he wouldn't be a good parent. He wouldn't be.

But I would. I should have told her that I wished I was eighty pounds overweight, like her, with a bunch of butt-ugly kids and an ugly husband, too, but I just hadn't pulled it off yet. That cheered me up. I put the drawing of the cattails aside and started sketching Billiam and the rag rug he was sleeping on in front of the wood stove. He was nuts about the wood stove, it was so cozy. That was another household fight. I wanted to replace the electric baseboard heaters in the house with a gas furnace. It was ridiculous to heat the house with a wood stove. What were we, the

Beverly Hillbillies? I remembered Kevin singing *Green Acres* to the pig, the night we moved in.

Kevin's solution was to bring home more wood and spend his mornings in the driveway, chopping and stacking, chopping and stacking. Also gave him an excuse to miss work. Our house was his work now.

"There's too much to do around here today," was his standard line. So off to work I went, selling other people's art and not doing my own. And another thing... I was becoming more and more irritated with Kevin's art choices. Or what he liked to think of as art. He put this weird crap all over the house. Not just LaLa. He spotted my shrine in my studio/spare room. He apparently had never seen one before.

"It's your what?" he kept asking me, transfixed by it. "Your shrine? What do you do with it?"

"I use it to meditate." It was the same small one I'd had at the apartment; I guess he never noticed it. I collected little things; I had since I was a kid. Shells from our beach trips, when Kevin and I were teenagers; feathers and rocks; weird little newspaper clippings.

"To get centered, you know," I said. I pushed the candles back a couple of inches. It made me self-conscious, talking about it. It usually held a few smooth black rocks JoJo had given me, worry stones; two candles; and a handful of little plastic toys.

Next thing you know, Kevin had to build a shrine, too, for both of us to share. I didn't want to share a shrine, but it was kind of thoughtful of him, I guess. I didn't want to hurt his feelings. He started out small, copying my shrine. He nailed it to a wall in the living room, above the television. He put just a few small items on it.

That lasted about three days. Pretty soon, it was littered with everything: palm fronds from Easter Sunday (that and Christmas were the only times we made it to church), Jesus and Mary art, three sizes of cheap-o paintings of The Last Supper. I tried to get in the spirit. I donated a framed picture of the Kennedy brothers, and some snow globes. But it really wasn't my thing, where he was going with it.

JoJo saw it and shook her head. "Your energy is all jumbly and confused now," she said. "Your juju is a mess, Kevin. You need to get some sage and cornmeal and sprinkle and smudge this place."

Kevin told JoJo his shrine was "splendid." That was the exact word he used, "splendid," then he added more splendid crap to it, built additional shelves on either side, and almost set the house on fire every time he lit his candles.

There was such a thing as too many candles. That thought had never occurred to me before; I always thought the more the mo' better, but no. Kevin became very taken with novena candles, to the point of obsession. He and I were both intrigued with all the Catholic stuff, having been raised as heathens. But he went over the top with the candles decorated with pictures of the Virgin Mary, and the bleeding Jesus with his heart pierced through. I took JoJo's advice and smudged the house, then the yard, and sprinkled cornmeal all around the perimeter. Couldn't hurt.

Then Kevin started in with masks, hung on the wall behind the shrine. He had cleared everything off the top of the entertainment center and made it the deluxe shrine. The shelves below held the television, VCR and stereo, plus speakers. It was out of control, but that was Kevin. The largest mask in the collection was from Ghana – he had picked it up at an import store downtown.

"It's called a 'good spirit' mask," he told me, animated, "Cool, huh?" He was reading from the card that came with it. It was a stark black face, with gold designs swirled over it. Rows of beads surrounded the eyes; shells outlined the nose. It was a beautiful mask, but I didn't want to look at it constantly. It was the focal point of the living room – the eyes followed you wherever you went. And he was going into debt buying all this stuff.

"Maybe he should buy some 'get more money' novenas," I told Jo. Between the masks and LaLa, I felt like I was being watched any time I was near the living room. He had started burning incense constantly too, to cover up the smell of all the pot he was smoking.

I wished he had never seen my shrine. I was going to go all minimalistic and just start keeping one red candle on it.

I glared at the good spirit mask, shut the sketchbook and went in to start dinner. Maybe the house was haunted. I hoped the sage and cornmeal would help. Or maybe the shrine was bringing some kind of bad juju on us. At least the house didn't feel as haunted as the house I'd grown up in. It always had weird sounds and unexplained things going on – strange lights, the feeling that someone was in the room with you when no one was. But my new house was where my mother had grown up, after all. I had some fond memories. Granny and Grandpa had been over to visit a few times. They were happy we'd rescued the house. They liked seeing the updates we were making. Granny especially liked the plantings Roscoe had put in – the pink rosebush she had requested, which fit in nicely with the other roses; some more daphne; a row of arbor vitae.

"I helped!" I told her.

She patted my arm. "I'm sure you did, honey." She was scribbling down notes on an old menu she had scrounged from her purse.

"Here. Give this to Roscoe for me, would you?" It was another list of plants. Some of the names I didn't recognize; I think she'd been discussing my yard with her garden club ladies.

We had wallpapered and painted, and Roscoe was doing something to the windows. Glazing? He was a putterer. He even let me in my own kitchen sometimes.

Kevin liked guy food – pork chops with stuffing, barbecued chicken with twice-baked potatoes, meat loaf. I found it to be a little tedious. So I pulled out all of the lettuce and vegetables I could find in the fridge and made a salad. Chopped celery, parsley, a little mint, butter lettuce, red pepper, tomato and a cuke. There was some smoked salmon in the cabinet, so I put that on a plate on the side, with capers and some cheeses. No need to make guy food tonight; Kevin had called to say he wouldn't be home until late. It was peaceful without the fighting.

Times I couldn't concentrate on making art, I was making food art. This was something Amber and I bonded over. Her bad attitude went out the door as soon as I broke out the cookie cookbook. We had done this since she was a baby, making stack after stack of cookies – gooey chocolate chip; cinnamon-crunchy snickerdoodles; chocolate crinkles, lacy with powdered sugar. Amber loved the recipes we made up together – Mexican wedding cakes with miniature chocolate chips hidden inside; double chocolate cupcakes with cream cheese filling. But her favorite was one we called peanut butter balls. It was a variation on buckeyes and was a no-cook recipe, consisting of Rice Krispies, peanut butter, butter and powdered sugar, rolled into balls, and dipped in melted chocolate chips. They were only about eight thousand calories per cookie.

We spent a lot of time in the kitchen together; sometimes Roscoe joined us and we made enough food to fill up the freezer I'd scrounged from the Nickel Ads. We made pans of beef enchiladas, lasagnas and tuna casseroles, chicken and stuffing and whole turkey dinners, stuffing and cranberry sauce and everything else.

We all loved to eat – it was the one thing we agreed on. Kevin? We stopped fighting as soon as I fed him. I had learned this trick when I was still a teenager. He and his friends ate like horses – it was how I learned to cook, feeding them. And my mom didn't really like to cook, and worked a lot, too, so it was that or TV dinners. Skyler liked chicken with rice, chicken cacciatore, anything with meatballs. The way to his heart, like Kevin's, was totally through his stomach. I wished I could get him to come over for dinner with his girlfriend, but they were always busy.

The more Kevin and I fought, the more I cooked. I also started making things for the house. My Grandma Ryan taught me to sew and embroider as a kid. She tried to teach me to knit, too, but I never got the hang of it until I was grown. Mom gave me a portable sewing machine for a housewarming gift. I made curtains, tablecloths and napkins. Simple things, but in pretty colors – forest green and deep purple, to match the dishes Kevin's mom had given us. She wanted us to get married.

Anyway.

I had been doing a lot of reading, too. Mainly books about artists. I checked out as much stuff as I could carry from the library. We had a branch not far from us; I was in there once or twice a week. I'd been reading reams about Matisse, Paul Klee and Georgia O'Keefe, Frida Kahlo, Diego Rivera, Jackson Pollack, Lee Krasner. What disasters those last four were, God rest their souls. I read a quote from Kahlo once, saying that the traffic accident she was in and Diego were the two biggest tragedies of her life. I could identify.

I grabbed the rest of the joint from the ashtray and smoked it, then started on some chores. *Note to self: Stop smoking pot.*

That night I dreamt Kevin was hurting me and I was trying to get away, then it turned into that damn car dream again. I woke up, crying and feeling as if I were being choked. My bed was empty. Kevin and I were on different schedules. His involved using ecstasy all the time – going to parties at abandoned warehouses. Raves, they were called. That was probably where he was. He said he had to drink lots of orange juice and iced tea so his spinal fluid didn't get depleted too much.

"What the hell?" I asked him.

"It drains your spinal fluid. It's not that bad. It's just, like, dehydrating is all. Like when you drink too much."

But it probably wasn't like that at all.

"I thought you were giving up dealing?" I asked him. A look crossed his face, like, Don't mess with me.

"I just need to do this for awhile, until I get some more jobs lined up."

Gotta go see a man about a horse, as his family was fond of saying. What the hell did that mean, anyway? A horse? It was just pot, and it wasn't in the house, but that didn't make it any easier to, uh, deal with. To cope with. And now it sounded like it was ecstasy and possibly meth, too.

I brought it up again the next night. I was so scared he would get caught. He screamed at me, called me names, alternating singsonging them, then screaming as he ran around the house. Scary and creepy. That was ecstasy, huh? I was trying to pay the bills and had asked him when he was expecting money in; he wasn't. That was what started the whole fight, then I told him again I didn't like him dealing, and he flipped. Finally he grabbed his cigarettes and left.

Maybe I was just getting old. A lot of our friends were trying heroin – smoking it or shooting it – and acting like it was no big deal. Kevin smoked it, or had smoked it in the past, but didn't shoot it. People had done it in college, too. Like it was a fun risk to take or something. People talked about it more openly now, that was different. Even my own cousin and brother had tried it, together.

"It makes you throw up the first time," Gwen said. "Everybody does. But then after that, it is mellow, mama."

"You used needles? Or smoked it?"

"Needles." Gwen looked away from me. "Clean needles, don't worry! Look, it was fine, it was just for fun. You and Kevin used to smoke opium, you told me. Morphine and opium are heroin, it's all the same."

"Yeah, we had that opiated Thai stick, a couple of times," I said. "But I wasn't throwing up! I just got relaxed, then crashed."

"Kevin told me he's tried heroin a few times; it just wasn't his thing. And you used to smoke hash all the time."

"Chasing the dragon," I said, "That was fine."

"This is fine," Gwen repeated.

"It's not fine, or fun," I told her. I was shook up. I didn't want them overdosing. We both knew we weren't going to agree, so the conversation ended.

When I asked him about it, still upset, Sky told me, "Don't worry so frickin' much, Liz, you are the most anxious person I've ever met." (He was the one who used to be anxious, not me. *They's mustards down there.*)

"You're my brother, I worry."

"We're not doing it all the time," he told me, then hurried the conversation along. "Just once in a great while. It mellows me out." Fine and fun, yeah, just like Gwen had said.

39 *I Have Never Seen So Many Unsavory Characters in My Entire Life*

NOVEMBER 1993

The weekend before Thanksgiving, I took Amber, Mom and Grandma to the Saturday Market to shop for Christmas gifts. It smelled of patchouli and car fumes under the bridge where the market was held. Grandma kept her purse clutched to her side the entire time.

"I have never seen so many unsavory characters in my entire life," she said. "Lizzie honey, maybe we can just stop by the mall next time? Naw. I don't like the mall much, either. Maybe just Bi-Mart, or Costco."

"Sure, Grandma. But I thought you might get a kick out of this!" I said. Amber gave a little kick, to demonstrate.

"Kick, ha!" Grandma said, glaring at a homeless man who was lurching her way.

He gave her a smile.

"No, thank you," she said. Off he went.

She smiled at Amber, then grabbed for her hand with the hand that wasn't gripping her bag. She always carried a big black purse that looked like a doctor's bag, like the ones for house calls? I fully expected her to be able to perform surgery out of it, if needed.

"You come stand by Grandma, sugar."

I bought a scarf for Amber to give to Kim, incense and candles for JoJo and Gwen, and an Indian figure, Ganesh, the elephant god, for Sky. I had called him a bunch of times, since the last time we talked, but he wouldn't pick up. His girlfriend was always at work. I dropped by; no answer. So I just kept leaving messages. I knew the code for his answering machine – 10, just like everyone else's. We all had the same cheap machines from Fred Meyer – that was the default code.

So I would leave him these frantic messages, then call back later and punch in the code, to see what messages were on there, but nothing gave. It would be some guy saying, Hey, bro, it's me, give a call back, and that was about it.

Gwen had clammed up, too, but claimed they weren't using heroin anymore. It was like when they were kids, keeping their secrets so they wouldn't get in trouble.

"It was just for fun, not serious," was what she told me, with a look that said mind-yer-own. Well, they *were* my own. My own brother and my own cousin. At least Gwen answered her phone. I shook them both out of my head and looked at the wooden toys Amber wanted to show me.

Grandma got small bouquets of dried flowers for the women in her garden club.

"I have little vases at home I can put these in," she said in a big voice, loud enough for the woman who ran the stand to hear. "These ones here are just overpriced."

The woman smiled at me. I'm sure she had a grandma or two of her own.

Mom bought handmade earrings for the women in the family and wallets for the men. Amber begged money from me to buy me a Christmas present and made a big production of sneaking off with Mom to buy it, then keeping it hidden in her pocket, away from my sight.

"I hope you like earrings," she said, giving me a big bright smile.

"Oh, I do, very much." We picked out a hand-carved chessboard for ourselves.

"We can buy a book and learn to play, huh?" I asked her. "Don't they have a club at your school?"

"Yeah, they do! Maybe we can stop by the bookstore on the way home?" she asked. Amber loved the big bookstore downtown. She was enthralled, at the moment, with books about horses, and those wacky gag books where you fill in the blanks and make up the story.

"You should sell some of your art here, Lizzie," Amber said.

"Naw, it's too weird for this place. The people who shop here wouldn't like it."

"It is not too weird!" my mom said, protective of me. "I like it. Mostly. I don't like the more violent work you do. I don't get some of it."

"It *is* pretty weird, Grandma," Amber said, laughing.

"Huh. How weird is it?" Granny asked. I ducked the question.

A tall, gray-haired man walked by, out shopping with a little girl who must have been his granddaughter, or great-granddaughter, maybe. She was about six years old and wore a leopard-print coat and bright red shoes. Her grandpa had on jeans; a red, Western-print shirt; and a battered denim jacket, along with well-polished brown cowboy boots. The little girl had a huge elephant-ear pastry in her hand and was spilling sugar, cinnamon and butter all over herself, chattering away to her grandpa. He was trying to get her cleaned up with a napkin. They looked happy.

"Now that is what I call one good-looking man," Grandma whispered to me. "Not as handsome as your grandfather, though." She liked cowboys, of any sort.

"Guess what y'all are getting for Christmas?" she asked me.

"Grandma, make it a surprise! OK, tell me." I hated suspense.

"Flannel shirts! I heard that grunge thing is real hot right now." Humming to herself, she went over to look at some handmade jewelry.

"Is this real?" she asked the girl behind the stand.

"Real what?" the girl asked back.

Flannel shirts, that was a good one. I'd never worn any flannels in my life that weren't hand-me-downs from my uncles and grandpa.

"New flannels, did you hear?" I asked my mom.

"What?"

"Nothing." I was still watching the old guy and the kid from the corner of my eye. I caught a whiff of his aftershave as they strolled off. The market was fun for people-watching; Amber's eyes were busy, too.

"Hey, Ma! Old Spice! Hey. Do you miss Dad? I mean, around Christmastime and all?"

"Your dad?" Mom stopped to think.

"No, someone else's dad. Yeah, mine!"

"Not particularly. I miss the idea of him – the idea of what we all could have had. Does that make sense?" At least she was honest.

"Yeah, I guess. I miss him around his birthday, mostly. And Father's Day. And my birthday." All the time, mostly. I missed him enough for the entire family. I stopped to look at some wooden planters one of the vendors had on display. They were wall hangers, with pretty designs carved on them, flowers and butterflies and things like that. They had mirrors above, and a spot in front of the mirror for the plant. I caught a look at myself for the first time in hours.

"Dang, what is up with my hair?" I asked, faking like I was upset. "I knew I should have washed it this week!" My hair was always a dark, curly mess. I never even brushed it, just added more product to it. I shoved the curls back. They fell down in my face again.

"You look like you could having something living in there," Amber said. "Little people or something."

"Yeah, let's hope there's nothing living in there, cutie."

Mom reached over and tousled my hair. "You and Sky got your dad's hair. His always went like that, too. Cowlicks." I bought one of the planters. I had a fern at home that would be perfect for it.

"Hey," Amber said, spotting the elephant-ear vendor, "let's go get one!" That was our next, and final, purchase for the day.

"Can we get one for Mom, too? So she'll feel better?"

"Maybe next time," I told her. Kim had been in a fender-bender a month earlier. Said she might have whiplash.

Also, her back hurt.

"What is true is that I am too scared to drive now. So I haven't taken Amber to school in a week." That's how I found out about the accident – she called to see if I would come take Amber to school.

"She's already missed a week of school?"

"Um. Yes," Kim said. "I was wondering if she could maybe come stay with you and Kevin. Just for a short while, until I'm feeling better. Also, what is true is that I have a urinary tract infection."

Amber had been with us ever since. When I picked her up from her mom's, she came out with two grocery bags crammed full of her stuff.

"Where are all those backpacks I keep giving you?" I asked her.

"Huh?"

Always with the paper bags. And Kim usually didn't crash, physically or mentally, until after the holidays. That was her new routine, anyway. But it would be nice to have Amber with us for awhile; I was fine with that. She loved Thanksgiving and all the rituals we did at Mom's house. If Mom and her sister weren't fighting, everyone would come over, and Gwen and Skyler, too, and whoever they brought. And Kevin.

We needed to work on Amber's room at our house, but it was mostly put together. Kevin was at home waiting for the guys to deliver the bed we had ordered – we could use her room as a guest room when she wasn't there.

"My mom's not feeling good, you know, Grandma?" She had called my mom and Grandma "grandma" and "granny" since she was tiny. "Whiplash runs in our family!"

She seemed quite pleased about the whiplash, as if it were a gold star or something.

"That's what I heard, hon," Mom said. "I'm sure she will be feeling better soon."

"Or not!" Amber said. "Sometimes it takes her awhile to get better. I mean, like a loooooong time." She seemed cheerful about it. Mom and Granny gave each other a look over the top of her head.

"Thanks for the elephant ear, Liz. You're nice."

"Anytime, Amber. You are nice, too." We headed off to see the Christmas tree at the square; the guys were just getting it set up. It was supposed to be the best one ever.

Afterward, we dropped Mom and Granny off at Mom's house. Mom lived about five minutes away from us was all. Made life easy. Together, Amber and I headed home.

Kevin had worked the entire time we were gone.

"Come see, come see!" He was like a little kid, wanting an audience.

"Cleaned out the wood stove, swept and mopped, did all the dishes, caulked around the sink, started the laundry and ... Come here, pooches!"

Thud. I heard the dogs jump down from my bed, then they trotted out, bathed, brushed and beribboned. Sasha, the female, had pink ribbons tied to her collar; Junebug, the male, had blue.

I laughed and petted them. "You won't even come meet us at the door anymore? How was your nap, you lazy things? They're so soft. What did you do, use my conditioner?"

"Yes, ma'am. That herbal stuff of yours. They're just delicious dogs now. Skylab stopped by while you were gone."

"Yeah, what did he want?"

"You know." Yes, I did know. His own herbal stuff. Sure, my brother wouldn't return my calls, but he'd come over when he knew I was gone, to get some binky from Kevin.

Amber started wrestling with both dogs at once. Junebug, who was small but didn't know it, knocked her over and licked both of her ears, then stuck his tongue up Amber's nose. Amber was loving it. She snuggled against the dog, wrapping her arms around Junebug's neck. Junebug licked her ear again.

"Junebug, gross!"

"My sweet little friend, I have a special surprise just for you. Right this way."

We followed Kevin down the hall.

"Close your eyes!" Kevin told her. She did. "Ta-da!"

Amber's room had been completely transformed: the single bed replaced with a double; a new quilt thrown on it, with an orange, blue and purple star pattern; a matching throw rug on the floor; a poster of the solar system on the ceiling and her U.S. map on the wall. Amber didn't like things all girly-girly. This was perfect. Now we could use it as a guest room, too, when Amber was with her mom.

Kevin had put together a wooden rack that had multicolored plastic bins for storage. I spotted a new laundry hamper in the corner, bright red to match the bins. But the biggest surprise was the drafting table – one just Amber's size. She sat down on the wheeled stool that went with the table and started spinning around.

"This is mine? Lizzie doesn't even have one of these!"

"No, I sure don't. Maybe I can borrow yours?" Amber nodded yes, yes, yes.

"Where did you get all this stuff?" Amber asked.

"Yeah, Kevin. Where'd you get it?" I knew the bed was going to be delivered, and I had bought the bedding and rug myself, stashing them away from Amber. But the table and the rest was a surprise.

"Oh, you know, from a buddy of mine."

That meant it was stolen. Aw, shit. At least Amber would never be the wiser. I shot Kevin a look.

"Really?"

He gave me a palms-up shrug.

"It was all out in the garage, OK? I was thinking I'd like to take you two out to an early dinner. Lizzie?"

"Yes!" Amber said. "I'm ready!"

She was already heading for the door. All we had done was snack all day.

"Wash your hands first. Kevin, for Christ's sake – no more hot stuff here, OK?" I told him when Amber was out of earshot. I punched him in the arm.

"Who said it's hot? Geez my knees, Liz, you're about suspicious. It's just some little plastic bins for the kid. Where am I taking you for dinner?"

"Are you writing a bad check for it?"

"I am wounded, Elizabeth." He left the room, then turned to give me a sweet smile.

"You with me? Or not?"

"Not. Sure, I'm coming." I flipped off the light, then flipped it back on and looked at the room again. It did look nice. Shit. Most of it was paid for, anyway. What was I supposed to do with the rest? Take it back?

"Damn, Liz, what's up with your hair?" Kevin ran his hands through my hair, then pretended they were stuck and he couldn't yank them out.

He tickled my ribs. "Baby, you've got some kind of Rastafarian-Martian thing going on here. I mean, really."

I laughed and moved up against him. "Fuck off, Kevin."

"I ironed all your clothes for you – they're in your closet."

"How does he do it, folks?" I asked. "Thank you!"

"You really do need to learn how to iron some day."

We went to Champs for dinner. They let kids in until midevening, as long as they didn't sit right at the bar. We ordered all the appetizers on the menu, per Amber's request – crab puffs, jalapeño poppers, stuffed mushrooms, nachos, onion rings. And french fries. And cheesecake for dessert. So much for a healthy dinner.

"How has your mom been, Amber? Is she still seeing that one guy?" Kevin reached over and stole a crab puff from her.

"I don't even like those," Amber told him, smiling like nyah-nyah, then took four of Kevin's french fries. "No, she has a girlfriend now, Sondra."

"A girlfriend?" I asked.

"Long story," Amber said, finishing Kevin's fries and reaching for mine.

40 *Beer and Potato Chips*

NOVEMBER 1993

I dropped by Skylab's apartment to see him, one night that week after work. I wanted to ask him about Thanksgiving. That was my excuse, anyway. I suspected that Kevin was doing speed, and I wanted to see if Sky knew anything. I had caught Kevin that morning with his eyes all swollen, looking exhausted. He was already skinny and jumpy; he didn't need any help with that. He slept on the couch in the living room, more often than not. Meth made you sweat and stink, he didn't want to be next to me when he was doing it. If he was doing it. But he and Gage might have just been working on cars, that made you sweaty and stinky, too. How was I supposed to know? Follow him around?

I didn't think Roscoe was using, but he sure liked his binky. He'd found a job working at the hot tub place up the street; they did massages there, too.

"No funny business, it's hippies who run it," he had told me. Roscoe was looking into massage school, he thought it would pay more than garden design. Both jobs sounded kind of iffy to me, but I was sure he would figure it out.

Sky's girlfriend, Amy, arrived home from work, right after Sky let me in. He was on the couch, watching TV and inhaling potato chips and French onion dip. He had an open beer in front of him on the table and an almost-full half-rack on the floor beside him. His dog was lying next to him on the couch. Occasionally Sky threw a potato chip at him and he caught it.

He didn't offer me a seat, or a beer. But he didn't throw chips at me, either.

Amy was a sweetie – hair that fell into long, blond ringlets, huge blue eyes. She was so much more in love with my brother than he was with her. I hoped she didn't know.

"I got a raise today!" she said the minute she entered the door. "And a bonus, too. This is so great ..." She dropped two bags of groceries on the kitchen counter.

"Now you can pay me back the money you owe me," Skyler said, not looking up from his show. He grabbed another chip out of the bag and dipped it into the half-empty container. He fed one without dip to the dog. Spike was a cattle dog and a little kooky. He seemed calm enough at the moment. I helped myself to a beer.

Amy looked crushed and went into the bedroom to change out of her uniform and shower. She had worked at the same grocery store since she was sixteen, first stocking shelves, then working her way up to checking. The store was near our place, and whenever I dropped by to say hi, Amy was always working her tail off. She was hoping they'd make her a manager someday. She told me that.

"God, Sky, that was mean," I whispered to him.

"She knows I'm kidding," he said, eyes still glued to the TV. He wasn't watching anything in particular; he kept flipping the channel. He shifted on the couch and stretched out a little bit. He wasn't kidding. I knew him. He was tight with a buck, and Amy wasn't good with money. Or so he said. I was guessing that a big chunk of Sky's money went to beer and drugs. He'd been mean to her before in front of me. One time Amy threw her arms around him affectionately and he stiff-armed her until she let go. He was my brother, but he wasn't the sweetest guy in the world. He could be, when he tried. He was always sweet to Kevin.

I tried talking with Skyler about Kevin and he kept ignoring me, so I finished my beer, said goodbye to Amy and left.

"Maybe you should go unpack your own groceries," I told him on my way out the door. Still no eye contact.

"Amy will get them," he said.

That next summer he was gone, Skyler was gone, and I didn't know what hit me.

41 *If He Could Take It Back, He Would*

JUNE 1994

"**B**abe, are you sure it's OK I'm not going today?" Kevin called out from the bathroom. He was shaving and getting ready to leave town – he had been working some construction jobs, helping build new houses down at the beach. He needed to get back. I was glad he was working, maybe he'd stay straight for awhile. I was in the kitchen, finishing my coffee and a sesame bagel.

"No, it's fine. Don't worry about it."

Skyler was gone, nothing was going to change that. It was the day of his funeral. I hadn't been able to think, sleep, work. My bosses told me to take a couple of weeks off, whatever I needed, but I knew I'd have to go back, eventually.

The day was too beautiful for a funeral. The weather was warm, in the 70s by midmorning. Kevin emerged from the bedroom, carrying the small

Pan-Am flight bag he used when he traveled. He set it down by the front door.

"I've got to get going. I left the coffee on for you," I said. "And there are bagels, too."

"See you in a few days?" Kevin said. "I'm not trying to make excuses or anything here, but Sky wouldn't care one way or the other, if I went."

No, Sky wouldn't care about something like that; Kevin was right. He would rather have Kevin smoke a joint in his honor or something. Go to some hardcore show and bash around in the crowd. A worthy tribute.

"It's fine."

I didn't want him going because he was a liability in social settings. He always said or did the wrong thing, tried too hard to make a joke and offended people. I had long since stopped asking him to go to social functions, openings at the gallery, brunches at friends' houses. I made excuses for him – he was working on a job, or finishing up a project at the house. In reality, he was usually out in the garage, smoking dope with his buddies, or playing guitar, "practicing," at someone else's house. And making excuses for the drugs. He was sleeping in the guest room or on the couch most nights, telling me the next day that he was out late and didn't want to wake me. I knew it was speed, those nights. When he was working, he didn't do as many drugs. So work was good.

No, I didn't want him at my brother's – his friend's – funeral, and he knew that. He wasn't welcome. Even though he and Skyler had been closer to each other than they were to most people. Maybe that's why he didn't want to go – he felt guilty, because of the drugs. He shouldn't. Skyler made his own bad decisions.

So we kissed goodbye, and I grabbed my bag and left to run last-minute errands before the funeral. It was scheduled to start at one o'clock. I put gas in my car, picked up the funeral programs at the printers and dropped off some videos I had rented. The programs had turned out nicely. Mom asked me to do them; she didn't like the tacky little ones the funeral home did. Graphic design wasn't really my thing, but they had turned out well. My boss Xavier helped me.

There was a large photo of Skyler printed on the front. It was one his girlfriend, Amy, took at the beach last summer. He was leaning against a log, sitting on the sand. He had his head tilted to the side and was grinning. He looked happy. He loved the beach. He loved Amy; it was so obvious by the way he smiled into the camera at her. I had my doubts about how committed he was to her, but he loved her. In his own way. He loved his life. Wrong, wrong, and wrong. He didn't love anything enough to stay. I didn't realize how sad he was – that he'd been blowing off his friends for months until they eventually stopped calling. I heard about his death from Amy, hysterical after she found his body, dead from a gunshot wound to the head. People said later that he'd been acting strangely at work. He worked at a music store. He would show up late for shifts, then not talk to anyone the entire time he was there. He almost got fired over it. The bosses had put him on probation, and he didn't seem to care. Amy said she had wanted to tell me, but Sky told her not to. Gwen hadn't even known.

If he could take it back he would. I knew this. I knew it in my bones, the same way I knew that if our father could take it back he wouldn't. I liked to think he would, that he would put us first, but he wouldn't. He was too sick, the schizophrenia had him by the throat. He thought he was doing us a favor. Skyler wasn't schizophrenic; he was just high. And low. Untreated depression that he was trying to self-medicate.

No taking this one back, though. Too late. If Sky could see what had happened to everyone, how miserable and lost Amy was since he was gone? How devastated Gwen was? She was blaming herself – she wouldn't even talk about him with me, her mom, my mom or anyone else. Maybe it would have made a difference to Sky, maybe it would have changed his mind, knowing how people felt about him.

Or maybe not.

Most of the time I didn't know how I was going to go on without him, my brother, my friend. I was struggling to even remember to eat, shower, return phone calls. It was all too much. He drove me so nuts, but I was so lost without him. It was too final and too fast.

If he could see how Mom had changed. How she thought everything with dad was her fault. She always had. *Sky knew that.* We both knew in our hearts. For two decades Mom had been trying to tell herself that it wasn't her fault. And now, with Skyler, it had to be her fault.

That was how she looked at it, see?

Dad was her fault and Skyler was her fault. She couldn't shake it.

It wasn't. It wasn't her fault at all. Everyone told her that – her coworkers, her friends, her neighbors, her family, everyone. I told her, daily.

But she did not believe us.

"It was his own decision," Aunt Tisha said. "Now, I wouldn't make that decision. No, I wouldn't. I think it's …" she paused, then kept going, "cowardly. It is. It is the coward's way out."

We were at Mom's house at the time. It was early evening, earlier in the week – Tisha had stopped by with one of her stupid casseroles. Chicken with rice. Not as good as Mom's, but better than the Taco Fiesta thing Tisha usually made. Or the one with green beans. Gah. She was trying to "show support." But really? I think she just wanted to get a dig in. She and my mom went from zero to sixty in about four and a half seconds. Meow.

"You're saying my son's a coward?" Mom screamed at her. "My

husband? He was, too?"

"Well, Sue," Tisha said. "They just weren't strong enough for life."

"They were not cowards," Mom said. "I will thank you never to say that again."

Tisha, realizing she'd stepped over the line, backed down and left the room, then left the house and drove off without saying goodbye.

I pulled into Mom's driveway, picking her up for the service. She was at her dining room table, the same table Skyler and I had grown up with. She was chain-smoking and looking straight ahead. No tears. The ashtray next to her was stuffed full.

"Mom, it's almost one," I said, touching her on the shoulder. "We'd better leave. You want to see one of the programs?" I pulled one out of my purse.

She gave it a glance, then broke down.

"It looks really nice, honey. Let me go splash some water on my face, OK?"

The service was at the Hollywood Funeral Home, down the street from Mom's house. It was named for the Hollywood neighborhood, which was named for the Hollywood Fred Meyer store, I guess. Who knew. Which came first – chicken? Egg?

From the outside, it almost looked like a nightclub – all neon and bright lights, landscaped with tropical flowers. They must have replaced them yearly – this was not the climate for them. Roses and rhodies, yes; little boy flowers and birds of paradise, no. The owners had even planted a couple of palmetto trees. Those seemed to be holding their own.

A large waterfall, surrounded with lush greenery, took up most of the entryway. The name of the business was outlined in careful script in pink neon along the roofline. The exterior of the building was decorated with work, including doorways that led to nowhere and three balconies too tiny to stand on. It was an odd place.

It was where we had my father's funeral, too. Same '70s decor – they had done a little here and there, in the years since. They added a mural in the entryway, with cherubs and clouds, across from the waterfall.

Gilt and tackiness and really schmaltzy. All of the neon and plants were soothing, in a way. Like sensory overload. It was Skyler's style – the tacky/kitschy '70s crap that he loved.

"We ought to turn that place into a club," Sky said every time we drove by the chapel. "We could call it the Hollywood Funeral Home and Nightclub."

Inside the building the decor got even better – a large painted mural of the pearly gates, including heaven and clouds, was on the wall just behind the pulpit. It went with the cherub mural in the entryway. Two large gold-plated chandeliers decorated the chapel. The carpet was pale pink, and another waterfall, this one a bit smaller, was off to the side of the chapel in an alcove. It kind of reminded me of a baptismal. It made me have to pee, the sound of all that running water. I would have hated to have Sky's service at some a cookie-cutter chapel. It just wouldn't have done.

We were burying Skyler in the same cemetery with Dad, in a nearby plot.

It was all so confusing. It happened so fast, at first, then everything slowed to half-speed and took forever – the flower arrangements, the food for the wake, all the phone calls, getting the obituary in the newspaper. Gwen had been kind enough to take over this task, and she had made most of the phone calls to friends and relatives. Then she shut down and refused to talk.

About thirty people were flying in from out of state, and out of the country, for the service. It was short notice; I hoped they would be able to get a grieving rate or whatever it was called, for the flights. None of them were staying at Mom's, they didn't want to impose. They were crashing with other family members, at Gwen's and Tisha's, and at motels. A bunch of them were staying at Granny and Grandpa's – they had a big place, and one of their neighbors was loaning them an RV to park in the driveway.

Where were you when he needed you? I kept thinking. I knew that wasn't fair, placing blame like that. They didn't know. How could they? Even I hadn't known, really. I had known, but I hadn't known just how bad it was.

Everyone was dressed properly, except Gwen's dad – Uncle Dan, Tisha's ex-husband. He showed up wearing a white suit, huaraches and a Panama hat.

"He looks like he's going to a fucking Jimmy Buffett show," I said to Mom, once I got her alone in the bathroom. She was sneaking a cigarette right next to the "No Smoking" sign.

"Yeah," she said. She gave me a tired smile. "I've never liked that asshole. And Tisha's high – she's all doped up on antidepressants and booze."

"You're not supposed to take those together," I said.

"Not according to Tisha. 'They're my happy pills! I made sure to have the doctor prescribe the kind you can drink with!' Jesus. I need a pill just to deal with her."

A bunch of my brother's friends showed up, and mine, too. I mean, loads of them. People kept coming over and grabbing my hand, telling me they were sorry. I had no idea what I said to them, it was a big ol' blur. There were about three hundred people at the funeral – guys Sky worked with, friends from high school, friends from the clubs, ex-girlfriends – a whole gaggle of them, alternating between crying their eyes out and being happy. They spilled into the entryway and out the front doors.

It was more like a wedding than a funeral, really. People were calling to each other across the room, squealing and hugging. Sky would have liked that, I think. He wouldn't have wanted it to be all somber and depressing. Granny's minister did a nice job with the service. He was saying this, that and the other thing, nothing important or personal, really. He hadn't known Sky. Sky was always too hungover to make it to church.

Then the minister said, "There are some who say that those who take their own lives are committing a sin against God, that they will not be admitted to heaven. That God would not make room for them."

You could hear this "pfft" inhale of breath from all over the room. I was sitting between Mom and Gwen. Granny and Grandpa were on the other side of Mom. I gave my mother's hand a quick squeeze. She looked like she was ready to pass out.

"But this is not true," Granny's minister continued. "This is not the way God loves. God is a loving God. When someone is in that kind of pain, the pain that makes you think you cannot go on – God knows that those people need the most love, and he takes them in, he holds them to his heart, first. First of all, he loves those who are sick, and who are in pain."

I didn't expect that at all. Maybe the fire and brimstone bit, tell everyone they needed to get baptized in one of the waterfalls or go straight to hell. I had been trying so hard not to cry, all day. But this little hot tear escaped, then another one, and after that I couldn't stop. I let out these huge, wracking, ugly, embarrassing sobs. I wanted Sky back. I wanted my father back. I wanted my baby back. I was so pissed off at myself for all the bad decisions I'd made. I was sick of dating assholes like Kevin, Michael, the others. I wanted to date only nice men from here on out, who would stick around for awhile. Longer than awhile. I was sick of being scared all the time. ("*They's mustards down there.*")

It was so fucking wickedly unfair. From the pew behind me, I felt

257

someone reach out and give my shoulder a squeeze. It was JoJo. I hadn't even known she was sitting there.

I laid my head down in Mom's lap. She stroked my hair.

"There baby, you let it out," she said, "We don't care what people think. You just let it out. We loved him, didn't we?"

And then, it was done. We all drove to the cemetery, ashes to ashes, then back to Mom's. Mostly everyone who showed up for the funeral came to the reception. Tisha must have gotten the keys somehow, because everything was set up when we got there, and it had Tisha stamped all over it. She left the funeral early with some of her friends and they took care of everything. There was too much goddamn food. Uncle Dan held court in the corner, in his huaraches, talking about some auction he'd been to, what good deals he'd scored.

"Something fell off the back of a truck," Sky would have said to me, on the sly. None of us could stand Dan.

Dan was never going to get over Tisha; he kept looking her way. Gwen said they drove her nuts and she hoped they never got back together.

Tisha's main friend, the Vulture, Mom called her, helped serve up the meatballs and slices of turkey, scooped mounds of macaroni salads onto plates. She took this big pile of cream puffs from Costco and made it into a Christmas tree-looking thing. She drizzled chocolate syrup all down it. It was fucking bizarre. I didn't even know what her name was. She seemed to thrive on death.

Why would anyone eat right now? How can they eat right now? I remembered summer sausage and burned rice, a merry-go-round, spinning, and wanted to throw up. There was a board in the entryway with pictures of Sky – playing ball, playing guitar, out in the sunshine, at the river, swimming. Pictures of him with Peaches, our dog, when he was a kid. I couldn't look at them now. It was like, all the rage now to set up these picture boards at funerals and have people write notes on butcher paper on the table for the family. Smiley faces. Hearts. *(Everyone grieves in their own way.)*

The guys he played softball with retired his number, after they heard he was gone. It was a beer league; they had fun together. It was one of the few social things Sky did up until the end. All these people had left nice messages on my home machine, or sent notes. They called Gwen, too, and she passed their sentiments on to me.

I let out a sigh. I'm sure that some of the people felt guilty for staying away, for not helping. Tom was there, at the reception, our friend Heather's husband. Heather was there, too, somewhere. Tom had known Sky for years. They played ball together, chased girls together.

He came over to check on me. "I loved him, Liz," he said, looking straight into my eyes, "but he could be such an asshole, couldn't he?" I smiled and nodded my head.

"It's the first time anyone's had the nerve to come right out and say it," I told Tom, then I smiled a little and started crying again.

"He could be such a jerk. But I loved my brother. I loved him."

"I know you did. We all did." Tom held me, and then Heather walked over and she held me, too, and I cried all over Tom's black dress shirt, one he probably purchased specially for the funeral. I cried all over Heather's nice dress, too. They didn't care. They held me until I couldn't cry anymore.

42 *Things Kevin Said to Me*

JULY 1994

I dreamt all the time that Sky was still alive. He was at my place, sitting at my wooden kitchen table, maybe cracking open a beer, and I was saying, "I thought you were gone," and he was saying, smiling, "No, it was a mistake. Really I'm here."

But he was far away, even sitting just across the table, and mostly he didn't say anything, just looked at me and smiled this kind of Cheshire cat smile. I said "Oh." When I went to hug him or touch him, to feel him just for a minute, because I missed his skin, and I wanted to know he was real, then he faded right out, like the Cheshire cat would have, right as I was saying his name. *Sky, Sky.* I sometimes woke myself up, yelling out my brother's name, as if I were warning him of danger. Trying to keep him from being hurt. Kevin wasn't home much at night, so he didn't hear me when I yelled out, but Roscoe did. He was worried, wanted to know if I was OK. I wasn't OK.

"My uncle went out that way, too. There is just no explaining why people make that decision," he said. "No explaining it. Someday it won't hurt as bad. But it will still hurt." I already knew that.

Kevin wouldn't talk about it. He said he was crashing at Gage and JoJo's, but he wasn't. We weren't sleeping together anymore. It was over. We had a raging fight the week before, my soon-to-be-ex and I, because I found a pipe he'd been smoking meth out of. He hated needles, so he just smoked the shit. I mentioned rehab, and he flipped. No, actually, I just mentioned maybe cutting back on using, and he freaked. (I was thinking rehab, though.) Guys like Kevin never went to rehab. And the way he talked, the things he said... It wasn't him talking, it was someone else.

"I tell you what to do, and you don't do it. Or we decide what's going to happen and it doesn't." He was raging. I didn't even know what he was talking about. You know what started it? Besides the pipe? He had built this crazy Christmas tree, way back in late November, almost a year earlier. He called it Frankentree. He took two-by-fours and nailed them together, like a cross, then screwed cedar branches up and down it. He got them from the neighbor's yard; they had about a dozen cedars in their yard. The trees were so big they dwarfed their house.

He said this way he wouldn't kill a tree. I got sick of it – I kept asking him to take it out of the living room. It was a fire hazard – he had it next to The Shrine, where he burned candles nonstop, even when he wasn't home, or awake. I got fed up and ripped off the branches, threw them in the yard debris and carried the rest of it out to the garage. I would have put it in the garage, but I had no key.

Because it was Kevin's garage, not mine.

I left it by the garage door.

Roscoe said, "Oh, thank God," when he got home and saw it was gone. But Kevin freaked. I had this beautiful peace lily that my bosses gave me for a housewarming gift. He tore all the leaves off of it, then threw the clay pot on the floor. It shattered.

"You ruined something of mine, so I'll ruin something of yours." Roscoe got him settled down, but I had to go spend a couple of nights at Mom's. She was having a hard time, too. We had been going to the movies a lot, and out to dinner, just to stay distracted.

Sometimes I kept Sky in my head all day, like a mantra. It would start low in my head, the chant, then get louder. It was relentless, it hurt so much. Amy was devastated, of course. She gave up their apartment and moved back home with her folks. She called me sometimes. She and Sky had had a huge blowup the day before he died. She had freaked out on him about his drug use. She kept replaying the fight out loud in her head, and talking to people about it. It wasn't helping her, any.

"Why didn't he tell me?" Mom kept saying. "Why the hell didn't he talk with me? He could talk with me; he was my kid. He should have told me." She had friends, thank God. They called all the time, took her out for lunch, or shopping. One of her neighbors stopped by a couple of times a week and made her go to Fred Meyer with her, so they could do their shopping together. It was Sandy – she had been our neighbor forever. She called me to check in and keep me posted. I took some time off from the gallery, but I had to go back. I needed my routine.

The bills were getting paid at least. Kevin had this strange habit – after we got in a fight, he would pay all the bills and give me whatever money he could scrounge up. Guilt. Roscoe always ponied up, too.

Sky, oh, Sky, oh, Sky, chanting and counting every crack in the sidewalk. When I woke up in the morning, the first thing that popped into my head was Skyler is dead, Skyler is dead, Skyler is dead. It was making me go crazy. But then, Sky and Dad had always been crazy-makers.

I started pretending, just like I'd done with Dad. I pretended that Sky was still alive and living on the north side of town. He hadn't called because why should he? He was out of contact a lot, when he was alive –

dropping from sight for a few months at a time, even. So this wasn't a big stretch, imagining that he wasn't dead, he was just incommunicado. It could be the case, if you really thought about it long enough, made it pretty enough. I could daydream all day long, if I put my mind to it.

Our family was nothing to get too excited about, honestly. Best avoided if possible. I could see Sky's point, wanting to stay away. In hiding. He wasn't dead, he'd just gone undercover. Not returning calls.

I liked the time I spent with Mom, but I drew the line at Tisha. And once Sky killed himself, she was at Mom's all the damn time, fuss-fussing. The woman was a nutbar, always so negative and putting everyone down, while slapping a sunny face on top of it. I hated her for how she treated all of us.

"Skyler, I cannot stand hearing this anymore," she once told him, almost cheery when she said it. He had mentioned he'd been "a little" depressed and wanted winter to end.

"I have never been depressed a day in my damn life. You've just got to pull yourself up by your bootstraps and face life!" That effectively shut Sky up. He didn't ever talk to Tisha after that. How long ago had that been? Two years ago? Now that I looked back, I could see when his depression started – when he was 13, 14, sometime around then.

Granny had become beyond demanding since Skyler had died. Her favorite trick was calling at 7 a.m., then braying, "Did I wake you?" and demanding a ride somewhere. Maybe Costco, to buy pounds of meat and large tins of cashews; to the fabric store to get more material for tablecloths and napkins for Christmas gifts; somewhere, anywhere.

She told me, "I know it's still summer, but I want to get a leg up on my sewing."

I knew it was because she wanted to check on me, make sure I wasn't dead, too, but I was exhausted. I wanted to reassure her, but I wanted someone to reassure me even more. Gwen called to say hey once in awhile. The rest of them I just ignored. Saw their numbers pop up on caller ID and let 'em go straight to the answering machine.

When I couldn't sleep, I wove a simple, happy and completely imaginary life for Skyler. Skyler-on-the-North-Side. It went like this: He and Amy had split up. She found someone more steady. Sky found a sweet wife, Jessica, who none of us knew that well. They had twin four-year-olds, a boy and a girl, Dylan and Stacy. They lived in a little bungalow – yellow, with a couple of lilac trees out front, an apple tree and a garden in the back. A sandbox for the kids. Skyler had quit the music store and worked at a... silk-screening place? He was a foreman; he liked it.

Maybe he would call next week and I could see how everyone was doing.

It kept me going, the fantasy. Except for, y'know, when I let it in that he really was gone. There were variations on my denial. Sometimes I would become convinced that I saw Sky somewhere – on the train, or at the store. Only he was wearing a baseball cap and sunglasses. *Look at that one,* I'd think. *It's got to be Skyler – same hair. Sky has that same shirt.* It made my day go better, thinking there was a chance that he was OK, after all. These games were all familiar – they were the same ones I'd played before, only it was Dad then. A man the same height, with the same smile. Longer hair, or shorter. A blue Chevy instead of red. That kind of thing, on and on for years.

I could talk about him with Gwen, at least. (Except I didn't discuss the fantasy with her, about the little house. No need to worry people, who might think I was losing my mind, too. No need to go there.) Gwen had that same dream, about Sky, the kitchen table and the beer.

"Then he just fades out, right?" she said. Yes. Weird.

I last saw my brother in the spring, at a brunch at Tisha's house. I had been so busy with the house, with work, with Amber. Skyler had always had periods of going into hiding, almost. Wouldn't return calls, and no one knew what he was up to. Then he'd re-emerge, his old sweet and surly self. It wasn't anything out of the ordinary, my not having seem him for awhile. We didn't live in each other's pockets. He kept in better touch with Kevin than he did with me.

Sky wasn't speaking to Tisha, that day or any other day. Mom and Tisha were visibly hostile to each other. They often were, but that day it was more obvious than others. They wouldn't speak to each other or make eye contact. As always, they refused to discuss it with anyone, preferring to let it fester and grow.

"There's history there," Mom said, with a dark look and a darker tone, when I asked her what had gone down between them. It was a Sunday brunch. Our entire family was there. Tisha's house was immaculate, as always. The House of Immaculate Deception, Mom called it behind her back. No wonder Gwen preferred our house. All those little pastel sachets and potpourris strewn about; deep, emerald green, thick-pile carpet (Tisha didn't know shag was out); and modern furniture. She treated herself to a new "suite," as Granny called it, every year or two, all financed by Dan, her ex. And chickens galore – chicken potholders, chicken welcome mat, chicken pictures. She kept a little crocheted cover, with a chicken on top, on the spare roll of toilet paper in the guest bathroom downstairs.

Cluck, cluck, I always thought, in a distracted kind of way, whenever I saw Aunt Tisha. An image of Big Bird would jump into my head, and I wouldn't realize until later, oh, yes, Tisha = chickens. Even though Big Bird wasn't, technically, a chicken. What the hell was he, anyway?

"My mom and her chickens, Jesus," was what Gwen said.

"Granny and her cows," we would both say, and laugh.

"I used to know my sister," Mom always said following a visit. "I knew her when she was a little girl."

Everyone was tense during the brunch – no one really wanted to be there, but Granny and Grandpa were staying with Tisha for the weekend, and she thought it would be fun to do a family thing. So we had been summoned.

We were all half-assed trying to make conversation, trying not to piss each other off, eating food without really tasting it, enjoying it or thanking Tisha for assembling it. Gloppy spinach dip; monster trays of tasteless cold cuts, sweaty cheeses and almost-stale breads; vast quantities of three-bean, potato, and macaroni salads out of tubs from the deli; two kinds of homemade pie – cherry and apple – from Granny, along with one of her huge chocolate cakes, mounded with frosting. Ice cream on the side. Fruit cocktail from a can, with miniature marshmallows and Cool-Whip.

Tisha flew around, pulling a dish of some hot appetizer "dunk" thing out of the microwave. "Have some spinach dunk!" she said. "Try the bacon cheddar dunk, it's really good!" She opened up another bag of chips and poured them into a big, bright blue bowl, lining up the bowl with the chips and the bowl with the dunk alongside all the other matching bowls on the kitchen's island. Everything was either cobalt blue or stainless steel. She made sure the three refrigerators (the big side-by-side in the kitchen, and the two mini-fridges – one in the garage for the guys and one in the family room) were stocked with beer and soda. Tisha checked the box wine status, pouring a glass for each of her hands.

Tisha's calico cat wandered in from a big hunt outside, started rolling around at Tisha's feet, began convulsing and puked up half a mouse. The cat immediately darted down the hall to the laundry room to find her food dishes.

"Oh, ew, Mom," Gwen said. I looked away. Tisha cleaned up the mess in a hurry and pretended like nothing happened.

"So, then," she said, washing her hands at the kitchen sink.

"Who needs a freshen-up on their drink?"

Everyone was drinking heavily, not just Tisha. Sky was watching a ball game on TV in the living room and got up to grab a can of beer. He brought a couple over for Gwen and me, too. Mentioned, out of the blue, that he was going deer hunting in the fall with his buddies.

"Oh yeah, deer hunting, sure," I said, thinking of all the hunting trips we'd taken as kids, and how Sky, Gwen, and I had always identified more with the deer than with our grandpa, uncles, their friends and their gun collections. I thought he was joking.

Gwen laughed. "Since when do you hunt, man?" I remembered for a fleeting moment the little dead doe we'd found one hunting trip. I glanced at Gwen, wondering if she was remembering that, too.

I must have been twelve, Sky and Gwen were eleven or so. We were walking in the woods to the ramshackle outhouse and almost tripped over the deer, lying dead in the path. She looked more asleep than dead, as if she was taking a nap in the wrong place. Dumbstruck, we stared into her blank, glazed-over eyes. Didn't say a word, any of us, thinking about Grandpa and "the boys," as Granny called my uncles and their buddies, off shooting in the woods to our left. We all wore bright red or orange to make sure they didn't hear us moving and shoot us by mistake – that was the reason we were going in a pack to the outhouse.

We ran to get Granny and dragged her back with us. She looked the doe over and said, "Now that, that is a shame. Your grandpa would have known better than to shoot a doe. And he takes clean shots." We stared at the doe, transfixed, then left and tried to forget we'd ever seen her. We never talked about it again.

"You gonna kill Bambi, Sky?" I asked him, laughing. "C'mon, man." Neither Gwen nor I paid that much attention to how Sky was standing, stiff, his hand holding the banister while we were talking. While I was talking. While I was rambling. We didn't notice how his body collapsed a little, and he sank onto the bottom step of the staircase. I didn't ask him if he wanted another beer; it didn't look like he needed one.

I didn't think about it until much later, where he'd been, how he'd stood. I didn't think about it until after he was gone and I was trying to remember every single little detail about the last time I'd seen him. He was standing so quietly, the whole time Gwen and I were laughing. And then everybody else was laughing. Where was Amy? She must have had to work that day.

We were laughing at the thought of the person who had always been our sweetest, laziest, most peaceful family member, going Rambo in the woods. Laughing at him.

I could die at the thought of it.

Skyler, we were just teasing, we didn't mean it. We always teased each other, remember? You remember, don't you?

It got worse, because Gwen asked again, "Really, you're going to go hunting?" and after that I had to launch into a story about my friends from college. Sky had already heard this one – he knew these guys, too. City boys, who decided they wanted to hunt, and were undiscouraged by my family hell stories about all our hunting trips growing up: the guns on the kitchen floor when we got back, waiting to be cleaned; the deer heads in big cartons in the front yard.

"They decided to go anyway," I continued, "And they bagged a buck. Only they didn't kill him, because they didn't know what the hell they were doing. They shot him in the spine."

Gwen, who had never heard the story, broke in, serious, and said, "Oh, shit."

"...and the one guy's dad killed him, to put him out of his misery. Then to try to be funny, they nicknamed the deer 'Lucky.' After that, they all three went into these depressions for weeks, wouldn't work, wouldn't leave their houses, and they wouldn't eat any of the meat!" This got a big laugh.

"They brought it all over to my house. So I made ribs, slathered them with barbecue sauce," and Granny interrupted, "Whose recipe? Mine or Marie's?" Marie was her sister, and they always competed over their cooking. "Why ribs? You know deer ribs don't have much meat." And I said yeah, I knew, I just did it for effect. And added that I made venison stew, too, which they also wouldn't eat.

"You know you have to cook it right," Granny added. "Lots of oil, lots of pepper."

"I know, that's how I did it, how you taught me," I said. "Big babies."

"Yeah, bet they never went deer hunting again, though," Gwen said. She finished off her beer.

"Yeah, probably not. You know what Kevin brought home last week?" I asked. "A mounted deer head. I kid you not. He got it from those people with all the cedars? They were having a garage sale. Does he hate me?"

"Yes," Gwen said. She took my empty and went and got us a couple more beers.

Sky said nothing. He left the room at some point and didn't really say goodbye to anyone when he left. And that was the last time I saw him. I called him; I left messages with Amy. I think Kevin ran into him at a show, but that was it. I don't remember when Sky went from sitting on the step to leaving. Two months later, he was dead.

"I didn't know," Gwen told me, after we'd spun the story out one more time, thought of every stupid detail – where was Granny sitting? Where was Grandpa? What did Skyler do after I told that dumb story about Lucky? Why did I tell that story, it was just mean.

269

"You didn't mean to be mean," Gwen said, "We were just being smartasses." Did he go back to watching the game? Did he say goodbye? We couldn't remember. He had his own apartment; he had Amy; he was working; we thought he was OK. He never said anything. We thought he was busy with work and his friends. We didn't know his friends had stopped coming around. I hadn't forgotten that he and Gwen had messed around with heroin; she swore it was just a few times. Maybe for her it was.

"It's always the wrong people who kill themselves," Gwen said, "You ever notice that?"

I inherited my brother's dog. Amy had never liked him that much; he was too rambunctious. Spike got along fine with my dogs. I also inherited Skyler's jean jacket, his CDs and tapes, his books, and his collection of wind-up toys. There was a monkey, banging a drum; a dragon that shot flames from its mouth; a few vegetables – a cucumber, a tomato and a bell pepper – with sweet, painted-on faces and funny legs; a kitty that bounced a ball; a boy on a bike pulling an ice cream truck; a baby in a buggy. There were about two dozen altogether. It was his favorite collection. He also collected stamps and snow globes. I let Gwen have those. Amy kept everything else. There wasn't much. Mom paid off the money he owed, for credit cards and utility bills and all that. He didn't have a life insurance policy, or kids, or any savings. There was surprisingly little left and that was it for my sweet, pissed-off, and confused baby brother. That was about it.

≈

Things Kevin Said To Me

by Lizzie

"You're a fucking idiot."
"This house is a pigsty."
"Demon."
"Evil."
"Evil bitch."
"Lazy."
"Lazy bitch."
"Shit lips."
"Unproductive."
"I'm ten times more productive than you."
"Don't we have any food in this house?"
"I will not bow down to you."

⁓

You know that gut feeling I had, that I shouldn't marry him?

One of the last things he said: "Why are you leaving me?" Then he told me, over the phone, after I moved out: "I know you'll come back to me."

I said, so quietly he almost couldn't hear me: "If I ever really feel like I need it, I'll call you up and say, 'Please, Kevin, will you tell me I'm a piece of shit?' "

He burst into tears. I could hear him sobbing over the line. I hung up the phone and smiled for the first time in weeks. After that, when he figured out I wasn't coming back, that was when he started trying to kill me. He grabbed me by the throat once, when I went back to pick up the rest of my stuff. He came after me with an ax, then threatened to chop off his own arm.

271

Fine with me, it wasn't my arm.

He came after me and my friends with a hammer. He tried to run me down with his car. It was meth. He was so high on speed, all four times, I don't think he even knew what he was doing. But I did.

43 *A Twelve-State Killing Spree*

December 1994

I left the dogs behind when I moved out, except for my brother's dog. Kevin started crying when I suggested taking Sasha and Junebug.

"How can you split up our family?" was what he said. Sheesh. The dogs would have been the closest he could get to a custody battle. So I took Billiam, my sweet, loyal male cat, and found a playmate for him, LuLu, so he wouldn't get lonely, missing the dogs. He had liked them. LuLu was an older stray I found at the pound. I felt bad for Amber – she was so attached to the dogs. But she was more attached to me and I had to stay safe.

Kevin kept calling and threatening to kill me, or the pets. He was always high. At that point, I took out a restraining order and rented a small house in a part of town where I'd never lived before. I had my mail delivered to Mom's house, and had the utilities put in JoJo's name so Kevin couldn't track me down. I couldn't believe I had to do this, considering I'd known the man my whole life.

I was glad to have the pets for company. Amber came over sometimes, but she was busy with her friends, more often than not. She was always going to someone's birthday party or something. Swim parties, Chuck E. Cheese's, this other place she loved that was full of bounce houses. Kids' parties were so fancy nowadays. Her grandparents spent a lot of time with her, too. They missed Michael. He was indeed gay *("Come out, come out, wherever you are")* and moved to Key West with Kimchi-David, the delicious love JoJo and I met at the movies.

His parents were a lot more understanding than I would have expected. They loved David. Who didn't? And David was great with Amber, that was a blessing for me and her both.

I thought Michael was omnivorous, as far as sex and partners went, but whatever. He stopped running around, according to Kim. Good. He promised to have Amber stay with him during school breaks, and whenever he could he'd fly back to Portland.

I got stuck staying late with some buyers at the gallery one night – they were big spenders, and I couldn't very well rush them. It was cold as hell and of course my car wouldn't start. I was sitting there, feeling miserable and sorry for myself. I started missing Kevin. Everything about him was running through my mind – the way he washed my hair for me and brushed it, the way he made me laugh. How he had always ironed my clothes since we were teenagers. Even his stupid Rice-A-Roni thing he made. The shrine he'd built for me. *I hated that stupid shrine, now I was crying over it? What the hell?*

"Lizzie, you're the kind of woman I'd go on a twelve-state killing spree for," he told me once. But would I have been the first one dead on his spree? I felt like Judas for leaving him. Judas. The day I left, he didn't know I was leaving him. That morning in bed he pulled the covers away and kissed me on the back. Betrayer. He didn't deserve this. He was trying to do the best he could. He had an addiction. Several. *When am I going to stop feeling responsible for him? He is responsible for himself, not me.*

I didn't know who I meant – Kevin. Dad. Michael. My brother. When I was a little girl, my dad worked swing shift, at a factory not far from our house. When I heard the eleven o'clock train go by, I'd know I would hear his key in the door, soon. Click. The light switch would flip, another click, his footsteps on the stairs, going to the basement to feed his tropical fish. What happened to his fish? Mom got rid of them, I guess.

I could sleep, once he was home. I could finally sleep. Dad told me once that his family didn't believe in grieving, or being sad at all.

"If you don't think about it," he said, "it won't hurt." Such a big lie for a father to tell his little girl. You don't think about it, it still aches. Another memory flew in: One afternoon when I was around nine, it was in the fall, I think. The leaves were turning? We were at the park, but I didn't want to be there. I loved this park, it was my favorite, and Sky's, too. It was right by our school. My dad used to pick us up every day from school, then we'd go home to have a snack. I'm getting this wrong, I know. I walked home by myself, he never picked me up. Unless we had a doctor's appointment. Or I'd walk with friends, and then Sky, once he started school. Who knows. Dad must have walked with us, sometimes. We'd have a snack – usually peanut butter and banana sandwiches on fluffy Wonderbread – then we'd head to the park. This particular day, I hadn't wanted to go.

"Can't we just stay home?" I asked. I was reading a Nancy Drew mystery; I was right at a good part. Dad was distracted and seemed in a hurry to go. Sky wanted to leave, too, so we left.

I forgot my coat. My dad wrapped me up in his coat... then there was... something. The memory was gone. I loved his coat. It was brown corduroy, really thick, with a red lining.

I was fully spacing out now. I tried the motor one more time. It still wouldn't turn. I gave up and headed for the pub down the street for dinner. It was eight already. It was almost Christmas. The lights looked pretty downtown, and the women I passed on the street were so festive, all glittery and dressed up in red and black.

The waiter appeared.

"What sounds good?" he asked.

I scanned the menu. "Soup and bread would be great. And a pint of the winter ale." He clicked his pen shut and gave me a sweet smile.

"No problem. I'll be right back with the beer." I grabbed a magazine someone had left on the next table over. It was an old issue of Cosmopolitan. "Five Sure-Fire Ways to Please Your Man," it said on the cover. I turned to an article about the top ten ways to "de-stress." I could use that one. I flipped through some fashion pictures, all the women sparkly, like the women I had passed by to get here. The waiter reappeared with the beer. He handed me an envelope.

"You have an admirer, baby," he said. It was a pre-printed Christmas card addressed to the pub.

Someone had crossed out the company's name and written, "I realize you don't know me and vice versa, but Happy Holidays." It was signed The Mystery Employee. It made me smile. I glanced around the room, to see if someone was looking my way, but no one was. I ate my soup, drank my beer, called a tow truck and headed for home.

44 *Nobody Says Swell Anymore*

MAY 1995

I hopped on one foot through the park, trying to sum up my life in thirty seconds for Christian Howard. First date. Cute Chris. Heather and Tom set us up, his housemates, our mutual friends, and the original owners of LaLa. They were married and happy, and wanted everyone else that way, too. They felt bad about Sky; it had wrecked all of us. They felt bad about Kevin and me, too. Also, I think they felt guilty about LaLa. Personally, I blamed her for the breakup of my relationship. JoJo said she did a hex, it wasn't LaLa at all.

"I will take credit for this," she said. Who knows.

Chris and I were both a little nervous.

"I saw this in a movie once," he told me. "I thought it was a swell idea." It made me laugh.

"Nobody says swell anymore. It's a swell word, swell." He made this "aw, shucks" face for me. He really was handsome, but a goofball at the same time. Good.

"Lizzie short for Elizabeth, born in 1964, year of the Dragon; danced when I was a kid, ballet; my dad killed himself when I was nine, but I tell people he drowned; my mom is a nice lady, very shy, and sweet." Didn't mention to Chris that I had a brother, that I used to have a brother, and that he had been gone just about exactly a year. I'm sure that he already knew, from Heather and Tom.

"I have a nine-year-old stepdaughter; I like to make art, that's what my degree's in; trying to get a show together, I work in a gallery to pay the bills; I love my dog and cats; I wish people were better to each other; my favorite color's green, am I out of time? No? I love my granny but she's a pain in my ass. Done!"

I stopped. I could feel my face, all flushed. I straightened my sweater and pulled my curls into a ponytail.

"Go!"

Chris flashed me another smile.

"What are your cats' names?"

"Billiam and LuLu, and the dog's name is Spike." Didn't mention Kevin. No need to scare the man off on the first date; we could talk about him later. Besides, I was sure Heather and Tom had briefed him on everything.

Chris started hopping with ease. "Born in 1965, rat or snake I think; liked to build model rockets when I was a kid, grew up in New Mexico, miss the sunsets; mom lives in Los Angeles, tests software for a living; dad lives in New Mexico still, teaches history; one sister, she's all right; I was married once for about ten minutes, no kids; love to climb, ski, play trumpet, spare me the jokes please; I've worked at the same grocery store for too long, that's it."

He stopped.

"That's it?" I asked. I'm not sure what I expected. Some drama, maybe. Some kind of hitch.

"Yeah, that's pretty much it," he said with a big smile. "What about you?"

"No, that's not it," I told him. "I forgot something. My ex-boyfriend keeps trying to kill me. He's tried four times. I'm not very safe."

Chris paused for a few seconds, then asked, "Is he going to try to kill me, too?"

"No. He mainly wants to kill me."

"You wanna go get a drink?" Chris asked. I did.

45 *To Bad Art*

MAY 1995

Second date. "I got fed up with all the deer-head decor," I said, when Chris asked why I left Kevin.

"That, and he was a prick. I left a note on the table that said, 'Hope you and LaLa have a wonderful life together' and split." I took a sip of my wine. All right, it hadn't gone like that, but close enough. Chris raised his glass.

"Here's to bad art!" he toasted. We were at the river, having a picnic. Chris had brought a nice bottle of red wine, real wine glasses, Greek olives, a baguette, cherry tomatoes and goat cheese sprinkled with chives. I brought a pint of cherries, sun-dried tomato hummus, bagel chips, lettuce and pickled green beans. He and the breast woman, one of the models for LaLa's many breasts, had split up a few months earlier. It was amicable, but not too amicable. If you know what I mean.

"Did you guess I had a crush on you?" I asked him. He handed me a hunk of French bread with some goat cheese spread on top. I layered it with pickled green beans and lettuce. He handed me another piece of bread with cheese. I handed him the one I had just fixed and started preparing another.

"Teamwork," I said, "Eat up." He began slowly chewing. I was still at the stage where I didn't want him to know how much I adored eating. I seriously, completely, loved food. That freaked guys out, that I wasn't on Weight Watchers constantly or something. You would think it would make them happy. Anytime I dropped five pounds, Michael praised me like I was a good dog. Kevin, too. Anyway, it wasn't working, trying to keep my love of good food hidden. It was a great picnic. And Chris was too sweet – he liked feeding me. He kept popping cherry tomatoes and bagel chips into my mouth.

"I thought you were way out of my league," he said, answering my question. "Olive?"

"Please. You know what I think? I think you worked a hex with LaLa and didn't even know it."

"You're on to me," Chris said, smiling at me. "It was my secret evil plan." He pulled me toward him. It was the best date I'd ever had in my life.

46 *LaLa the Lifesaver*

Third date. We went out for vegetarian sushi, then to see some lame romantic comedy. Excellent date. He bought me popcorn and Milk Duds and we shared. Fourth date, fifth, sixth, seventh... it was going fine. Super-fine. I talked nonstop about Chris with Jo and Gwen, who were kind enough to listen. As if they had a choice. How I didn't know he was interested in me. How he asked me to go away to the beach for a week, to stay at a friend's place. How I said yes.

"Just the two of us," I said.

"No, really?" Gwen said. The three of us were out shopping. We were planning to have lunch after. "So you might actually, you know, finally have sex with him?"

"We've been waiting," I said, "What's wrong with that?"

"What's wrong with that?" JoJo asked Gwen.

"Nothing," Gwen said. "It's refreshing, really. I mean, I wouldn't know, but I've heard." She was dating a drummer for some hardcore band, he was large and sexy. He was like a big puppy dog until he got onstage.

282

She had just broken up with one of her neighbors. Actually, that was how she met the drummer, through the neighbor. It was Portland – one degree of separation, everywhere. JoJo was going to be married to Gage until we were all dead. He still saw Kevin sometimes, I was pretty sure, but didn't give us, or him, details. That was how we all wanted it. Except for Kevin, probably.

"Also, we didn't go to school together, how cool is that?" I asked them both. "I mean, for real."

"Also, did she mention he loves to go hiking?" JoJo asked Gwen.

"Did she mention that he took her for sushi? Vegetarian?" Gwen said.

"There is such a thing as vegetarian sushi," I said. "You know – cucumber rolls and veggie tempura. Miso soup."

"Of course, honey," JoJo said. JoJo liked ribs.

"Let me think," Gwen said. "Loves art, loves sushi, is willing to wait for sex, loves the stupid cats, puts up with the stupid dog, and he's a musician. And he has a real job. And, they're going to the beach!"

Jo gave me a wink, "So now you can play our game, 'Hey, Chris!' all the time."

Life. Was. Good. Finally. We had been seeing each other as often as we could, and talking on the phone in between times.

He had waited until our fourth date – he took me for a hike in the Columbia River Gorge – to ask for more details on Kevin.

"So, how many times did it happen, altogether?"

I counted on my fingers. "Once, when I went to pick up some of my stuff, he tried to strangle me. I was by myself then, it was scary. After that I took people with me."

"Heather?" he asked, "She told me what happened when she and Tom went with you that one day …"

"When he lunged at me with the hammer? Yeah, that was choice. All I heard was 'I'm going to fuckin' kill you,' then Tom, thank God, got him up against the wall. By the throat. He held him back. Heather and I ran out the back door."

Chris said, a little disbelieving, "But you never saw the hammer? That's what they told me, that you didn't see the hammer."

"No. Isn't that crazy? It must have just looked like a blur to me or something. I was in shock. Then when we were in the car, Heather kept asking 'When did he grab the hammer?' and I didn't know what she was talking about. Tom saw it, too. Tom knocked it out of his hand when he grabbed him, that's what he told me."

"God, what a horrible thing for me to put my friends through." I shook my head. I didn't like to talk about it, it still made me shaky.

"Don't even think that. They didn't want you there alone. Heather was so pissed off at that asshole. She was going to go after *him* with a hammer. She wanted to."

"Can't blame her there."

"So that's twice."

"One time, earlier, he threatened to chop off his own arm, then he came after me with the ax." I was already letting the edges go blurry on the memories. "I ran out to the car and climbed in. Then he came outside …"

"With the ax?" Chris asked. He seemed calm, but there was an edge to his calmness. Inside I think he was turning it all around. There was something he was starting to feel, I could see it in his eyes. A protectiveness, wanting to look out for me. He was looking like a husband. That was new for me. It felt natural. It felt like about goddamn time.

"Naw, he'd already put down the ax."

It had only been a few months earlier that all of this had happened, but it seemed like a thousand years ago, a thousand miles away.

"Our friend LaLa," Chris said. "She can take the credit for all this." I smiled.

"Or JoJo, it was one of them," I said. We always brought it back to LaLa; it was already a little joke for us. We were sitting at a lookout point. It had been a great hike. A hawk flew over. She was so close I could see her markings underneath, light brown and white, her feathers ruffling in the wind. Pretty. The only other critters we had seen so far were banana slugs and a couple of chipmunks. I hoped the weather would hold and we could come up here again soon. June was always so iffy in Oregon. Chris took a candy bar out of his daypack, broke off a hunk and held it out to me. Dark chocolate, with hunks of orange peel. I took a gulp from the water bottle and traded him.

"To LaLa!" Chris said, taking a bite of chocolate and swigging some water.

"Yes, to LaLa, for saving my life."

Chris smiled at me. "So, when can I see you again?"

47 *Tranquility*

OCTOBER 1998

Then there was our daughter, born in October, two days before our first wedding anniversary, Cecelia Elizabeth Ryan Howard. Born with her father's dark hair and her great-grandmother's brilliant blue eyes. Her eyes were shaped like her dad's pretty eyes, but weren't as dark as his. She had my long fingers and big ears. And my big mouth. Cute as hell, the little bunny rabbit. We were still in hiding, sort of. That was fine with me. I never heard from Kevin, or Michael, thank God. I had an unlisted number.

Kevin called over at my mom's a couple of times, and dropped by there once, but she told him to leave us alone. "I'm not fucking around here, Kevin," was what she said. He always listened to my mom. So he left us alone. I went through the paperwork, signed all this shit, then got a check from his lawyer after about a year and got my name off the house. He was still living there with Roscoe, as far as I knew. I could see them being happy there even when they were old men – patching up the roof, planting some more daffodils. They got along much better than Kevin and

I ever did. Maybe it was the binky that bonded them. As far as Kevin's meth addiction? Who the hell knew. I hoped for his sake that he would quit someday, lit my candles and said my prayers and all that. What else could I do? I hated him, sometimes, and I felt bad for him, for what we lost, other times. My family didn't care that I didn't have the "family home" anymore.

"That house was cursed," was all my mom had to say about it. End of subject.

It was possible.

Our wedding was small, just our immediate families, JoJo and Gwen for me; a few of Chris's buddies. It was exactly what I'd wanted my whole life. Tranquility. No curses, that I knew of. Knock wood.

We still saw Amber, when we could. She was almost thirteen, a good, sweet kid, like she always had been. No crazy hormonal puberty stuff, at least so far. No shenanigans. I think the adults provided enough of that – she didn't need to. Girl was steady. I apologized to her not long ago, for her childhood. She just laughed.

"Lizzie, you're a good stepmonster, don't worry about it." Then she gave me a big hug. She still made cards for me, for my birthday, Mother's Day, Valentine's Day. That was a tradition for her with a lot of people – her beautiful handmade cards. She sent them to her grandparents, her dad, her mom, friends and me. She had something. Something inside that made her bebop along, not taking people, idiots, especially, seriously. It was a gift, and it didn't come from me or her parents. Kim's mental health stuff was fine, as long as she wasn't using and remembered to sleep and eat. She was off all the medications. The meds messed her up more than helped. I knew they were good for some people; they just seemed not good for Kim. I still wondered, with my dad, what could have helped.

Amber liked Chris just fine – she was an attendant at our wedding.

Kim never called panicked anymore, wanting me to rescue her and Amber. Once she didn't need a babysitter, she forgot all about me. That was good. She was a user, even when she wasn't using. I didn't have time for that. I was busy with Chris, the gallery, life and... the baby. The baby, the baby, the baby girl. We called her sweetie-honey-baby.

One quiet Saturday morning in November, when Cecelia had just turned six weeks old, Chris was working outside, turning over the soil and putting compost on the garden so we would be ready for spring. The cats were out there with him, hunting for mice. They loved our new place.

The weather had been rainy, but the skies cleared for the morning so Chris was taking advantage of it. He had changed jobs – no more working produce, getting to work at 5 a.m. to unload delivery trucks. He worked for the city now, in the water bureau. He liked it. Now he worked with vegetables for fun, and had time for music, evenings and weekends. When he wasn't changing diapers.

"We'll have kale and lettuce and greens, baby," I told Cecelia. "You can eat all of that when you're a bigger bunny, see?" The baby smiled. She was easygoing, sweet and happy, most of the time. She kept trying to hold her head up.

"You're too young for that, slow down!" I told her, and ran my finger down her plump cheek. So yummy.

I carried her in a basket into my studio and began painting her first portrait. I would paint it in soft pinks and warm shades of peach and lavender. She looked up at me and blinked in the morning light, ready for the day.

I finally had enough work together for a show, and there was a small gallery not far from our neighborhood that was interested. Not assemblages, not paintings – photos. I had a ton of work ready and framed, mostly of bridges and rain, and Portland scenery, and a few pictures of flowers and plants. Some black and white, some color. I was happy with them.

I was trying not to think about the bleeding.

The blood started and once it started it ran fast. It ran like a red waterfall.

We'd been out to dinner a few nights earlier, before it happened. We had the baby with us, of course. Cecelia was a good baby, right from the beginning, and slept in her little car seat pretty much wherever we put her. There was a café by the house we were renting in Multnomah Village, and we treated it like our second dining room. They served breakfast all day – home fries and chilaquiles, and French toast made from brioche. It was buttery and too rich, with homemade raspberry jam. Their coffee was good. The waitresses never remembered who we were or what we liked, but that was OK. It had sort of a vortex feeling, that place. It was odd. I ran into Gwen there once and she didn't even recognize me, at first.

We'd been in the garden, cleaning up after the harvest earlier that day. When the weather was nice, we sat out there in the evening, too, after dinner. We would watch the stars come out and cuddle the baby. She loved the fresh air. Our rental had a guest house, and a huge garden took up the space between the main house and the "out house," as our German landlord called it. Chris had planted a huge garden for us – potatoes, lemon cucumbers and roma tomatoes, big handfuls of them, for marinara, and an heirloom slicer, a tomato that Chris liked for salads. And the tiny, yellow pear tomatoes I loved and he didn't. We had basil, for the marinara. And zucchini, that we both grew to hate. We put it in stir-fries and cakes, breads and salads. We gave it to neighbors, who gave us more of the same in return. Always the goddamn zucchini. But then, finally, the pole beans were spent and the raspberries, too. We froze as much as we could. We ate all the lettuce, replanted, and ate the second crop, too. Once the morning sickness was gone, I was starving all the time. We both loved to cook. Chris had waited to pick the miniature red peppers that looked like bitty ornaments on a Christmas tree just the right size for fairies. He waited until after the baby came to pick them.

Four summers later, Cecelia and I would hunt for fairies in the backyard of the house we bought and moved into after the rental, Cecelia's brown hair floating around her face in little wisps, her eyes luminous. Her two-year-old brother would chase along behind us, laughing, falling down, and picking himself up again. We'd pull aside the calendula and heather to see if we could find traces of their footprints. A volunteer pumpkin vine sprouted up in the middle of her secret garden, her fairy garden. Nearby, I planted a rose bush with miniature pink buds, in honor of the roses I had left behind at the other house, my grandparents' house.

"But do they leave footprints? Do they walk anywhere?" Cecelia asked. "Or just fly?" We left them notes. At night, while Cecelia slept, I left tiny notes with precise, perfect penmanship. Fairy writing. Their names were Dawn and Forest (those were the junior fairies) and Summer and River, their parents. "Yes, we do walk some places," the fairies wrote. "Yes, we have wands. But we don't really have ages. We like to draw and color, do you?"

I ran up and down the stairs too much, after the baby came, doing laundry. Chris's mother came to town to help, thank God. I had frozen all of this food ahead of time – two pans of enchiladas, three pans of tortellini with sauce and cheese, cookies and pounds of vegetables and on and on. Chris bought a big upright freezer for me and kept running to the store to buy more pans, aluminum foil and freezer bags. I did it all while I was hot, pregnant and losing my mind, crying and baking and cooking and hanging green, yellow, pink and white onesies on the clothesline.

They call it nesting.

I was nesting like a mofo. I washed every tiny item of baby clothing that people had given us and arranged it all, ahead of time, in her little dresser. Usually Chris and I hung out the laundry at night, and brought it in in the morning. (That was his trick, from when he was single.) We had some gorgeous hot weather. But I wanted to get caught up and was doing laundry nonstop. Never caught up, though, never ever.

My friends, family and coworkers had thrown me three different showers. They were too generous. We even had one at the gallery, that was the best one of all. A bunch of our regular patrons came by, we had all these yummy appetizers and played crazy games with sex toys and baby food. Not approved by Parenting magazine, no, not at all. One of the guests brought me a stack of Dr. Seuss and P.D. Eastman books, my favorites from when I was a kid. *Are You My Mother?* was the best.

I went to part-time at work, those last couple of months. I was taking my full three months maternity leave, after. Unpaid, but still… I sat on the patio every afternoon, waiting for the baby to arrive. I was relaxing in front of the out house, eating natural fruit juice popsicles and talking to her, my baby girl, asking her what she was doing in there. We had some good conversations. I weeded the huge flowerbed that ran along the driveway. I took Spike for walks, until the day some freak in a van followed me and I got scared. I was too huge by then to run. After that, Chris and I walked together at night.

After the baby came, I got scared when I couldn't stop bleeding. I didn't know what to do. I asked my mom and Chris's mom, too, about the bleeding, if it was too much, and they both said everyone bled a lot after they'd had a baby. My grandma told me the same thing. What the hell did I know? I'd never had a baby before. Chris's mom stayed a week, then flew back to Los Angeles.

Chris, when he saw all the blood pouring out of me, called 9-1-1.

"Baby, it's OK," he said. "It'll be OK. Are you OK?" He knelt by the toilet, folding his skinny six-foot-two body to fit in the tiny space between the toilet and the sink. He reached out and wrapped his right arm around me, strong and warm, balancing the phone against his left ear.

"They want to talk to you." He tried to hand me the phone. I took a big breath and it made kind of a catching, choking sound in my throat.

"I can't. Just tell them..."

"There's a lot of blood," he told them. "She's postpartum a month."

The blood wouldn't stop. There were big clots in it. The nurse in the maternity ward had told me clots were normal. She also said, "But if they're bigger than a lemon, you've got a problem" and "I've seen people bleed out in a matter of minutes, so be careful." I couldn't tell how big these were, but they looked lemon-sized, maybe. There was too much blood. I flushed the toilet. That was a mistake, because later they would think there was less blood than there actually was. They would want to know the exact quantity of blood, and I wouldn't be able to tell them, and Chris wouldn't be able to tell them, either.

Chris gave them our address and pushed the off button on the phone. He set the phone on the bathroom shelf, just as Cecelia woke up wrinkle-faced and screaming from her bassinet in the next room. Chris kissed me hard on the head and went to her. The fire trucks and ambulance got there in less than seven minutes. Chris held Cecelia, shushing her and packing a diaper bag. There were five male EMTs, who all seemed seven feet tall, taller than Chris, even, with big boxes of medical gear. There were more outside, I think. I felt hemmed in and was starting to hyperventilate. Sometimes I forget to breathe, or I hold my breath. You know those Tennessee fainting goats, the ones that just fall over when they get startled? I'm like that. Everything starts spinning, my stomach goes flip and I have to sit down fast, or else I might pass out.

I'm like that even when I'm not maybe possibly bleeding to death. The EMTs had me sit in a chair in the kitchen, and the lights were too bright and my blood pressure, once they took it, was way too low. No, I didn't know how much of my blood had filled up the toilet. More than what was in there at the moment.

"It looked like it was going to overflow. I flushed it once."

"Was there more than that in there when you flushed?" one asked. He didn't even look thirty. He had a tattoo of barbed wire wrapping around his upper right arm. His arms were tough – muscular and tanned. I'd never had anyone younger than me take care of me.

"I don't know, I don't know. Yes, I think there was." I wanted to go lie down in my bed, with my baby girl, even though I was still bleeding and it hurt and was scaring me because where was it all coming from? The cramping was horrible. But Cecelia needed to nurse. She needed me.

Chris's dark skin looked pale and his pretty eyes were almost black. He looked guilty. He had Cecelia in one arm, trying to get her to take a pacifier, and the diaper bag over his other arm. She didn't want a pacifier, she wanted me. I wanted to tell him it was OK, but felt too much like shit to comfort him.

"Yes," he said, "there was more than that. It was like a waterfall coming out of her." They strapped me on a stretcher and jolted me out the door. We went bump-bump down the front stairs and my head was spinning again. From the corner of my eye I saw all the neighbors hovering in their front yards as the guys carried me on a stretcher into the van. I didn't want them to worry it was the baby going in the ambulance. The neighbors knew we'd just had Cecelia – they'd all brought over gifts.

One gave us a scrap of satin for the baby to caress, "a snuggly," the woman who brought it called it and told me, "both my boys still have theirs." They brought blocky little board books with pictures of goats and ducks, two copies of *Goodnight Moon,* a gift certificate for a massage for me. Another pan of lasagna. They brought over a big green salad, homemade vinaigrette in a jar, a loaf of olive bread, and a bag of chocolate crinkle cookies with it. I didn't know any of the neighbors' names until I read them on the cards they left with the gifts. It was a rental – we weren't planning on staying in the neighborhood. It was sweet, how sweet they were. It broke my heart, in a way.

Barbed Wire rode in the back of the ambulance with me. He knew what I was thinking before I had a chance to say it. "You're not going to die and leave your baby, I promise," he said and jabbed an IV into my left arm while the ambulance hurtled down the freeway.

"The right arm is easier," I told him. "The vein's bigger." But he said he could reach the left arm more easily.

"I'm getting good at this," he said. "I'm going to have them give you something to calm you down, once we get there."

"I can only do morphine," I told him, "All that stuff, hillbilly heroin and all that? The synthetic crap? It makes me throw up." I knew that from having dental work done, and from after the baby was born. I got torn up from the delivery. It was morphine or aspirin for me, nothing in between.

"Morphine it is, then." Once we got to the hospital he badgered the staff to give me a room, and drugs. They put me in a room but no one came in, they were all busy with other patients.

"I thought if you were bleeding to death they took care of you in the ER," I said. I tried to smile at him but started crying a little instead.

"You're not going to bleed to death," he said, and tucked the blanket around me more tightly. "You want another blanket? You're not going to leave your baby, and you're not going anywhere, OK? So stop worrying." He grabbed another blanket and spread it over me.

"Thanks." I couldn't talk anymore after that, the words didn't come out right when I tried.

A nurse finally came in and started interrogating me. "When did the bleeding start? Have you had unusually aggressive sex recently? Are you allergic to any medications? Are you breastfeeding?" Chris answered for me. When had he gotten there? He was holding the baby. She was asleep again.

"She took a bottle," he told me. "Just a few sips, but that was enough." I was finally floating from the ceiling down to the bed.

"I'm fine now," I told her, dodging the sex question. Yes, we had; no, it wasn't aggressive, and it was none of her fucking business, our fucking. You were supposed to wait like six months or something after you had a baby, but we hadn't.

"Chris, I'm fine. Can we go home now?"

"Baby, you're fine cuz she just gave you a big dose of morphine," Chris told me.

"You did?" I asked her, confused.

"I did," she told me. "Welcome to better living through pharmaceuticals." She left the room without telling us when she'd be back. Barbed Wire had left without saying goodbye. I wanted to tell him thanks, for the IV and the pep talk and all.

"Chris, really, I'm fine," I told him. "I mean it." I tried shifting from my side to my back and felt another gush of blood.

"Dammit!"

It spread underneath me, warm, then cool. "When is this going to stop?"

"Bleeding always stops eventually," Chris said, and gave me a little kind of smirk. It faded so fast, maybe I imagined it. The words smushed together then twisted into a different shape. Bleeding always stops eventually. Eventually stops always bleeding. Stops bleeding always eventually.

I poked my head up through a morphine haze. "What the fuck do you mean? Do you want me dead?"

He shifted Cecelia from one arm to the other and wandered over to the counter. I couldn't believe she was sleeping through all this. She seemed to sleep better with background noise – the dishwasher, the radio, Chris playing drums or trumpet. Ambulance sirens.

"Jesus, Lizzie, stay still, it'll only make it worse."

He picked up a syringe and fingered it. "Your nurse left half a shot of morphine. Can I have it?"

48 *We Used to Be Dinosaurs*

MAY 2001

Our children, our joy, Cecelia, who was almost three, and Leo, who was nearly six months old, were eating breakfast in the sunny kitchen. It was Sunday – the only day we were all together. Leo crowed from his high chair; Cecelia skipped back and forth between him and the kitchen table, chattering. I was washing the dishes and planning the day. Chris had to run errands – grocery shopping and the library – so we weren't really together-together, but still. We'd have all afternoon and the evening, though. In an absent-minded sort of way, I was worrying about the kids. I did this too much. Leo's birth had gone fine; I took it easy afterward and hired a doula to come help. I avoided the vacuum cleaner and made Chris do most of the laundry. People helped when they stopped by. I think they were worried I would bleed to death if they didn't.

"The little punks," Chris nicknamed the babies. I called them Thing One and Thing Two.

I was able to nurse them – that was a comfort. It was hard at first but we got the hang of it. I was still nursing Leo. It was the most tender part of our day, and the only time he held still. He was already crawling like a maniac, wanting to keep up with his sister. I cuddled them and kissed them and peeked in on them hours after they had drifted off to sleep, *Goodnight Moon* tossed on the floor, teddy bears thrown aside. Sky's dog, Spike, slept every night right outside their doors. He was good with them, even when they threw things at him. He liked the food they gave him – "floor d'oeuvres," we called it. Their bedrooms smelled soft, sweet, sweaty. It made me weepy. They were so little, my babies, so delicious. I spooned yogurt into a bowl and set it in front of Cecelia. I refilled Leo's sippy cup with some watered-down juice. He was never into bottles but liked his sippy. He gave me a look and threw it on the floor.

"Ahhhhh!" he said.

"The future can wait," I said under my breath. I said it fast, like a chant. I wrung out the dishcloth and draped it over the sink.

My list for the day: Plant flowers in the window boxes, finish the laundry and fold diapers, get dinner on the table. Naps. After lunch. No, how about finish breakfast first. Meals, one nap, meals, walk, two naps, meals and diapers. Play play play play play. Night-night. Chris was making vegetable potpies for dinner – Cecelia's favorite. Especially the crust, flaky and buttery. All our free time was spent at the store, or cooking, or in the laundry room. After we got the kids to bed, we sat in the backyard drinking wine and listening to jazz, Coltrane or Monk usually, through the speakers Chris hooked up. Sometimes we played cards and ate cereal, or worked in the garden in the moonlight. We still hung out the laundry at night, like when we first moved in together. It felt good, that some things remained the same. Like the kisses, and the laundry. But not my body. It was never going to be the same. I adjusted my bra straps and lifted my black tank top up off my sweaty skin. Time to nurse again.

"Leo," I heard Cecelia tell the baby, "we usta be animals. All us, long time ago." She was wearing the cutest summer dress – white, with a pattern of strawberries, and a red collar. Leo didn't have anything on but a diaper. He was in his high chair gnawing on a teething biscuit. He already had four teeth; two top, two bottom. It seemed like everything was happening faster with him than it had with his sister. Cecelia was eating cinnamon toast and smearing butter all over her dress with her hands. Leo made a grab for the toast but she kept it away.

"No, no, baby," she said, smiling and playing keep-away with him. I could bake her an applesauce cake later. Roscoe's recipe. That was what I would do.

"Nyah, sss-sss-sss," he said, smiling his goofy grin at her. It sounded like "sis" and "Cece" combined, but that was probably only how a mama would hear it. He laughed and snorted at the same time. "Nyah, sss." His first word was "Da-da." Of course it was. Cecelia's first words were "ha sa." "Hot sauce?" Or "What's that?" We could never tell the difference. Now she jabber-jabbered and communicated nonstop.

She made her hands go into claws and grimaced at him. "Nails, usta be claws. Now they nails! We were animals, all us."

I hid a smile so Cecelia wouldn't be distracted. Really verbal kid, just like Mama. And Great-Granny. Ha. She was learning all kinds of stuff at preschool. I liked the daycare where they were; the caregivers were nice. I worked Saturdays, usually, and they were with Chris then. I had Sundays and Mondays off from the gallery.

"You got wild animals inside." With a flourish, she pointed to his stomach, then her own. "I have eggs inside. We usta be dinosaurs." The baby listened, blue eyes, identical to Cecelia's, unblinking. They were both dark-haired, with my lips, my granny's eyes, Chris's and my long legs. They were funny kids, and liked to laugh. Leo threw his biscuit on the floor, gazed at it for a moment, then yelled for it, like it was going to magically levitate back to the tray. His sister picked it up and handed it to him. Helpful. I was surprised the dog hadn't nabbed it first.

Leo looked at Cecelia with awe. She could be reciting her ABCs, or telling him the secret to finding true love, and he would always listen. She was the most important person in his universe.

I gave the baby a fresh teething biscuit and tossed the other one in the compost bucket. Spike gave me a woeful look. Cecelia handed Leo what was left of her gnawed-on toast. He took it. He wasn't supposed to eat wheat yet; the biscuits were made of oats or something. Rice flour. Who the hell knew, there were so many more rules than when Amber was a baby. I gave up and let him have the toast.

"We usta be dinosaurs, now no more dinosaurs! They all dead now! Yep. They died in the... 1960s." She had been talking with my mom again. Ha.

("It was different in the 1960s. We stood up for what we believed in!" – my ma)

("Yeah, it's tougher than a nickel steak." – my granny)

("Seriously?" – me)

49 *The Bridge*

AUGUST 2001

T hat summer Chris and I did a ride called the Bridge Pedal, a benefit for one of the hospitals. The city closed off the bridges to traffic and let bicyclists and walkers take over the roads. We had planned it out in advance; Mom was watching the kids. He was willing to let me back out, though, right up until the last minute.

"Are you sure this is cool?" Chris asked as we rode downtown. Part of the ride was over the Fremont Bridge, the highest bridge in town and, you know. That one.

"I'm fine. And if I'm not, once we're up there, I'll have to deal. Won't I?"

"We don't have to stay up there long," he said, giving me this worried look.

It was a gray day that started out with a light drizzle, then turned to sun. We flew over four of the bridges (the route included six total) and soon were more than halfway through the fourteen-mile ride. We got to a hill and walked the bikes partway.

"Out of shape," I said, breathing fast and guzzling a bottle of water. We had gone for some rides ahead of time, to condition, but it hadn't been enough.

"You're doing great," Chris said.

Then we were approaching the Fremont, the second-to-last bridge on the route. From a bike, it seemed to hang even higher in the air. I felt little, next to it.

The view was tremendous. The view was the last thing my father saw, before he jumped. The west hills rolled green behind us, the Willamette River was powerful and wide, sparkling diamonds of sunshine in its dirty, greenish-brown water. The buildings of downtown, the shipyards, the industrial wreckage, the train yards. A person could see it all, from every direction. It wasn't a bridge that was ever open to non-motorists, except during the bridge pedal.

"Look, Mom," a preteen on a mountain bike yelled to his mother, who rode behind him with the rest of their family, "suicide counseling!" He gestured to a sign, posted on the on-ramp to the bridge, that listed the number for the suicide hotline. His mother ignored him. *("Ha-ha!" – Nelson, The Simpsons)*

In fact, there were signs on both sides of the bridge, coming and going. I looked for them every time I drove across it. They weren't there when my father died; the bridge was brand-new then. I remembered my uncle Russell, Mom's brother, mentioning the signs when they were finally posted, years after Dad's death.

"About goddamn time," he'd said, growling. Even after so many years, it still hurt us all, in different ways. Mostly we avoided talking about Dad. My dad, Leo Ryan. (Our son's full name was Leo Ryan Christian Howard.) Our entire family also avoided the bridge, going extra miles to take other routes. I tried not to avoid it. It wasn't the bridge's fault.

We were at the top.

"Chris?"

"Yes, my love?"

"You know when you said that, about 'bleeding always stops eventually,' when I was so sick, after Cecelia?"

"Oh, God, Liz. That was the most thoughtless thing I've ever said to anyone. I'm sorry. Really."

"Really?" I asked. "Because if you meant it, now would be a good time for me to give you a little push." I motioned to the edge.

"Very funny."

We stopped riding, parked the bikes and took it all in. He drank from his water bottle, then uncapped the extra one for me.

"It's high, this bridge. I mean, really high," I said.

"It's pretty goddamn high," Chris said.

I gave him a look. "And then you wanted my morphine, remember?"

"Hey, you're the one who needed the morphine, not me," he said, laughing and hugging me.

"Here, drink. And forgive me, please."

I already had. I stopped to grab handfuls of Oreos and peanut butter cookies from one of the break tables. They had a whole party going on up there, volunteers, stickers and hats for the kids, all kinds of stuff. Free water. Chris took two more bottles to replenish our supply. I helped myself to more cookies.

"Cookie monster," he said, grinning at me. We wolfed down our snacks and guzzled water. A group of riders in their early twenties rode up, attired entirely in pirate gear – bike helmets stickered, T-shirts covered with designs of skulls and crossbones. The girls had wench outfits on, purple, green and black velvet, and the guys were wearing puffy shirts.

"Kinda hot for velvet, isn't it?" Chris asked me in a low voice. He started kissing my neck. "Mmm, salty."

Pirate flags waved from the back of their chopped-off black bicycles – man-powered versions of low-riders. Chris and I gave them the thumbs-up and they smiled. One of the wenches waved a cookie at us in greeting.

"He must have stood there," I said, pointing to the ledge on the other side of the railing. "Before he jumped. He must have balanced there."

"We can go, baby," Chris said, reaching out for me. I went to him.

"No, it's pretty up here," I said, tears starting. "I need to think of it in a different way, from now on. I always imagined he had to balance, on the railing? But he would have had to climb out on a ledge, he would have had to stop and think, right? For a second at least. He could have changed his mind right then, if he had wanted to."

"It would have been all blackness," Chris said, "Except for the lights from the city and the hills." Chris knew, from what I had told him before, that it was the middle of the night when it happened. The police found his car, then called my ma and woke her up. I didn't know this at the time, she didn't tell me until I was grown.

"Does your husband have suicidal tendencies?" the officer asked.

Bastards, telling someone that way.

Mom, the next day, called the cops and told them she didn't want anything in the newspaper.

"I've got two kids."

"Ma'am, we can't control what the newspaper prints."

"Where do they get their information?" she asked.

"He paused!" she told me. "Then he said, 'Uh, from us.' "

"So I told him that if they gave the newspapers any more information than was absolutely necessary, 'I will fucking firebomb the goddamn police station, do you understand me? I have two little children over here.' He said he understood."

Oh, my mom. Left alone like that, thirty years old. So there was no big story, just a small blurb inside the Metro section. I saw it, later. It was small and factual. I was OK with that. It had happened. There was no denying that he had lived and then died. I heard that the television stations covered it, but we just kept the TV turned off.

Bike riders kept arriving – thousands of people came out for the bridge pedal. Families, couples, teams in matching jerseys. It was like a carnival.

Chris held me tighter. "He would have jumped into blackness."

"It was freedom for him, you know?" I said. I smeared my face on Chris's sweaty T-shirt and wiped off my sweat and tears. "In a way, it was like he was flying. Free. Like he was finally free." I threw a peanut butter cookie over the railing. It arced, heading for the water, far below.

"What are you doing?" Chris asked. "Don't throw those cookies away!"

I smiled and leaned back into Chris's strong arms. "My dad loved peanut butter."

50 *My Favorite Housekeeping Tips*

AUGUST 2001

I decided, spur of the moment, to throw an eightieth birthday party for my granny, my mom's mom, because my mom and her siblings said they'd rather burn in hell than throw Miss Grumpy Butt a party. Or words to that effect.

"She can go to hell," was what Tisha said.

I loved her, that was why I decided to do it. I guess she wasn't that sweet to them, when they were growing up. But she was a good grandma. You know that expression, "Should have skipped being a parent and gone straight to being a grandparent"? That was her.

Granny Joanie wasn't a typical granny, or whatever a granny "should" be. (My dad's folks, rest their souls, were classic grandparents.) To my way of thinking, a grandpa should smoke a pipe, have a hearty laugh and dole out the money when your parents aren't looking. A grandma should have these features: white hair, plumpness, an ability to empathize more than parents, a sweet personality and preferably a knowledge of the game of bridge. Or golf. Grannies should golf or play bridge. She should be the kind of woman who spends her days at committee meetings for neighborhood beautification and takes her grandchildren out for lunches, perhaps an Arnold Palmer and a club sandwich at The Club. She should maybe take classes in flower arranging.

That wasn't how any of my four grandparents were, although they were all nice. Mostly nice.

My granny's idea of neighborhood beautification was sticking some fake flowers in pots and lining them up outside her front door. Live plants ran in fear from her.

We lost Grandpa not long after we lost Sky. I think he was heartbroken. Maybe because of stress and possibly because of general stubbornness, Granny had lost more than one hundred pounds since Grandpa had been gone. Yes, she was big before. But now she was just big in spirit. She had thick black hair, streaked with white, that had thinned over the years. She sewed her own "short sets" every summer – blue or bright pink polyester, usually festooned with a tropical flower pattern, with a sleeveless top and baggy shorts. Her arms sagged and bagged. She did not care.

"I sew myself a new one of these every summer," she would say, pivoting to model it. She never offered to sew me one, thank God. Since she had been losing weight, she made them in smaller and smaller sizes.

"Granny, you invented that whole surfer boy-Hawaiian thing," Sky told her once. Granny thought that was hilarious and said, "Oh, you!" and swatted him on the butt. Oh, my God, she loved Sky; he was her favorite. I liked to think I was, but it was always Sky.

Behind her back, we referred to her as the banty hen. She refused to apologize or give in gracefully, was frequently in error and pitted members of our family against each other. To my mother, she once said: "You know that nice picture you gave me? Tisha took it! To have it reframed, supposedly. Well, I've never gotten it back! I think she threw it away, probably. You two never have gotten along." Then Tisha, bewildered, told my mom, "She said she didn't want it! She never said it was yours." Mom retrieved it and kept it for herself.

Granny clipped her toenails in the living room when company visited and served whiskey to the minister when he dropped by. ("Why do you think he visits so much?" Granny asked me. "A little bit of whiskey once in awhile is just fine." Another bit of advice was: "You know what's wrong with you? *You don't eat bacon.*")

She screamed in person or over the phone at anyone who got on her bad side. Over the years, this group had included, but was not limited to: Betty Crocker (cake mix wasn't up to par) (*"You sweet talker/Betty Crocker!"*); the newspaper (numerous misdeeds, including employing an incompetent, opinionated female columnist – "She just thinks she's so smart."); Bi-Mart, to tell them their store manager was rude to old people; Quaker Oats (they shorted two cereal bars in the box she bought) and many others. The light company. The president of the United States (who, in turn, sent her and Grandpa a card for their fiftieth wedding anniversary). Her insurance company received calls weekly or monthly, depending on her mood. The funny part was that everyone sent rewards, treats, coupons, whenever she complained, trying to placate her. Little checks and vouchers to make up for whatever crime they'd committed – charged her too much to repair her vacuum cleaner, looked at her wrong.

Common refrain: "I got that coupon in the mail, that's how I paid for it!"

She was not pretty but was too lively to be called plain. Even when she was at her heaviest, she had an undeniable spark. Something. She was usually described by others as eccentric or "a hoot." (My daughter and son would inherit that spark, along with her mean streak.) She rarely slept. She lived solely on candy, cookies, and pie. ("And whiskey!" Sky used to say.) She refused to cook for our family, after years of slaving for us, but also refused to go out for meals or eat food we brought her. It caused mealtime difficulties. I missed her spaghetti sauce so bad I could have wept. I begged her to make a batch for me. All she said was, "Ha!"

Grandpa became Saint Robert after his death from a heart attack. Everything that was nuts about him – the unpredictable temper, his fondness of booze, the resentments regarding his family ("I never wanted any of you," was one of his direct quotes, and he said it more than once) – had been forgotten or forgiven.

Granny revised all of his opinions, once he was gone. I guess decades of marriage entitled her.

"I never liked that house," he said about their old place, the one I had bought with Kevin. (I didn't ask him if he, like Mom, thought it was cursed. He didn't say boo when I moved out; I think he was glad I dumped Kevin.) Or, "No, I have never particularly cared for cake. Pie is better."

Granny told me, in regards to my first house, "Your Grandpa and I just loved living there, those were some happy times" or "This was his favorite cake I made." The father of six and angry husband of one had never been particularly happy anywhere they'd lived, when it came down to it.

I loved her, for a whole list of reasons. She was funny as hell, for starters. She wasn't my mother. ("Lucky!" my mom would say, in a dark tone.) And she was the only grandparent I had left. So we would have a big party, in her honor. We had some family we were expecting from the South – they came out every year when the weather got rough back there.

"You don't have the 'humididity' out here in the Pacific Northwest that we have back home," as my cousin put it. One night, after the decision was made, the relatives from Louisiana, Arkansas, Kentucky, Tennessee and all parts of the United States notified, the country-western band reserved, even after everything had been arranged, my mom was still trying to talk me out of it. She wanted to reason with me, she said.

"Honey, don't you think this is, maybe, a little much for you to take on, planning this huge thing for Grandma?" she said. "Maybe cancel the band and just play some CDs? Or skip the potluck and just serve cake?"

"Look," I said, "don't try to back out now, Mama, I mean it."

"No, sweetie, I wouldn't back out, it's just – you know how she is. She's upset about the food. She wants to cook everything herself, and it's too much."

"God, seriously? I thought she'd given up on cooking." No wonder Mom was worried. "Has she said yet what she's going to make? She won't tell me anything when we talk. You know everything will have a pound of bacon grease in it. She is making me crazy, see? Maybe I shouldn't have started this whole thing."

"No, baby, it's sweet of you."

"The party's not even until next month and she's already crazy. It's my own fault. I told her I was worried about her microwave and wanted to buy her a new one. At the party, you know everyone will want to heat up their stupid hot pots. Stupid lima beans and ham. Who eats that crap?"

"That's not crap, that's some good home cooking. Ah, the vintage microwave," Mom said, snorting. "She bought that when? 1975?"

"Yeah. The door doesn't seal anymore. She's radiating all of us."

Mom gave a big loud laugh at that. "Honey, that door hasn't sealed right since they bought it. She probably said, 'X-rays are safe, so this is too!' Am I right?"

"Oh hardy-har. Now Granny calls me Miss Einstein because I'm so dang smart. When I call her, she's all, 'Hello, Miss Einstein! I was wondering if you were going to call this morning.' And she tells me no, the microwave is fine."

"Um, she called me, actually. She showed you the manual or something? She wanted me to come out and look at it."

"Seriously?" I said, starting to really get pissed. "Oh, she is insane. She tells me, 'Here's the manual from my microwave, Miss Einstein, see? It says right there that radiant waves at low levels do not hurt you' and 'I called that man from Montgomery Ward and he told me you are barking up the wrong tree because microwaves are not harmful, that has been proven to be a fallacy.' "

"She's always been a brat," Mom said, sounding all cheery. "That's no damn surprise."

"Mama, it is driving me nuts."

"Welcome to the club."

"If someone was throwing you a party and wanted to bake you a cake, wouldn't you be happy?" I asked, without waiting for an answer. "Wouldn't you say, 'Hell yes, bake me two cakes'?"

"Yes, honey, I would," Mom said, "I'd let them bake me as many cakes as they wanted." And with that, the conversation ended.

Unlike the cleaning at Granny's, or should I say, the "trying" to clean at Granny's, which never ended. I kept going over there, dragging the kids with me, to help her, then she wouldn't let me help once I got there. She would bring out the photo albums and want us to go trippin' down memory lane together. The kids did not have the patience for that and neither did I. Apparently she had forgotten what it was like to wrangle a baby and a preschooler.

Granny called me one morning, a couple of weeks before the party, to

311

tell me everything she had planned for the day.

"Miss Einstein, you there? Whaddya know?" Without waiting for a response she launched into her to-do list for the day. Leo crawled into the room, looking for me. He pulled himself up on a chair and pointed up to the cupboard, wanting cookies. It was 8 a.m.

"No cookies," I whispered to him. "Crackers." He sat down on his bottom. I handed him one cracker for each hand and he fed them to the dog, who had trotted in behind him. Spike was getting chubby. Leo pulled himself up on the chair again.

"Uh! Uh!" Cookies. He was determined. I filled a sippy cup with milk for him and handed it over. He threw it at the dog, who left the room.

"First I'm shampooing the rugs, just the ones in the living room and hallway. Then I'm planting those petunias!" she said, sounding defiant. "Tisha said she would help me but she hasn't. Then I'm making up the spare bedrooms. When it cools off tonight, I am weeding that yard. Looks like no one's helping me with *that*, either."

The extended family was supposed to show up soon, RVs and all. They could help her. I was hoping, anyway. I had to work. I located the diaper bag and got it ready for their daycare.

"Let me help you with all that, OK? I'll be over this weekend." I needed to leave, I was running late. Why had I picked up the phone? Because she was my grandmother. What if she'd fallen or something? But had been able to reach the phone? You wouldn't want to miss that call, would you?

"Fine, come over." Granny said. "Y'all just want me sitting on my hands. I am perfectly capable of doing all this. You think I don't know how to clean my house anymore! Well, I do. My house is clean, honey." (That was debatable, honey.)

"So Violet went to stay with her daughter and son-in-law last month."

"Violet?" I asked, confused. Leo had crawled after the dog; I tried to find him. He was under the dining room table. Cecelia came in.

"Did you give Leo cookies?" she said, hands on hips.

I handed her crackers, whispering, "Eat these ones, don't give them to the..." Too late. The dog had taken them from her hand. He was nice about it, but still. Cecelia started wailing and hit the dog on the head. He sat down and looked ashamed. He was a good dog; he just liked food a little too much.

"Honey, you know Violet, our old neighbor. Anyway, she said she had to change for dinner. So she goes into their bedroom – they'd given her their room to sleep in. They have a hide-a-bed for a spare bed. Well, they thought it would be too uncomfortable for Violet. She's had that back surgery and all. I cannot stand a hide-a-bed, they're just a worthless invention. Anyway. Her daughter is a college graduate. She is! She graduated with a degree in … in … psychology I think. She's a smart girl! By the way, I read somewhere that most people who have college degrees end up not even using them for their jobs. Anyway." I looked at the clock. If she wound this up in five minutes I could be on time for work.

"She married this bozo, well my God, he doesn't even have a high school diploma I don't believe. And he's not the nicest man in the world, either. Doesn't take very good care of his wife and the kids. I think she supports them I don't think he even has a damn job.

"So Violet is changing and she says to me later, 'I don't think those sheets had been changed in two months; they were filthy!' "

At which point I said, "Maybe she's depressed and doesn't feel like cleaning her house?"

"Ha! Depressed my ass! She needs to get up and clean her house. That will make her feel better." Then she hung up on me.

You better not mess with Texas and you sure as hell better not mess

313

with Granny. It got me thinking: Would Violet's daughter have felt better, had the dust bunnies disappeared?

Magic 8 Ball sez: In all likelihood, no.

JoJo loved stories about Granny. I usually called her right after I hung up with Granny. I called Jo once I dropped the babies off and got to work.

"Didn't you hear about that survey?" JoJo asked. She was always quoting from a reliable survey she read "somewhere." She was the queen of Cosmopolitan magazine.

"For real. They asked people if they'd rather have great sex in a dirty house or average sex in a clean house, and more people said they'd go for the average sex."

"Do they mean clean sheets?" I asked. "Cuz I don't care how dirty the house is, but that bed had better be clean."

Kevin hadn't cared how clean the sheets were; he just wanted me between them, waiting for him to show up at night. Kevin once commented about a friend, "I never really understood it with them, what his deal was with her. It wasn't like she was that good lookin' – and she didn't keep his house that clean."

He added, "Not that that's important," when I shot him a look. Housework wasn't my favorite thing in the world, but I did hate for things to get nasty.

"Housework equals World War III," that was JoJo's expression. In her house, Jo fought the good fight with Gage and lost. She did all the cleaning. If they had had kids, he would have called it "babysitting" if he spent any time with them.

"Gotta go," I said, "Customers." We hung up. They weren't interested, just took a quick look around and left. I grabbed some paperwork from my in-box and started filing it. Why did girls get stuck with the damn housework, anyway? Morning sickness and housework, welcome to being a woman. My brother used to bitch all day long about having nothing to eat in the house, but he never took the time to clean the fridge, shop or possibly cook. *("Depressed my ass!" – Granny)* He had been. But I don't think cleaning house would have helped.

When neat-freak Michael and were together, he did most of the cleaning. Kevin did none of the cleaning, although he had a thing for mopping the dining room floor. Not the kitchen, not the bathrooms – just the dining room. It didn't put much of a dent in the chore list. My routine was to dust first, then vacuum, strip the bed, put in a load of laundry, run the dishwasher, scrub the bathroom, call it a day. It all seemed so pointless – even if you cleaned a room a day (someone had sworn to me once that this was the only way to clean), everything still needed a do-over all the time.

Krystal, Kevin's sister, was a cleaning fanatic. She would put on Christian music and clean the entire house, including windows, in less than four hours. This amazed me. She was a walking, talking version of a Good Housekeeping Barbie. Her family visited one time, when I was still living at the house. Krystal's oldest kid, Sherrie, smacked her hand hard on the arm of the couch; dust flew through the sunny living room.

"Hey, Mom!" she said with a hoot, "look at that!" Krystal winced. Not because her daughter embarrassed her, no. Because my housekeeping bothered her. Her other two daughters took it all in with mild interest. Kerry, her husband, smirked at me. (Dirty slut. Too busy doing "art" to clean.) Yeah, thanks for stopping by.

I gave them a big ol' fake smile, and mentioned the time. "It's getting late, isn't it?"

My "to-do" list, in no particular order: Vacuum the fucking furniture, change the litter boxes, take out the fucking compost, pick up the dog crap in the backyard, ignore the weeds for the time being, consider watering the fucking garden, fucking head back into the house where there will be more fucking laundry, even though you just finished it. (Each baby added to the household increases the laundry four-fold.) (Why?)

On to: Transplant the houseplants, water them, do another load of laundry why-does-it-never-end? Then scrub the toilet. Thinking of Violet's daughter, change the sheets on the bed. Never mind all this; Time to make dinner.

Chris was different. He did the dishes not just once in awhile but daily. The grocery shopping, too. He was the best roommate I had ever had. He cooked — not just the gourmet stuff, like risotto or some kind of fancy pasta thing — but the everyday stuff, too: scrambled eggs, a big pot of soup, a stir-fry.

Like Mom always says, "You've got to have the meat and potatoes." We didn't eat red meat, but I knew just what she meant. Chris cleaned our place, too. The serious cleaning, not just the dishes. Our personalities could be summed up by the way we mopped a kitchen floor. I mopped frequently, but mostly wouldn't move the furniture out of the way. He mopped infrequently, but did it up: bleach, with lemon in the mop water, and he moved everything – pet bowls, kitchen table, chairs, musical instruments – out of the room while he worked. He liked to play guitar and whatever else he felt like – drums, horns – and we had instruments in just about every room.

I thought of something else to ask JoJo and called her back.

"Yes, ma'am."

"You know about cobwebs?"

"No, but you do. You just don't know it. Liz, cobwebs are not that hard to deal with. Use the dust mop on them."

"No, no, listen. They're not even dust. They're, like, ninety percent human skin! How gross is that?"

"Ew! Gotta go." She hung up too fast. I called her back again.

"Here is my final thought: Fuck housework."

"Exactly my point," JoJo said. "Fuck *worrying* about housework. It is not worth getting so stressed out about. You've got two kids now, you have to lower those standards..."

"...says the Magical Cleaning Lady. Really, Jo, I'm serious. You know how much you have to clean once you have a kid? And cook? Now I'm hanging up, and I will not call back."

"Promises, promises," Jo said.

MY FAVORITE HOUSEKEEPING HINTS

by Lizzie

- Stash the dirty dishes in the oven when expecting company (for drinks, not dinner). What – they're going to ask you to bake a loaf of bread or something?
- Put the dirty laundry in the trunk of the car when the in-laws are in town – because they'll check the closet, but they won't check the trunk.
- If you've got kids, play with them.
- You like to do art, build some.
- Make some love. Watch a special on UFOs. If you feel like it, bake some cookies. Then leave the cookie sheet in the oven until the next time you use it.

Granny phoned again that night. We were just getting the kids to bed;

Chris was doing their bath.

"Lizzie. It's her grandma. Call her." Granny had never been able to get that whole first person/third person thing straight. I grabbed for the phone before the machine clicked off.

"Yes, ma'am. What's going on?"

"Oh!" Granny said, "I wanted to tell you. Don't buy paper plates, see? I got plenty. I'm keeping them in my spare bedroom."

I sighed. "Granny, we wanted to pay for this party, not have you pay for it. Everyone already chipped in." It was the least they could do since they weren't doing anything else. The invitations, dealing with the band, arranging the food, weeding, all left for me. Jerks.

"I haven't bought that much," Granny said. "It's just a big expense for you all."

"It's a big expense for you, too. You already bought napkins, a canopy for the backyard, I don't even know what all."

"You kids don't need to waste your money," she told me. Uh-oh, she had that tone in her voice, it was building. "I bought two hundred more Styrofoam coffee cups, too. I don't care if you can't recycle them, they were cheap! And you don't need to mail out the rest of those invitations, after all, I'm going to call everyone and personally invite them."

⁂

MY FAVORITE HOUSEKEEPING HINTS

by Granny

- Buy items, such as paper towels and toilet paper, in bulk. Stuff so many into the cabinets that the doors won't close right.

- Buy items, such as liquid cleanser, in bulk – store extra in Hershey syrup containers. Make sure not to label them. Invite the

318

grandkids and great-grandkids over.

- Save time on cleanup – don't cook for anyone. Unless it's your birthday party, and people want to cook for you. Then insist on cooking everything yourself, and complain loudly about it.

⁓

"You really want to call all those people?" I asked. "Last time I saw the guest list you had about two hundred people on it."

"You exaggerate. It was a hundred. No, a hundred twenty-five. Or so. Now Lorna, you remember Lorna, no, I guess you wouldn't. No! You remember her! You met her in Arkansas when we all took that trip."

(*Your Aunt Tisha was the little flowergirl,* I continued on in my head.)

"Your Aunt Tisha was the little flowergirl in Lorna's daughter Elsbeth's wedding," Granny said. "She was only five and oh! She was so cute. Your Aunt Tisha, that is. Elsbeth was 20 or so. She was never much to look at, Miss Tits..."

"Grandma, you can't say that about people, it's just wrong."

She ignored me. "But, oh! That was a nice wedding, they had one of those big, fancy ice sculptures, of a swan, and lots of food, coconut cake, not as good as my coconut cake. I don't think we need an ice sculpture for my party, that would be too much."

"I love your coconut cake, Granny."

Chris came out to the living room, signaling "hang up" at me.

"I'm planning on making my own cakes for the party, did I tell you that?"

Granny proudly baked her cakes "from scratch" from a box, and they were the best. She would be the first to tell you. "There is puddin' in the mix!" she said when people asked her what her "secret" was.

"Granny, take it easy. We don't want you all tired out by the time we

319

have the party."

"I have enough energy for twenty people, you." Over the phone, I could feel the little banty hen drawing herself up. "I got plenty of energy, and you don't know anything about it. And I can do the food, you know. I have enough food in my pantry to feed a hundred people, any time I want."

I was tired and wanted to climb in bed with Chris.

"Thank you, Granny."

Granny said, "You're welcome, honey. Now, I know you want to go see the babies, but wait, let me tell you something else. I got half a dozen big bags of balloons at Bi-Mart. I bought these on sale for ninety-nine cents per bag. So there, smarty. But y'all will have to blow 'em up." Click.

Chris came over and handed me a drink.

"You are a good granddaughter. Now come hang out with me. I'd like to spend some time with you before all this party planning kills you."

51 *I'm In the Mood for Love*

A unt Tisha finally put an end to Granny's shenanigans a week before the party.

"Mother, we do not want to hear you complain for two weeks after the party about how tired you are," Tisha said. "I'm baking your cakes. The end."

I heard this from my mother.

"Then," Mom told me, "I believe Tisha told her 'And buy a new goddamn microwave.' " That made us laugh. Pretty soon I felt better.

The next time Granny called, she was fretting about parking – would there be enough room? What if everyone got there at once?

"It will be OK, Granny." Then I hung up on her for a change.

❧

We could hear the caterwauling as we came in through the back gate of Granny's backyard. Leo started struggling to get down from my arms and Cecelia covered her ears.

"Mommy, make it stop!"

"My God," Chris said, "What is that?"

"Sounds like..." I peered to the far end of the yard, where a small stage was set up. "My Granny. 'Crazy,' Patsy Cline. Not Granny. Although one could argue."

"I'm sorry," Chris said, looking embarrassed.

"Yeah, I was hoping she wouldn't sing today, either," I said.

"No, I didn't mean that!" Chris said, then caught my smile. "I didn't mean to insult her, was all. I just, you know..."

"You know what Granny would say, 'Ol' Patsy had her a hard life.' " Chris laughed.

"And Elvis? 'That poor boy had too much, too soon.' Hey, did you know it's Willie Nelson's song, *Crazy*? He wrote it."

"No kidding," Chris said. I spotted my mother sitting at a picnic table with some old friends.

"Hey, you!" I called to her. She waved us over.

"Everybody, this is Chris, Elizabeth's husband," Mom said, without bothering to give him any of their names. "And the babies!" She scooped Leo from my arms and gave Cecelia a plate with a big slab of cake on it.

"Here, sugar, I was saving this just for you."

"Hey, everybody," Chris said. He looked at me like, *Don't even bother, let 'em have cake.*

"Go get some food, there's about four hundred pounds of it in there," Mom said. Chris and I left the kids with her and went inside. We grabbed a couple of Chinet plates from the sideboard.

"Ooh, she got the fancy paper plates," I whispered.

"That's how you know it's a shindig, not just a potluck," Chris whispered back. Granny and her church friends had outdone themselves. I was told I did not have to help with the set-up one bit. But we could clean up, after. So the whole thing turned out to be a lot easier than it could have been, in the end.

The table was loaded. One platter held Granny's famous fried chicken, peppery, greasy and perfect; another, sliced pork roast. There were homemade rolls, ready to be ripped apart; biscuits with butter, with a honey bear and a bowl of gravy on the side; ten or twelve different salads, from black-eyed pea to Jell-O concoctions with mini-marshmallows and fruit cocktail to coleslaw and carrot slaw and Waldorf salad. There was my favorite – butter lettuce salad with buttermilk dressing. Someone had put out corn on the cob; and there was a green bean casserole with french-fried onions on top; a platter of cheeses, pickles and deli meats. On and on – it really was about half a ton of food. Granny had done some of it, but not all of it, I was relieved to see. I hadn't brought anything but a card.

"This is better than Thanksgiving," I said.

Chris passed on the carnivorous selections and loaded up on salads, vegetables and bread. We had pretty much stopped eating red meat, pork and chicken, but I still ate fish. The kids didn't like meat at all and shoved it away when we offered it to them. Chris started to spoon up some of Granny's scalloped corn.

"Don't – lard."

"Good to know," he said, and returned the spoon to the dish. Most of the salads, other than the ones made with Jell-O, had bacon sprinkled on. And Jell-O, sadly, was not vegetarian, either. I grabbed some bacon-free potato salad, fruit salad, and a roll. And chicken. I couldn't resist.

"Not much for the veg-heads, huh?" I asked.

"Never is at these things," Chris said, "I'll get some bites for the kids, OK? They can eat off our plates." He loaded up a second plate with cheese, deviled eggs, strawberries and rolls.

"As long as Mom's feeding them cake, you know they won't eat." I put some mac and cheese on my plate – they'd eat that, maybe.

Everyone was so engrossed in conversation that they ignored us. Most of them were Granny's friends. The relatives were all in the back, at the tables by Mom. They were having a good time. We had spent a couple of evenings alone when they got here, just the family, and caught up. Chris maneuvered me out the sliding glass doors onto the deck, ogling the dessert table on the way. Tisha had gone all out; the cakes looked spectacular. Granny had gone nuts on the pies and baked five: apple, cherry, Marionberry, chocolate, and coconut cream, for me.

"Diabetic coma," I said.

From the stage, Granny began harmonizing on "The Race is On," that George Jones song. One of the old guys was taking the lead. The band didn't seem to mind her sitting in. Granny was a fool for George Jones. The relatives were all whooping and clapping for her. It was three old-timey musicians, who must have been in their late seventies or early eighties. They called themselves The Orange Blossom Special. I found them at the farmers market, where they were playing an 8 a.m. set for the crowd.

"Play 'I Fall to Pieces,' " I yelled when the song ended. We found a couple of spots at an unoccupied picnic table and sat down. Mom was making the rounds with her grandbabies, showing them off. I saw Leo had two cookies and was shoving them in his face, and that Cecilia had scored an ice cream cone.

"We're starting to get some requests, folks," the banjo player said into the mike. "Come on up and tell us what you want to hear. We'll play them all, iffen we know them, that is." A couple of octogenarian groupies headed their way.

"Would you play *My Old Kentucky Home*?" I heard one call out, smiling up at the guitarist. Granny didn't like the competition. She pulled the guitarist aside and whispered to him.

"This one's dedicated to you, Lizzie!" she hollered to me, and began singing *I'm in the Mood for Love.* My smile was so big my face hurt. I nibbled at my food and scooted closer to Chris. He wrapped his arm around me and began tapping his foot. The old ladies started dancing in front of the stage.

Aunt Tisha walked up and interrupted us. "Sweet Jesus, when will she stop singing?" Tisha asked, grimacing.

"Hi, Chris," she said with a little coo.

I rolled my eyes. "Want to get us a couple of drinks?" I asked Chris. "I saw some coolers on the deck."

"No problem," he said. He nodded at Tisha and walked off.

"Cute," Tisha said, watching Chris's ass as he walked away. "I always forget how cute he is. But can you tell me something, Elizabeth? Why did you stay with Kevin?"

"I didn't," I said, flat. "Excuse me, please." I got up and walked off.

I was depressed and anxious after I left Kevin. Embarrassed to have left the family home behind, ashamed of the violence I put up with from him. I hadn't even called it violence at the time; I called it his bad temper. I felt stupid and tired. But I got over it, somehow. Saw a good therapist for awhile. Maybe the house was cursed. Mom was probably right.

At that exact moment, as if she knew I needed her, Gwen waved me over. She was sitting with a bunch of people. They had my kids up on the picnic table and were cooing at them.

"Let me find Chris," I called to them. On the deck, Granny's mail carrier, who had become one of Gran's dearest friends along with five hundred other people, was chatting Chris up. I strolled over.

"Hi pal," I said to Chris, and gave the mail lady a smile. "Got a drink for me? Gwen wants to hand off the kids, I think."

"So what do you think of the party?" I asked, as the discouraged mail carrier wandered off. "Want to go sing with the band?"

"No, no, thank you," Chris said. "I like having an audience of one."

"I like being an audience of one." I loved when he played music for me, sang for me. I hoped someday our kids would be musical, too. I was not. I could teach them to make art, though.

"God, you would not believe what Tisha just said to me." Tisha zipped past me, right as I said it. She didn't seem to hear me. I didn't know where Mom was. I needed to talk to her.

"So, how long until we can sneak out of here?" Chris asked. "I'm starting to hyperventilate." Gwen raised Leo's hand and made him wave at us.

"Hi, Daddy and Mommy!" Gwen called. We walked over to her table – I put my arms out to Leo and he dove under Gwen's chin, buried his face in her chest and held on. He looked out at me and grinned, then dove into her again. Ever since the kids were born, Gwen never visited to say hey to me, just the babies.

"Who's the big boy?" she sang at him. She picked up Cecelia with her free arm and tickled her. Cecelia giggled. Leo stayed buried between Gwen's breasts.

"She doesn't have any milk, funny boy. Hey, where did my mom go?" I asked Gwen.

"Haven't seen her," Gwen said. I heard raised voices drifting out through the screen door. It sounded like Mom and Tisha.

"Uh-oh," Gwen said.

"You want to maybe try to get the kids to eat?" I asked Chris.

"No problem." He took Leo from Gwen and held out his hand for Cecelia. "Who likes cake?"

I went into the house as fast as I could, with Gwen following me. Near the dining room table I saw Tisha and Mom gesturing angrily at each

326

other. They kept sticking their palms up in each other's faces in the universal sign for "stop." I could hear them yelling and so could everyone else. People were keeping their heads down and leaving the room. Tisha was trying to lower her voice but wasn't succeeding. Mom didn't seem to care who heard.

"He should never have been with you in the first place, he should have been with me," Tisha said. She almost spat at Mom when she said it.

"Thank God for him he wasn't," Mom said with a hiss.

"What is going on?" I asked. "Mom, who's she talking about?" Mom turned to me, her eyes flashing.

"Mom?" Gwen said to Aunt Tisha. "Are you OK?"

"Your Aunt Tisha was in love with your father," Mom said to me, "before he met me."

She turned to Gwen. "She thinks if Leo had been with her he wouldn't have killed himself. And Sky wouldn't have, either. She thought she could have saved him, and Skyler, if they were hers." She turned on Tisha again.

"Tisha, they weren't yours, they were mine. And there was nothing anybody could do. Nothing. And you don't do much of *anything* better than I do, got it?"

Gwen and I looked at each other, then looked away in a hurry. Gwen put her hands up to her face, covering her eyes. Man. We had seen them fight before, but not like this.

"Sue, I never said..." Tisha started, then stopped. "Skyler was your son, not mine," she started again, then stopped and started bawling her head off.

"This is our mother's birthday, you understand?" It was clear who the older sister was: Mom. "This conversation is over." Mom turned and walked off.

"Elizabeth, are the kids OK? They're with Chris?" She looked around for them. She wanted to make sure they hadn't witnessed the scene. Tisha ran down the hall, still sobbing, followed by Gwen. I tried talking with Mom, who insisted she was fine.

"God, Mom, what brought that on?"

"She asked how I was doing, with Sky gone. She was being her insincere self and I told her, 'Knock that shit off.'" Mom sighed. "It sort of went downhill from there."

"She's been in love with Daddy, all these years? Even though he's been dead forever now?" I couldn't wrap my head around it.

"They were lovers. It was a long time ago. That is none of my business. But my business is my business. I'm fine, honey. Thanks for checking on me. Now, go spend some time with your grandma, all right? Maybe get her to take a break from her singing career and eat something? I'm fine. I want to see my grandbabies now." She went through the patio door to Chris, who was in the yard, holding Leo and looking worried. Mom scooped up Cecelia, who was next to Chris.

"It is so good to see you," I heard her say to a guest. "I know Mother will just be real happy you're here. She'll be done singing in a bit. Or maybe not!"

"Your granny... She takes the image of the country grandma and turns it right on its head," Chris said as he drove us home.

"Then takes it out in the street and beats its ass," I finished. The kids were in the back, passed out and sweaty. They had played so hard.

"What about your aunt freaking out like that?" Chris said.

"She dated my dad! How icky is that? She could have been my mom! I mean, I guess not really, huh? But you know what I mean."

"Pity whoever gets her for a mother-in-law," Chris said. "I'm glad I got your mom, instead. Poor Gwen."

"I can't believe I never knew that before. My poor mom, getting blamed like that. She did everything she could, I mean, what more can a person do? Throw themselves in front of the person? 'Halt! Thou wilt not kill thyself!'"

I reached over to take his free hand. Chris kept his eyes on the road, driving with one hand and holding my hand tight.

52 *A Gentleman and a Hothead*

SEPTEMBER 2001

"Lizzie, whaddya know?" Granny said. "Let me tell you something. You got a minute?"

It was 7 a.m., the morning after the party. Chris and I were in bed, trying to sleep in. I had the worst headache. The kids, after their big day, were out cold. At least until the phone rang. Chris was snoring.

"Come on out here and help me clean up," Granny said, then hung up. I gave Chris a quick shoulder rub.

"Be back soon," I whispered, as he tried to grab on to me and wrestle me back into bed.

"We just got here!" he said, eyes still closed.

"We've been asleep for hours," I said, laughing. "What are you talking about? I'll be back in two hours, max. We can have lunch. You got the kids?"

"I've got the kids," he said. He stuffed his head beneath his pillow, then uncovered it for a second. "Are they awake?"

"I don't think so, not yet." He dove under the pillow again.

"Chris, c'mon. I have to go pump really fast."

He reached up, head still under the pillow, and felt up my boobs.

"Gah, don't! I'll leave the baby a bottle, OK?"

"I'm good, I'm good," he said. "Go."

"I'll put on a pot of coffee, OK? Bye."

⁂

My Top Favorite Baby Names That Chris Said "Absolutely Not" To

by Lizzie

> Boo Radley
> Frida Kahlo
> Diego Rivera
> Ransom
> Rowdy Yates
> Lil Dizzy
> SK8er Chick
> Che G.
> Baby DeLuxe

⁂

Granny met me at the door without saying a word. I grabbed a garbage bag and started picking up debris from the sideboard. Her friends had done the dishes and packed up the leftovers before they left. Only no one took any leftovers with them. Good thing she had an extra fridge in the garage.

"Ha!" Granny said. "Look at this mess. Ha. You take half this food home with you. It's way too much for me. You and Chris and the kids can eat it up."

"My kids are on an all-cake diet now. Where are the relatives?" I asked.

"They headed up to Multnomah Falls or somewhere, took one of the RVs with 'em. They got a real early start. I didn't want to go, I'm pooped. Chris stayed home with the babies, huh?"

"Yeah, they're all tired."

"I like that Chris, he reminds me of your grandfather. A gentleman. Only not with the temper, that's good. Your grandpa, God rest his soul, he was wicked." She winked at me.

"He's not a hothead, am I right?"

"You are, as always."

"Skyler was like your Grandpa," Granny said, "a gentleman. And a hothead."

I didn't disagree with her on this. We started pulling food out of the fridge, to figure out what to send home with me. I didn't want any of it. I was dehydrated and tired.

"Can't you call someone from church, see if there's someone housebound who could use some of this?" I said.

"That would work," she said. We put everything we had just pulled out back into the refrigerator.

"Yeah, send it to a good home, someone will appreciate it. The relatives will eat a bunch of it, I'm sure."

"Of course they will," Grandma agreed. She seemed extra happy. None of the surliness of the previous weeks.

"Hey, Grandma, you knew that, right? I mean, about Aunt Tisha and my dad?"

We went out to the living room and I started straightening things up, smacking the couch cushions and setting them right, pushing the end tables back into their spots.

"Oh, that? That was nothing. Tisha's an idiot." Granny came over and rearranged the way I had done the couch.

"There. Better." She folded the afghan that was over the back of the couch. It was the same one she'd had since I was a little girl. "She's my daughter and I love her, but she's an idiot."

"Do you think it runs in families?" I asked, picking up a stray cocktail napkin and some plastic cups that were shoved under the end table.

"What, being an idiot?" Granny asked. "Or do you mean Skyler and your dad?" She saw the look on my face.

"Skyler," she said, "and your dad. No, I don't think it runs in families."

"Look at the Hemingways," I said. "And Katharine Hepburn's family. They're like us. One kills himself, then another, then another, and you never know when it's going to happen, or who's going to be next. It all just dominoes. It dominoes and doesn't stop."

"Now, that's not necessarily true," Granny said. "Let's head outside. You fix me a cup of coffee first." So I did. Extra milk and extra sugar, the way we both liked it. She sat on a bench on the deck, and I brought out the coffee and a plate of cookies. She took a deep breath.

"That party just wore me out. Lizzie, your brother, his whole life, everyone always told him 'Don't be.' 'Don't be this...' 'Don't be that...' "

It was true. Sky just wanted to be left alone, to play music, hang out with his friends. He loved playing guitar and harmonica. He sang, too. He had a nice voice, like Dad. Mom was always frustrated with him, wanting him to be more responsible. His teachers thought he wasn't trying hard enough. One time he told a boss, who wanted him to come in to work on his day off, "My life is not an empty book for you to pencil in." As if it were the most unreasonable thing ever, to get called into work. Big surprise Sky hadn't lasted at that job, either.

Grandma offered me a chocolate chip cookie from the plate on the table, then took two herself.

"It was like they were telling him, 'Don't be alive, don't be yourself, don't be human. Don't be,' " she said. "So he decided to not be. That's as near as I can figure it, anyway. I miss that boy every day. Your dad, too. He just wanted to be left alone."

"But is it catching? Or what?" I asked. "Suicide?"

Granny paused. She took a long drink of coffee, then waited for a little bit longer, thinking it over.

"It's like they open a door and it just makes it easier for anyone else walking by to go through it. That's all."

"What if it happens to me?"

"Don't let it," Granny told me, then she hugged me as tight as she could. "You don't go anywhere, all right? You and Chris have the kids now. You have responsibilities." She pulled back abruptly, holding me at arm's length and looking at me as if it were the first time she had ever seen me. The fleeting moment of gentleness was gone. She was not a sentimental person.

"Besides, honey," she said, no-nonsense. "A person's just got to pull himself up by his bootstraps ..."

I mouthed the second half of the sentence to myself, as Granny strutted away, carrying our empty cups and the plate. The little moment was gone. Granny was herself again, saying what Sky, Gwen, and I, and the rest of our family had heard our entire lives.

"... and you got to do it your own damn self, because no one else is going to do it for you."

Granny walked back out to me, slowly.

"Oof," she said as she sat down. "Let's skip the party, for my ninetieth."

"If you had told me when I was a little girl back home, that I'd have all this someday? A washer and dryer right in my kitchen, a freezer that makes ice, a dishwasher? We had an outhouse, growing up. We had to leave the milk and butter down the creek to stay cold. We didn't have a refrigerator, oh no. I'd never have believed I'd have all this someday." She gave me a happy little smile. I patted her arm.

"I love you, my grandma."

"I love you, too, honey. Always have, always will."

53 *Beyond Loneliness*

I knew JoJo didn't want to talk about it, but I needed to. So I woke her ass up and took her out for coffee one Sunday morning. I left the babies with Chris. You know what? After all those years of being left alone with Amber, I loved having a partner who told me things like, Take a damn break, would you? I loved it.

We went to our usual hangout, the little café by JoJo's house.

"What were you thinking?" I asked her, once we had ordered poppyseed scones with lemon icing and two large iced vanilla coffees.

"Liz, you know I don't want to talk about that," JoJo said, blue eyes clouding. "Because of Sky, you feel guilty, right? Don't feel guilty."

"Ha, ha," I picked off the scone's corners and nibbled them. "Sure, no guilt. That's cool."

"He didn't do it because of you. Or because he was lonely."

"So why then? I keep thinking, 'If only I'd dropped by his place, maybe he wouldn't have,' or 'If only I would have called him, just in time, I could've stopped him'." I drank half my coffee in two swallows. "I want

336

him back. I want my brother back. I want my dad back. I wish I hadn't had the abortion; I want my first baby back. I've lost everyone."

"No, you haven't, you still got me! And Chris. You two are going to build the nicest family, I know it. Look at those sweet little kids you've got. They need you. Amber, too."

"I need them more," I said.

"Listen, it was beyond loneliness. It was some crazy place beyond loneliness," JoJo said. "Your dad – he was so sick. The baby? Was not meant to be. You had the measles, remember? Not. Meant. To. Be. If Sky needed you, he would have called. He knew to call. It was just beyond that for him, see?"

I nodded, but I was inconsolable. I drank the rest of my coffee and wadded up my napkin, stuffing it into the empty cup.

"Sky would take it back, if he could," JoJo said finally. "But he can't. Your dad, too. He'd take it back in a minute, wouldn't he?" I began crying. I wasn't so sure. JoJo went up front for more napkins.

"Lizzie, honey, I love you," JoJo said. Before she sat down, she hugged me, kissing me on the cheek. "No more crying. I mean it. You have to stop beating yourself up over this. They would take it back if they could."

"Now, enough about you. We talk about *moi* now."

I wiped off my face and smiled.

"Are you seeing someone? You act like you have a boyfriend or something."

"Yes, and I filed for divorce," JoJo said, grinning.

"What? When?"

"Last week. I'm done with Gage. He's not going to stop seeing her, the girl he was seeing. He lied. I don't have time for his shit anymore. I filed for real divorce and now I'm filing for, like, a mental divorce."

"So, who is he? The guy?"

"That night manager, at the bar," JoJo said.

I groaned. "Oh God, not from the bar."

"No, he's pretty nice," JoJo said. "Remember? He sent me that huge bouquet when I was... sick. And get this – he goes to school during the day. He's studying for his M.F.A., his, y'know, master's degree!"

"He's an artist? What does he do? Paint?"

"No, no, in business," JoJo said.

"His M.B.A.?"

"Yes!" JoJo said. "I meant B not F. See? I like smart boys, too. And he's never been married, and he has no kids. And so," she finished. "So there."

"So there," I said. "So things are kind of different now, Josephine."

"Yes, things are kind of different."

54 *Memories Flying By*

Right now, it's a few days after Labor Day. Still hot, but it's already feeling like fall. It feels like that day I didn't want to go to the park, the day Dad wrapped me up in his coat. It was autumn, the leaves were falling off the trees. A merry-go-round, just kids at the park, no grown-ups. Except Dad. Dad lying flat on his back on the merry-go-round, his head hanging off the edge, onto the ground, hitting his head over and over and all the kids jumping off the merry-go-round, stopping it, stopping him. Standing there with sad, scared looks on their faces. My brother and I standing there, too, not knowing what to do. Helping him home. Was he bleeding? Did anyone stare? Did the kids walk partway home with us?

They would have.

They were protective of us, the kids in our neighborhood. Most of them were real nice.

Memories flying by. It wasn't in the fall, when that happened. It was blossoms falling, not leaves. My memories made me twist it. It wasn't in

339

the winter. It was in the spring. It happened in the afternoon and then that night he died. It was the night Dad left.

☙

JANUARY 1, 1974

Dear Diary,

I am nine I will not be ten until August. Last night we went to our friends house for a party. At midnight all us kids went outside to bang pots and pans and shout "Happy New Year." We stayed up there till 1:05 a.m. in the morning. I slept till 12:30 today and we ate breakfast at 1:30. I wish it could be X'mas again. Until tomorrow.

Your friend,

Elizabeth Ann Ryan

☙

JANUARY 2, 1974

Dear Diary,

Last night I slept in my sleeping bag on the frontroom couch. For X'mas I got a stuffed dog with long shaggy hair, 7 kinds of fingernail polish, a sleeping bag, 2 diaries, perfume etc. In school I'm in Miss Kenney's class and I am top in reading and spelling. My name is Elizabeth but Lizzie is what my family calls me. But I tell my friends call me Betsy. My brother is a brat. I want my own room with purple shag rug and painted white walls. My friend Tammie M.'s room is like that. Until tomorrow.

Sincerely,

Betsy Ryan

JANUARY 5, 1974

Dear Diary,

I am very sorry that I've forgotten to write in you for the last 2 days. I am keeping you in my secret box. I love dogs. I'm writing with one of the 15 pencils that has my name on it. My grandma ordered them for me through the mail. Today my mom went to the store and tonight we are going to have hotdogs. In school everybody in my class except me is going to some kinda music concert. I have my 9x tables memorized. I like the show "M*A*S*H". I just finished watching it. Tomorrow night I'm going to watch "Walt Disney." Until tomorrow.

Love & Peace,

Liz Ryan

JANUARY 10, 1974

Dear Diary,

In school today in spelling I did pages 34, 35 and 36. I am the highest of my class in spelling. We also made pictures of a movie we saw. In the pictures we folded our papers in half and the top half was something like a kid playing doctor and the bottom half shows the kid grown up & his job is being a Dr. I made mine a little girl playing with a dog & when she grew up she worked in a pet store. We had U.S.S.R. otherwise known as Uninterrupted Silent Sustained Reading. Then you have questions after it like what time was it when the dog got lost? I have a doll named Amy Jane and she's almost a antique.

Until tomorrow.

NANCY ELLEN ROW

Liz A. Ryan

❦

JANUARY 25, 1974

Dear Diary,

I am in a higher reading level now. Tonight we had chop suey. It's the good kind – out of a can. The chow mein noodles come in a different can. My brother is staying the night at Grandma's so I get to sleep in a sleeping bag in the T.V. room. I'm going to write in my diary even when I grow up. I don't think I'd like to have it published. Too many secrets. Well,

Until Tomorrow,

Elizabeth Ann

❦

JANUARY 26, 1974

Hang in there, baby! (that is the poster in my room with a picture of a orange cat hanging down)

Dear Diary,

I like Kevin in my class. Today my whole family (mom, daddy, me, Sky) went to the dentist for a check-up. Not one cavity! We went to the store and I found out they just got a whole lot of groovy posters 2 bucks apiece. Tonight I'm going to sleep in my sleeping bag again. I'm not relegious.

Lizzie Ryan

❦

JANUARY 27, 1974

Dear Diary,

Last night my dog Peaches slept with me in my sleeping bag. I made the dinner tonight, spaghetti. In my class I was enomanated Mission Impossible that's what my teacher calls the person who takes the lunch money but I didn't win. Traci is the class president. I personally think Kevin likes me. Tammie likes Mike she wears his coat. In gym we danced some dance called Johnnie something. I am going to have a slumber party next Friday! We are going to all sleep in the basement. I will invite Traci, Katherine, Tammy J., Tammie M. and whoever I want. My dad is reading to Sky and I have to write everything down before he finishes. Tonight me, Daddy and Sky went with Grandpa and Grandma out to eat buffet. Mom couldn't come she was at ballet class. She says ballet is not just for kids, but moms can take it too. Kevin is maybe going to get suspended from school because the new kid said Kevin threatened to beat him up, which was a lie.

Lizzie Ryan

FEBRUARY 17, 1974

Dear Diary,

My slumber party was so much fun I didn't have time to write in my diary. My cousin Gwen came to the party and spent the night with us and her and Skyler slept downstairs with us. Tammie M., Traci, Katherine and a bunch of my other friends came over. We played records and danced & some of the records didn't even get played. We had 2 pepperoni pizzas, pop, popcorn, hot chocolate, hot apple juice, dip and potato chips and lots of other stuff. Some of the girls stayed till four o'clock. I made a chocolate cake. Traci and Tammie M. got in a fist fight. We made slam books, that's when you write how you really feel about someone and pass the book around and everyone writes about the same person in it. They write about you too. Well, now I'm in a hurry & can't tell you about all the things except we had lot's of fun. Well, goodnight until tomorrow.

Love,

Lizzie R.

MARCH 9, 1974

Dear Diary,

Tammie has a high temperature and hasn't been at school for 4 days. I'm not so crazy about Kevin anymore. In gym class Mr. Wu made us do somersaults (about 4) on a mat & the log roll. I got sick. I could of thrown up. I'll do a drawing here's me going over, over, fast, fast, dizzy, dizzy. And also Mr. Wu yelled at Kevin and Mike a lot (especially Kevin) and that got me upset so I came home. I'm not supposed to tell Tammie but Traci has been wearing Mike's coat all week. Tammie's mom can't support them so Tammie might have to move away with her brothers to their Dad's after she just got her beautiful floor-length curtains, shag rug, canopy bed and her own room. My Mom has pnimoni. I know I spelled that wrong.

MARCH 20, 1974

Dear Diary,

I'm not really writing on March 20. In fact, it's June 12th today. Dad's dead. He commeted suicide on the Fremont Bridge. He took Peaches with him, she is dead, too, so now we have a kitten (carmel colored) named

Carmel for Skyler, and a dog (white with tan spots) named Honey for me. Tammie moved Saturday. I had a going-away party for her (my present). All the girls from our class except Katherine came over. Tammie wears a bra I don't. I'm still awful flat. My job is to feed the fish downstairs. They were Dad's fish before.

❦

THE END

❦

About the Author

Nancy Ellen Row is a writer from the Pacific Northwest. She blogs daily at wackymommy.org and msnancy.org. You can reach her by e-mail, wackymommy@wackymommy.org, or through her website, nancyellenrow.com

She lives with her husband and their two children in the suburbs of Portland, Oregon. This is her first novel.

Made in the
USA
Middletown, DE